Book One of the Pr

Specialist One

The Price of Victory

ORRIN HURLBUTT

Specialist One: The Price of Victory

ISBN: 978-1-922532-25-1 (Paperback)
978-1-922532-28-2 (eBook)

A catalogue record for this book is available from the National Library of Australia

Editor: Beverly Streater
Proofreader: Sarah Kate Hill
Cover Design: Ocean Reeve Publishing
Design and Typeset: Ocean Reeve Publishing
Printed in Australia by Ocean Reeve Publishing

Published by Orrin Hurlbutt and Ocean Reeve Publishing
www.oceanreevepublishing.com

Ocean REEVE PUBLISHING

Acknowledgments

De Cao Raelkin Sanjs Translation Group Pty Ltd
[Version 387.24.19.75]
C:\LogArchive\Dataset176
>Run 'Specialist_One_the_price_of_victory/'
<Notification>
<New Standard English detected>
<Localising High Imperial Creole>
<Translation Localised>
<Some linguistic obscurities will be noted in brackets, others will be clarified in the attached glossary.>
<Thank you for supporting the De Cao Raelkin Sanjs Translation Group>
<Translating alien texts since 2235>

Acknowledgements

To my sons and daughters,

Preparing for the finest military force the universe has ever known. I know you were raised in the arms of a rifle; born to be warriors, though nothing can compare to the moment Condition One is sounded: To the first crack of weapons fire. None of your training will prepare you for it, nor will this near-fantastical tale. But I hope that it will show you one thing; something I could only learn in the heart of a firefight, while bleeding on a barren rock. The steadfast reliance on your brothers and sisters in arms. A lesson taught to me by lies, betrayal and misfortune, transgressions that should never be committed ... but will be all the same.

~ Sara

I put these words to tablet as a detailed account of her life. But her life alone lacks context, her decisions and actions in the name of security did not happen in a vacuum. As such, I have conducted hundreds of interviews, pursued documentation from security footage to recorded memories of events. As such, of the men and women I knew personally or had had direct access to their lived experiences she records them here in the first person. To the servicemen and women, I knew through after action reports she has kept your actions in the third.

~ The Historian

Prologue

My boots thumped across the roadway, the light afternoon breeze catching the strands of my long black hair as I marched through the streets of Albonii. To my side, the cries of protests echoed over the immovable wall of naval special police, army military police, and corrections soldiers and marines, their riot shields held tightly as gas grenades were fired over the phalanx and into the crowd by grenadiers. A bottle careened over the line and clinked harmlessly at my feet. Side-stepping it, I made my way through the hatchway of the field Command Post (CP). The post was abuzz with activity as officers' aides relayed reports and senior non-commissioned officers drifted in and out of the post. After passing through the post's Command Centre, I made my way aft and slipped into the commanding officer's tent connected ad hoc to the field CP.

The stern stench of chemically heated rations wafted from the tent as I slipped through the tent flap, the orange hue of lamps illuminating the quarters. The room was spartan by necessity; a table, chair, and bed filled the room, with a computer tablet sat propped on the table. I snapped to attention at the door, my hat tucked under one arm.

'Grond Kapitan Jen, I have the report you ordered,' I relayed, my jaw stiff and my words precise. With a quiet sigh, Elenskis Jen spun on her chair to face me, her crimson eyes piercing through the orange glow.

'We've known each other for long enough to drop such formalities in the privacy of my own quarters, haven't we, Sara?' she inquired in reply. I relaxed.

'Aye, ma'am, but as your Regiment Sargent Madjor, it's easier for me to lead by example so I'm always demonstrating proper military etiquette regardless of audience,' I replied with a smile.

Elenskis chuckled. 'Ah, yes—like military bearing is a concern for the soldjers and mariins of the Two hjak Two Ten Seven Meikkorek Bataljon,' she remarked in reply as I advanced towards her.

'Well, someone has to demonstrate it; it may as well be me, out of respect for you, at the very least,' I replied as I looked at the tablet on her desk. 'What were you reading?'

'Oh, just a report from the Kaiserkriig Mariin; apparently one of our detection buoys near the old-Earth Aether junction picked up some sort of craft in its vicinity,' she remarked.

I leaned towards the tablet, frowning as I read the report. 'Didn't our ancestors record all of that space as lifeless?' I asked.

'And didn't the old Earth destroy itself with capitalist globalisation?' Elenskis finished for me. I nodded in agreement. 'Well, four-something centuries of negligent ignorance will do that—leave everyone confused as to what in the gods' names is going on out there,' Elenskis added sourly. With a glance, her gaze snapped down to her tablet, and she powered it down before turning back to me, her platinum hair harsh in the artificial light as she turned. 'So, what happened now?' she queried, knowing full well something had to have gone wrong.

'In the last thirty-six hours, the Meikkorek Bataljon has had eleven drunk-and-disorderlies, two unconfirmed hooker murders, one incident of attempted theft, and thirty-seven DUIs, ma'am,' I reported.

'I'll write up the necessary Formalnai Meikruls,'

'That's seven fewer FnMs than the average, ma'am,' I remarked dryly.

'Still too many. Any repeat offenders?' Elenskis asked with a sigh.

'Liider Mariin Ela Tremblej has again been apprehended for assaulting a barkeep and the attempted theft of a server droid, ma'am.'

'She gets worse with each passing rotation,' Elenskis commented.

'She has nothing to do, no purpose; she's lashing out in response.'

Elenskis nodded in agreement. 'We're all lashing out in some way or another; Meikkorek Bataljons tend to do that.'

'Purpose is the cornerstone of the warrior,' I recited.

'Especially for lifers like us …' Elenskis remarked in agreement. 'How's your adjustment period been going?' she asked abruptly, her eyes locking with mine. I opened my mouth to speak but words failed to form.

'It's … going, ma'am,' I replied.

'You shouldn't continue to dwell on your decisions at Nuleningrad, Sara; you did the service proud regardless of what the Courts-Martial Board said,' Elenskis remarked, a comforting hand settling on my bicep as my eyes darted to the floor at the thought.

'Pride …' I began, my voice trailing off. 'I always thought I could find that in service to the state, through sacrifice in the name of Ympiirista Aleksandra …' I muttered.

'The state and the service didn't and still doesn't deserve your pride; it treated you like a blunt cudgel rather than the intelligent and discerning scalpel you are,' she said with firmness.

An awkward silence descended upon the room before I broke it. 'Ela is currently cooling off in the brig; the SPs'll release her in the next nine hours.'

'Is someone going to be assigned to her? This unit can't receive any more flak, otherwise we'll be classified as being "self-destructive and dangerous towards authority figures" and we'll all be sleeping in Fort Yomii,' Elenskis remarked, her jawline tensing at the thought.

'I'll look after her in the morning, ma'am. But I'll let her cool her fists first,' I remarked in reply before an explosion echoed through the tent, followed by a pressure wave. Digital whistles began to ring, followed by a flurry of instructions shouted over comms and in-person. A corporal rushed into the tent and snapped to attention.

'Kapitan! Protestors just broke through the sentry line!' he reported, his voice squeaking with nervous tension. With an audible sigh and a scowl, I pivoted away and ran out to meet the breakout riot.

Chapter 1
The Morning After

31/11/2436 (Military Calendar)

I wrenched forwards, my breaths sharp as pain pulsed across my temples. A shiver ran down my spine, the icy touch of the bulkhead registering behind me. My eyes opened to the claustrophobic confines of a steel container. As I began to struggle out of my seat, darkness fell over my vision. The five-point harness pinched at my chest, shoulders, and sides, while the cold hands of the collar tightened at my throat as I struggled. Wildly reaching for the release mechanisms on my harness, I realised the metallic cuffs that encompassed my wrists and were holding my hands evenly spaced. My eyes began to quiver and the panicked fire that rested within began to flare as my fingers curled into fists and a final pleading call tumbled from my lips.

'Is anyone here?' I called, but the words fell from me as though strangled by a malevolent spirit. I attempted to let out a scream of anger and frustration but all that came was a weak whimper of air, desperately desiring to create sound. The cold utilitarian design of my chair was now suddenly obvious to me as thoughts abandoned me and focus on escape from my new prison ceased.

What have I done?

What went wrong?

What happened to everyone else?

Who did this? I wondered as I lay there slumped in the harness, my racing mind slowing to a standstill. In the silence of my thoughts, my brow furrowed into a frown. Something was off: the subtle, incorrect tug of gravity, the delicate movement of my body as my seat was adjusted by unknown forces. *I'm in space! I could be light-years from Imperial territory!* Fuming, my body tensed at the thought. But even as my fury began to rise, it just as quickly abated as the harness reminded me of the shackles. *Not as bad as that time you shot Derjantu Morei,* I thought with an amused smile as I sat back up to ease the coarse straps off my chest. However, the rough grip of the harness continued to dig into my shoulders. I drifted in and out of consciousness for hours on end, the subtle sway of artificial gravity a soothing hand to my drained mind.

After my initial awareness, I awoke with a start to the prolonged whine of a klaxon and the shimmer of emerald emergency lights that pulsed through the room followed by a series of rapid instructions: a voice boomed out from a speaker, their urgent tone unmistakable despite the alien words.

My mind began to race with questions—*What are they saying? What language are they speaking?* I wondered before pausing on a tendril of thought … *I can see and hear!* With a jump of excitement, I rapidly scanned the lifeless room's tightly packed chairs, each loaded with people. As the unknown speaker continued relaying information, the room's pulsating deep orange emergency lights flooded the compartment with intense waves of light only to be followed by all-encompassing darkness.

The male voice continued over the speaker, his words cycling down in a numerical fashion, as my gaze darted around the room, fearing my vision would abandon me once again. Squinting through the fluctuating brightness, I locked onto the brash velvet hair of Ela.

I desperately tried to call out to her as the countdown continued. But once again, screaming at the top of my lungs, the words merely tumbled from my mouth at random. Non-verbal grunts and chokes echoed through the room, quickly shifting

Ela's attention from the raucous noise occurring around us. Her eyes widened as she recognised me, and a smile split across her soft cheeks. 'Sara!' she signed with excitement as the speaker finished his report and the telltale psychophysical detachment washed over me as we were thrown into the alternate dimension known as the Aether. The speaker rattled off another series of reports before a digital chronometer winked on with the digits 35:59:58 counting down.

As the klaxons and emergency lights subsided, I began to notice the small running lights and faint bunker lights embedded along the walls that provided subtle illumination to the room, as well as the faintly glowing control console beside the hatchway. Now able to see each other clearly, Ela and I began the difficult task of signing to each other in manacles.

'That's chiif to you, mariin,' I rebuked the marine for her use of my first name. Ela simply shrugged. 'How in Asfod did we get here?'

'Brafiki if I know; last I remember was passing out in the brig,' signed Ela in reply.

'You find anyone else from the unit?' my mind shifting back into operational gear as I signed.

'I only just got my eyesight back; I've been writhing in this gods-damned contraption for the last four hours.'

So that's how long I'd been out for, I thought before continuing to converse. 'Got a way out?' I pressed.

'Well, the cuffs don't seem to react to changes in wrist position so I'd say as long as you can slip your wrist out, you'd be good to go on that.'

I looked at her, dumbfounded. 'Who'd be able to do that?'

'You think I just sat on my hands every time I was thrown in the brig hungover or FnMed?' she hissed.

I tucked my shackled arms up to my chest in a defensive gesture, palms out. 'Fair point, fair point,' I conceded, 'but can you get out of the harness?'

Ela looked at me with disappointed eyes. 'This joke of a contraption? With free hands, it'll be a joke.'

'Fine, fine—just do it,' I ordered.

With a wicked smile, she turned back to her harness, and with blinding speed and violence, an unsightly image began to take form as she dislocated her thumbs and slipped her crooked hands through her iron cuffs, before rapidly picking apart the metal casing below her chair. Blood snaked down her hands as she removed a magnetic coil. A loud thump echoed through the hollow room as the gravity around Ela returned to the one-G constant of the deck plating. A moment later, she'd slammed the coil at the base of her collar's chain, her head yanked forwards as the electromagnetic field in the wall released. She disengaged the interlocks of her safety harness in much the same way before leaping to her feet, snapping to face me and saying, 'Easy as piss,' tossing the magnetic coil to the floor.

'I am not breaking my thumbs!' I signed in reply as she stood there defiantly ecstatic as klaxons and emergency lights began to screech through the room followed by the meaningless instructions over the speaker. A security alert had been broadcast in response to the candidates that had just escaped ... namely us.

'Shajst!' she hissed as she snatched up the magnetic coil and began selectively releasing other prisoners.

'Well won't need to worry about the security cards these *bladsa brafiks* use then,' she muttered as she undid the magnetic locks on my cuffs and restraints. With a start, I leapt to my feet, glancing around before moving towards the hatchway with everyone else who had been released.

'Kapitan,' I remarked as I advanced towards the hatch.

'Good to see you, Starshiina Hart,' Elenskis replied. I glanced back at the emerald-eyed man behind me as Ela brushed past me towards the console to my left.

'Who's he?' I asked, pointing back towards him as Ela began typing in commands with her intact middle fingers.

'A corpse waiting to be disposed of,' the man absentmindedly remarked as Ela focused in on the work in front of her before turning around, finger still hovering over the console.

'The entire schematic is written in a language I've never seen before, but if I'm reading the outline correctly, and I know my warships, the engines and reactor should be aft. Given the size of this ship, I'd say it's fair to assume the armoury is somewhere near these chokepoints,' she explained, indicating towards a pair of triangular rooms to the aft.

'So how do we get there?' I inquired, looking over the shifting, rotating 2D outline.

'From the looks of it, crew quarters are in the upper decks, so with that alert, they'll be crawling with salors and mariins.'

'Not to mention our decks are going to be flooded with them any moment now,' I added as I looked across at Elenskis. 'Orders, ma'am?'

'We don't want to be fighting them head-on just yet. But we can't be seen using the ladders or passageways. So, two of us will take the ventilation shaft up to the crew quarters while another two of us head towards the armoury,' Elenskis instructed.

'Aye, Aye,' Ela and I replied. The man behind us just sighed as we began searching for an access hatch. A frown creased my brow as I followed the burly man's hobbling trajectory. 'You alright there, old man?'

At this, the man simply scowled. 'I'm only twenty-eight, and I'm fine—I didn't drag this corpse of a body out of the marshes of Nufiripin during the spiral offensive just to be mothered by children.'

At this I frowned, thinking through the areas of operation and engagement from the last four years of the spiral offensive, the uncertain expression coalescing in recognition as I spun to face Ela.

'Mariin, you mind telling me why you released a veteran of the harshest amphibious island-hopping campaigns in the last four years?'

Ela simply shrugged as she lifted herself up onto a pair of central impact chairs. 'He said he was prior service *korman, chiif.* I wasn't going to say no to a *medik*, especially one with that death stare,' she replied, brows raised, and left foot hooked back towards the man. 'I've found an access shaft; can somebody give me a hand here?' She continued resting her feet back against the chairs.

'Roger that,' I replied as I scaled the chairs to begin lifting the cover off.

'Y'know, *chiif?* Anybody mention your eyes cut like the cerulean stare of Anki?'

'Stow the sarcasm, *mariin*. Y'know, comparing *chiifs* to *latos* is only technically sacrilege,' I jokingly rebuked as we lifted the covering off.

With the cover removed, I boosted Ela into the shaft, followed by Elenskis before turning to the man. 'Old man, you coming?'

He sighed again as if exhausted by the mere thought of effort. 'I am not an old man; I am Tomas, and I am not being dragged into some gods-forsaken black hole dungeon by paramilitary filth!' he said with a grunt as he stepped up and was eased into the ventilation. A moment later, Ela and Elenskis hoisted me in, and we eased the ventilation cover back into place. The ventilation shaft we'd crawled into was a junction of sorts, welded into the shape of a crooked Y.

'Mariin Tremblej, what's our heading?' Elenskis questioned.

'If my memory is correct, two of us are headed right towards the armoury and another two of us are headed left towards the crew quarters,' Ela explained.

Another sigh echoed from behind. 'Gods-damned fantastic, following the plan of a child who *might* know what she's doing,' he grumbled. Ela began to reply, but I grabbed her upper arm and squeezed till she dropped the matter and turned back to Elenskis.

'Orders, ma'am?' Ela inquired. Elenskis paused once more, her crimson eyes staring intensely at the divide before she spoke.

'I'll go with Starshiina Hart. Tremblej, go with our friend here to the armoury,' she ordered with firm determination.

'Alright, come on, corpse-man,' Ela hissed as she began to crawl right. Tomas huffed out a gruff sigh before following suit. Elenskis turned to me.

'Come on, Sara, we've got some ground to cover,' Elenskis remarked before crawling left. A small smile began to sneak across my lips as I followed behind her.

The crew quarters were in chaos when we finally reached the access hatch that led up into the upper decks. Sailors nervously secured themselves to their rooms' impact chairs while others still moved to man gunnery stations and damage control centres. Amidst the chaos, it'd been relatively simple to slip into an empty berth. The rectangular berth was packed with bedding, built as if stacked on shelves. At the foot or side of each bed was a tall slender locker, its electronic lock glimmering green in the low light of the berth. The vinyl flooring felt aged and grated against my bare feet. As I glanced around, I noticed a peculiar seal emblazoned on the far back wall of the room. At its centre sat a contour drawing of a planet under a star, wrapped in digital wings and guarded by two upraised swords and an anchor. Printed in block letters along the outside of the circular symbol was the name 'Unified Security Group'. I frowned in confusion before turning Elenskis.

'Who do you think we're dealing with? This has to be some rogue Spetsjalist Polits Kor operation. It's too professional, and the Gaponno Fist certainly wouldn't mark themselves with such elaborate imagery,' I remarked indicating towards the emblem.

'I don't know; their equipment doesn't seem right, and ultimately it won't matter if we can get off this ship,' Elenskis calmly replied before opening a footlocker. 'I think this is women's clothing—put this on,' she remarked before passing up a two-piece general work uniform. I slipped out of my Imperial combat uniform and into the new, foreign clothing, the ship's cold air causing my skin to prickle. As the final auto-compression band snapped tight, I looked across the room to the pale face of my commanding officer. Elenskis began to linger, her stern façade beginning to waver.

'Come on, Kapitan, we've got an armoury to raid,' I remarked, my hand settling on her shoulder. As I inched close to her, her sharp jaw began to move in a nod.

'But … first, we've got to take off these gods-damned patches. While it may look strange, it'd look stranger if we're wearing chefs' patches and about to walk into an armoury,' she reminded, her tone strengthening.

'Aye, aye,' I responded as I tore off the patches from their clasps.

'Now. Let's get moving,' Elenskis instructed as she slipped out of the berth.

++++

We'd made our way through the crew quarters and down to the deck just above the security station, peeking down the steel ladder at the forms of two armed sailors who stood on either side of the door, their weapons held at ready-carry. As I continued to look down from my perch, I heard the vulgar tongue of Ela in-between questions.

'"Elaelah Tremblae". That is your name, correct?' asked one of the security personnel in fluent Ympiirno Spraak.

'Wouldn't you like to *brafiksjoti* know? If you've got no gods-damned clue who I am then maybe you are a part of the Gaponno Fist! You change uniforms as often as I change gods-damned tampons!'

'Ignore her, she's just a child who hasn't been buried by her sanity yet,' muttered Tomas. I looked across at Elenskis.

'Well, the decoys worked. Try walking in?' I signed.

'Don't have a better idea,' she signed in reply. With a stern nod, I began to clamber down the ladder to the lower level. The sailors ahead of me quickly noticed my approach, their grips tightening on their weapons before seemingly recognising me and snapping to attention.

'Evening, Lieutenant,' the pair replied as I silently stepped through the hatchway between them. Elenskis followed close behind me. I paused at the heart of the triangular room; the hum of the reactor was quite obvious now, and the wall climbed inwards, its ribbed design in dramatic contrast to the smooth steel aesthetic of the rest of the ship. The officer questioning Ela stopped and turned to face us as we turned in the direction of the armoury, the silhouette of a sailor stepping through the armoury's hatchway.

The officer began to bellow at us as we stepped in. His words were lost on me but his fury obvious as he began to stride towards us, his hand raised in a knife shape. At that, Ela leapt from her chair, swung her arms under herself, and began to run screaming, *'Brafiki jaitsi tormoz zhopas siim shvandik sluka bladnitsa shajstii!!'* as she dashed to the hatchway. At this, the officer pivoted away from me and reached for Ela, quickly followed by the other man who'd been beside him. With her distraction, Elenskis and I raced to the armoury and ducked inside as the hatch slid shut, my palm reaching for the locking mechanism.

I spun to face the room that was now behind us. The silent vibrations of the reactor became much louder as we ventured further into the compartment. Unlike the rest of the ship, the armoury was well-lit with overhead lighting, presumably to ensure that munitions couldn't easily be lost. The sheer volume of equipment was claustrophobic. The room's two main passageways could barely fit one person at a time because of the amount of equipment stored here. The locker's rows of rifle grips tugged at the sleeves of my uniform as I walked through the room towards alien body armour, its sharp, steel frame as if pulled straight from a digital revolution holo or history itself, from its Kevlar-like inserts and its medieval cloth.

'Look at this stuff; this is some capitalist collapse stuff,' Elenskis muttered as she plucked a compact weapon from one of the racks. 'Actual bullets and electromagnetic coils!' she remarked, lifting up a stripper clip of munitions from a locker nearby.

I simply shook my head. 'This just gets stranger by the second,' I muttered to no-one in particular. I turned back towards the armour and lifted the sharp, steel-coloured helmet off its stand. Its outer shell was cool and smooth as I ran my hand over it, yet its visor was warm to the touch. I immediately flipped it over to peer inside at the padded technical intricacies of the protective equipment. The padding was coarse to the touch, yet fresh, as if only recently replaced.

'Let's get geared up; they'll have figured out what happened by now,' Elenskis remarked as she began donning the various pieces of the armour.

I quickly followed suit, adjusting the various metallic plates across my chest, back, and sides with difficulty.

'What is this stuff made of? Actual steel?' I remarked with difficulty as I rested it across my body.

'You hate Union power armour till you remember people used to actually wear *shajst* like this,' Elenskis remarked.

'Apparently still do,' I replied, my voice trailing off.

'Alright, let's stack up,' Elenskis remarked as she slipped her helmet on. As I fitted the cover over my head, its all-encompassing nature perturbing me, an unusually loud thud echoed through the armoury. I lumbered around the stack of rifles in the centre of the armoury to where Elenskis had been, to see her on the floor, convulsing as if in shock, before feeling a sharp pulse through my neck, my vision disappearing in an instant.

I woke with a start, my heart racing, my eyes wide as I caught up with my surroundings. I rapidly realised my hands were in electronic cuffs, and my clothes had been stripped back to my undergarments. More importantly, I wasn't in the armoury anymore.

'Where am I?' I called, expecting the words to fail me once again.

'On the bridge of the Unified Naval Vessel *Kau*,' called a voice in front of me. I took a deep breath to focus myself. To my right kneeled Elenskis, Ela, and the man named Tomas. Around us was the trapezoidal expanse of a bridge. Its floor burned my naked knees, while the dark shadows of armed guards hovered around us. Blue lights flickered and the unintelligible chatter of sailors echoed around us as the black of the Aether curved around the glass viewport. A chair in front of us spun back to face us from its elevated position. A man, his hands curled around his chair's armrest, sat before us.

'You know, when the navy requested that I start this whole "testing breakouts" thing, I didn't expect much of it, but you four surprised me,' he began, his cool features unbothered as he spoke.

'Wait, you speak Ympiirno Spraak?' I spat out.

'I'd be concerned if I didn't. Wasn't raised in the Greater Imperial Union of Sovereign Realms for nothing,' he remarked.

'So, you are a Spetsjalist Polits Kor Agent,' I hissed vehemently.

'Gods no, even after leaving the Imperial War Navy I wouldn't sign onto the Secret Service Bureau if it gave me a gods-damned palace rivalling the empress's throne,' he replied, swatting the idea away as if swatting an insect. I frowned in confusion at his words and his bizarre reverb, but my confusion was interrupted by the muffled writhing furies of Ela. If the situation hadn't been so confusing, I would have laughed. 'Well our candidate seems to want to speak. Lance Corporal Mathers, if you'd be so kind, deactivate the woman's neural inhibitor collar so we can get past her blathering rage.'

'Your troops speak Ympiirno Spraak?' I questioned before the marine could execute her orders.

'Most can, though Lance Corporal Mathers is from old earth. No; as well as inhibiting your body's ability to send signals to your vocal cords, it's also providing a simultaneous translation of our conversation for the convenience of my marines,' said the man before he nodded to Mathers. In a single motion, the marine deactivated the collar and a series of words exploded out of Ela's mouth.

'So, you're Gaponno Fist!' she proclaimed.

'No,' the officer replied, 'I am Colonel Ronald Nelis, Commanding Officer, 1st Marine Corps District, Unified Marine Corps. We—' he paused, gesturing around the bridge, 'are the Unified Security Group. Better known to you as the Taskforce.' At this, emotions of shock, terror, and hatred exploded from all three of us with the man continuing to sit there quite apathetic to the proclamation.

'Are you *brãfiksjoti* kidding me? The Taskforce? As in the children's story?' howled Elenskis, her crimson eyes ignited with fury. 'I've heard it all now. Whichever rogue Spetsjalist Polits Kor Kapitan Lutenant thought up that excuse for kidnappings should go *brafiksjot* themselves!' she spewed.

'We have another twenty-seven hours till we arrive at our rendezvous, so I have all the time in the world to show you the evidence that we are who we claim to be. Here let me show you,' Nelis began before Tomas interrupted.

'What do you want?' he asked plainly. This was reason for pause.

'I beg your pardon?' Nelis said as he turned to look down at Tomas.

'I looked over the people in those rooms. Some are civilians, others prior service personnel, and a lot of them are war heroes in some way, shape, or form. And most of them are criminals which is the other important unifier—Elenskis Jen, formerly Grond Kapitan, Ajnster Rank responsible for the Union defeat at the Siege of Nuleningrad, as well as her Chiif Starshiina Sara Hart and Liider Mariin Ela Tremblej of KKN Grondfors Tu Ten Tu Komando,' he muttered. An air of shame cast over the three of us as he spoke the words.

Nelis bounced off Tomas' remarks. 'He's dead on the money. Imperial War Navy Land Force 22 Commando's failure at New Leningrad wasn't your fault, and we all know that the 227th Correctional "Punishment" Battalion is entirely a waste of your talents. We're offering you employment, escape from your current duties to the Union of Sovereign Realms to make use of your talents to preserve life and peace through prowess; in the sciences, in the art of war, and the arts of espionage.' Nelis paused before changing tone dramatically. 'Of course, escaping prison sentences and being able to fight actual enemies of peace are also on the cards if that's more your speed,' Nelis said nonchalantly as if having missed the volatile bait that'd just been cast into the room. 'I'll tell you what. I'll give you the enlistment papers, and while my marines escort you back to your transportation berth, you can mull them over,' he calmly said as the guards behind us lifted us to our feet and passed us the paperwork. Before we even began walking, Ela was already trying to bite open the folder to begin filling it out.

My face contorted in shock. 'Ela what are you doing?' I called out, leaning closer as we walked.

She looked at me, perplexed. 'You're kidding, right? This is literally a one-way ticket out of prison.'

'Into another one. They could still be sexist like the old Earth for all you know!' I retorted. Ela's face knotted.

'I thought you of all people would be the first to jump at this kind of opportunity. You're the one who was planning to be a lifer; you are one of the only people I know who joined up to actually do something good,' she replied.

I frowned. 'And never seeing your family again is fine?'

'When your own family conscripts you to the Kor Mariin Infantrii to get you out of their hair, they can jump off a cliff for all I'm concerned. Besides, this Taskforce gives me everything I want, the flexibility to *brafik* around with nigh whatever technology I can get my hands on, and gets me a real fight, not some peasant commoners pissed that their crops were bombed.'

I turned to Elenskis as she looked over the folder in her hands. 'You're not seriously considering this too, are you?' I said in distress.

'Why not?' she asked sincerely. 'Since your court-martial, I've been sidelined and my career has been stonewalled. Meikkorek Bataljons are where outcasts go to die in the IUM. But I'm not done, I couldn't see myself outside the service period, and this gives me something I've sought after for a very long time.'

My eyes widened. 'And I'm sorry about that, but seriously? You'd give up your commission?' I was reeling from what I was hearing.

Elenskis couldn't help but choke on her own breath. 'I couldn't bear to hold a commission after Nuleningrad,' she admitted.

I walked in shock, my heart pounding as I looked at her fill out the paperwork.

'If you want to return to a Meikkorek Bataljon, raised simply for deterrence, be my guest, but I'm with Ela on this one. You were always the idealist of us, always looking to do more, to serve the people like we should,' Elenskis replied with a subtle shrug as she looked over the paperwork.

My posture slumped as I looked down at the papers in my hands. *Why am I arguing this?* I wondered to myself. *You've done worse for infinitely less! And isn't this the very reason you shot Lutenant Foksel?* I fumed to myself before finally awkwardly opening up the khaki dossier as we walked, its freshly pressed card soft yet alien to the touch. Inside sat a single pen and a single sheet of smooth paper, its sensation foreign to me. The form had the watermark of the Taskforce logo. The form itself was relatively straightforward, albeit alien to a woman from the twenty-fifth century. Simple things such as name, date of birth, height, weight, preferred Military Occupational Specialty (MOS), and preferred branch. After filling out the paperwork, I folded the folder in on itself and marched on in silence back to our berth. Instead of leading us to our berth, however, the marines lead us into the large open space originally marked on the schematics. The grey-white deck was packed with armouries and operating theatres to rival almost any Imperial Combat Support Hospital. Here, formation after formation of trainees were being briefed, berated, and intensely exercised in group 'smokings' by Taskforce instructors. After lining us up into orderly rows, one of the instructors stepped forward.

'Welcome to Combined Basic Military Training, trainees!' she boomed as she stood in the centre of the doorway, her long shadow casting an imposing image into the room. 'For all you numb *shajst,* that abbreviates to CBMT!' she roared before continuing, 'I am Senior Taskforce instructor Hejding! You are to refer to me as STFI or ma'am! I am the literal manifestation of Eri herself! My word is law, my word is final, and my word will bring you pain, suffering, and torment, and until I am told otherwise that will be the case! Now, I have been told by the *siim* buckets in OPSI that you are some of the finest Imperials we've ever found! And that you may just be the finest soldiers, sailors, marines, and airmen this Taskforce ever makes! Well, I don't care if you're the gods'-own golden *Slukas!* You are, all of you, *tormoz*, who couldn't wipe their own *zhopas* if they tried!' she screamed, the vein in her skull rising as she howled. We stood in silence. 'This silence is not the appropriate response, *brufik* rags!' the STFI barked.

'Yes, ma'am!' we cried in response, snapping to attention.

With that, Hejding and her fellow instructors threw themselves at their jobs with enthusiasm, spewing verbal abuse quickly and without discrimination as we were herded into rows upon rows of barber chairs that lined the centre of the deck. The barbers threw their blades into our hair, slicing it off with unparalleled and terrifying speed and precision before a woman temporarily relieved the instructors of their duties. She stood before us a moment, her golden tan skin bright in the overhead lighting. As we continued to look on in confusion, she quietly sighed before screaming, 'Trainees! You are not demonstrating proper military etiquette!' We finally realised the importance of her collar-mounted pins. We snapped to attention and saluted as we realised she was an officer.

'Trainees! Welcome to Composite Surgical Armoury One. I am Lieutenant Junior Grade Michiko Stratton. I'm a part of the administrative staff for CSA One. Any questions?' she queried.

'Yeah, what is a Composite Surgical Armoury?' questioned one of my former commanders. The lieutenant drew a deep breath.

'Did I authorise you to neglect your reporting statement, trainee?' Michiko exclaimed.

'Ma'am! Trainee Veitenberg reports! No, ma'am!' former Kapitan, Zvajter Rank Veitenberg barked back.

'Then why did you neglect to show the proper respect?' Michiko barked.

'Ma'am! Trainee Veitenberg reports! No idea, ma'am!' Veitenberg replied as he shifted to parade rest.

'Did I instruct you to move to parade rest trainee?' the lieutenant barked.

Veitenberg quickly corrected his instinct. 'Ma'am! Trainee Veitenberg reports! No, ma'am!' he continued as he snapped back to attention.

'Lose the ma'am sandwich, trainee!' Michiko bellowed with fury.

'Trainee Veitenberg reports! Yes, ma'am!' Veitenberg replied.

'Now, what was your question, trainee?'

'Trainee Veitenberg reports! What is a Composite Surgical Armoury? Ma'am!' Veitenberg yelled in reply.

'Composite Surgical Armouries, or CSAs, are where you will receive armour adjustments, medical treatments, and Cephi 7—a Biological-Nano-Machine that acts as a combat enhancer, improving your battlefield survival and success rates by altering your neural, musculoskeletal, arterial, and optical systems,' she explained as if flicking a switch. 'Surgery will be in ten, but first, we need to get you cleaned up,' Stratton remarked before tending to another batch of trainees.

A nearby Taskforce instructor threw themselves at us, hauling us into a spare latrine before spitting us back out, freshly clothed in surgical gown and soaked. *I do not miss boot camp*, I thought to myself. Now cleaned up, the instructors ordered us into one neat column, the barber's chairs now safely tucked into the deck as we awaited the surgeons to complete preparations. The deck was smooth like marble but sturdy like steel. I was freezing in my gown. When it finally came time to begin operations, the instructors began relaying operating theatres to individual trainees before authorising them to walk across to their theatre. I was called last and allocated Operating Theatre 220, which I strode into silently and as calmly as I could. The doors sealed behind me as I walked up the ramp. The smell of chemical disinfectants permeated the air. At the centre of the room sat a long operating table, overshadowed by a cluster of imposing mechanical arm-like appendages. To the left was an observatory of sorts where a man now stood, concentrating on his work. The man looked up.

'Trainee Hart, correct?'

'Yes, sir,' I sharply replied.

'I'm Doctor Felta; please take your gown off and lie down on the table, Ms Hart,' he clinically replied, looking back down at his console. I disrobed and slipped onto the memory foam-like table, the liquid material reacting and hardening as it matched my form. My skin quivered in the cool theatre.

'This is Surgeon-Major Dane to all trainees,' boomed an unseen woman. 'Do not be afraid of what is to come. Under anaesthesia, your assigned surgeon will implant cybernetic enhancements to critical joints and key neural pathways throughout your body. Following these alterations, Cephi 7 will be administered directly to critical components of your body where Biological Nano-Machines will adjust your physiology to improve operational performance. Doctors, administer the anaesthetic now,' Dane instructed.

'Mr Marr, could you please administer general anaesthetic,' Felta instructed over the intercom.

'Yes, doctor,' replied a quiet male. A door near the observation room snapped open, revealing a lanky male nurse who slipped on his airtight surgery suit and stepped out past the containment field. He strode over to me and activated a cluster of buttons on the side of the table. As an electrical hum fluttered into the air, the nurse gently tugged a translucent mask out from below the table and pressed the mask close to my face. I quickly fell unconscious.

When I slowly began to reawaken from my slumber, my vision was blurred, my skin numb, my senses blind as I regained consciousness; my body burned from the inside. My cells felt violated; my heart twisted as it struggled to find its rhythm. My breath felt like sulphur. When the theatre's decontamination protocols were completed, Dr Felta re-opened the door and Elenskis Jen strode in, also struggling to find her feet. She lifted me off the table and helped me back to our meagre squad bay. Elenskis lowered me down before sneaking off to the ship's wardroom to dilute the pain. I simply passed out.

Chapter 2
Familiar sights, familiar sounds

0600 Hours Zulu. Unified Naval Vessel Kau

The pitched sound of a whistle echoed through the ship's 1 Main Circuit (1MC) before the clean voice of the ship's Boatswain's Mate of the Watch echoed over: 'Now reveille, reveille, all hands heave out and trice up. Give a clean sweep down fore and aft. The smoking lamp is lit in all authorised spaces.'

My eyes flickered with each word, but my mind remained in a haze as my limp limbs struggled to move. My mind faded back into unconsciousness as an alarm screamed through our squad bay; blood-red light and the scream of klaxons flooded the bay. 'Attention, trainees!' exclaimed the Senior Taskforce Instructor. I recoiled in shock. The berth was bright like fire and the TFI's instructions were a piercing whine that punctured my ears. My body pulsed with pain.

'I said get up, trainees!' the STFI continued to bark. 'I don't got all day you dumb-*zhopas brufiks*!' she continued to scream. Fellow instructors entered the room and dragged us to our feet. My knees felt weak as if bashed in with a club, my back and skull whined with pain. 'Instructor Grigs! Instructor Breker! Give 'em their eyes and ears back,' instructed the STFI.

The other instructors nodded before snapping to and stepping down the line, going through a short process of acclimatisation with each trainee. A pulse of bright light, distinct from the incoherent smattering of inputs, pierced to the heart of each eye. I blinked as the light hit my iris and the screaming brightness began to fade. The instructor lowered the small handheld torch that she'd just pulsed across my retina and raised a small circular clicker that she again rapidly clicked beside either ear. As the sound pierced through the white noise, my hearing began to return, and the muted drone of the berth's klaxon returned to my senses as the instructor moved on down the line.

'Now that you *brufiks* can see 'n' hear again, I said 'Attention!' the senior instructor barked. We drearily snapped to attention, our posture sloppy and our form poor. We stood in silence. 'This silence is not the appropriate response, *brufik* rags!' the STFI barked.

'Aye, ma'am!' we exclaimed.

'Now! Fall *in*!' continued the STFI. We quickly fell into two columns. 'Platoon! Mark, *time*!' she continued. We began to march without moving. My legs were weak, my balance out and my arms wide in a vain attempt to balance myself. 'Platoon! Forward, *march*!' she boomed. As we unceremoniously began to stride out of the berth at the STFI's command, each of us swayed precariously as if heavily intoxicated, our naked flesh boiling to the touch. The Taskforce instructor directed us down to the lower level where we loosely fell into three rows. The surgical operating theatres had been sealed up and the barber stations had been replaced with an intricate gym. Hejding intercepted our stares. 'Now, *zhopas brufiks*! Before I send you off for the Hakon, you're gonna get reacquainted with your *bladsa zhopas* bodies!' she boomed as fellow instructors marched down the three rows that we had formed, handing out cross-branch physical training uniforms. The grey and black two-piece PT uniform was designed around Taskforce black shorts and pants with reflective stripes along the sides with the letters 'USG' written on the left leg while the Taskforce grey shirt and sweatshirt bore the same lettering on the left chest and centred on the back of the silvery shirt. Lastly, among the other Taskforce-issued underwear, socks, and watch caps was the standardised Taskforce issue bright orange (*brafiksjoti* sunspot) reflective belt that was required to be worn everywhere and at all times, especially during PT.

'Platoon! Un*brufik* yourselves! Asap! Your naked *zhopas shajst* ain't worth the looks!' Hejding howled.

I began to lower the pile of neatly folded clothes onto the cold, smooth deck, my joints aching as I bent, before seizing up like many of my fellow recruits as we finally saw the extent of the operation, beyond the boiling pain, blinding light, and deafening sound. My eyes widened, and my heart began to race as I looked down the length of my arm and gingerly touched the edges of my right elbow, the skin red-raw and the pain near excruciating where a dumbbell-shaped object had been forcefully slammed through my cartilage. As I reached across, I glimpsed the grey shimmer of another of these 'bolts', this time buried in my left elbow. My gaze drifted toward the four that cut through my knees and thighs, before settling on the pair of medical ports embedded in my abdomen. My face began to convulse as fear and panic began to settle in. *What have I signed up for?* I remember wondering to myself. I clenched my fist as I started to spiral into anxiety and closed my eyes almost wishing it to be a dream. *No, no, there's got to be something to it, it can't be what it seems,* I rationalised, slowing my heart rate and letting my worries flow through my body before returning my thoughts to the task at hand. I unfurled the pile of clothes and began to slip on my undergarments, my thighs screaming as I slipped on the first part of my underwear, before raising the rigid sports bra over my head and sliding it down around my arms where it snapped tight to my skin, sending violent impulses down my spine and out through the tips of my toes. I frowned in discomfort, and fear picked at my thoughts as I reached down my spine and felt the pricks of six pin-sized holes each exactly spaced down the length of my back. I clenched my teeth as I pushed through the cloud of emotions that roiled within. *There's got to be a reason,* I thought to myself again and again as I slipped on the rest of the uniform. Its automatically tightening and straightening fabrics made the whole process of clothing oneself even more mindless than it already was.

'Okay *brufik* stains!' Instructor Hejding boomed as we finished slipping into our uniforms. 'The surgeon-major ain't here just yet, so to keep entertained ...' the instructor trailed off. 'Pair off! Let's get off easy here!' Hejding roared. With that, instructors strode down our lines and dragged us together, regardless of who exactly we were paired off with. I looked at the woman I'd been paired with through ever-so-slightly warped vision. I couldn't help but smirk at Elenskis. 'Positions!' Hejding boomed. I pulled back onto my right leg, bending my knees as I raised my fists to protect my chest. 'Three-stage sparring! Right to left! One!' Hejding continued as the entire platoon stumbled forwards. I stumbled backwards, my knees feeling like elastic under my weight as Elenskis lazily advanced, her fist gliding through the air as if wading through water. I smirked.

'Taking it easy now, are we?' I mocked.

'And you aren't?' she retorted with a smirk. The two of us frowned as we moved through the motions of stage two. Neither of us was holding back.

'Three!' Hejding cried before adding, 'Contact sparring! Try not to kill yourselves.' As her instructions carried through the room, the whole platoon erupted in a flurry of kicks, punches, and blocks. Elenskis and I just stood there for a moment before throwing ourselves at each other. My fists immediately went for her throat; one after the other, she easily threw them away as if they were blind flails before she swung a boot towards mine that I easily stopped with my hand. Both of us frowned as we reversed the other's strikes and threw our opponent into the ground sending bursts of pain through our backs. 'Alright! I said not to kill yourselves! Your white *zhopas* bodies are too damned expensive for you to be killin' each other!' Hejding bellowed.

'Officer on deck!' Grigs screamed, causing each of us to crawl from the deck that we'd been violently tussling on and snap to attention, saluting. The officer returned the salute before Hejding began.

'Platoon! Fall *in*!' Hejding barked, and each of us quickly complied, falling into a series of mostly neat rows. 'Platoon! Open *ranks*!' Hejding called before continuing. 'Now, Surgeon-Major Dane is gon't explain to you how to *unbrufik* yourselves!' our Senior TFI bellowed as she stepped aside to give the Surgeon-Major centre stage, her face uncurling from a scowl as it passed the instructor.

'Thank you, Senior Instructor Hejding. Platoon 1234!' Dane boomed, clearly used to this part of the process.

'As you know, last night you were administered Cephi 7 alongside a number of cybernetic enhancements, more commonly known as a "combat enhancers". However, you certainly lack the understanding of what any of that actually entails or, more importantly, what that changes,' Dane began to explain. 'This is a safety brief issued to all trainees immediately after augmentation and is not supplementary to your usual safety briefing,' Dane continued. I mentally sighed. 'All trainees are reminded to utilise the handrail at all times when ascending and descending the stairwell as your body adjusts to its accelerated nervous system and augmented auditory system.' Dane paused. 'Trainees are also reminded to avoid the following: lifting in excess of 311 kilograms, running faster than 26.83 kilometres per hour, imposing over 4,364 newtons of force, exposing your eyes to over 700 lumens or your implants to water for the next ninety-six hours,' Major Dane explained. *That's what that is,* I thought to myself with mild concern as memories of the red-raw pinpricks along my spine came flooding back.

'To piggyback off what the major just said: that means do not throw yourselves at walls, do not throw yourselves at each other, do not point lasers at your eyes, do not point flashlights at your eyes, do not stare at the lights and do not shower in unfiltered water,' Hejding reiterated.

'The more technical aspects of how this was achieved will be available to peruse when we arrive at the *Hakon* with your official materials. But for the time being, are there any questions?' Major

Dane added, her tone softening as if anticipating the nature of the questions.

I frowned, rubbing the inside of my palm as I spoke, my heart already racing. 'Trainee Hart reports. Permission to speak, ma'am,' I requested.

'Go ahead, Trainee Hart,' she replied. I hesitated.

'Exactly how strong are we now and what are the long-term side effects?'

The Surgeon-Major paused again; her grimace spoke for her. She'd gone through this part of the briefing before and it hadn't ended well. 'So, your strength, speed, durability, and reaction times are more or less about double the numbers I just rattled off. As for the long-term effects of Cephi 7 …' her voice trailed off. 'Because Cephi 7 is biomechanical in nature—' she paused as if stumbling for words, 'we have extended your normal life expectancy beyond the naturally possible. To date, not a single Taskforce service member, with Cephi 7 or any of its previous iterations, has died of natural causes in over two hundred years, and the projected life expectancy has risen closer to a little under five hundred,' the doctor explained. The hush of shock carried through the room as we realised the long-term implications we had just signed up for. We would outlive our children's children, our wives, our husbands, our brothers and sisters. I would outlive my sisters, mother, and father, and their families before I was even teenage. We had signed a lifelong contract with Jioma himself and even age couldn't escape that fact. Of course, we didn't even know the half of it. I didn't even know the half of it.

'So, wait; are there actually any drawbacks to this Cephi 7? Long life and stupidly powerful? I don't see any downsides there,' interjected Ela. I clenched my fist in frustration before releasing it with a sigh as the TFI lit up like a furnace but was restrained by Dane.

'There are certainly biological drawbacks. First and foremost, because your body can lift over three times the average person's, the pain you will experience is also exacerbated and, as you also quickly discovered this morning, your eyes and ears are now susceptible to extreme shifts in EM frequency, electromagnetic pulses, and abnormal electromagnetic phenomenon, leaving you blind and deaf to the outside world.' She paused once more. 'With that in mind, you are now lethal weapons; you are the culmination of billions of years of biological and technological evolution. You are the pinnacle of biomechanical engineering in the universe; you are weapons, waiting to be unleashed against chaos itself, the gates of Hutama, Valhak, and Hel itself will not stop you,' she explained with renewed vigour. Her prophetic words hung in the air as if we'd just attended the speech of a 1,000, when the priesthood of Nuberlin had collectively immolated themselves in protest of Emperor Vasili the Third's loosened eugenics policies or the Declaration of Xendarin Independence, when the exiled Abetra, in one voice, had said no to Imperial rule. But that moment faded as Surgeon-Major Dane lowered her right hand.

Our STFI kicked back into full gear, running us back through the wringer thanks to Ela's remarks. By the end of it, our lungs were screaming in pain as they struggled to keep up with our bodies' needs, and our skin was boiling as our muscles poured piss and vinegar into our veins; by the end of it, pain rippled through me.

Chapter 3
Bad knees and boot camp

Our Senior TFI glanced down at a small, loosely rectangular touchscreen pad strapped to her wrist.

'Alright, *brufik* knuckles! Fall *in*!' she barked. We broke from our exercise and formed up in front of her. She paused for a moment, a sigh slipping through her implacable façade before she spoke. 'So, I's got good news and bad news,' the Senior TFI paused. 'The bad news is you'll be leaving me to get your battle dress uniform!' We all gave out a sigh of relief. The torture was over. 'But! The good news is, I'll be correcting you *tormozed brufik*-knuckles down on the surface,' she exclaimed with glee. The torment was only delayed. 'But first! You'll need to get cleaned up! Instructor Breker! Get 'em squared away for their date!' she instructed.

With that, a pair of TFIs began to bark as loud as they could, dragging all thirty-two of us through the '*shajst*, shower, and shave' routine in the paired set of showers and heads that divided the CSA in two. Under the screaming whine of our TFIs, all of us were thrown into an open bay shower. The water hit me like a freight train, my entire body screaming as water washed over me. The aching rushed off my body with the water; as I stood there, my hands scrubbed down my skin, pushing the discomfort out as if by magic. But without the muscle ache, old torments re-emerged; my spine cried out in agony as the purple water/soap concoction was kneaded into my back by another recruit. My knuckles wept in anguish as they ran across my body, the skin thin and raw from the implants, my bones ached under the frigid water, as if split down the bone and pounded into putty. My lungs pulsed with fury as I inhaled, the freezing air rattling my entire body as the water was abruptly cut off and I was shoved into the head across the way. I reached out to stop myself as I slammed into the head in front of me. Its cold angular frame sent a chill straight up my shoulders as I slowly propped myself back up and sat down on the metallic frame, the cold surface enflaming my injuries further. I sat there confused, panicked, in shock. *What have I signed up for? Have I been lied to? Is this worth it all?* My mind was racing. Suddenly, the head's frame shook around me, and I was thrown back into the present, shaking as my still-naked body shivered in the frigid warship air.

'Get out of there, trainee!' boomed one of the TFIs. My muscles convulsed in fear as the TFI continued. 'What the *brafik* are you doing, trainee?' the instructor continued to boom. 'If you don't get out of there right this minute trainee, I will break down this door; do you understand?' she finally boomed, kicking the door this time. My eyes widened, and as if abruptly aware, I rose and burst out, practically into the instructor's boot. 'Trainee, what in the gods' names do you think you're doing?'

'Trainee Hart reports! No idea, ma'am!' I replied, snapping to attention as best I could.

'Then get out of my sight, trainee! Locker rooms are that way!' the instructor boomed, pointing towards the door to my right.

'Trainee Hart reports! Yes, ma'am!' I replied before immediately striding off towards the lockers where the rest of the training platoon was already dried, dressed, and at attention awaiting instructions. Instructor Breker stepped into the room as I finished slipping on my unified combat utility uniform. Her eyes swept across the locker room, her gaze unwavering.

'Trainees! Dismissed!' Breker finally boomed. With that, the entire platoon responded to her instruction and filed out in silence. My thoughts began to drift, the world became a pale cut-out before my eyes as I processed the life I'd mistakenly agreed to as a voice filled my mind.

'Trainee Sara Hart. It'll be fine, just breathe,' the voice muttered, almost disinterested. My eyes widened, and I froze much to the amusement of naval security patrolling along the catwalks above. My gaze searched around frantically for the voice, quickly realising that we had all heard the same voice.

'Trainee Hart. If you can hear this, my name is Konstans Chia, and I'm your integration supervisor—take a deep breath, I'll walk you through this. It's going to be alright, trainee,' she reassured me. My heart rate stabilised, my muscles relaxed, and my vision began to return to me. 'Now you're back with the land of the living—I think that's the metaphor,' Chia remarked with a nervous chuckle. I couldn't help but smirk, much to the glowering stares of TFIs around the deck who couldn't do a thing to us right now. 'If you turn to your left, you'll see a very familiar face,' she explained, her tone ever-reassuring.

I looked out across the colossal deck towards the indents that lined the walls, housing thousands of armour bays, each manned by an armourer and containing everything an infantrywoman in the twenty-fifth century would ever require. As my gaze swept across the bay, all I remember thinking was how similar they were to armour stations aboard Imperial vessels (even today), but in the middle of all that, something caught my eye. Not the smooth, utilitarian design of the armour bay, nor the multi-appendaged armour mechanism that would string me up like the Vitruvian woman, or the alien furnace that blazed away behind all of it. No, the man staring intently into the screen of an operations station was who'd caught my eye; my mind began to race, through shock, disbelief, excitement, and confusion. *That's impossible, how could he? Why?* I began to wonder, my thoughts cutting themselves short as I squinted at the familiar face, the armourer's sharp but scorched jaw unmistakable. I froze, and my heart skipped a beat as a familiar feeling began to wash over me. I broke into a jog before I was thrown forward, my face slamming into the cold deck and my feet resting on a single strand of Tangible Holographic Plasma

(THP). The TFIs quietly chuckled to themselves as the armourer gave me a rebuking finger wag.

'Do not run in my armour bay. If I need saving, then is fine. Am I clear?' questioned the Russian man.

'Yes, sir? Um, do—' I began as I rose from the deck before being quickly interrupted.

'Do not call me "sir", I am neither instructor nor officer,' he quickly chastised me. 'Now walk over to the *tvastar*,' he instructed indicating towards the mechanical monstrosity at the heart of the bay, clearly preoccupied.

'Wait! Can I ask you a question?' I interjected.

'I'll ignore that rude and blatant disrespect for protocol, trainee. Yes, what is it?' the man asked, though not nearly as interested in the conversation as I was.

'Are you Dimitri Malekova, formerly of the Rojal Ympiirno Field Artileri Tu Ten Tu, Bataljon Trei and uncle to Sara Hart?' I continued, hoping it was him.

'Yes, but how do you know so much?' This time, more interested.

'Because your niece is standing right in front of you!' I exclaimed. He looked up from his desk, and when he saw me, his face lit up with joy.

'Darling!' he exclaimed with delight, his strong Russian accent truly breaking through this time. 'Since when did you join the Corps of Naval Infantry?'

I blinked at the translation of Kor Mariin Infantrii.

'Just after your convoy went missing, Uncle Dimi, and you never return—' I began to explain before Uncle Dimi interrupted me.

'Wait, I had a flash clone, what happened to it?' he asked, confused.

'You mean a *primsjns*? Never appeared. You were the only marine registered MIA from Rojal YFA Tu Ten Tu after your two-week stint in the Shroud,' I replied.

'Well, I must file a complaint about that, but another time. Welcome to the Taskforce, darling Sayra. Normally I'd only be assigned to your training platoon for the duration of CBMT, but I am going to take you under my wing, and we will have very *korosh vremja*. Now, please, disrobe and step up to the *tvastar*, but don't run in my armour bay. You may be my niece, but you will still not run in my armour bay,' Uncle Dimi instructed.

A moment of embarrassment pulsed through me as I disrobed and tucked the clothes back into the bag they had been issued to me in before pausing with mild confusion. 'Right-hand side, there is a bin to place your gear in,' Uncle Dimi remarked as if distant. I quickly located what he was talking about and tucked my clothes into the bin, eyeing a small alcove in the wall where a neatly folded one-piece body glove was materialising before my eyes. After quickly glancing at the odd alcove, I turned towards the *tvastar* and stepped on. A wave of confusion washed over my mind as I advanced towards the oddly empty podium. At the centre of the podium sat the white lines that marked out where I needed to stand. I quickly obeyed as the floor below me dropped unexpectedly before stabilising.

'Okay, Sayra, let's do this,' he said, a weak cheer returning to him. 'Beginning phase one. Initiating geometric scan … now, scan in progress.'

Thousands of blue gridded triangles exploded out of the projectors in the roof and began to circle my body, tracking up, down, left, and right.

'Okay, geometric scan complete. Starting up molecular moulding forge … now. Okay, moulding complete. Cooling.' He waited a moment. 'Collect your body glove now please,' he explained, enthralled in his work.

I quickly obliged, stepping down from the *tvastar* and striding across towards the alcove I'd previously seen. I remember feeling the wave of self-consciousness fade from memory as I slipped into the black body glove, its skin gripping tight to mine, moulding around my shape and form to perfection, slipping over my joints flawlessly and matching my every curve.

'Step back up to the *tvastar* please,' Uncle Dimi instructed. I followed the instruction without question. 'Okay, phase one complete,' he paused. 'Please raise your arms,' he instructed. I quickly complied, my body now shaped like the ancient Vitruvian Man. 'Applying phase two components … now.' Uncle Dimi continued as the floor burst open to reveal a cluster of arms carrying a variety of gauntlets and chest pieces that were fervently fashioned to me. Pain began to pulse through me as the plates were rapidly clamped onto my body's impact dampeners. I now began to truly understand the ramifications of my enlistment. I began to panic. My heart raced, and I began to struggle, fight out as I panicked. *It can't be real. What have I signed up for?* I remember wondering. Uncle Dimitri quickly noticed and paused the process.

'Do not be afraid, Trainee Hart,' Chia interjected.

'Cancel interaction, Chia, I can handle this,' Dimitri interrupted. With that, Chia's voice faded away.

'What the *brafik* are you doing to me?' I howled in terror.

'I'm applying your battle dress uniform,' he began to explain softy. 'Due to the limitations of the human body, particularly joints, Project Phoenix introduced impact dampeners constructed of a graphene-based carbon nanotube to keep your joints intact. Otherwise, you'd pulverise your cartilage the second your fist connected with an immecrete wall,' Dimitri calmly explained. 'As well as this safety measure, the impact dampeners were installed with magnetic hardpoints to allow you to wear your body armour without physical combat webbing and in a precautionary effort to avoid plate interlock failure,' he explained. My breath began to slow, and my heart rate slowed in tandem as I nodded in acknowledgement. 'Are you good?'

'Good,' I said with timid strength. Uncle Dimitri quietly returned to his station and recommenced. The tvastar's mechanical arms returned to rapidly clamping the eighteen-piece battle dress uniform. As each piece was affixed, a flexible, self-correcting interlock switched on as the plates were pressed against my body glove. Shin and thigh plates were wrapped around my legs while shoulder plates and wrist guards were rapidly slipped on and automatically tightened to fit my contoured arms; finally, the thick, loosely H-shaped, rear-mounted reactor housing and curved ballistic chest plate were lowered and locked together with magnetic clamps across my shoulders and waist before a heavy collar was fitted around my neck. As the tvastar made final adjustments to my body armour, another arm began to lower, its dark shadow skirting around the podium as it lowered. My eyes widened in fear. *Shajst, shajst, shajst, shajst, shajst!* I thought to myself as the object continued to descend towards my head, my armour's collar impeding me from looking around as the object surrounded my head and a crisp seal formed around the rim, the last vestiges of foreign O2 expelled as the two-piece helmet sealed. My heart rate slowed, and my mind calmed. *It's a helmet, brafikwit,* I thought to myself, embarrassed about my panic attack. Amidst the pause, the quiet hiss of medical ports echoed in the suit.

'Armour fitting complete,' Uncle Dimi faintly called through the armour. 'Okay, bringing your suit online,' he muttered. 'Connecting micro fusion reactor to the grid now,' Uncle Dimi added. A surreal hum began to echo through the suit as the variety of environmental sensors, computers, magnetic plates, and wireless transceivers whirred to life. The dark interior of my helmet faded away as internal lights and displays began to flicker to life; sporadic pulses of pain pierced through my back and up through my spine as the armour awoke before quickly settling into a subtle pattern of jolts.

'Micro fusion reactor within acceptable safety margins, memory crystal functioning within parameters, wireless transceiver online. Switching over to suit comms, is that better?' My uncle's voice came through the suit's crisp high definition speakers.

'Reading five by five,' I reported. As the rest of my pain began to wear off, the thunder of a headache, began to echo through my skull, and I winced.

'Is everything all right?' Uncle Dimi immediately asked.

'I've got one Azvod of a headache, and I don't know why,' I replied with a wince of pain.

'I'm presuming that would be your subdermal implant and your neural interface,' he replied.

I frowned. 'Subdermal implants? Neural interface? I feel like I'm missing something. The Major only said not to expose them to unfiltered water.'

'Wait? You don't get subdermal implants in the union military anymore?' he said as he rubbed the side of his skull. I shook my head.

'It's an implant no larger than a nail. It works as a tracking beacon and digital dog tags. While we still issue physical dog tags, these allow you to be found and identified in case you—you're killed.' Uncle Dimi stumbled over his words. A frigid silence fell upon the bay.

'*Et Kolosh*,' I attempted; he laughed at my poor attempt to speak Russian.

'I must teach you Rashaano Spraak again, darling!'

'And what's this neural implant?'

'Your neural interface is what bridges the gap between the biological and the technological; what it feels, you feel, and vice versa. Your battle dress uniform is both metaphorically and practically an extension of you. The difference between woman and machine is very difficult to define,' he explained.

'And why would I have a headache?'

'Because both of them are screaming electrical signals that are bleeding into your brain; the neural implant is the easier one. Once your body acclimates to the slightly different electrical pattern, it will simply feel like nothing is different; your subdermal implant, however …' Uncle Dimi's voice drifted off, '… it'll hurt to high Azvod for the rest of life, you just gotta deal with it or con some Mort out of your corpsman,' he explained.

'Okay, bringing your suit's operating system online,' Uncle Dimi continued, throwing his attention back to his computer. The various displays in my helmet flickered and lines of code began to roll down my helmet's visor as my suit moved from standby status. With a final flicker of code, my helmet-mounted display appeared before me, the top-mounted compass spinning erratically as it attempted to find magnetic north to little avail. In the left-hand corner, dozens of blue markers appeared stretching for kilometres, beyond the scope of the IFF tracker. 'Operating system functioning within acceptable margins,' Uncle Dimi remarked before moving on. 'Commencing AI integration.' Uncle Dimi moved to activate a switch before hesitating. 'What the *shto za chjort*? Don't even know if the hardware can support such a thing.' He paused to look over the armour specifications again. 'So that's how they're accounting for it,' he continued before activating a switch. My eyes began to blur, and foreign thoughts began to roam through my mind and my skin fell numb. 'AI integration complete, correcting audio-visual organs ... now,' Uncle Dimi continued. My vision began to return.

'What the *shto za chjort* was that?' I cursed.

'Language!' Uncle Dimi hissed with joking disgust before continuing, 'That was your suit processing a Tier Three AI. Remember, you and your body armour are now intrinsically linked, meaning anything it feels, you feel. Your armour has a thick layer of micro superconducting memory crystal, known by most in the service as an SMC, within. To ensure that the crystal doesn't overheat, your BDU pumps the memory crystal with liquid nitrogen. And while your armour protects you from the adverse effects of the liquid nitrogen, the extreme cold is translated back to your hypothalamus. Best way to describe that sensation is an impression of numbness. That's what you just felt,' Uncle Dimi explained.

I frowned. 'Wait, wasn't I supposed to be issued a Tier One AI?'

'You should have been,' Uncle Dimi replied with an exasperated huff of air. 'I'd say it was an error on NAVLOG's end, but your suit specifications included an externally mounted liquid nitrogen supply to keep your body glove's SM crystal layer from overheating, so I have no idea. I'll hit up logistics command when we get to UV-25-38,' Uncle Dimi replied before shrugging nonchalantly. 'Well, while you've got a Tier Three, you're stuck with it,' he said. 'To finish answering your question, I'm assuming you saw a variety of bizarre and foreign thoughts during the transfer,' he anticipated. I nodded. 'That's because your body's fibre optic linkages were transmitting the thoughts of your AI; your body armour acts as a conduit for two minds to exist in a single body,' Uncle Dimi explained before pausing. 'Now, Mariko! Are you there?'

'Affirmative, Armourer Malekova. Good gods, how am I supposed to operate out of this prison?' hissed the thick accent of a Japanese woman over my suit's speakers before remembering protocol. 'Trainee Hart, excellent to meet you. I am Hiroshi Mariko, Service Number 02918-76521-HM. I am your Field Combat Assistant, or FCA. I am designed to improve and maintain Field Combat Efficiency, FCE. To do so, I have been loaded with broad infiltration and analytics protocols.'

'Well, hello, Hiroshi,' I replied. The AI broadcast a tutting sound.

'Hiroshi is my surname, Trainee Hart, a Japanese name is given surname first. My name is Mariko, as Armourer Malekova has been demonstrating.'

I tensed with frustrated embarrassment.

'Okay, you can step down from the *tvastar*,' Uncle Dimi remarked. I quickly complied as the *tvastar* sealed back up. I found the suit was surprisingly light considering its protective capabilities.

'Now, the first thing you should know: although Research Command officially refers to this thing as a semi-powered combat suit, it's all bull*shajst*. The force hasn't had the *jaitsi* to produce even one of those since the Concealer War; what you're wearing is more accurately a battle dress uniform which is effectively a glorified ballistic vest with air conditioning and a Kinetic Plate Matrix, or KPM. Even a semi-powered exoskeleton would be better than this!' Uncle Dimi hissed. 'This, it's very basic, very un-classy, not good. Having worked with mobile defence suits here and there, the original combat suit, even the old, powered combat skeletons—these are child's play,' he said with mild frustration.

'In saying that, your armour's crystalline layer and neural fibre were all kept, thank the gods, from our networking days, despite

OPSI's concerns after the Concealer War. Now, let me explain your equipment,' he said with a nod.

'Firstly, as you may have noticed, your black body glove is heavier than the kind you would be issued by the CNI. That's because your body glove is now the base for a thin layer of micro superconducting memory crystal, as I have explained, and a thick layer of hydrostatic gel. The hydrostatic gel will enable you to survive falls harder than your body can currently survive and will regulate your internal body temperature to keep you alive,' he explained, pulling up a holographic breakdown of my BDU's design. 'For your equipment's greater design, your BDU is made up of eighteen plates of Carbyne-A2, a carbon-titanium alloy designed to absorb extreme impacts. As well as this, your BDU is equipped with an adaptive camouflage system constructed from photoreactive panelling lined throughout the armour.' Dimitri paused. 'Lastly is the basic *shajst*.'

'Language,' I jokingly replied with a smirk on my face.

Dimitri paid no attention to my comment. 'Your suit runs on a micro fusion reactor, but you will still require the requisition of a set of replacement liquid nitrogen canisters for extended operation until LOGCOM decides it screwed up.' He paused. 'That pretty much wraps up everything,' he finished.

I looked down and began to inspect the armour quickly settling on the weight of the gauntlets. 'Why're these heavier than the rest?'

'Oh, because that's where the "semi-powered" comes in,' Uncle Dimi explained, with air quotation marks. 'They basically pulled up the old AE10 actuation cylinders from the MDS and loaded six of them in each gauntlet. While I adore the MDS for being a combat suit, it wasn't without its problems. The AE10s were never particularly reliable and had a tendency to overheat, and their liquid nitrogen cooling systems were never particularly well designed. During basic, they'll run you through the exact process of shutting down your gauntlets, because if deactivated too quickly, they'll suffer from catastrophic failure and fuse the entire gauntlets together, at which point your suit's automatic repair systems will have to clear out the fused metal and the actuators will have to be ejected,' Uncle Dimi explained, raising a gauntleted fist. 'Like this.' He engaged a switch on his gauntlet that threw the armoured covers away from each other and forcefully ejected the actuators from their housings.

I nodded in understanding as Uncle Dimi slipped the gauntlet off and slid the actuators into a bin beside him. I looked back down at my new body armour, its grey colourisation revealing little of interest, except a small control panel on my right gauntlet, something akin to the Imperial Common Tactical Interface, or ICTI.

'What's this?' I asked, pointing down at the glass rectangle attached to my gauntlet.

'That's your command pad interface, or CPI for short; it's what you'll use to network to explosives, access the software of your suit, and access the higher system functions of your armour. When you are asteroid-side, you'll be issued a personal CPI that you can strap to your wrist and will function identically to the CPI integrated into your armour currently,' he explained as the ship's klaxon flared up and emergency lights flickered on.

'All Stations prepare for drop. This is not a drill. All Stations prepare for drop. This is not a drill,' barked the Boatswain's Mate of the Watch over the 1MC. As the klaxons blared, my mind began to drift, the monotonous drone of alarms almost soothing. Dimitri tapped on my helmet what felt like seconds later but had apparently been minutes according to my suit's chronometer.

'Sayra! You heard the order! Move!' he barked. I quickly snapped out of my trance-like state and left the armour bay just as the doors sealed.

Instructor Breker hissed over my suit's comm piece, furious at my inaction: 'Trainee Hart! The *brufik* have you been? You are to report to your squad bay in the next six minutes!'

'Reporting to rack, aye ma'am!' I replied.

'That was not the—!' Breker began to howl, but at this, I shut the comm line off.

'Mariko?' I called.

'Yes, ma'am?'

'So, you're a Tier Three AI, I'm assuming that means you're specialised,' I deduced.

'Yes, ma'am. While all field-assigned AI are classified as field combat assistants, Tier Three AI are also designed as combat enhancers, improving natural reaction times and taking over all automated functions within a combat specialist's body,' she explained. A pulse of fear echoed through my mind as the childhood mantra came to me in my thoughts: *Intelant in mind, two be entwined.*

'Intelligence and soul in mind, two are entwined. Cute little fearmongering about AI-induced neuro-electric bleed-through,' Mariko observed. I frowned in confusion as to how she'd heard me before assuming I accidentally muttered it.

'Then plot a course to squad bay—' I paused searching for the information as it appeared on my HMD. 'Seven dash thirty-seven dash fifty-three dash L and take control,' I instructed as I looked up at my HMD's chronometer.

'Taking control, aye ma'am,' she reported. Before me, my muscles, breaths, and motions were snatched from my mind, and I became a passenger in my own body as I dashed up to the squad bay, disoriented and panicked when I finally stopped.

Where the brafiksjot am I? I wondered as I looked up at the series of digits above the door to the berth before me, the digits and numbers 7-37-53-L stencilled in black. *What am I reading, for that matter?*

'Berth fifty-three, ma'am,' replied Mariko. 'And the bullseye translates to: seventh deck below the main; in line with or aft of frame thirty-seven; it is the fifty-third compartment and, therefore, starboard of the centre-line; and it is living quarters,' she explained

'What the—?' I spluttered with shock. 'How did you—?' I continued shakily, but Mariko cut me off.

'Your thoughts are merely rudimentary electrical signals that are now simultaneously moving through your SPCS as well as your body. I can "read" those thoughts,' Mariko explained 'Also a bullseye is the serial code above every compartment aboard a ship ma'am,'

'Never do that again without my express written consent,' I replied, unnerved by the idea. My ten-year-old sister's declaration repeated in my thoughts: *Mama was right; first* skarants *take your body, then they take your* anki.

'Aye, aye,' Mariko replied.

'Mariko, SITREP,' I requested.

'All systems nominal. Moving to standby stat—' Mariko began.

'Oh, and write up a protocol for that, to keep in reserve for an unfortunate day,' I interrupted.

'Moving all systems to standby status and writing Protocol 37, aye ma'am,' Mariko replied.

As my suit reset, Breker crackled over the wireless. 'What the *brufik* was that, trainee? You just ignored my communication and violated twenty-two different naval protocols!'

'Apologies, ma'am! I was instructed to move punctually, ma'am! I have been indisposed for the last thirty-six hours. I have not had the time to read up on Taskforce naval protocol, ma'am!' I barked.

'Well, just—just don't do it again ... and lose the ma'am sandwich!' she hissed, her arguments rebuffed and her online format limiting her options for corrective punishment. Eventually, the rest of my platoon caught up to me, all wearing the same gunmetal grey–plated BDU as myself.

'How'd you get ahead of us?' Rebeka asked.

'Magic!' I replied, mimicking a plume of smoke. Everyone just rolled their eyes and entered our berth.

'Sound off, Chiron Platoon; left-to-right, people!' called Breker over the intercom as we settled into our drop seats and strapped ourselves into our five-point harnesses, emergency lights shimmering in the dark. Each of us began to report our status and presence. I was last.

'Trainee Hart reports as ordered!' I answered.

'Good, we're all here. Engaging magnetics now.' The sound of magnetic clamps echoed through the room while the emergency lights changed to a solid colour before returning to their intermittent state. 'Wait, no, no, no, no; that can't be right!' exclaimed Breker.

'What is it, ma'am?' asked Elenskis.

'There's been a power failure: your impact seats' magnetic induction fields won't engage!' Breker replied with a grave tone in her voice.

'And that does what?' called out one of the ex-officers.

'It keeps your *zhopas* on that chair and the wall in front of you intact!' she barked as she tapped a switch.

'Platoon Office Fifty-Two Twenty-Three One to Combat Information Centre, Platoon Office 52231 to CIC!' she called out in frustration, panic settling into her throat, a deathly silence engulfing the room.

'This is CIC, send traffic, Platoon Office 52231,' replied one of the operations specialists, obviously unaware of the issue.

'I have Chiron Platoon on their deathbeds in two minutes due to a magnetic induction field power failure!' Breker exclaimed.

'Wait, what?' questioned the operations specialist, now confused as to the situation.

'You heard me, *brafik*wit!'

'Um—um right … um, what do you want me to do?' he asked, now quite clearly distressed.

'Can we abort the drop?'

'Negative, we're already halfway through the drop sequence, there's no turning back.'

Our internal suit alarms began to flare up, alerting us of our impending doom. We began to panic, some of us began to say our prayers.

'Then do something!' our TFI barked.

'Right!' the specialist replied before changing main circuits. 'CIC to Repair Officer Control! Magnetic induction field power failure! Reroute power in compartment seven dash thirty-seven dash fifty-three dash lima!' he barked over the 54MC.

'All Stations, all Stations, stand-by for drop. All Stations, all Stations, stand-by for drop,' monotonously reported the Boatswain's Mate of the Watch.

With a purring hum and a loud thump, our seats began to come back online. I clenched my eyes shut in fear as I dissolved, my mind ripped from my body, left drifting through the universe of impulses and flickers, matter and dark matter, before rudely reawakening intact once more.

'All Stations, all Stations. Drop complete.'

'Hello? Chiron Platoon! Are you there? Alive?' the Petty Officer questioned, quite clearly shaken by the ordeal.

'We're here!' we exclaimed as we all exhaled.

'Oh, thank the gods!' he replied, audibly relieved to hear our voices.

'Well, gods-damned. Trainees, we'll be arriving at the *Hakon* in three hours' time. I'd recommend you read up on your Taskforce Field Manuals and get some rest. It's gonna be a long thirty-five weeks,' Breker explained as she flicked off her comm line and returned to her work.

We all nodded and turned off our comm pieces. Chiron bumped fists, nestled on each other's shoulders, did whatever we could to calm down; it was at this point I decided that sleep was my best option. When you've almost died, the next best thing is always soothing.

Chapter 4
One step forward

'Sara! Sara! Come on, we've got to move! Now!' groused a trainee, their haggard voice barely a whisper through my helmet's hearing protection.

'Trainee! I will personally fry you in that chair and then drown you in your own *blad* if you aren't up and out right this second!' screeched Breker over my comms.

'Trainee Hart, it is recommended you wake immediately,' requested my AI. I began to shake my head, the haze of my sleepiness wearing off much faster than any normal human. I awoke to see the roof lit up in colours of red and black, klaxons blaring.

'Welcome back to the land of the living,' Ela said, gesturing as I rose from my chair.

'We didn't want you to miss out on the view,' remarked Elenskis, her smirk hidden by her helmet.

We walked out of the squadbay and slipped into a nearby elevator down to one of the starboard observation bays. A pair of watchmen manned their stations, eyes steadfast on their digital scopes and instrumentation, searching for any danger. As we looked out into the black sea, we saw one of the greatest feats of humanoid engineering. At the heart of the gas giant's monolithic rings was an installation that ran as far as the enhanced eye could see. Asteroids linked together by inconceivable chains made from an impossible substance. At the heart of each asteroid was a multi-layered complex. There were thousands of them capable of training billions of recruits and trainees.

'Welcome to the *Hakon*; this is where all trainees and recruits are trained to become the finest warriors in the universe. Take a good, long look, trainees. This is the first and last time this place won't seem like hell to you.' She paused to let us soak in the vastness of the space in front of us. 'Okay! Show's over—get down the well deck.'

'Okay, where the *brafiksjot* is the well deck?' I asked aloud, as the platoon dispersed.

'Fourth deck, ma'am,' Mariko chimed in, as she set a waypoint on my HMD. With my heading set, I made my way down to the well deck. As I arrived, the ship's trainees and recruits began to form up into their new training platoons and larger training companies near the fore rampway. The captain strode in moments later, standing firmly to our left. The Petty Officer of the Deck snapped to attention.

'Captain on deck!' the Deck Officer exclaimed.

'Regiment! Attention!' instructed Instructor Hejding. We turned ninety degrees and snapped to attention.

'Regiment! Present *arms*!' the STFI continued as we slammed our right foot down and snapped our right hand to the brim of our forehead.

'Regiment! At *ease*!' barked the captain as he returned our salute. He paused, his gaze drifting over us, his stern jaw and piercing gaze unnerving to some. 'Trainees!' he began. 'I am Captain Kanin. I have skippered this ship, the UNV *Kau,* for the last forty years. I have watched generations of warriors disembark for the *Hakon* and I have some wisdom. Past this door is the fire of ancient Earth's Hell! On the surface, you will meet the Taskforce's finest: recruit division commanders, drill instructors, drill sergeants, and military training instructors! They will beat you, mould you, and from the mud, blood, sweat, and tears you will emerge the finest troops this universe has ever seen! Capable and enabled to do anything and everything to ensure the security of this universe! Of everything we hold dear! Hooyah!' he exclaimed. The entire well deck screamed their various cries in reply.

Hejding turned to the captain and snapped a salute. ‘Permission to go ashore!’ she bellowed as the captain returned her salute.

‘Permission granted!’ the captain replied, before turning and striding off.

Hejding turned to the outline of the Taskforce flag emblazoned aft—the image of a planet brought to life by contour lines and surrounded by planetary orbit rings—and snapped a salute before quickly turning around.

‘Regiment, right *turn*!’ she instructed. The regiment snapped to and turned ninety degrees right. ‘Regiment! Mark *time*!’ We began to march in place.

As we began to step in time, the well deck’s fore-bulkhead began to withdraw into the floor below, revealing a large docking collar, its monolithic bulkheads receding into the floor as it folded away. The collar went on for kilometres.

‘Regiment! Forward, *march*!’ Hejding exclaimed. We marched out of the ship and onto the foreign station. We marched for two hundred metres before we were called to a halt at the first bulkhead. Hejding turned to the nearest Taskforce logo and snapped a salute before marching ahead of us to the periphery of the bulkhead and turning to the Officer of the Deck (OOD).

‘Request permission to come aboard!’ she called as she snapped a salute.

The OOD returned the salute as he replied. ‘Permission granted!’

Hejding turned back to us. ‘Regiment! Forward, *march*!’ We strode forward, entering the impossible asteroid. ‘In this here hell, I did see!’ Hejding began to exclaim in tune; we repeated her cadence as we strode. We marched for close to ten kilometres before we reached our destination. As we passed through the last set of defensive bulkheads, we entered a monolithic cavern of finely finished metal sides; ledges lined the wall, their railings constructed of THP while bridge ways connected the two walls.

‘Regiment! *Halt!*’ Hejding called. We quickly stopped. ‘Regiment! At *ease*!’ We relaxed into parade rest. I dared a look around and saw that our formation had engulfed what felt like a third of the entire lower deck of the atrium.

'Welcome to the hub! Welcome to hell!' remarked another instructor as they approached, coming to an abrupt stop just metres away from Instructor Hejding. The two instructors snapped each other crisp salutes as the new instructor reported, 'You are relieved.'

Hejding replied, 'I am relieved,' before turning about-face and marching back towards the UNV *Kau*'s well deck.

As Hejding strode away, the new instructor stepped forwards and began to speak. 'Regiment! Uncover, *two*!' the instructor began as the column responded in kind, and we each slipped off our helmets, revealing our bald heads to the cool air. I took a deep breath of 'fresh' air as light water vapour began to condense below my eyes. 'Welcome aboard the Unified Naval Space Station *Kaery*, everyone! Today marks your first day of being true warfighters! I am Senior Taskforce Instructor Saeto of the Hakon Combined Military Training Depot, or HCMTD. In the next two hours, you should receive the details of our training regime for the next thirty-five weeks. You will be divided into a series of training companies. From there, you will be further divided into your respective training platoons. Your service-specific instructors will serve as Company and Platoon Commanders for the first component of your combined basic military training here at the HCMTD. When you shift to Combined Technical Specialty Training, known as CTST, the distinction of command will become broader for some MOSs and more refined for others. You will be filled in with more by your respective instructors.

'Regiment! Fall *out*!' he barked.

With that cue, we broke from our lines and formed up with our respective training platoons, my platoon's information appearing along my retina.

'Godfather Actual. Kanji Actual. Standing by to transmit. Over,' came the balanced voice of Drill Instructor Kisae before the high-pitched scream of another pierced our minds.

'Attention recruits!' the man boomed over our suit speakers. 'To all the ignorant *zhopases* that mistakenly enlisted in combat MOSs, I am Taskforce Instructor Davidson. In the infinite wisdom of OPSI, they have elected to ensure that you have the most comprehensive understanding of the interconnected battlefield that you will be operating in. As a result, not only will I be educating you on the finer points of logistics, but I will be standing in for your Company Grade Officer, Logistics and Operations Handler. During School of Infantry Field Training Exercises, I will be your first point of contact! Furthermore, unless otherwise stated by myself, I will be referred to from here on out as "Godfather Actual"!' he boomed causing us all to curl in pain. 'Kanji Actual, distribute squad bay coordinates now. Godfather Out,' Davidson instructed.

'Received. Out,' replied DI Kisae as the data was transmitted through before he switched over to TEAMCOMM. 'Platoon commanders, distribute squad bay directions!' Kisae instructed over the din of the hub.

'Aye, sir!' our platoon commander replied in response before turning back towards us and looking down at his CPI to send out the squad bay data.

'We've received squad bay directions, ma'am,' Mariko reported.

'Send wireless acknowledgement,' I instructed.

'Sending wireless acknowledgement. Aye, ma'am,' Mariko replied. As I waited, my HMD lit up with wireless acknowledgements from other members of the unit.

'Kanji Company! Fall, *out*!' Instructor Kisae barked.

With that, my squad made their way to the squad bay; we marched on in relative silence. For the first time since Imperial Combined Recruit Training, I barely knew anyone. After we'd selected our enlisting branch, we were rotated into recruit training companies pertinent to our branch. To my left was Ela, loud and proud, fragments of her velvet hair defiant to the last. To my right strode Elenskis, my shy but confident old CO, her lean body honed from years of fighting, the shimmer of silver along her bald head a by-product of her Kaltri descent. I brought up my CPI's SPS; It read 20-110-15-L. My eyes widened in shock and confusion. How many decks are there? I wondered.

'One hundred and fifty, ma'am,' Mariko replied.

I gritted my teeth. 'Mariko. What did I say about reading my mind?'

'To not. Although I'm not exactly reading your min—'

'Mariko,' I interrupted.

'Apologies, ma'am,' she replied. With that, we moved off in silence. Fifteen minutes later, I arrived at our squad bay, and the door reacted to our presence. 'Could you wire me, ma'am?' Mariko requested.

I frowned at the request. 'I don't understand.'

'*Muzukashii*,' Mariko cursed in Japanese. 'Could you plug me into the wall? It's called "wiring" in the Taskforce,' she practically spat. I moved towards the console and paused. 'Back of your helmet, you'll find a crystalline matrix, put your helmet back on, I'll transfer over to it and then you can wire me into the wall,' Mariko impatiently explained. I did as instructed and inserted her AI matrix into the wall, her hologram appearing adjacent to my rack. 'Ah, much better. So much more room!' she exclaimed. Mariko had decided to project her avatar this time. She looked like a typical ancient Japanese woman, fine silken kimono, her left eye obscured by a cluster of hazel hair. That was day one.

The next thirty-five weeks was Asfod made manifest as every waking moment served to break us down and rebuild us, each of us relearning military life from the ground up, from the structure of the Taskforce, the customs, courtesies, and values of the Unified Marine Corps to even the fundamentals of marksmanship with our M32s before transitioning into our military occupational specialty schools for the remaining twenty-two weeks, where we were instructed in our specialist skills and equipment of our trade. For most of us, the harshest difficulty was acclimatising to just how much of the Taskforce was automated. While it had been prevalent during our induction, most of us had been so spooked and disorientated by the whole situation that we had barely noticed the number of artificial intelligences that worked in tandem with organic instructors and specialists. The blue shimmer of Tier One instructional AIs that hovered ominously beside us as we fired round after round at the range or pulled ourselves up past the chin-up bar was unnerving at first. We each expected our AI overlords to suddenly snap and fry the neural implants embedded in our skulls as our Imperial instructors had often warned at the mere mention of computer mathematics, but each of us eventually came to see them as amazing tools of peacekeeping, and they'd saved my life more times than I could begin to count.

Chapter 5
Two steps back

36/12/2436 (Hakon Military Calendar)

Thirty-six weeks later ...

Automatic rifle fire rang out from the far end of the forest, followed by a rapid shuffle, then a loud thud; a cry of orders would engulf the air soon after, and weapons fire would quickly follow. It was the final day of the weeklong optional junior non-commissioned officer course that selected trainees with markedly successful prior service careers and demonstrated leadership qualities during CBMT and MOS school. For the course, I'd been promoted to platoon commander (PLC) and assigned along with my fellow JNCO applicants to blue force, or BLUFOR for short; it was the Field Training Exercise, or FTX, immediately before we were to be assigned to the fleet. Our objective was to neutralise the Opposing Force, known as OPFOR, based in the Ang Var Valley. We were given broad latitudes as to our method of destruction on the singular condition—General Order One—that prohibits actions that exceed the realm of plausible deniability, in turn violating Silentio Super Tumultum. It was a simple clearance op; nothing we hadn't done a thousand times before. What we hadn't counted on was the presence of a battalion strength unit, and uncharacteristically for my platoon, the plan fell apart from the moment we dropped in. In our eagerness to get the job done, the approach was almost immediately compromised by a pair of man-portable laser interferometer gravitational-wave detectors.

With a positive ID on our dropship's magnetic resistors, we'd been subsequently caught between a pair of man-portable air-defence systems and forced to land in an ambush where we experienced complete equipment failure. We'd been on the run for the last forty minutes. A large military force was now in pursuit.

'Ma'am, rear guards report our pursuers have broken off,' said Elenskis.

'Thank the gods. Tremblej, what's our status?' I questioned.

'Not good, ma'am: SPS is down, environmental receptors are offline, wireless communication's a no-go, even our suits' memory crystals been *bȓafiksjoti* fried!' Ela howled in anger as she listed off the problems. I grabbed her by the shoulders.

'Refocus, marine,' I instructed. She sighed.

'Sorry, ma'am.' She took a deep breath. 'Our KPMs are down, the static couplings for our hydrostatic gel have been fried, photoreactive panellin's been disabled, our force amplification actuators have fused, and our power packs have been fried, anything else?'

Down to Dark Age ballistics, then, I thought to myself as I inspected my M32.

'What's the situation with our comms?'

'I can get local comms back online in the next five mikes but long-range capability ain't gonna happen,' she answered bluntly.

'Okay, set it up and transmit the RV point,' I instructed nodding.

'Uh, which one, ma'am?'

'Rally point Zulu,' I elaborated. Ela looked at her physical map in confusion.

'I don't—' Ela began to respond.

'It isn't on the map because OPFOR's been issued our rally points. If you find a walled building that we didn't note in our mission plan, transmit it by courier to the rest of platoon until you get local comms back and augmented by a new security format,' I instructed.

'Aye, aye,' Ela replied as she knelt to inspect the map, a marker in one hand and her suits comms gear in the other.

A multitasker as ever, I thought to myself as I began to patrol the perimeter of our defensive line.

'Heads on a swivel, people! Those Delta Bravos could be anywhere!' exclaimed Elenskis, my 2IC. Our marines shifted their gear and quickly refocused.

'TEAMCOMM is live!' Ela exclaimed moments later as marine couriers rushed back and forth from her to their team leaders, coordinates in hand. I turned to Ela.

'Tremblej, you got that new encryption online?'

'Negative, don't broadcast anything risqué just yet,' she replied, still buried deep in her comm gear. I nodded before tapping my comm piece on my helmet. A spark of electricity pulsed through my ears; my eyes snapping shut in pain before reaching for the handset from Ela's suit's wireless gear.

'Kanji One Actual to all elements. Sound off and execute your orders, wireless silence protocols are in effect. Only mission-critical information will be transmitted. Actual Out,' I instructed.

The platoon quickly reported in and then dispersed, disappearing into the woods, headed for the rally point. With our momentary regroup complete, our pursuers had also completed theirs and resumed the hunt. When Kanji arrived at the RV point, we quickly began to dig in. Ela had found an old, abandoned town built by the artificial pocket universe's local inhabitants—or as local as you can get for an accident of natural selection—the Kisai. Surrounding the town was a six-metre stone perimeter wall, lined with small crenels to offer clear line of sight when firing.

'We don't have the combat effectiveness to beat them back, ma'am, and from the looks of it, they've procured combat armour as well, which'll mean they have the offensive advantage,' Elenskis reported into my thoughts. I simply nodded.

'What's our ordnance situation?' I asked, turning to her as she prowled up beside me.

Elenskis just scoffed. 'Tango Uniform: we've got two satchels of C13 explosives, two shots for the 40 mike-mike, seven siphon charges, and a pair of gravity mines. Don't know why the *bř̃afiksjot*, but apparently Casi has some weird fetish with gravity mines or something; I don't know,' Elenskis reported with a noticeable bark to her voice. I nodded in response.

'Okay, so what's our SITREP?' I asked.

'All squads have reported in, ma'am. We've dug a fifteen-metre perimeter trench around the town,' Elenskis explained. 'Against the cliff behind us,' she added.

'Tremblej?' I inquired turning to Ela as she stood behind me, still fiddling with her comm equipment.

'Gear-wise, we're still *Brafiki*. Fourth squad apparently have a couple turrets that aren't completely *brafiki*, I've jerry-rigged a short-wave local comm net and a substitute wireless encryption that's made our comm situation a little more stable. I've also been able to reroute most of my gear's fried static couplings, and I'm confident I'll be able to replicate that in the other suits,' Ela explained.

'Still no LRC?' I queried, hoping for long-range communications.

'Still just TEAMCOMM, ma'am,' Ela solemnly replied.

I sighed. 'What is wrong with our BDUs?'

'From the looks of it, Makos' BDU was compromised by a trojan horse. The virus was processed by her BDU as a priority communique and was automatically opened. The trojan then pretty much hijacked her security firmware and piggybacked to our gear through our wireless transmitters,' Ela explained.

'So, our core firmware is just locked down then?'

'Yut, quarantined,' she acknowledged.

I frowned. 'So, wait, why'd our actuators fuse?'

'Our suits' nitrogen distribution system prematurely shutdown before the actuator shutdown cycle.'

'And the components fused themselves together …' I finished, trying to hold myself together, but I couldn't; I began to panic, my heart raced, my hands jittered. My platoon had never failed me—but in our last exercise, I was going to freeze, and I was going to choke our defeat.

‘Orders, ma’am?’ called Elenskis.

‘Ela, switch all elements to SQUADCOMM!’ I called out, trying to strangle the fear that crept into my heart.

‘Yut!’ she exclaimed. She gave me a thumbs up when it was live. I picked up the handset, due to my fried comm piece.

‘All elements …’ I began, my voice quickly trailing off as I looked around the town. ‘All—’ I muttered over the comm line, momentarily clicking off the handset.

I smirked; a pinch of pain flickered up the side of my face as I looked on. ‘All elements,’ I said with renewed resolve, my voice strengthening with every syllable, ‘Kanji One Actual. Bury defensive ordnance twenty-five metres outside our perimeter and consolidate our defences to our ten, twelve, and one. Take up defensive positions within the town!’

‘Rah!’ replied the platoon. I clicked off the handset, smiling at the use of the marine corps creole’s absurd word for a question, an exclamation, and ‘yes’ as I turned to look at Ela.

‘Tremblej, synchronise every BDU in the platoon. Sync them to your CPU and start them on that lockout.’

‘Yut!’ she replied with contained excitement as she realised the plan. I clicked the handset on again.

‘All elements *do not* engage the enemy under any circumstances. Hold your ground. Only move to engage the enemy if they are within one metre of the perimeter. Be advised supplies will be low. Check your shots and count your wishes. Out,’ I finished. Acknowledgement lights winked on from the squad leaders, and the wait began.

Chapter 6
Hunted and hunter

Ela turned to me, she snapped her free hand to the brim of her helmet before following with the numbers *2* and *5*. The platoon had identified movement 25 metres from our position. Nodding, I raised my free hand palm-out and snapped it down to my side, ordering the platoon to open fire. Ela nodded and repeated the gesture. An explosion engulfed the forest in a sea of red and orange. Ela paused, checking her CPI's display before turning to me and signing to me with hand signals and Imperial Sign Language. *Seventy-five percent ion lithium charge.*

I nodded before waving my horizontal palm in an arc at my waist, Ela quickly relayed the command, and Elenskis and another marine nodded in reply before quickly firing two rounds from the platoon's pair of M406 underslung grenade launchers over the town's perimeter wall. The raw fire was soaked up by OPFOR like a sponge. They continued to advance towards us, unable to fire upon us through the dense perimeter wall. Moments later, a cluster of grenades came tumbling over the wall before they were quickly reflected back by something akin to the hand of gods. I smirked. *Gravity mine fetishes,* I thought to myself amused as the modified mines hung above the perimeter wall.

'Now!' I barked. Ela hit a tile on her CPI with a smile, her helmet held high to announce the emotion. Moments later, an echo, like a sonic grenade, reverberated through the forest and the crunch of footsteps ceased. A weary smile returned to me. *Finally, some good luck,* I thought to myself.

'Contacts secure,' Ela reported.

'Everyone, ten-metre defensive positions; police those troops and weapons—we need what they have: magazines, power packs, anything. And we've got sixty seconds before their buddies figure out what's happened. Rah?'

'Rah!' cried the unit in reply.

'Someone want to tell me what *did* just happen?' muttered Tomas as he rose from his fox hole.

'We overclocked their suits and I hacked their force amplification safeties,' explained Ela, her cheery tone almost out of place.

With that, the platoon spread out. Half of the marines covered the frozen members of OPFOR, stripping them of weapons and equipment while the rest screened the area for further contacts.

'Tremblej, SITREP!' I cried.

'I've bypassed the quarantine and I've got LRC but it's spotty thanks to a rogue EM field passing through the system,' she replied.

'Rogue, my arse,' I remarked in an attempt to break the uneasiness. Ela continued to look concerned. 'Patch me through,' I instructed.

'Yut,' Ela replied as I picked up the handset.

'Kanji One Actual. Godfather Actual. How copy? Over,' called Davidson over the comm line, his voice smothered in static and barely readable.

'Godfather Actual. Kanji One Actual. Reading three by three, connection unstable. Over,' I replied, attempting to speed things up.

'Roger, be advised friendly craft moving in to facilitate extraction. ETA one mike. Over,' he replied.

'Negative, Godfather Actual. Requesting triple-R procedures. Over.' A sigh came over the mic as I looked back to Ela; she just gave me the 'it's royally *Brafiki*' gesture.

'Wilco Actual, initiating triple-R procedures. Out,' he replied, disbelief settling into his voice. Moments later, our armour pinged, informing us of a freshly received program. Attached was an automated text:

BE ADVISED. ORBITAL REPAIR, RESUPPLY AND SYSTEM RECOVERY UNAVAILABLE. AIRDROP OF TRIPLE-R MATERIEL TO BE DELIVERED AT GRID REFERENCE FS245–223. END.

A quiet 'rah' rang through the platoon. Ela frowned.

'We've got contacts! Twelve o'clock! Thirty-three foot mobiles closing fast! ETA five mikes!' relayed Elenskis.

'Looks like they were tipped off by our resupply!' Elenskis added.

'Brafik!' I hissed, pulling up my satellite positioning system. 'Okay, the valley is south-east of here. We've got forces moving west and reinforcements moving out from Ang Var. We need to disappear,' I turned back to Elenskis.

'Then we're moving in one. Have the platoon move out to the mouth of this cave system directly west of us. We'll drop down into the cave system below, find a position with a lot of physical noise, and wait for OPFOR to roll right over us,' I instructed. 'From here we can move onto Ang Var.'

'What if they're equipped with imaging gear?'

'Then it's a gamble we lose,' I said in sharp reply.

'Rah,' Elenskis replied. She turned to the platoon. 'We are Oscar Mike! Follow me!' she exclaimed.

The constant thunder of OPFOR's manoeuvres was louder than before. They were right on our tails this time, and we had no other choice. I reached the mouth of the cave system. It was a two hundred–metre drop into an underwater pool that fed the entire region. *How were we going to get down again?* I asked myself. I flicked up my visor and gazed through the waterfall that cascaded into the cave system. The wall was jagged. A pain in the arse, but structurally stable. As the platoon neared my position, I gestured to the rock wall.

'You've got to be kidding me!' Tomas hissed as he threw himself against the rock wall. With that, I stowed my rifle and leapt into the current of water; my hands felt the shock, and I immediately recoiled, gravity catching up, but I refocused and slammed my right hand into a piece of stable rock. I settled in. The platoon followed suit.

'We wouldn't happen to have some stealth systems still?' I inquired, the patter of footsteps hanging ever ominously overhead. Ela simply shook her head. *The iron ball paint, the water, and the angles are gonna have to do,* I thought as the heavy patter of full battle rattle echoed through only moments later. The sound ceased; the click of rifles rang through the cave system. Two riflemen, both armed, had broken off to investigate the cave system.

'You see anything?' one of them asked.

'Negative, you think they went down?' the other replied.

'Kanji must have some serious balls if they dropped down there.'

'Well, may as well be thorough. Drop a hunter down there,' the second rifleman instructed.

'Roger that,' the first replied. He holstered his weapon and unclipped two charges. He flicked on the arming switches and reached through the wall of water, his hands mere metres away from my back, before releasing the charges, gravity dragging them down towards the pools below, their manoeuvring thrusters activating just before they hit the water. They made an initial sweep, their search pulse tracing across the area before vanishing into the labyrinthine cave system. As the riflemen moved to rejoin the main group, I let out a deep breath.

'Gods,' I cursed.

'Ma'am, we've got another issue,' Ela reported.

'Explain when we're safer, marine.'

'Agreed. Down we go,' she said with hollow enthusiasm. 'By the way, how're we dealing with those hunter mines, ma'am?' Ela added.

'Well, you've got two hundred metres to figure it out,' I jokingly replied as we began to descend into the cave system. We got about a hundred metres into the descent when Ela began to speak.

'PLC, I've got an idea.'

I smirked. *Of course, you do,* I thought to myself. 'Let's hear it,' I replied.

'So, we piggyback the mine's wireless signal and transmit a falsified termination signal,' she replied with glee in her voice.

'And that does what?'

'Firstly, it gives us an alibi. The termination signal is released if the on-board computer knows it can—with reasonable certainty—kill a target, which means that if we do have to destroy it, we can keep our platoon capabilities a secret, and second—' Ela began.

'Of course there is,' I replied before nodding for her to proceed.

'We can re-program them,' she explained. 'I've dismantled a few HMs in the last twelve weeks out of boredom; anyway, their hardware isn't EMP-hardened like most pieces of Taskforce gear. Once I've piggybacked its feed to OPFOR, I just need to get within a range of five metres and I can overload one of my BDUs SM triple-Cs; that should do the trick,' she elaborated.

'You only have six cooling cells that aren't burnt out, so explain to me where you're going to get the required triple-Cs?'

'I only need two to maintain crystalline integrity. I can lose a couple,' she explained.

'Now, explain to me how a triple-C is going to work as a jerry-rigged EMP?' I continued, sceptical.

'Triple-Cs store a small quantity of liquid nitrogen within an electrical field housing. Now, the cell, in lay terms, carries a temperature probe that detects the heat levels of the SMC; when the crystalline structure reaches temperatures of sixteen twenty degrees Celsius, the cell's electrical field collapses and liquid nitrogen is poured into the micro superconducting memory crystal. The triple-C is then ejected into the wilderness before another triple-C is "chambered",' she explained. I ran my thumb in a semicircular arc across my helmet's head, indicating I was rolling my eyes.

'I did qualify to use my BDU, you know?' I replied sarcastically. Ela simply ignored the comment.

'So, if I overload the triple-C's EFH and connect it to the mine, the two objects will overload each other,' she explained.

'So how do we go about that?' I inquired, even more sceptical now than I had been.

'Distraction, obviously. Once I've isolated them from the wireless grid, I'll need two volunteers to bait the mines into striking range. There I'll be able to throw the triple-Cs onto the mines and nabbing us two hunter mines,' Ela explained, madness most certainly in her eyes.

'Fine, but if we lose, you're buying all of us a round,' I instructed. She gave me a thumbs-up as we continued down. 'XO, what did we recover from OPFOR?'

Elenskis simply shook her head below me.

'Jack *shajst*, really. In our panic, we missed a lot. We got a couple satchels of triple-Cs. A few technical kits and a couple M42 Mod 9 MVR grenades. But that's it,' Elenskis reported.

'*Brafiksjot*,' I cursed. 'And what happened to the resupply?' addressing both of them.

'LOGCOM dropped it north-east of our current position,' Ela hissed. 'It's almost like we're meant to fail,' she muttered to no one in particular. Most of the platoon was now just above the water before we quickly dropped into the pool below. As soon as we hit the water, the weight of our gear began to drag us down at an alarming rate. I began to swim as hard as I could to the edge and propped myself up onto the rock wall with difficulty. My skin burned as I sat on the edge, my rifle nestled on my knee as the last few marines fell in.

'You know they've heard our splash, right? They're gonna be after us,' Ela interjected into my solemn thoughts.

'Agreed. Prenalta, Baua—you're with Tremblej! Everyone else, make yourselves scarce!' I barked. We all quickly scattered into the various corners of the cave system as the bait formed up on Ela.

Chapter 7
Trapped in a web

Ela sat behind one of the cave's central support beams and fiddled with her pair of triple-Cs as Privates Baua and Prenalta struggled in the water, their armour offering them no support. As the two marines flailed awkwardly to stay afloat, the buzz of hunter mines rang down the main tunnel vectoring towards the disturbance as Ela patiently counted.

'One… three… five… six…' she mumbled as she rocked the cooling chips between her fingers. As she reached ten, she thoughtlessly tossed the chips to her right hand, their delicate frames balanced like playing cards between her fingers as her left hand traced across her CPI, the computer wrestling with remote weapons security and communications systems. With a smug nod of triumph, she uploaded the falsified report and deactivated the communications systems as the mines rushed into the cavern mere moments later. They hovered only a moment before zeroing in on the pair of helpless marines and throttling towards them. In a flash of motion, Ela threw the two chips into the air. Both hit their marks and the mines harmlessly tumbled into the water.

'Okay! Get those mines and marines out of the water!' I barked. Ela and Kanji rushed to their aid, hefting the practically drowning privates out onto the edge while Ela calmly fished the mines out of the cave's large ocean. 'SITREP!' I barked.

'Baua and Prenalta are gonna be good,' relayed Tomas.

'These mines will need some rewiring, but they'll be good to go,' Ela reported.

'Okay, everyone be ready to move in five,' I instructed, Elenskis relaying the orders.

'Rah!' the platoon replied. The echo was near-deafening. I strode over to Ela, who was already tweaking the mines.

'So, explain to me what we're going to be using these for?'

'Well, realistically we're going to be blowing something up, so we're going to need some firepower. Figured why not commandeer these little sparks,' she replied, not looking up from the mines as she spoke. I nodded. I couldn't argue with her logic. When Ela finished tinkering with the mines, we quickly vacated the reservoir and moved south-east through the cave system towards the Ang Var Valley, the Valley of Souls in old Kasiri.

'PLC!' Ela called out.

'What is it, Tremblej?' I called back.

'Ma'am, we may have a problem,' she reported. I mentally sighed. *Can't catch a break.*

'What is it, Private?'

'I've got my wireless transmitter back online—' she began as I interjected.

'It was down?'

'Aye, but that's a separate problem. I just intercepted communications between Ang Var and the main assault forces that were hunting us. MAFs One through Three are returning to base. They've completed their sweep and they are heading back as we speak. They've got a projected ETA of fifteen hours.'

I frowned at this information before silently cursing. 'Well, that certainly complicates things. Now, what was this other problem?'

'When UNSS *Kaery* transmitted their antivirus programs and override commands, we instead received more viruses, and the override commands actually disabled more of our equipment,' she explained through gritted teeth. 'In the rush of our withdrawal, I hadn't noticed till now,' she reprimanded herself.

'Specifically, we're currently host to a sophisticated logic bomb, an inglorious successor to the "ILOVEYOU" computer worm. It'll adapt, overcome, surpass everything I throw at it, and it'll in turn *brafik* with everything and anything. Everything from your HMD to your O^2 supply,' Ela explained.

I nodded, comprehending her explanation. I cursed to myself. 'I wonder why they would do such a thing?'

'If I had to hazard a guess, I don't think we're supposed to continue operating surface side in this FTX.'

I grimaced. Brafiksjoti *brilliant*, I thought to myself. 'So where do we stand?'

'Well the bad news is I can't get rid of the virus and I'll have to rejig everything I got working again, but I think I can trick our nano-repair systems into un-*brafiksjoti* our suits' memory crystal and clearing away the superheated *shajst* show that is our actuators,' Ela replied.

'Rah, good find,' I replied.

'Yut,' she answered before striding off.

They were my brothers and sisters. I was home. It was a long march. Without basic systems, we were practically blind moving through the cave with only our physical map and our gut instincts. After a couple of weak stalactites and a few near cave-ins, we reached the entrance I'd been looking for. The cave opened up. I moved ahead with a couple of marines, rifles raised. We were directly east of the Ang Var Valley. I smiled.

'*Gospadinas*, we've got our target,' I remarked to my marine companions. They each tapped the chins of their helmets, smirking. 'Cover the entrance,' I instructed as I re-entered the cave, the pair of them replying with a crisp, 'Yes, ma'am.'

'Sentaura, Makos! We're roughly three klicks east of the Ang Var Valley. I need teams two and three up in that valley. I want detonation points marked on a physical map and wireless silence. That's building struts and weak points in the canyon as well as anything that'll cause blunt force trauma, chaos, confusion, and isolation. Understood?'

'Rah,' replied Sentaura.

'Errr,' responded Makos in her marine corps drawl of agreement.

'Time's a-wasting *gospadinas*,' I replied. With that, they strode off to muster up a reconnaissance party. We remained in the cave for twelve hours before Makos and Sentaura returned, their sections intact.

'What's the situation?' I inquired.

'*Gat tou nen!*' Sentaura exclaimed, his Kitari tongue taking over from the anger he held.

'CATFU, ma'am. That place is Fort Kow,' Makos explained.

'Then let's see what we can do about that,' I jokingly remarked as Makos passed on his initial summary. We strode over to the flattest rock we could find, and Makos set his map down. Makos was right: the map was littered with marks denoting various weapons emplacements and bunkers.

'They've dug six AA batteries across the entire valley; they're dispersed in an asymmetric pattern and placed with effective overhead cover and overlapping fields of fire. At the mouth of the valley, directly north, are six heavily entrenched MG positions with flexible, hundred-and-eighty–degree fields of fire. Those six emplacements can deal with forces engaging anything ahead of them and they've been embedded in bunkers. Looks of it, they're old Taskforce facilities. Concealer-era kinda *shajst*. In the centre, you've got six barracks entry points. Based on their size and the units we monitored entering and exiting the facility, there's a large underground complex that houses all OPFOR personnel. At the heart of this valley is their CP. Its surrounded by a kinetic field and has manned watchtowers at every corner with fields of fire that encompass the entire valley. This place is impenetrable,' Makos explained.

'Not if we can help it, marine.' I paused to inspect the map. There was a cluster of circles scattered through the valley. 'Makos, what are these?' I inquired pointing to the circles on the map.

'From the looks of it, they're wells, accessing the underground reservoir that we're currently hiding in, ma'am,' he promptly explained.

'Then that's our ticket in,' I replied with a smirk, my helmet under my arm.

'Rah?' he questioned, confusion in his voice.

'You're right. Their defensive entrenchments have immaculate fields of fire, range of fire and defensive advantage. But that's only advantageous when waging a conventional defensive war. We can safely move ordnances such as mines, grenades, and C13 with a good throwing arm up through those wells into the enemy base. They'll be helpless to stop us. Now, your report mentions an ammo dump, where was that?'

'We IDed several ammunition dumps on either side of the valley. Materiel at the far south of the valley and materiel at the far north. Just off the edges of their AA and MG positions, ma'am,' he reported.

'Then those are our targets. We hit those, we can cripple their defensive emplacements.'

'But, ma'am, what if they seal the ordnance off from each other?'

'Then we hit hard and fast. Light the fire starters before they even realise what's going on,' I explained.

'Are we directly assaulting the CP, ma'am?'

'If the majority of the camp's battalion is holed up underground, that means that we'll need to close on the CP and barracks quickly and destroy the hatchways on each building to contain the subsequent response they'll field once they realise what's going on topside.'

'And how are we going to get that close, ma'am?'

'Tremblej?' I questioned as Ela rose from her crouched position, her gaze not leaving the map.

'Platoon sergeant!' she called out. Elenskis rose and quickly ran over.

'Rah?' reported Elenskis.

'Did we recover our siphons from our last encounter?'

'Six, but we lost two in transit.'

Always the professional. *Brafiksjot!* I thought to myself. 'Did you eyeball their generators?' I asked turning to Makos.

'Kinetic field and base power generators are here,' he replied, directing his index finger to the far end of the valley. 'But I don't know how you're going to get close to disable them.'

'Luckily, we don't need to get that close,' I replied. 'Ela, did you get those hunter mines up and running?'

Ela began to lick her lips, a smile growing on her exposed face. 'Aye, ma'am.'

'Lastly, did you see any structural weakness in that mountain?' I questioned. Makos just shook his head.

'Ang Var has been structurally reinforced, then reinforced again to ensure against rockslides and any tectonic movement. They've got support beams and nano-meshing that runs up and down the valley,' Makos replied.

'Then we hit the supports if they're meshed to the rocks; if the structure falls, so does the mountain.'

'And how would we break a carbon nanotube? That *shajst*'s used in space tethers, for *brafik*'s sake,' he replied.

I turned to face Ela. 'How difficult would it be to destroy the molecular bonds of these nanotube support beams?'

Ela leaned in to look at the technical details recovered by Makos. 'Not difficult. As long as we're able to rustle up enough acetone, we'll be in good company,' she casually replied.

'Get it done,' I instructed before turning to Elenskis. 'Platoon sergeant, round up the squad leaders.'

'Rah.' With that, Ela broke off to begin making preparations while Elenskis disappeared into the crowd of marines to begin distributing the word of the gods. My word.

I balanced on a nearby rock as the team leaders arrived.

'Okay, *gospadinas*, this is our situation and game plan. From communications intercepted by Private Tremblej between Ang Var and the MAF, the force is RTB as we speak, with an ETA of forty mikes. As such, we will be conducting this operation at zero one hundred hours Zulu. We will be conducting a three-pronged assault on the Ang Var Valley. As the MAF enters the valley—Squad

Commander Murakami,' I called forward as I gestured to the map, 'fourth squad will move in and cut off the valley entrance. Fire grenades at these four points when the power goes out,' I explained, indicating the mouth of the entrance.

'With the entrance blocked, move around and take offensive positions at the top of the valley. Squad Leader Makos, you and second squad will be hitting the facility's main power grid. Tremblej has rigged our pair of acquired hunter mines to emit a localised EMP. That should give you enough time to move in and place the platoon's remaining siphon charges, which should cripple their ability to react to us. Squad Leader Sentaura, we have identified six wells designed to access the underground reservoir that we are currently standing in. These six wells will enable you and third squad to target enemy munition dumps along the perimeter, as well as the reinforced cliff wall, accurately and safely. You will be carrying most of our ordnance, including a series of improvised acetone munitions to be deployed against the reinforced cliffside. Second and third squad, while your objectives are not operationally taxing, they must happen in tandem without wireless communication. Understood?'

'Rah!' replied Sentaura.

'Yut,' responded Makos.

'Errr,' acknowledged Murakami before adding, 'what will first squad be doing, ma'am?'

'First squad will be distributed between all three objectives to boost your troops,' I explained. 'If there aren't any more questions, we're moving out in ten, gear up in five,' I instructed, as the squad leaders dispersed.

I unclipped my watch from my belt to check the time: 0020. The watch was a gift from my mother, passed down from her mother's mother. An ancient Earth watch, from the first flotilla to arrive in the Primera Cluster. My good luck charm.

Ela strode up beside me. 'Ma'am, I've completed adjustments to the hunter mines, and I've completed all platoon suit repairs except yours,' she remarked before beginning to unlatch armour plates and reroute wiring. 'Looks like your comm piece's been fried, ma'am; you'll have to keep using my handset for any wireless commands. I'll switch squads with CSO Deimos,' she muttered as she continued to work. I looked around, scanned my platoon as they conducted weapon and armour checks in their combat pairs and quickly formed up with their squads. A thump on the back of my gear soon followed.

'Okay, good to go, ma'am,' Ela remarked before snapping to attention and striding off to talk to Communications Systems Operator Deimos and finish collecting her gear.

'Welcome back, Mariko,' I remarked.

'Ma'am,' she replied as my suit's memory crystal kicked back into gear. 'Updating logs and initiating repair cycle; call me when you need me, ma'am,' she added as my wrist armour and shin guards parted to eject several spent micro force amplification actuators.

I strode out onto the early morning dirt. The landscape had shifted drastically from cool lush forestry to desolate desert. The dust from OPFOR vehicles rose in the distance. They were returning home to a graveyard; they just didn't know it yet. I joined second squad to get the best seat in the house as the fireworks ignited.

++++

We flanked around back and began to scale the pair of monolithic mountains that enclosed the valley and protected it from southern attackers. The mud was thick, the trees colossal. Without many foundations of solid rock and few boulders, we struggled to the top, but when we did, Gaia-damned was it a sight to see. At the *Hakon*, this artificial galaxy operated on a completely different timesheet to the universe. Sunset was at 1100 hours and sunrise, at 0100 hours. We didn't have much time before our positions would be compromised by the rising sun. Second squad began to barrel down the mountain with controlled speed, ensuring that we didn't stumble, but as I slid, my left foot locked up, and instead of easily avoiding a large fallen tree, I hit it and went tumbling down the muddy mountain, my hands desperately reaching for something to hold onto.

Got it! Hgh, brafiksjot *that was close,* I thought to myself as I clung desperately onto yet another fallen tree. My armour was soaked in mud, my heart raced as my eyes swept the perimeter; my fall hadn't been nearly as damning to the operation as I'd originally thought. The base was still unaware of our presence. *Thank gods,* I thought to myself. I readjusted and resumed my descent. *There's the generator.* It was just behind the command post. Always guarded by six heavily armed marines and surrounded in a security field that prevented any physical contact. Well, almost any physical contact.

Second squad had formed up beside me, and I began to wave them off to their positions where they'd patiently wait for the security barrier to fall and the marine positions to lose power before rushing in and placing their siphon charges. I turned to one of the men behind me and ordered him to get eyes on the wells. He nodded and began to track the openings with his helmet-mounted acquisition calculation binoculars as Ela sidled up beside me and passed me the pair of hunter mines she'd overloaded. I looked around to see a cluster of thumbs up from the various groups. Second squad was ready. I looked up to the edge of the valley as I lay there with my rifle nestled on my chest to see the first flickers of fourth squad edge over the horizon. The enemy was in, and they were ready to begin. An explosion from the valley mouth rumbled back as my spotter began to tap me on the shoulder. Third squad was setting up. I held my breath as my spotter inspected the throws. He gave me a thumb up. With that, I rose from my position and activated the pair of hunter mines before throwing them towards the generator's security field. Violent rumbles of electrical static pulsed out from the impact site; mounted positions erupted in balls of flaming plasma and shields faded as second squad leapt from their fighting positions and rushed in, slamming their siphon charges into the ground just metres from the generator before retreating to their foxholes. The entire camp fell dark, and a cry of orders soon flew as OPFOR struggled to ascertain the situation. As the base was called to alert, a cluster of explosions rang out across the valley; the ammunition dumps exploded in a ball of fire, ripping through the anti-air emplacements and MG nests in the camp, and the hillside began to tumble into the valley as the acetone-weakened supports were destroyed by explosives. As the crumbling rock echoed through the valley, a plume of dust barrelled through the camp and up into the sky. Our cover had been established, their communications had been cut and their ordnance ripped from them. We had the advantage.

The crack of weapons fire began to echo through the valley. I slid down onto even ground and kicked a struggling marine back down as I moved towards the barracks. I lowered my helmet-mounted thermals, the quiet beats of my enemies visible to me once again as we systematically collapsed the staircases that led down to the underground facility. From there, we swept through the valley, clearing with unparalleled speed and precision. For years after Ela swore that Lati Freja swept through behind us, her bondmate Lati Athia howling in the triumphant night of the other realms. Years after, a Kisai infantry soldier would dispute her claim, instead attributing the violence to the calmed Valley of Souls, which hungered no longer.

Moments later, our long-range transceiver (LRT) crackled to life.

'Ma'am, we have comms!' called out Ela. I strode over and unclipped Ela's handset as her LRT wire extended from the back of her BDU.

'Godfather Actual. Kanji One Actual. Insurgents neutralised. Over.'

'Kanji One Actual. Godfather Actual. Hostile QRF inbound on your position. Over,' Davidson replied.

'Affirmative. Interrogative: what are we looking at? Over.'

'Thirteen infantry brigades and six armour columns. Over,' he replied.

Brafiksjot! I thought to myself. 'Understood. Requesting triple-R! We'll hold out in the valley. Over,' I said, confidence building in my voice as I spoke.

'Negative Actual. Triple-R will be provided but Air Corps Command is overriding General Order One and has authorised a bombing run on your current location. Exfil is in seven mikes. Fall back to grid reference Foxtrot Sierra two two three, four five niner. How copy? Over,' Davidson responded. Anguish flashed through my gaze. *We've failed, then. Can't focus on that right now, though.*

'Lima Charlie. Resupplying and falling back to grid reference FS223459. Out,' I replied as Ela immediately rerouted my signal to TEAMCOMM. 'All Elements, Kanji One Actual! Resupply and air support are inbound; rearm and fall back to grid reference FS223459, best speed possible!' I barked.

I pulled up the map as the dozens of canisters precisely impacted into the ground around the platoon. With the arrival of the replacement parts, each marine quickly rearmed and reequipped what they needed. The LZ was east of our current position and towards the edge of a colossal ravine that divided the FTX arenas. I quickly worked out the distance. 'Five klicks,' I muttered to myself; seven minutes was going to be a stretch, but we could do it.

Elenskis tapped me on the shoulder. 'Ma'am, squads two and three are equipped and ready,' she reported.

I nodded. 'Have two and three move out; four and one will leave soon after,' I instructed.

'Aye, ma'am,' Elenskis replied, snapping to attention before turning on point and relaying my orders.

'Anything you need?' I asked Mariko sarcastically.

'A better suit. But that's beside the point,' she replied as I snatched up a batch of liquid nitrogen tanks and actuators from one of the containers and attached it to the back of my BDU.

'Gods, you complain a lot,' I retorted.

'And you're too serious,' she replied ironically. As I inspected my equipment and saw its condition, I turned back to the squad.

'Then let's get ourselves underway,' I remarked. 'Squads one and four, are we ready?' Elenskis turned to face me.

'Rah,' both Platoon Sergeant Elenskis and Squad Commander Murakami replied.

'Then let's get going,' I instructed. The pair nodded before relaying my orders.

'Dropship ETA five mikes, executing Protocol 37, ma'am,' Mariko interjected, her words cleansing my mind as I took off, the world around me blurring, my body burning, my flesh boiling. As I neared the landing zone, Mariko screamed a desperate cry before my HMD went dark, my legs flew out from under me, and I slid past the landing zone, careening towards the two-kilometre-deep ravine. My HMD began to flicker back on, and the screams of Mariko were the first thing I heard.

'Ma'am! Brake!' she exclaimed.

'How?' I screamed in confusion.

'Just *brãfiking* think!' she boomed. My body slumped, my mind amused by the AIs cursing.

'Thirty metres! Twenty metres! Ten metres!' Mariko hissed out in a panic as I inched closer and closer to death. I began to calm, and my feet instinctively dug straight down, as my back struck the fragile soil, while my hands grasped for a handhold. As I edged closer to the cliff, something else clicked. My mind now focused, I quickly rolled onto my chest and punched straight into the ground that was now rapidly sliding out from under me and it was here that, as I slid, feeling the ground disappear from under my feet, legs, stomach… I stopped.

Mariko's audio line appeared to the side of my HMD. 'Never do that again!' she exclaimed in misdirected and pointless fury.

'Agreed!' I replied, shaking as the adrenaline began to wear off.

'Excuse the new complaint, but we have fifteen seconds before the Condor leaves without us,' Mariko explained, her voice returning to its previous monotone state.

I crawled back up the cliffside, and I began to jog up to the dropship, my muscles screaming as I ran. I could see Kanji, already entering the craft from its aft hatch. When I looked up at the centre of my HMD, my timer began to flash red as it passed 10 seconds. I thought I was done for: I still had fifty metres to go, so I just ran, as fast and as hard as I could, the weight of my dead armour dragging me down as I moved. Soon the last fifteen metres was crossed, and I boarded to quickly collapse onto the dropship's deck, poorly nicknamed by infantry the 'meat tray' due to the frequency of injured aboard dropships.

The pilot called out over the intercom. 'Welcome aboard Kanji One. Touching off now!' his thick southern accent cutting through the comms like a piercing howl.

'*Gods Hand*, this is Tango Hotel Five-Five Seven. Extraction complete. Moving to minimum safe distance. Out,' he reported over the wireless. We sat in silence as the dropship cut out across the arid continent before arcing up towards space.

Elenskis turned to face me. 'We failed to maintain General Order One, right?' she said into the silence. I simply looked on in silence before clenching my hand, shaking it in acknowledgement.

'I think we did. Irritating a battalion and exposing our insertion craft to instrumentation is the quickest way to scream "we aren't Imperial, and this wasn't an accident",' I finished as our pilot resumed communication with the Squadron Leader of Air Training Wing UAC.

'*Gods Hand,* Tango Hotel Five-Five Seven. Have reached minimal safe distance. Good hunting. Out,' he called over the comms, excitement building in his voice. As our craft climbed into the air the pilot screamed, 'Boom!' over the intercom. 'And then there was none!' he gleefully remarked as the training pilots glided over the valley below us activating their practice munitions.

'Charlie Tower. Tango Hotel Five-Five Seven. Requesting clearance to land. Over,' reported our pilot.

'Tango Hotel Five-Five Seven. Charlie Tower. Transmit Security Codes now. Over,' replied the air traffic controller.

'Charlie Tower. Tango Hotel Five-Five Seven. Transmitting Security Codes now. Over,' responded our pilot. There was a long pause as the air controller verified his security codes.

'Tango Hotel Five-Five Seven. Charlie Tower. You are cleared for approach. Speed one zero five. Automatic Approach, checkers Yellow. Over,' instructed the air controller.

'Copy that, speed one zero five. Automatic Approach. Checkers yellow. Over,' replied our pilot. I looked around the troop bay as we sped towards the station's flight deck. I took a deep breath.

'Kanji!' I boomed, my platoon slamming their feet into the hull in reply. 'What have we done?'

'Failed!' they replied.

'What did we fail?'

'The mission!'

'Who did we fail?'

'The corps!' they boomed.

'So!' I began, pausing, 'do we carry our heads in shame?'.

'No, ma'am!' Kanji replied.

'Do we sulk?'

'No, ma'am!' Kanji barked in reply.

'You are gods-damned right we don't! We are marines! We are the universe's finest! We survive, adapt, win!'

'Oorah!' they boomed in reply.

'Kanji! Touchdown in five seconds,' our pilot reported over intercoms. Moments later, our Condor touched down, its magnetic clamps holding it to the elevator below. With our ship now stationary, the lift below it began to pull us down onto the hangar bay. The rear hatch began to lower, and light began to flood the troop bay.

'Helmets off!' I barked. With that, I took my helmet off, my controlled black hair splayed into the open air. My face was fresh with not a single scratch on my skin, let alone a scar to mar my defined cheeks. I was Platoon Commander Private Sara Alaja Hart. Alongside me was Platoon Sergeant Private Elenskis Jen, her elegant platinum blonde hair glistening in the pale light. Across from me was Communications Systems Operator Private Ela Tremblej, her auburn eyes filled with fury. The last of the command group was

Hospitalman Tomas Plimis—the only male to be a part of Kanji's upper echelon—his cheeks subtly flushed from the fighting.

As we stepped out onto the deck, Kanji behind us, Sergeant of the Deck Kovalcik exclaimed, 'Attention on deck!' The entire hangar froze and snapped to attention. 'Present *arms*!' the Deck Sergeant continued. Regardless of rank or rate, uniform or assignment, the entire deck saluted us. We strode up to four of our drill instructors. They too were saluting us, each of them dressed in formal attire which was, needless to say, abnormal. Without knowing how to respond, Kanji simply returned the salutes and the Sergeant of the Deck returned the hangar to parade rest.

'Instructors?' I asked as they lowered their right arms, myself and the others shocked at the whole 'parade'.

'Private Hart, you and your platoon have done the near-impossible,' replied Instructor Ine.

'You're going to have to clarify that a little more, sir,' I replied in confusion.

'Private, you and your platoon have just beaten the Hakon Exercise. The Hakon, as you know it, was never this station, this realm or even CBMT. The Hakon is the name of this JNCO Field Training Exercise. The Hakon Exercise is intentionally rigged for failure. No matter how you planned your operation, you were always destined to violate General Order One. The Hakon is designed to test a leader's strength, not in their direct-action thinking but their creative thinking, endurance, and dedication—to both the objective and the unit. The Hakon Exercise was developed by the late Director Halloway herself to instruct leaders on the costs of war. To teach leaders sacrifice, to prepare them for the impossible, it forces leaders to reconcile two quintessential components of military life—the mission and the unit. Since its inception, less than forty percent of candidates have survived to initial exfiltration and of that forty percent, less than five percent of that group have successfully beaten the Hakon Exercise. But you—' he explained, pointing to me, 'you're something special. You're one of only five units to have ever survived the Hakon Exercise without sustaining a single casualty,' Instructor Ine explained. Shock rippled across the platoon.

'Victors of the Hakon Exercise will be, upon graduation, awarded the Colonial Star. A medal offered only to the champions of the Hakon Exercise, acknowledging complete dedication to the military way life, to the Taskforce values and mission statement. Also, because of your success, you can be moved out to your respective commands tonight. You've earned that much already,' Instructor Rei explained.

I chuckled. 'With all due respect, we'll stay for our graduation. We're no better than any other marine, sir,' I replied.

'Very well, Kanji One,' Instructor Rei replied, and with that, we snapped to attention as they left in silence.

Chapter 8
H-Day

Our final day of training and graduation. The day was business as usual with drills, runs, and theoretical exercises. The graduation parade was at 1900 hours Zulu time. Every graduating platoon was organised into their company and dressed in their branch or command-approved culture-specific military dress uniforms. Kanji Company was at the front of the column formation. Makos, who'd had the misfortune of becoming the platoon guidon bearer, stood in front of and to the right of First Platoon, the pennant bearing the unwieldy swallow-tailed flag of the UMC, its contour-line planet held up by the Marine Corps eagles' talons as they clung to an anchor. It cried *Semper Fidelis*, with the words *'per Mare, per Terram, per Astra'* wrapped below it. I adjusted my uniform one more time, noting the earpiece that I couldn't help but keep on me tucked away in one of my pockets. I never enjoyed being kept in the dark about anything, from the smallest life detail to the greatest inter-galactic decision, and carrying an earpiece on me kept that itch at least mentally scratched.

'Company! Mark, *time*!' barked Instructor Kisae. Kanji began to march in place. Moments later, the doors in front of us opened to reveal a parade ground more akin to the gladiatorial arenas of ancient Roman and Akati empires. High above the ground level sat a glass ring that encircled the parade ground. There, Hakon staff would observe us as we conducted ourselves demonstrating military bearing and professionalism. The tradition was a carryover from the hundreds of old-Earth militaries that were integrated into the USG's precursor.

The Joint Signals Intelligence Group's Direct-Action Special Mission Unit was known as Joint Special Operations Taskforce 4 (JSTF4), or simply, 'The Taskforce'. However, with the USG's formation and the unofficial reactivation of JSTF4, secrecy was paramount and the tradition of march out parades changed under Director Halloway. The march out parade, rather than a sobering moment for family and friends of the candidate, was instead a gruelling twelve-hour individual assessment where recruits would be subjected to a variety of tests and exercises to demonstrate their aptitude in the arts of espionage, direct action, and many other operational portfolios critical to the execution of the Taskforce Charter, all under the watchful gaze of the director. Of course, that was a thing of the past: the director was rarely seen at ceremonies such as these when the Taskforce operated hundreds of training facilities just like this. The march out parade had also changed, returning to its roots of being a military inspection as improvements in artificial intelligence and the all-seeing nature of the Hakon became a reality, allowing Taskforce analysts to have a complete understanding of the troops they were training and their progress.

'Company! Forward, *march*!' Kisae exclaimed. As we strode out into the parade ground, the bright lights blinding us temporarily, we marched out into the cavernous bowl-like coliseum. To our surprise, Director Mizuka herself and each of the four component branch flag officers stood overhead, looking on our march from the viewing pocket above in an unprecedented turn of events. Each platoon filed out and filled the large coliseum. Our Regimental Commander broke off and stood beside us to our left.

'Regiment! Open ranks, *march*!' he barked. We obliged, spacing ourselves out for inspection. Holographic models of Director Mizuka and the four flag officers appeared in front of the regiment and began their inspection. On this rare occasion, our march out inspection was overseen by the director and our flag officers. Normally, this wouldn't be the case. More commonly, the five roaming holographic models were in fact facsimiles of the Taskforce's senior staff and completely AI-driven. Of course, as they strode through our ranks, on-board AI continued to sift through live and historical data on each trainee and recruit, searching for any last unsatisfactory component.

Suddenly, the parade grounds shook violently as waves of artificial gravity fields crossed paths and competed for dominance. I grimaced as my mind began to race: *Who would be flying that close to the station?* Then my earpiece began to vibrate with network-wide traffic before fading quickly into static; I began to frown before forcing my expression to remain neutral. As we stood there, the entire parade ground was engulfed in emergency lighting followed by a deafening klaxon. The holographic avatars evaporated into thin air as a sailor exclaimed over the 1MC.

'All Hands, all Hands, General Quarters Condition One! All Hands, all Hands GQ1! This is not a drill! Air Threat Warning Red. Air Threat Warning Red!' Instantly, the director and four flag officers were rushed from their observation lounge and presumably to either the bridge or a station hangar.

'Regiment! Fall out! Get to your muster stations!' our regimental commander exclaimed. My mind instantly started decoding the instructions as Ela pulled up her SPS. *Condition One* meant all station personnel were to man their fighting positions; *Air Threat Warning* meant the current priority threat were fighters. The last direction, to a muster station, would've been an empty sentence in any other military sense. Aboard training space stations like the UNSS *Kaery* that hosted thousands of trainees and recruits daily, the civilian concept of a cruise liner's muster station had been adapted to a warship's armoured citadel for situations where evacuation wasn't necessarily required, but where recruits and trainees were a hindrance.

'You heard him, *gospadinas*! We're Oscar Mike!' I barked, gesturing for the door. I threw my earpiece to Ela. *Glad I brought it,* I thought. 'Do we have comms?'

'Local net only!' Ela reported. I gritted my teeth; local network meant that we could only receive what was broadcasting within a fifty-metre radius.

'Can you raise Godfather?' I asked as I followed our new waypoint.

'Trying!' Ela barked back. 'No response! They must have wireless jamming!' Ela reported.

'We need weapons! Where's the nearest armoury?'

Ela looked down at her CPI's SPS. 'Nearest armoury on the eleventh deck is ninety-forty-four-Mike! Through here!' Ela exclaimed pointing to a nearby door.

I moved to grab the release lever on the manual bulkhead to open it, but the system was stuck. I looked up at the pressure gauge; it was in the red. *They've already reached us,* I thought to myself. Moments later, the asteroid rocked as station-side batteries and enemy fighters clashed for dominance.

'That door's a no go,' I explained.

'Here let me give it a try!' Ela barked. I reached out and stopped her.

'No, it's not the lever.'

'The entire compartment?' she inquired, stunned as she realised what had happened. I nodded. '*Brafik!*' Ela exclaimed.

'Okay, put us back on course for the muster station,' I instructed.

'Aye, aye,' Ela replied. We continued down the passageway we had momentarily broken off from.

We ran for over twenty-five minutes attempting desperately to make our way across Kaery Station towards our muster station. Kaery Station, being one of the first stations installed in this sector of artificial space some three hundred years ago, while not unliveable by any means, was quite condensed compared to other stations in Taskforce-controlled territory, making it difficult to navigate at the best of times and impossible to traverse at its worst. As we neared within forty-two metres of our designated muster station, Ela paused, her tension lines abruptly changing as she listened intently over the crackling boom of naval gunfire.

'Canton Two-One is currently taking losses to enemy boarders,' Ela relayed.

'Can we raise them?' I inquired.

'Negative,' Ela spoke as she shook her head.

'Can you vector in on their signal?'

'Rah,' she replied with a nod.

'Do it,' I instructed. With our adjusted heading, I indicated the end of the passageway with a knife-hand and Kanji Company, First Platoon began to run in the direction of gunfire.

'Go, go, go!' screamed a staff non-commissioned officer as he fired down the passageway. 'Get in before the bulkheads close!'

Marines paced back from their cover, firing as they went, quickly ducking as the bulkhead lowered above them. 'Come on! Get in here!' the gunnery sergeant exclaimed. 'Damn it, Hodjson! Get in here now!' he barked as the bulkhead was close to sealed. 'Hodjson!' the gunnery sergeant exclaimed to the marine now trapped in the other compartment. The sound of the locking clamps thundered out from the door as a burst of weapons fire soon followed. '*Brufik!*' the gunnery sergeant exclaimed, in a fit of rage.

'You Canton Two-One?' I asked as I neared the gunnery sergeant.

'Oh, *brufik*'s sake, what do you need, Boot?' he snapped.

'We're responding to your request for assistance,' I replied. He began to laugh.

'Of course! Oh, the galactic irony! This facility has over two hundred thousand marines and the gods send a newly minted *brafiksjoti* boot!'

'If you don't need our help then we'll just be on our way,' I hissed back.

'How I'd love to say that we don't. As it stands, you're not going anywhere,' he replied.

'Why's that?'

'I think I know who you are, and your muster station's behind me, isn't it?' he asked.

I looked past him at the door number. 'Rah.'

'Well, you're out of luck. These Echo Tangos cut the control lines to the muster station doors. We can't open it, and the guys inside can't either,' the gunnery sergeant explained. 'So even if I didn't need your help, you'd be stuck here anyway,' the sergeant continued.

'Who dropped the bulkheads?'

'Operations did. We've got boarders on decks three through forty-nine. To contain them, they sealed the bulkheads. It ain't gonna work, however ...' the sergeant replied as if dreaming.

'And why is that?' I asked. I was becoming frustrated with the sergeant's attitude.

'Because it won't! We've been retreating from these damned UESes for the last ten compartments of this gods-damned deck and they've blown through at least twenty-five bulkheads!'

Unidentified Extra-terrestrial Species, I translated in shock. It isn't a known enemy of the Taskforce

'How long does it take them?' I asked.

'Three to five minutes max,' he replied.

I looked over at the bulkhead, the red-hot flames of their cutting utensils already beginning to show. I turned to Ela.

'Private Tremblej!' I boomed.

'Rah?'

'Get me a bypass on that door, I need it reconnected to the station, and I needed it yesterday.'

'Yut!' she barked. She immediately ran over to the control panel of the door and began to peel away the metal coverings.

'Gunny! We need to hold them off. Regardless of our situation, we need to slow down their cutting operations. Shooting at them should do the trick.'

'It ain't gonna work,' he replied.

I quickly struck him in the jaw.

'Just shut up and listen to what I say, then!' I barked.

He looked at me, shocked. 'I am going to NJP your *zhopas*!' he bellowed in fury as I strode past him. 'Do you read me, marine?' he howled, spinning to grab me by the arm. I spun back to face him with a stare that could kill a sun.

‘What do you want me to do?’ I growled back. ‘Stand here and lie down dying?’ I hissed.

‘You can’t stand and lie down dying!’ called Ela, already multitasking as she worked.

The gunny sighed as he lowered his gaze before calling out, ‘Marines! At the ready!’ Every armed marine readied their weapons and aimed at the bulkheads on the left and right.

With grim determination, I walked the line of marines as I instructed. ‘Jumper rounds!’ They all twisted their weapons, unloaded their current ammunition, and replaced it with a specialised magazine before they settled back into their sights. Their HMDs synced into the compartment feed. They were right there. Gunny once again snatched my wrist. ‘What are you doing? None of those targets have emitter tags!’ he informed me.

‘I know!’ I boomed back. ‘Let me do my job,’ I said, with more unspoken fire in my eyes. He let go of my arm as I strode across to Ela, snatched up my earpiece from her, and switched it to TEAMCOMM. ‘Mariko, you there?’

‘Affirmative,’ she coldly replied.

‘I need you to connect to the marine targeting computers on twenty-eight–ninety–forty-seven–Lima and do the mathematics to directly translocate all jumper rounds to their targets in the adjacent compartment—is that possible?’

‘I’m a Tier Three AI, not some back-alley parrot process—’ she began to reply.

‘But can you do it?’

‘Affirmative,’ she responded.

‘Then do it!’ I instructed her.

‘Already done, ma’am,’ she replied. ‘Anything else, ma’am?’

‘Negative, thank you,’ I remarked before turning back to the marines.

‘You have a Tier Three AI?’ the gunny inquired. I ignored him.

‘On my command!’ I barked. ‘Ready!’ They adjusted. ‘Aim! … Fire!’ I barked.

The marines opened fire, the whine of gunfire deafening in the passageway as round after round screamed through the air, each round vanishing and reappearing moments later on my CPI's streamed camera footage. The shots slammed into a trio of monsters with brutal precision. Each tight cluster caused a bright golden shimmer of energy that pulsed across their white and gold armour plating, their shimmering plasma cutters hacking away at the door as each round connected. They hadn't made a scratch. They hadn't killed a single one. My eyes widened. *What the* brafiksjot! I thought to myself. My fist tightened as I pointed a furious index finger at the gunnery sergeant about to speak. As the rhythmic slashes of plasma cutters echoed around me, the rapid clicks of emptied magazines clattered around. The sounds of chaos roared everywhere. My eyes narrowed and my lips pursed together.

'Marines! Fall back to the muster station door!' I barked. Without reply, each marine quickly turned back towards the doorway and began to tuck in close to the door.

'What are you doing?' the gunnery sergeant asked.

'If the conventional won't kill them, then the unconventional should, right?' I explained. I strode over to Ela. 'Private! How's that bypass going?'

'Slowly! It'll be done in another ninety ticks,' Ela reported.

'Well belay that bypass, I've got something else in mind. Rip out the power cables and connect them to Canton's equipment,' I instructed. Ela looked at me, shocked.

'Are you insane? That *shajst*'s well above their armour tolerances!' the gunnery sergeant interjected.

'So are our hostiles! Now get me those cables!' I barked.

'Yut,' Ela replied as she lifted off another covering.

'Marines! Get me a pair of guinea pigs!' I ordered.

The gunnery sergeant strode over to me. 'What the *brufik* are you doing?' he roared.

'My job. Stacking bodies,' I briskly replied.

'Yeah, ours!' he retorted.

'And how is that?'

'You're about to detonate a micro fusion reactor!' he exclaimed.

'And? Unless your KPM isn't rated for CBRN then I'd suggest you shut the *brafik* up!' I barked.

'But—' the gunnery sergeant began.

'But nothing! That is a micro fusion reactor! It ain't a nuke in atmo! Once this compartment is spaced, that detonation will do *brufik* all!' I exclaimed. 'Now! Everyone! If you missed the word! MOPP four is now in effect! Seal all equipment and adjust kinetic plating in keeping with CBRN protocols and get up against the door!' I barked, pointing behind me.

'Ma'am, are you aware that neither you nor your march-out platoon are sufficiently equipped to keep the current in-theatre CBRN protection level of Mission Orientated Protective Posture four that you just set?' Mariko chimed into my ear.

I ignored her question, fully aware that none of us were safe from the potential radiological effects of detonating a fusion reactor.

The marines ran up to the muster station doorway as I pulled a pair of them aside. 'Stop. Hold up,' I instructed as I grabbed one of the marines' reactor housings. I unclipped the access panel in front of his fusion pack and carefully removed the Micro Fusion Reactor, inspecting the reactor's water cooling before placing it on the floor. 'You're good to go,' I said, waving the first marine off. 'Tremblej! You done?'

'Yut!' she replied as she passed up the conduit that I quickly plugged into the second marine's suit.

'Private—' I began as I searched his shoulder for his name tag, '—Degata. Activate your KPM and generate a single field. Width two point five metres. Distance six point zero metres.'

'Rah,' he replied. Moments later, a field appeared around us.

I mentally began to count down twenty seconds. As the cutting became louder, their blades cut through the Carbyne-A swiftly and without a struggle. Moments later, the bulkheads exploded open. The liquid centre spilled onto the deck; smoke filled the room. Amid the haze, red eyes pulsed intently, their white armour shining in the fire. I smirked. 'Zero seconds,' I muttered to no-one in particular as the whole section vanished in a thick cloud of radiated steam. I paused for a moment, shocked as the plume rapidly thickened. 'It worked … it *brafik*ing worked,' I muttered, the gunny looking on in shock at my mutterings as I stepped towards the kinetic field. I peered out into the soup-like air as an intense deep glare gazed through the shroud right back at me, the pulsing red emergency lights illuminating the imposing form.

'*Brafik*!' I spewed. I threw myself back, and the marines to my left and right raised their rifles as the brutes began to rail against the kinetic field that stood between us and the irradiated hallway. *Thud, thud, thud* reverberated through the room, followed by a sharp whine that pierced our minds with each blow as the brutes desperately threw themselves at the shimmering field, their animal-like legs buckling, their hardened strikes lessening with each passing moment as the radiation sapped them of their strength. Silence fell upon the passageway as the desperate fists of the monsters tapered off. I let out a sigh as I turned to face Ela. 'Private Tremblej—' I began as the slam of an alien palm rang back from the field. I whipped back to see a circular device planted at the centre of the field. My eyes widened in realisation as I spoke. 'Ela, ETA on that bypass!' I queried, not looking back.

'Another thirty ticks!' she called forwards, not looking away from her work.

Brafik! I thought as I tapped my comm piece. 'Mariko! Vent the compartment!' I barked as static hissed into my ear. 'Mariko?' I called as I stood beside Gunnery Sergeant Koroljov.

'We've lost communications, Lance Corporal!' reported a Communications Systems Operator.

'Tremblej! Get us comms with Operations!' I barked, panic rising as Ela rose from her resting place, dragging another marine up beside the one generating the kinetic field. Without even looking, Ela tore the second marine's reactor housing open, reached in, and yanked cabling out of the rectangular indent, only to loop into the first marine's still-exposed casing before entering a series of commands into their CPI. An instant later, the explosive charge was flicked off by the kinetic field with the casualness of a marine swatting at insects. A moment later, the charge exploded, tearing through the floor and sending the irradiated steam and corpses careening out into the black of space. We both looked on in shock as Ela casually made an about-face, strode back to her work, and calmly sat down to continue rewiring the door. The station's emergency decompression measures were already being enacted. Ten seconds later, a spark of electricity pulsed out of the wall, and the door behind us began to rise.

'Got it,' Ela replied cheerily, shrugging as she sat on the ground. I turned towards the door before looking to Koroljov. 'Gunny, I don't think you'll be getting out this way. Wanna join us?' indicating back towards the blackened passageway.

'From the wireless chatter I'm receiving, we'll be in here sooner, rather than later. Besides, your word goes, ma'am,' he replied, shocked at my unconventional reaction.

Chapter 9
The blind coffin

The lift started down, and we began to descend into the belly of the box. As we neared the lift's termination point, I noticed the drop in the hexagonal container's deck. The lift pad was designed to integrate directly into the escape capsule's deck. As we were lowered into the vertically engineered escape unit, sections of deck would part as hydraulic motors tugged them away. As our lift cleared the last of the capsule's access hatchways, automatic hydraulics clamped the overhead above us with a metallic click. As the lift continued its descent, I scanned the container, its internal doorways sealed to prevent personnel from falling under the crushing descent of the lift. Another click later, the half-a-dozen doorways snapped open. The lift terminated on the container's main deck. First and second levels were comprised of the capsule's living quarters while the second deck through to the eighth comprised the hexagonal rectangle of armouries, galleys, heads, and showers, as well as the capsule's message centre, control compartment, and reactor room. Cramming hundreds of sailors and marines made it a tight fit, but it was still better than most barracks in the fleet.

Ela tapped me on the shoulder. 'Lance Corporal Hart,' she called out. I turned to look in her direction.

'What is it, private?'

'I noticed something odd about those UESes. While they were cutting through, I noticed a sporadic set of subspace anomalies,' she remarked.

'Not just subspace communications?' I said with a frown.

'No. Didn't generate the same pattern of interference as subspace communication would,' Ela replied.

'When we get out of this, the Office of Strategic Intelligence'll want to know about this,' I explained. Ela nodded in agreement. With the lift stopped, we stepped off and quickly made our way down through the capsule's hatches to its message centre. A collection of field units and training platoons hovered intently around the centre.

'Lieutenants, chiefs: Lance Corporal Hart and Kanji Platoon reporting,' I reported as I stepped through the waiting crowd of officers and enlisted troops into the message centre, my boot clanging with the deck as I snapped to attention. The officers and senior NCOs turned to face me, but their eyes were weary with distress.

'At ease. Glad to see you made it out in one piece. What happened to you and your platoon? We lost audio-visual contact with you,' asked one of the lieutenants.

'We were ambushed by our new friends, sir.'

'Yeah, but how did you beat them? Conventional weapons didn't seem to faze them,' Lieutenant Drake continued.

'We may have detonated a micro fusion reactor, sir,' I remarked casually with a smirk. They looked at me, shocked.

'She's not lying, Lieutenant. She did, sir,' reinforced the gunnery sergeant. The officers and NCOs continued to look at me shocked. Never in a thousand lifetimes could anyone from the Taskforce envision an enemy so resilient and so impossibly strong.

'Speaking of, what's the situation top-side, sir? We've been wireless silent,' continued the gunny.

'Not good, Gunny,' replied one of the lieutenants as an explosion rocked through the capsule. 'These Echo Tangos have neutralised over sixty-seven percent of our defensive emplacements. Point defence is inoperable. Station-side LRT is offline, Shields are trying to power cycle, and a third of the planet's ring has been displaced by strategic bombing,' he reported.

This time it was my turn to look shocked as another shell hit. 'What kind of firepower are their battlecruisers packing, sir?'

'We haven't seen their battlecruisers,' he reported.

'So, their destroyers? Battleships, sir?' I quickly rattled off, agitated by his specificity.

'No idea, all this destruction's been caused by their Starfighter Corps alone,' the lieutenant replied.

I stood there shocked. 'Sir, permission to be patched in,' I requested.

With a sigh, he passed me a comm piece.

'Ball Court, watch it, you've got a bandit on your six!' called one of the pilots over the wireless.

'I see the bandit manoeuvring to engage. No effect! I'm gonna need some assistanc—' the pilot screamed as the wireless feed died.

'Hakon, where's that AA? We're being chewed up out here!' barked the flight leader over comms.

'Working on it, Flight!' replied Commander Kiin. Moments later, the crackle of ionised shrapnel filled the wireless.

'AA's ineffective, Kaery Actual! Repeat, AA's ineffective!' reported the flight leader.

'*Br̃afiksjot!*' exclaimed Kiin. At this, the voice of Captain Izan echoed over the earpiece as he seemingly turned to face his executive officer and his Command Master Chief (CMDCM).

'Master chief, are all personnel at assigned muster stations and escape craft?'

'All surviving personnel have checked in at assigned muster stations, aye, sir,' replied CMDCM Takashi. A long pause seemed to drown out the chaos around the station before the subtle click of a switch echoed from the captain's command board.

'All Hands! All Hands! General Evacuation Protocol Seven. GEP7! All hands to your lifeboats. Cast off in two minutes. Kaery Actual, out.'

++++

'Okay, everyone, strap in!' instructed Lieutenant JG Haener over the intercom as he strapped into his impact seat and slammed a nearby activator switch.

'Magnetic clamps disengaged,' reported the capsule's protocol execution AI. We began to descend. With a shudder, our container had broken off from the station and began to drift towards the planet below before magnetic cables tugged us up into the stripped-away fuselage of a CH-108 Starhoist. Our momentum was stopped by two colossal clamps. The sounds of a boarding tube connecting the Starhoist's drooping nose-like cockpit followed soon after as we were snatched up and accelerated away, autopilot activated.

'Mackenzie, Chief! With me!' Haener called again as he and his co-pilot closely followed by their crew chief scrambled from their flight control stations, adjusted the O2 equilibrium between the Starhoist and the capsule and moved for the Starhoist's cockpit. Moments later, we began to bank hard as the pilots began manually manoeuvring the spacecraft, its unwieldy form leaving it unbearably vulnerable to interception. Explosions began to echo throughout the container as a pair of interceptors quickly zeroed in on the fleet of Starhoists that were abandoning the system, their cargo in tow. Explosions rocked through the ship; as they eviscerated the evacuation effort, a missile abruptly struck our starboard side. The Starhoist violently rocked. Another missile struck us. Our port side engine spluttered as the Starhoist's primary power feed erupted in a gout of fire. We began to lose velocity as the alien fighters closed the gap and prepared to fire. All of us grabbed for a handrail and closed our eyes, embracing the inevitable. But it never came.

'CAPs on station!' exclaimed the lieutenant as he received the news. The Hakon combat air patrol had stayed in-system to cover our jump out.

'Jumping!' the lieutenant exclaimed. The world around me began to twist and bend, my heart stopped as we slipped through a fracture in the universe, entering another realm of physics and laws of nature where time was irrelevant, and speed was incalculable.

After a few sparks and explosions, our Starhoist stabilised. 'We made it,' the lieutenant reported, relieved and shocked. He wasn't a young man, he'd been there and done that, like every one-hundred-and-twenty-six-year-old you meet, but somehow the ravaging of The Hakon was worse than everything he'd seen. More heart-stopping than every death-defying operation he'd been a part of. But more importantly, he had never lost. Until now.

Chapter 10
Bruised and bloodied

08/01/2437 (Military Calendar)
Taskforce Starhoist TH-986. Thirty-six hours since the fall of the Hakon.

We cruised through the Aether in silence. Our engines ran hot, and our blood ran cold. We'd been cruising for thirty-six hours when the message arrived. Initially, we were wary of the message. Its point of origin was 'directly behind' us. With hesitation and caution and time to kill, we decrypted the file and played it. The video crackled to life on the monitor. The capsule's complement of recruits and active personnel watched on from their racks in horror. The footage was from a damaged security camera at the heart of The Hakon's hexagonal Command Centre, the weary ghost of Captain Izan shouting orders from the central command table to the dozens of sailors manning stations around the cool grey centre before turning towards a marine.

'Marine! Give me your weapon!'

'Sir?' The marine paused in confusion.

'Just give it to me and get to your lifeboat.'

'Aye, sir,' he replied as he held his weapon out to the captain. The doors shut behind him as the marine left, the sound of weapon fire echoing through the reinforced security door behind him.

'Bolormaa, you still here?' called Captain Izan.

'Yes sir,' she replied, her ancient Mongolian avatar appearing beside the captain.

'Initiate clean house protocol,' he instructed.

'Aye, aye,' Bolormaa replied. The alert klaxon picked up as Captain Izan authorised the protocol.

As the security door exploded open, the alien creatures strode in with authority, their angular armour a striking visage. They quickly zeroed in on the captain but stopped just short of killing him. He armed his rifle as the alien commander strode in. His regal gold armour illuminated the room. He paused to activate a device on his wrist.

'Attention murderers. Heathens. Enemies of the Kukaerke. I am Sikaer five-five-four-three. You have violated solemn territory and stolen the honour of a people. We are their retribution. We are their reclaimers,' he proclaimed, clearly aware of the camera on the ceiling.

The enemy commander activated an energy blade mounted to his wrist. It was composed of three distinct pieces: a central brace and two curved sides. The golden blade hovered patiently as if sensing its prey.

Captain Izan tossed two grenades into the doorway before levelling his rifle towards the golden Sikaer, and he emptied a whole magazine into the bastard. 5543 simply stood there, patiently waiting. As Izan changed magazines, the golden warrior who would come to be known as Sikaer 5543 swung into action. He twisted Izan's right arm back and swung the blade upwards in a circular motion. The energy slashed through the commander's chest cavity. His lungs severed and his throat split, blood began to pour out onto the floor. As Captain Izan slumped to the floor, his heartbeat fading with every passing second, Bolormaa appeared to issue an immediate SITREP: 'All Taskforce units have evacuated the area of responsibility. Activating clean house protocol,' Bolormaa reported.

The video ended.

Captain Izan was now a legend in the eyes of the Taskforce. To the marines, he represented the highest individual kill count ever achieved. To the navy, he represented the finest sailor they'd ever produced, loyal and willing to the end, and to the wider Taskforce, he represented the greatest sacrifice an individual could ever make. To die for the Taskforce Charter. Commander Kisinthi Izan was posthumously awarded the Taskforce Decoration of Honour and a monument: carved from the wreckage of Starhoist Tango Hotel Nine Three Eight—nicknamed Igor—it was erected at the heart of Taskforce Headquarters, the names of the dead soldered into the twisted wreckage. It would become known as 'The Hakon Memorial'.

++++

It was another thirty-six hours before we arrived at the RV point, and when we did, we weren't exactly welcomed. The second we entered the system, we were surrounded by a combat air patrol of F-44 Interceptors, nicknamed 'Shriekers' by the marines. They began to bombard us with questions.

'Attention unidentified vessel. This is India Tango Two Eight Four. Transmit security codes, callsign, and cargo. Failure to comply within a timely manner will result in your annihilation. Over,' instructed the lead pilot.

'IT284, this is Starhoist Tango Hotel Niner Eight Six. We're transporting survivors from the *Hakon* to RV Point Romeo Zulu Two Six Three Seven Niner Eight. Transmitting security codes now. Over,' replied one of our lieutenants.

'Apologies 986. We've been pickin' up the pieces ever since GEP7, between the random *shajst* that's been droppin' out of subspace and the *brafiksjoti* shadow masses; it's been a nightmare. Skipper's been paranoid ever since, over,' the pilot replied.

'Roger that. Interrogative: what's the situation with Flotilla Rwanda? Over,' queried the lieutenant.

'See the vessels to your twelve o'clock high? Over,' the pilot explained. Our lieutenant acknowledged. 'That's all that's left: seventy-six percent of Rwanda was scorched in the firefight and less than twenty-two percent of evac birds even made it to FTL. Land when ready, we'll wire ahead. Out,' the pilot reported.

We sat stunned as we processed what we'd just heard. Our Starhoist glided up to the cruiser. The docking procedures that were usually quite stringent were noticeably absent. When we landed, the hangar bay felt alien. The usually bustling bay was now just a derelict husk. Combat hadn't been kind to her, wiring burst out of the walls like over pressurised veins, bodies lay in piles, soon to be disposed of. Sealant filled atmospheric leaks inside the wounded ship, sparks flew left and right as the ship's crew attempted in vain to bring the behemoth back up to operational status. The captain strode down to meet us, the Petty Officer of the Deck noticeably confused when Captain Anj waved off the formalities.

'Welcome aboard the UNV *Lion of Panjshir*, I hope you'll find all the comforts of home here; generally, she doesn't bleed around guests, but anything that's hers is yours,' he explained, clearly overworked.

'What's her status?' asked First Lieutenant Honberg. The captain just shook his head, finally giving in to the distress that had been niggling in the back of his mind for the past thirty-six hours.

'BUBAR would be the SITREP. Decks two through fifteen are open to the vacuum of space, the main reactor's venting every kind of radiation under the sun. Carrier air traffic control centre, navigation, combat information centre, helm—*brafiksjot* basic naval systems are completely offline. To be frank, I'm amazed we got back here in one piece,' he finished, weary from his explanation. 'Well, I'm sorry I can't be a better host, but I've got a repair list as long as my arm to complete. I'd transmit the coordinates for your berth, but our wireless system is offline as well, so I'll have Seaman Harrington escort you to your racks,' he explained, gesturing to a nearby sailor. The captain strode off without so much as another word.

As we set up in our berths, elsewhere the Unified Security Group Commander-In-Chief (USGCINC), Director Chihiro Mizuka, who had been one of the few to escape the Hakon unscathed, stormed down one of the many halls of Taskforce Headquarters.

++++

[FILE ACCESSED 2440]

'Get the committee in session now! We have just been kicked in the teeth by a military force we didn't anticipate! This is unacceptable!' Chihiro barked to her AI assistant, Ada.

'Ma'am, the committee is now in session, they are directly ahead,' Ada reported, her fine English emanating through the soundless passageway. Chihiro stormed ahead into the conference room. Before her stood twelve members of the Operations Personnel Security and Intelligence Committee.

Chihiro straightened her dress uniform. 'Take a seat, ladies and gentlemen,' Chihiro instructed as she slipped into her chair at the head of the table. The members quickly walked to their chairs and settled into one of the assigned spaces, their holographic 'shadows' flickering as they settled atop the solid object. 'Ladies and gentlemen. We are in crisis. The Taskforce has been threatened by an unforeseen adversary whose military strength rivals our own. They have threatened our charter, our mandate. So, we must react; we must respond. Suggestions?' Her cold eyes glanced over the room as she opened to the floor.

Field Marshal Blaire quickly offered his opinion. 'We could rescind Silentio Super Tumultum, engage this foe head-on. Draw them out. This enemy has power over us because they hide in the shadows. So, we draw them out. Force them into open conflict, rally the masses under a single banner,' Blaire explained.

The committee was quick to rile at the suggestion. 'Right, like that ever ended well,' sarcastically interjected Marshal of the Air Corps Sanderson. 'Do we want to wage war on three fronts then?' he added. Chihiro silenced the discussion before it developed into the all-out brawl it would traditionally become.

'An alternative then? A middle ground between direct action and covert intervention,' interjected Office of Strategic Intelligence Agent Sinamon.

'Go ahead, Agent Sinamon,' Director Mizuka replied.

'The Taskforce has run into an immovable object that has the technology to wipe us and our charges off the face of the universe. But open intervention has never ended in our favour. So, we let someone else do it. As you would know, due to Fleet Admiral Hurt's recent proposal to reactivate Project Reveles, Shadow Director Rokkaku began to mobilise our extensive political and espionage infrastructure to pave the way for a military authority at a planetary level that would answer directly to us three months ago. The original strategy was designed to supplement active Taskforce patrols and maximise the effectiveness of our revamped Stealth Corvette Corps without compromising Taskforce influence within Imperial space.' Agent Sinamon paused. The members of OPSI were shocked. Sasaki had apparently neglected to inform Director Mizuka of his strategy—something she wouldn't quickly forget. The room became awkwardly silent. As the pause lingered, the Agent's holographic representation fell limp, his eyes rapidly oscillating as he began processing the daily security report.

'Continue Agent Sinamon, regardless of OSICINC's disposition towards informing his Commander-in-Chief of his stratagems. Please continue,' she said, rising from her chair. At the director's instruction, Sinamon's jaw began to move as if a marionette.

'As I was saying, taking control of the Ympiirno Teritoriino Admin, known to most as the YTA and drastically restructuring and upscaling its daughter service the Ympiirno Teritoriino Meikseifno Osoriti, or YTMO, into the Ympiirno Shendars Kor, or YSK, would enable us to deal with the direct action presence of this—' Sinamon paused to bring up the data, '—"Honour Guard",' he continued, rising as he finished all his other tasks. 'To complement this direct-action mechanism, OSI would like to motion for the reactivation of Fifteenth Special Operations Group, reorganised as an integrated operations unit to specifically deal with threats like the Honour Guard. Functionally, with these two pieces in play, we would be able to effectively orchestrate an *umbra bellum*, a shadow war fought by proxy with spies and empires,' Agent Sinamon explained.

'Very well. The Office of Strategic Intelligence moves to reactivate Joint Special Operations Group Proteus, take control of the Imperial Territories Administration and restructure the Imperial Territories Security Authority into the Imperial Gendarmes Corps to wage a war by proxy against this new foe.' Chihiro paused. 'All in favour, say "aye",' Chihiro instructed.

Eleven of the twelve members exclaimed 'Aye!'

'And against?'

'Nay,' called out Field Marshal Blaire, his offensive proposal yet again crushed by the majority.

'Then it is settled. Operation Hidden Trident will commence. This session is adjourned,' Chihiro proclaimed. The committee members vanished from their chairs.

She let out a loud sigh as she slipped back into her seat. 'Ada, connect this room to all Taskforce comm nets. Audio only,' Mizuka instructed.

'Yes, Director. Setting up audio feed now,' Ada replied, her avatar now standing at the centre of the meeting table. Mizuka's glistening jade eyes reflected in the glass table. Seconds later, a socket ejected out of the counter.

'Connection is live. Wire in when ready,' Ada reported, her avatar disappearing. Chihiro reached down, tugged the cable out of its place, and plugged the cable into the back of her neck. The electric pulse was nearly unbearable.

‘You are live, ma’am, encryption stable, connection reading five by five,’ informed Ada. Chihiro took a deep breath.

‘Attention all Taskforce personnel; there have been rumours over the last forty-eight hours that Hakon Combined Military Training Depot and its support stations have fallen. For once, the rumours are true. At zero thirty hours Zulu time last night, HCMTD and UNSS *Kaery* were besieged by a superior force of bomber interceptor squadrons. Critically outmatched, Captain Izan issued General Evacuation Protocol 7 and ordered all Taskforce assets to retreat into friendly space, after which he detonated the facilities inventory of graviton warheads, consuming Artificial Galaxy UV twenty-five thirty-eight and the enemy force.’ Chihiro paused. ‘Despite Captain Izan’s valiant last stand, reconnaissance reports past the Red Line indicate this new enemy, known to us as the Kukaerke, is still a great threat that aims to destroy us. As of this moment, we are at war. All Taskforce units are to move to alert status and stand by for tasking. Counter-operations will begin shortly. Zeus out.’

Chapter 11
Blacked out

UNV Lion of Panjshir, thirty-five minutes after the director's official announcement.

I took a deep breath as I stared out into the blackness of space. Repair crews (nicknamed 'gimmits') scrambled to bring the *Lion of Panjshir* back up to operational status. Orders were being handed out by the minute, and Captain Anj wanted to get his ship back in the fight. No one blamed him: he had a score to settle. As I stared out into the vacuum of space, a dark-clothed man quietly approached me. I was so distracted that he practically sneaked up on me. I leapt in a panic as he tapped me on the shoulder.

'Easy, Lance Corporal Hart,' the man replied, holding his hands out in self-defence. When I returned to the present, I looked over the stranger before me. He stood a couple of metres away from me and actively avoided the floodlights erected by *Panjshir*'s gimmits to illuminate the wounded ship. The man wore a black and white suit if I remember correctly—very Maxim Isajev-esque.

'Lance Corporal Hart,' the man began, still actively avoiding light. 'Under Protocol Alpha Five Sixty, you have been selected by Director Chihiro Mizuka and the Operations Personnel Security and Intelligence Committee to join reactivated Fifteenth Special Operations Group: Proteus due to your prior service record and field experience with the Kukaerke. I am to escort you and your selected preference of support personnel to the earliest available transportation,' he recited perfectly. I simply nodded.

'This way, Lance Corporal,' the man instructed as he twisted to the left and put his arm out in the same direction. I strode ahead of the man, never daring to look back at him. We walked the length of the ship, always avoiding major thoroughfares and lifts, opting instead for ladders and maintenance passageways throughout the *Panjshir*. When we arrived on the hangar bay again, they'd repaired most of the damage. Lighting had been fully restored and many of the launch tubes had been brought back online. But the bay was still devoid of engineers. At the centre of the bay sat a lone Condor. The dropship's airframe was trapezoidal with sharp corners on its underside abruptly cutting the width of the undercarriage. Two hexagonal struts stood out from the rest of the craft while an integrated cockpit rounded out the curved frame. I stopped. *Where the Brafiksjot do I go now?* I wondered. I looked back to find my mystery tour guide, but he'd vanished. I panicked. *Brafiksjot! Where'd he go? What do I do?* I wondered. The Condor was black and unmarked, meaning it had to be OSI. Gritting my teeth, I strode over to the vessel. A Petty Officer of the Deck was assigned to the craft. I stopped just short of entering.

'Clearance, Lance Corporal Hart,' the PO requested.

'Um…' I replied as I mulled over the complications.

'Your security papers, Lance Corporal Hart,' the deck petty officer insisted.

'Um… yes, PO,' I replied as I reached into one of my fatigues' many pouches, usually filled with ammunition or other supplies. I fished around awkwardly as my mind raced over the possibilities. *Am I going to be court-martialled—ninja punched? I am so* brafiki, I thought to myself as I passed over my identification slip—a digital imprint of a servicewoman's DNA. The petty officer inspected it. Then handed it back to me and stepped aside.

'Welcome aboard, Lance Corporal Hart,' he curtly commented.

I looked at him, shocked. Shajst*! It worked. What now?* I wondered. Smiling awkwardly, I stepped onto the Condor. The troop bay was dark; shadows moved in front of me. I paused to panic as Dimitri emerged from the shadows to embrace me.

'Sayra!' he exclaimed as he came walking over. I smiled and returned the embrace.

'Uncle Dimi! You're alive!' I exclaimed.

'Of course, I'm alive! I didn't survive the Battle of Heidrianno Vali for nothing!' he replied jokingly. As I adjusted to the low light, I came to realise that Davidson and a small portion of Kanji One were also aboard.

'Godfather?' I queried, confused. Davidson looked up as if recognising his old call sign.

'Yep?' he called back.

'Why're you here?' I asked as subtly as a marine could.

'Was recommended for the position by your platoon. With everything that's happened recently. Figured I'd finally move out of the initialisation program,' he replied.

I looked at him, shocked. 'I didn't recommend you. I made no recommendations at all,' confused as to what he meant.

'Of course, you didn't! OSI doesn't have time for you to deliberate on candidates. So, they just take it from you. Access your implants and take the data directly from your mind,' Uncle Dimi replied with an odd cheer.

'Alright, if everyone could take a seat, that'd be great. While my spook buddies and I enjoy a good bit of blood, my Condor does not, and those servos can get easily clogged with your blood and guts,' called our pilot over the intercom, his bizarre accent catching us all off guard. I couldn't help but snort in amusement. *An aviator spy this obnoxiously foreign? OSI's really pushing the definition of "intelligence".*

'Who the *brafik* are you?' Ela hissed, irritated by the sound of his voice. I smiled. *They've snatched up Kanji's command team,* I thought to myself.

'Harmon Miles. Your new pilot,' he said with an announcer's tone.

'Great! A mortarded aviator!' Ela exclaimed as she rolled her eyes.

'Just take your seat, Ela,' I interjected. She nodded and settled into a nearby seat. Moments later, the Condor began to lift out of the hangar bay onto the flight deck.

'Magnetic clamps disengaged. Launch approved, moving clear of the *Panjshir,'* Harmon reported as our Condor accelerated into the empty void of space. The sound of a bizarre nodding doll rang through the bay as the cockpit's hatchway opened up. The man who had approached me aboard the *Panjshir* stepped through. Now, though, he was wearing similar fatigues as us, although coloured black. The man had black hair, tan skin, and white eyes with three small grooves at set intervals around his iris. Without a word, he took a seat in the crew chief's chair that was currently vacant and strapped in.

'All hands, jumping,' Harmon reported. Moments later, we leapt into the Aether.

'Gods, I didn't even feel the shift,' Davidson remarked, shocked. 'I've been on the *Kau* for too long,' he interjected.

'No, that's not your inexperience with conventional faster-than-light propulsion Handler Davidson. You're aboard the newest innovation from Min-Hei Industries,' the unknown man replied, pausing to regain his composure. 'Ladies and gentlemen, what you are about to hear requires Security Level Four clearance. Taskforce Internal Affairs have vetted you for this briefing, but this stays here,' he explained. We all nodded. 'My name is High Special Operations Inquisitor Mitchell Paladin. Before joining the Taskforce, I was a soldier, a part of the Special Air Service Regiment, a special operations unit based out of our origin planet, Earth. Your pilot,' Paladin pointed towards the cockpit, 'was a Royal Australian Air Force pilot, a part of the same military organisation as me. We served a part of the Australian Defence Force.' Mitchell paused.

'With introductions out of the way, as you know you've been assigned to Proteus, but I doubt you know what we are. Proteus is a temporary Joint Special Operations Group designed to disrupt guard operations within the Red Line. Our operational life expectancy is bound to the guard. As long as it lives, we live. Once we put it down, you'll be rotated out to traditional units,' he explained. 'For the operation, all combat personnel have been given the titles of "Special Operations Inquisitor". You will now answer to Director Mizuka and the Operations Personnel Security and Intelligence Committee directly and have the authority to access all Taskforce databases, installations, and operations necessary to achieve your mission objective. While you will retain your USM rank, you are, all of you, equals,' Mitchell explained. We all paused.

Elenskis was the first to question his explanation. 'If we're all equals, how do we refer to you?'

'First and surname basis now. No "ma'am" or "sir",' he replied. We all nodded. 'Moving on, the Taskforce has pulled assets from Min-Hei Industries, our premier research and development group and the galaxy's largest supplier of cheap medical supplies, to support your operation. Over a hundred and fifty shelved technical patterns have been reviewed and received renewed funding to augment your fight against the guard,' Paladin explained.

'Re-entering N Space in twenty seconds! Stand by,' exclaimed the pilot. We were shocked.

'Bull*shajst*! Nothing can create quark pairs that consistent!' exclaimed Ela.

'You're wrong about that, little miss,' Harmon replied. Ela clenched her fist. As she began to untangle herself from her seat's five-point harness, we dropped out of FTL. Ela was slammed back into her seat.

'Welcome to Echo Sierra twenty-two thirty-seven oh eight,' Harmon reported as he brought up a holographic map of the area.

'Harmon, what are we looking at?' I questioned.

'You are looking at nothing right now, but you'll see in a sec what I am talking about.' Mystery engulfed his every word.

'There! I see something!' exclaimed Makos as he pointed at the map.

'There you go, ladies, at point two three three,' Harmon explained. A small red light flickered on, amidst a debris field, a derelict starship.

'That's just a *brafik*ed Isoroku-class. The line was discontinued a hundred years ago!' retorted Petrov.

'Well if you're that dumb that you can't figure out why we're heading to a derelict starship, I don't know why you're here!' Harmon mockingly replied.

'It's a cover,' explained Ela.

'Three points to the pretty lady,' Harmon coyly congratulated.

'Oh, it's on, you Whiskey Tango mother*brufiken*! I'm going to beat you to a pulp!' Ela exclaimed with a fury.

Calling our pilot white trash is not a smart decision! I thought to myself as I interjected, trying to de-escalate the situation. 'Just elaborate for the boot over there.'

Ela paused to collect her thoughts. 'It's a cover; derelict vessels can move through a system relatively unnoticed, with the right EM coverings and radiation generators a "derelict" vessel can move from system to system with impunity,' Ela continued to explain.

'That's why you were chosen, not just for your dealings with the Honour Guard but your ingenuity. For example, your platoon leader's radical response aboard Kaery Station. Though certainly unorthodox—and some would even say overkill—that's what we are about: adapting in the field to combat situations that are beyond conventional tactics,' added Paladin. We all went silent.

'Ladies and gents, we are docking with the UNV *Yamamoto* in one mike. Beginning landing procedures now,' Harmon called over the intercom.

'*Yamamoto* Flight, Alpha Quebec Two Five Seven. Requesting to land. Over,' detailed Harmon.

'Alpha Quebec Two Five Seven, *Yamamoto* Flight. Transmit security codes. Over,' instructed one of the air traffic controllers.

'Affirmative. Transmitting security codes now. Over,' replied Harmon. There was a long pause.

'Security codes authenticated. You are cleared for approach, speed zero six seven. Hands-on approach. Checkers Red. Call the ball. Over,' called the control tower.

'Understood. Speed 067. Hands-on approach. Checkers Red. I have the ball. Over,' Harmon replied.

With that, our Condor glided into the flight deck, pivoting as it nestled onto the lift.

'Magnetic clamps engaged,' Harmon reported as we were ferried into the hangar bay.

'Air pressure stabilised, opening hatch,' Harmon stated. Moments later, the ramp behind us began to lower, and light began to spill into the bay. When the lift finally stopped, Harmon finished. 'Welcome aboard the UNV *Yamamoto*, LDD-One Fourteen, our home away from home. Now, if you could, please rate your overall experience flying with Air Harmon on the trip experience card that you will receive shortly, and thank you for flying Air Harmon. Have a nice day,' he sarcastically added.

'Message received,' informed my CPI. I opened the folder to see a picture of an island paradise and alien plants known as palm trees; of course, many of us recoiled in fear as we recalled a similar looking, carnivorous plant found on Belsarus VIII. The file revealed a collection of boxes stating whether the inflight entertainment was enjoyable, whether the pilot's skills were of high quality, bull*shajst* like that, so I quickly deleted it and moved on. As we stepped out onto the deck, we saw one hell of a refurbishment. A large assortment of engineers dashed around the vessel installing wiring, replacing tiles, testing lighting, connecting klaxons. You name it, it was happening.

'There are 20,000 of these derelicts currently being refurbished by the Taskforce. The plan was proposed some ninety years ago, but when Security Protocol Omega was issued, the plan never eventuated. Of course, with the new Honour Guard threat, we needed something with mobility and subtlety. These seemed to fit the bill,' Paladin explained.

'Your gear was transported to the *Yamamoto* ahead of time and your AI has already been transferred to your quarters. When you're done getting acquainted, I'll have you called up to the bridge; I've got some finishing touches to attend to,' Paladin instructed. He strode off without another word. I looked back at our Condor to see Harmon leaning on the airframe; he was mortarded all right: he wore a loose flight suit over an old twenty-first-century Hawayan T-shirt. His copper hair was barely within regulations, and he looked like he'd only just made the Taskforce body mass index of 33.0. I couldn't help but smile though, and I laughed as I strode off. We all quickly dispersed after that, admiring the plethora of advanced weaponry and targeting systems being installed in the *Yamamoto. If I didn't know otherwise, I'd have thought this to be an active warship,* I thought to myself. I opened my door to find Mariko's avatar tapping her foot. I'd gotten side-tracked, it appeared.

Chapter 12
Day one

'Ma'am, I have just received a Priority One Recall from High Special Operations Inquisitor Paladin; your presence on the bridge is required. Thirty seconds till Live Tangible Holographic Transmission,' reported Mariko.

I quickly turned off my shower and began to get cleaned up. Priority One Recalls, more commonly known as P1Rs, were commands issuable by members of OPSI and the High Special Operations Inquisitors under their command. They generated a hyper-secure tangible recreation of the caller and their location as well as the receivers known to techs as LTHTs. This was usually due to a critical issue that has recently arisen.

'Twenty seconds until LTHT,' Mariko informed.

'Wait one second! Emergency halt!' I called out, all the while attempting furiously to get my clothes on.

'Emergency halt overridden, fifteen seconds to LTHT,' Mariko reported as my clothes still struggled to slip on. Mariko began to count down: 'Live in five, four, three, two, one.' I quickly sealed up the front of my top as I hit the recreated deck. I breathed a sigh of relief as I inspected the room. A low shimmer of light wafted through the recreated bridge; the faint glisten of mist drifted around the empty compartment.

'Tangible Holographic Transmission active,' reported Mariko as she generated her avatar beside me. I turned to her and was about to give her a long rant in Rashaano Spraak when Paladin stepped out from the shadows.

'That was close,' he sarcastically remarked. I snapped to attention.

'Chief Inquisitor on deck!' I cried, instincts kicking in.

'Don't. Just because I'm a High Special Operations Inquisitor doesn't mean to say that I have any more sway over subordinates than you. I'm just the messenger. Every "order" I give you is the director's will alone, not mine,' he reiterated.

'Sorry, you get so used to taking instructions when your career's been gouged to death by bureaucracy that it almost feels alien to do otherwise, sir,' I explained.

'Lose the "sir",' he insisted.

'Also a bad habit,' I replied.

'And I'll add another thirty seconds onto that live alert, to avoid any further close calls,' Paladin said with a smirk.

'Thanks,' I replied, a smile returning to my face.

'Ladies and gentlemen. Now that you're all here,' Paladin initiated. I turned around to see my old command group behind me. For a fleeting moment, embarrassment fell upon me. 'It is my job to inform you that all assets from Proteus are to be broken up into expeditionary fireteams, small enough to work as precision instruments of war, but integrated enough to rally as a large capable fighting force if required. Director Mizuka has informed me that you four are to become Proteus' flagship fireteam. You'll be receiving daily operations from me,' he informed us. 'Any questions? Speak freely, this part of the ship hasn't been implemented with the variety of surveillance systems like the rest of the ship yet,' he informed us.

'Well, if this isn't an emergency, then why did you use a P1R?' asked Elenskis.

'Because it keeps people on their toes and working with the spooks from OSI has made me a little paranoid over the years, so a good terminal wipe always goes a long way to settle those fears.'

'So, where are we meeting once the bridge is operational?' I inquired.

'I'm having an operations room installed adjacent to the captain's ready room that'll be spook-proof,' he added to his brief explanation. 'Any more questions?' he again asked, the room went silent.

'Excellent. Moving on, as per OSI Protocol two ninety-five, all Special Operations Fireteams must have five members. So, we've assigned you one.'

Moments later, a red light flickered to life at one side of the bridge. It hovered silently, before slowly bobbing as its body chugged forward. It quickly entered the light, finally allowing us to see what it was: an advanced combat AI. Its frame mimicked humanoid muscle tendons; as it moved, the plates 'flexed', its monocular head the only component that felt truly inhuman, its reinforced housing creating an unnatural squareness to the structure.

'Marines, meet your new teammate, QT-2, he'll round out your unit as the fifth member of your section,'

'Good evening,' called the automaton.

'Great, I'm gonna have to rebalance the fireteam's *anki* again,' Ela whispered as she clutched the Crest of Kuzmoto around her neck tighter.

'I am Independent Operations Platform Quantum Template Version 2, designed from the ground up with a Hawkins matrix and modified virtual networking. I am equipped with critical analysis protocols and field adjustment processors to assist with combat operations,' QT-2 dutifully informed.

'QT-2 is one of a kind. He was created from the digital mind of Doctor Edmund Sans, co-developer of QT-2 alongside mechanical engineer James Fitsimons. He is the very definition of sentient; he learns like any other sentient species; he knows betrayal and can comprehend evil. But more importantly, he understands what needs to be done and why it needs doing,' Mitchell explained.

Ela scoffed at the explanation.

'Lastly, with your involvement a part of Proteus and to an extent, the OSI, Director Mizuka has seen it necessary to reclassify you. You are joining an elite caste of the Special Operations community, respected by even Special Forces Regiment. They've been the will of the director since the end of time. They're officially known as "Asymmetrical Combat Officers",' he said with reverence. We all stood in shock.

'Of course, you all know them as Specialists. As such, you shall be rechristened; from now on, you are to be known as Fireteam Lycaon, named after the cunning wolf-king of Arcadia, and your call signs are to be Specialists One through Five. QT-2 is the fifth and Sara, you are the first—you are fireteam lead,' Paladin explained. We looked at him in shock.

'But we aren't the first Specialists,' retorted Elenskis.

'This is correct—you aren't, but the number has never denoted seniority of age. The number assigned to a specialist is used as a rating system of sorts. The first five specialists are the director's right hand, the next five are her left. These digits demonstrate the values of a Specialist—adaptability, asymmetry, and loyalty. Is there anything else?'

We were silent.

'Good. When you're cleaned up, meet me on seventh deck, frame thirty-four, compartment seventeen Bravo. The engineering logs show that the bridge is getting its facelift now,' Paladin informed us.

Instantly, the feed died, and I was returned to my dimly lit rack. I had mixed feelings about all this change—the spectrum ranged from excitement to dread. As emotions swirled through me like a washing machine, my brow began to crease, and a thought crossed my mind: I haven't actually checked in on the fireteam. I hadn't been in a healthy mindset myself after the destruction of the Hakon and hadn't the chance to ask how it was affecting everyone and how the fleet was treating them. Even though we'd only technically been a part of the fleet for a couple of days, there is a different relationship between service members in the fleet, and past problems never go away just because you signed up with a new outfit. I knew Ela and Elenskis pretty well from my time as part of the 227th but Tomas, despite his initial revelation and the fact he'd being attached to our JNCO course platoon, was always quieter than the rest and a much more closed person. With that in mind, I made my way to his quarters. I tapped the key beside his door and waited as the echo of the electric bell rang through his room. Footsteps made the length of the room, and the muted click of a button on the other side caused the door to slide open. Before me was Tomas: he froze for a moment before snapping to attention. 'Good morning … ma'am,' he quickly replied, forgetting I still held the same rank as him.

'At ease. We're the same rank, Plimis, and if Mitchell's telling the truth, we're on equal footing here.'

'Yes, ma'am … yes,' he replied, struggling to simply say 'yes'.

'May I come in?'

'Yes, yes come in,' he remarked as he stepped aside and waved me in. 'What do you need?'

'So, I've only just realised, despite working with you for the duration of the JNCO Course during CBMT, I actually know nothing about you. I know Ela and Elenskis from my time as part of Tu hjak Tu Ten Seven and before that Grondfors Two Ten Two Komando but I've never gotten 'round to talking to you personally,' I remarked.

'Nothin' to talk about, practically raised in a power plant, joined the navy at seventeen,' he remarked, absentmindedly wiggling an unlit cigarette in his mouth as he spoke. I looked around his room; it was barebones like the rest of ours, so the face-down glass frame stood out like a sore thumb to anyone looking.

'What's that?' I said, gesturing towards the frame.

'Oh, its nothing, just a lousy Aion Krossno Ooda given to me by some pretentious officer,' he dismissively remarked. My eyes widened before returning to normal as my mind settled on the final comment … some pretentious officer. It wasn't out of the ordinary for prior service other ranks to have some animosity towards commissioned officers, as most company and platoon commanders were functionally incompetent and any higher ranks seemed to live in some ivory tower on high, but there was a venom to his words that ran deeper than the average salty sailor.

'You okay? You got a problem with officers?'

'Who doesn't? They try to speak like you, act like, talk to you like they understand you. But they don't; they truly treat you like a diseased animal out of earshot, filthy, uneducated an' expected to be put down. But when you grit your teeth an' stand your ground an' goddamned survive the rivers of Azvod an' back they act as if you're some grand achievement of theirs, some wild animal that's become civilised by their hand: a weapon of some godsforsaken empress. An' the middle-class pricks act like you're some goddamned hero to the state as you stand there with a broken arm, a shattered leg, an' pulverised knee receiving your medal, the whole damned event broadcast to the entire state. Then the thanks you get for your "exceptional service" is bloody retirement an' you're left in the tattered home of your parents after eight years of "dutiful service to the state", unable to walk to the damned brufiken pisser and dropped on your arse like you were an Asok's old breakfast.' By this point, Tomas had practically shredded his cigarette with his teeth, eyes dark with anger staring off at someone unseen, his mouth practically frothing. Then he turned to me, locked eyes with a fury I'd seen in few. 'None of you will ever understand me, the death I've seen, the brothers an' sisters I've had to bury with my bare hands, an' none of you will ever care. The three of you are just cold, calculated instruments of organised chaos, ticking away strikes on a board waiting for the rabid animal to finally die. Well, I ain't gonna die—you can bury me as best as you can, but no one has done it yet. Yet!' he boomed before spitting the torn-up remains of his cigarette into a nearby ashtray.

'Tom,' I said in a low voice, 'you want to know something? I do not pretend to understand you or your life; I've lived a completely different one to you, one that has been much easier and more privileged, but I am not one to sacrifice lives. You are not just another service number to me.' He didn't reply. 'I'll let you be, corpsman,' I replied before silently slipping out of his quarters.

I stepped into my quarters, shocked. I looked over to Mariko's avatar who also seemed to be bothered by something.

'Mariko, what's wrong?' I asked as I slipped back into the shower to finish what I'd started.

'Well, some bastard of an AI keeps denying me access to the ship.'

'So, name and shame,' I said as I kneaded soap-infused water into my skin.

'That's the problem, ma'am. He's the personal Tier Three Artificial Intelligence of High Special Operations Inquisitor Mitchell Paladin.'

My brow narrowed. 'Well, he's impeding your duties, correct?'

'Aye!' she said with fury.

'Then that's a breach of the Unified Code of Military Justice. So just NJP him,' I explained, but Mariko seemed hesitant.

'I don't think AI have the authority to execute Non-Judicial Punishments, ma'am,' she said after a moment.

'Just do it under my authority then,' I instructed.

'Aye, Aye,' Mariko replied with a smirk. The power flickered out momentarily as a digital war consumed the ship for less than a second. Mariko's avatar appeared moments later, blood dripping down her model, her kimono clinging to her skin as red liquid soaked into her digital cloth.

'Gods, what the *brafiksjot* did you do?' I exclaimed in shock.

'Don't worry, he'll be fine, I only flayed his avatar and forced him to say, "I will not tempt the goddess again," every time he tries to use an audio output device,' Mariko coldly replied.

I smirked. *That cold daughter of a* sluka, I thought to myself. After cleaning up, I left for 7-34-17-Bravo.

++++

I strode in, my head pulsing with pain as my eyes locked onto Mitchell and three others from my fireteam.

'Where's QT?' I questioned.

'Final maintenance checks to ensure that he's field-capable,' Mitchell almost dismissively explained. 'Now, onto your gear,'

Mitchell said with a hint of boyish excitement as we strode over to our assigned armourers. Uncle Dimi was right in the thick of it.

'Sayra! They did it! The force has *jaitsi* again!' he exclaimed with enthusiasm, fists held skyward.

'What have we got?' I asked as I looked over the manifest, ignoring the statue-like BDU behind my uncle.

'Oh, this and that; they've made another fifty-two metallurgical improvements to the shape and contour of the armour!' he began. My eyebrow quirked in curiosity at the choice of word *armour,* not *BDU.* 'They've finally replaced the old Gulf sixty-three power couplings which I've been complaining about for a literal century! And they've developed an eleventh-generation fusion-fission reactor!' he exclaimed. 'Software-wise they've streamlined the HMD, *again.*' I rolled my eyes. 'They've improved the tactical networking *again* and they've improved the waypoint updater, *finally*!' he explained. 'But that, all that doesn't matter, that doesn't compare to what you've been given,' he continued with a spark in his eye. 'They've introduced a curveball to the mix. A combat optimiser: something I thought was only a theory, not to mention they've brought back some much-needed firepower,' he replied with mystery. I was confused.

'And that is?'

'Dedicated power armour!' he cried with joy. My eyes widened; my heart raced. 'You're the first operator in near on a century to be issued pure, unashamed power armour! And that's not even the half of it!' he boomed. 'The suit, unlike your BDU or like any other suit of its kind, is made from nanomachine plate armour. As long as you've got Carbyne-A2 on-hand, your armour's nano-assemblages have the ability to repair and completely modify your power armour to assist you, wherever you're vulnerable. You're effectively a one-woman army now,' Uncle Dimi explained. I was shocked.

'Now, change out of those fatigues and don't even think to pick up your body glove; you won't be needing one of those anymore,' he instructed, distractedly waving me off. Without hesitation, I began to undress. My skin shivered in the cool air as I stood beside my new powered combat armour. The room was one of the *Yamamoto*'s many resource cargo holds that, with the infinitely smaller quantity of aircraft, had been converted into one of half-a-dozen testing grounds. Twelve *tvastars* and holding racks lined the room while a rifle range stood at the far end of the compartment; behind me sat a stack of ordnance and above the doorway was the observation booth where officers and technicians would preside over refits and exercises. Dimitri activated a tile on his CPI and turned to me as the armour's aft plating burst out.

The suit was larger than my now-obsolete battle dress uniform, with a thick mechanical underlayer that presumably housed the suit's extensive force amplification actuators. The surrounding ballistic plates themselves had also changed. Gone was the blocky rectangular chest plating, replaced now with a multi-layered T-shaped chest piece that ran from the reinforced collar brace down to the bottom of the ribs. Below those sat the suit's metallic ammunition belt that had been carried across from the BDU's original design. Apart from the obviously upscaled size, the suit had faithfully carried over the BDU's sharp, rectangular shoulder pads, single-piece gauntlets, and reinforced two-piece shin and thigh guards, all wrapped in a plethora of Tangible Holographic Plasma emitters that generated the suit's fantastical reactive webbing. Hesitantly, I ducked into the suit and slipped my head into the thick magnetic collar that safely secured my helmet before slipping into my suit's powered gauntlets and legs, my CPI seamlessly synchronising with my suit's network. The suit, as if sensing my presence, sealed up, leaving me in the dark but comfortable arms of my body armour, the snapping hiss of tubes connecting to medical ports my only stimuli, the suit's custom form flexing to my every motion and supporting my every need.

'Okay, I never thought I'd be saying this, but … activating powered combat armour, now,' Uncle Dimi reported. The HMD flickered to life and my vision filled with light, the circuits within my armour locked into the active position and I dropped to the ground.

Uncle Dimi paused to admire the suit as I rose to a standing position again.

'It feels even lighter, is that the servos or the plates?' I commented.

'Both,' Uncle Dimi simply replied. 'But those aren't servos,' he added. 'This armour outstrips even the mobile defence suits. Gone are the force amplification actuators that needed to be replaced after extended operations and suffered from chronic reaction lag; your suit, in lay terms, uses an ionic polymer-metal composite—' he began before pausing at my chuckle.

'Yes, those are very lay terms,' I jokingly remarked.

'—basically, it's a "liquid muscle" to amplify and double your already enhanced physical strength and speed, and all you need to do is think about moving. The suit will then automatically move in the intended direction,' Uncle Dimi paused. 'Okay, commencing AI integration,' Dimitri continued. My eyes began to blur, and my skin went numb. 'AI Integration complete, correcting audio-visual organs… now,' my vision began to return.

'How're you doing Mariko?' Uncle Dimi called as if realising something. 'It's been what? How many days?'

'So much room!' she exclaimed over the suit intercom, ignorant of my uncle's questioning as she settled into her new permanent space. 'To answer your question, Armourer Malekova: it has been thirty-two hours, twelve minutes, sixteen seconds since our last game of *durak*. You should get your internal chronometer checked, Gunnery Sergeant,' Mariko replied with a chiding tone. Dimi just scoffed at the thought.

'Furthermore, Lance Corporal Hart, Shadow Director Rokkaku has a gift for you,' Mariko informed me, her tone rapidly returning to a cold monotone. A waypoint appeared to my right, and I turned to follow it. There rested a large black case, settled on a pile of crates. It was a long but thin rectangle with a clasp on one side. I unclipped the lid and opened it up. The case held two blades. A letter, written in ancient Japanese, sat atop the largest blade. I looked on in surprise as I recognised the elegant design. 'A katana? I haven't seen one of these in years—not since the last Rojal Ympiirno Mariin Infantrii Kor *bal* my old unit hosted,' I mused before looking down at the letter.

'You're fluent in ancient Japanese?' Mariko asked as I shook my head.

'I can read and speak a little Japonno Spraak—otherwise, I couldn't have taken my oath to uphold the tenants of Bushdto,' I offered before Mariko began flawlessly translating the letter for me:

> *These two blades are the ratification of your oath as a warrior of the Taskforce, and manifestation of the director's will. The sword that sits before you is a katana, the ancient blade of the Japanese: once forged with the finest metals and an extension of a warrior's will in feudal society. But it is more than just a weapon. Though millennia on, the blade has adopted new features, such as electrical field projectors and a carbide blade. It remains a symbol of dedication to perfection, dedication to efficiency, to effectiveness, to the mission, to your team and your Taskforce. It is the physical embodiment of our Taskforce's martial values.*

Mariko paused.

> *Then, there is the Blade of Denici. The dagger that sits below is not as practical as the katana that I have just written about; the Blade of Denici is an unspoken oath. A Denici dagger is given to all commissioned and non-commissioned officers. The dagger and its meaning are steeped in the mythos of the Kitari people. Denici, according to legend, was a warrior-commander of unparalleled skill and charisma. She led her people against overwhelming odds; she was the Unifier of Miatha, the Kisir—the breather of death-herself, but, at the Final Battle of Kaefir, Denici's warriors were withdrawn by Monarch Haite. At the monarch's request, Denici was not informed of the withdrawal and was thrown headlong into the awaiting blades of the enemy. Denici fought valiantly to the very end, against insurmountable odds, before being finally consumed by the fighting. As the Fields of Kaefir remained barren, blood trickling down its mountains, a*

sorceress scoured the field for the souls of the damned. But when she came upon Denici's mutilated corpse and the sorceress saw the betrayal that had befallen the great woman, all she could feel was rage—fury at the injustice. From this, the sorceress cast a powerful enchantment that re-bonded her drifting soul to her body and rebuilt it from the ashes. Denici was reborn as Ka'asei, the daughter's grip. With her newfound strength and purpose, Ka'asei cut a path across Kitari space, earning her final vengeance against the monarch and all her offspring. This dagger henceforth was fashioned for all commanders as a reminder to never abandon your men, to never neglect your troops, lest the cold blade of the daughter's grip strike you down.

Carry these wherever you go and remember their meaning, for they will be your undoing if they're not heeded.

Mariko finished. I smiled as I finished 'reading' it. *He has quite a way with words,* I thought to myself as I clipped the sword and dagger onto my waist, my suit automatically shifting both out of the way.

'Okay, let's get you into the arena,' Uncle Dimitri instructed as he pointed to a structure across the way. The 'arena' was an elaborate weapons course that utilised Tangible Holographic Plasma to generate simulated combatants in a variety of positions. A cluster of 'flickers', as they were known to the 1011s (Marine Infantry), was spread out over the course, some covered the advance from atop a balcony while others remained close to the ground in tight cover. I strode up to the red line that ran the width of the deck.

'So, they've currently only got eight preset modes, but R&D has assured me that you can custom-construct whatever you need. The current list for Tasking 10.0 has Close Quarters Battle (CQB), Sharpshooter, Search and Rescue (SAR), Mission Orientated Protective Posture (MOPP), Reconnaissance, Infiltrator, Airborne and Enhanced Mobility Combat Protocol,' Uncle Dimi explained.

Uncle Dimi paused. 'So, you've got an M18 on your left or an M8A2 on your right.' I looked across to the M18 Aetherfield and plucked it from the weapon rack. I looked over the weapon. Satisfied with its status, I prepared for the test. I relaxed my shoulders and cupped the pistol in my hands.

BAMP! The signal rang across the room, and I bolted across the range, my aim tracing across the arena. Two flickers immediately popped out of cover, their submachine guns cracking through the air as I ducked right, firing as I fell. *One, two, three,* I counted to myself. I slid up to the barrier that stood between me and the remaining flickers. I held my Aetherfield low as I approached the edge, my breaths paced. *Let's see what this thing can do*, I thought to myself before barking 'CQB!' My suit began to shift around me, my chest plating became thicker, my visor widened as I turned the corner. With my greater field of vision, I glimpsed at the slender hand of one of the flickers. As if clairvoyant to outsiders, I whipped around the barricade, levelled my M18, and put a single round square in the hologram's head. *Gods-damned!* I thought to myself as I cleared the defensive line. I turned to face the second set of barricades as a flicker ambushed me, hitting me with stun rounds. The shots rippled through me, my armour's kinetic plates absorbing the shock. I smirked as I slogged the model with a single round to the head. The riflemen on the roof had finally responded to my action and levelled their weapons towards me. 'Airborne!' I instructed, wanting to test out as much as I could. Instantly my equipment reformatted. The suit's various plates shifted, becoming a sleek aerodynamic hull made of ablative plating. Jets appeared on my back and thrusters quickly rose out of my suit's skin. I leapt into the air. My computer tracked my trajectory as I glided up and mathematically tracked my firearm around the balcony, each shot finding its target. The buzzer abruptly sounded, and I dropped down to the ground in confusion.

'What's the issue?' I asked. Uncle Dimi just shrugged as force reconnaissance marines and army green berets rushed down the adjacent passageways.

‘Okay, what’s going on?’ I asked again as I strode over to Paladin.

‘All units are moving to REDCON One; OSI just got a hit. The guard’s mobilising. Honour Forces are attempting to set up footholds on Loinsek and Kahan Prime. ITSA Forces are moving in to secure the areas but they’re holding for Taskforce intervention,’ Paladin reported. Ela looked at him sideways.

‘Wait, Security Authority? Taskforce intervention?’ Ela questioned confusion rising in her voice.

‘Long story short, OSI’s taken control of the ITA and the affiliate Security Authority to act as our main military force while we act like the toothless watchdog,’ Paladin explained with gritted teeth. *Animosity towards Silentio Super Tumultum?* I mused.

‘I’m a former member of the regiment, what do you expect from Special Forces?’ he said turning to me. I looked at him with wide eyes. *He read my thoughts!* Brafiksjot*ing Taskforce,* I thought to myself.

‘So where are we deploying?’ I finally asked.

‘Lycaon isn’t going anywhere; ODA four-fifty-four and one-ten marines can handle that,’ he replied, his tone stern and final as I tensed in anger before releasing my fists and striding off in resignation.

For the first four months of the war, that was how it was for us: units always happened to be closer to the area of engagement or in a better state of readiness than us as we continued to acquaint and acclimate ourselves with our equipment and flash training. We quickly became restless as the constant ‘hurry up and wait’ began to grate on us, until …

++++

0430 HOURS, 16/05/2437 (MILITARY CALENDAR)

My boots thudded along the cold metallic deck, the subtle double tug of artificial gravity against my feet as I strode through the darkly lit passageway. It was the night watch aboard the *Yamamoto* when I'd been summoned by Mitchell, so only emergency lights illuminated the refurbished warship. Gone were its gaping holes and fluster of repairs that'd been a prevalent component of the *Yamamoto*'s early days. As I approached the bridge, nervousness began to creep into my step. *Why wasn't I P1R'd? Why is he trying to talk to me at this ungodly hour?* I floundered as I strode onto the bridge. The Junior Officer of the Deck (JOOD) turned to meet me as I stopped just past the doors, my feet tucking together as I snapped to attention.

'Good morning, Ensign Seihaya,' I formally intoned.

'Morning, Staff,' the Ensign responded.

'Is the High Inquisitor in his ready room?'

'Aye, he is,' Seihaya confirmed before letting me through to the room. The silver-panelled door snapped open to reveal a compartment sparsely styled. Behind him hung black and gold unit colours, a dagger tucked between a pair of wings with the maxim 'Who Dares Wins' written below the image. To the room's right sat a curved blade, nestled in a stand, as the only contrast to the sharp grey lines of the ready room.

'Good morning, Mitchell,' I began as I settled into the seat across from him, feeling more accustomed with the informal posture with each passing day.

'It's too early to be a good morning, and your face seems to agree with me on that point,' he tiredly joked. I gave him a weary smile.

'So, why the call then, if you weren't keen to be up yourself?'

'OPSI just got a hit on an Honour Guard Forward Operating Base on Aiken Prime at zero eight thirty local time,' he began. My eyes widened, my mind's morning haze instantly clearing as I focused in.

'So, do you need us on standby again? Because I'll have the fireteam brought up to speed according—' I began to add before Mitchell interjected.

'I want your fireteam running point on this one,' he calmly replied. My heart skipped a beat as I stared across at Mitchell, my blue eyes blank.

'A—are ... aren't there more tests and drills that need to be run? We're still fresh out of SOI.'

'There aren't any more tests to run—med techs confirmed that your flash training has been consolidated.' I looked on in shock. 'Final reports just came in this morning. In fact, the staff found that it's because you've only just recently graduated from School of Infantry that you acclimatised so well,' he added before continuing with his orders. 'Gear up and meet Harmon at the Hangar Bay. You'll be deploying at zero nine hundred,' Paladin finished.

Words evaporated from my lips as I tried to speak.

'I'll mobilise the fireteam,' I finally said as I rose from my seat and strode out. As I exited the bridge, I tapped my comm piece. 'Meet up in the briefing room at zero six hundred, Lycaon; Lati Athia sings her sonorous song on Aiken Praim.' A flurry of emotions and acknowledgements followed in reply to the old military mantra before I cut the communications line and made my way aft towards my cabin. There I worked tirelessly through the latest OSI reports, from enemy deployments to force multipliers and cyberwarfare capabilities. The Honour Guard had effectively capitalised on our weakness. In only four months, the Honour Guard had gained control of some twenty per cent of the northern regions. But in what could only be described as an alien move, they had seemingly ceased their advance. In the calm that had settled over the galaxy, UNS Fleets had plugged the gaps and secured the rest of the Andromeda galaxy from hostile takeover. Over the previous months, the entire front had been officially designated the Enzo Line while the enemy's enigmatic territory had come to be unofficially known as the Crimson Veil. I frowned as I looked across the strategic displays and reread the operations logs from the *Yamamoto*. While Proteus had been initially focused on containment operations, almost all operations in the last three months had been exclusively counter-operations in support of UA or UNS offensives. My frown deepened as I looked over Aiken Praim. It was situated as an FTL nexus that fed directly into the northern reaches, but besides that, it offered nothing any other nexus behind it could provide.

It lacked any strategic resource to claim or deny, which meant it was a relatively expensive endeavour to develop it as a staging ground or in a forward operating capacity.

If they were trying to mount a renewed offensive, there were half-a-dozen better positions to conduct operations from that they should have assaulted by now. Pushing the questions out of my mind, I left to give my briefing.

The *Yamamoto*, being a retrofitted Imperial Isoroku-class supercarrier, was equipped with over a dozen pilot briefing rooms. With the warship's transition from supercarrier to landing dropship dock, the majority of these had been converted into traditional briefing rooms with one being reserved for Fleet Logistics Support Squadron 77 (VRC-77) and Dropship Naval Combat Squadron-64 (DNC-64). When I made my way into the tiered room, the dim overhead lighting rose as the sensors recognised my presence. I took my place at the podium, looking over my notes once more as Lycaon began to stride into the oversized room. With my fireteam seated and a tap of my CPI, I began to speak, a wall display appearing behind me.

'As you are aware, we are being deployed to Aiken Praim, a relatively secluded and unimportant region of Ympiirno Space. It is a faster-than-light nexus into the northern regions. Ympiirno Shendars Kor elements on the ground have reported that The Honour Guard's Wayfarer Army elements have been deployed across the main continent to secure systems and facilities pertinent to the planet's command and control; communication; and intelligence, surveillance and reconnaissance; also known as C4ISR. Their attacks have not been directed at troop deployments; they seem to be exclusively directed at the planet's capacity to coordinate, communicate, equip, command, and control.' I paused to switch the display over. 'As such, Proteus has been deployed to systematically respond in kind. We, and four other fireteams, will be deployed across the main continent; we will not be within support range of each other. While other fireteams will be handling the majority of enemy C4ISR objectives, ours is to secure a high-value target. The HVT is an Honour Guard brood mother, call sign "Oya". Brood mothers are equivalent to Taskforce instructors, shaping broods into the warriors you see on the battlefield. Research into the Honour Guard threat has hit a wall, and Min-Hei has requested a live specimen. The committee has approved their request. To verify we've secured the correct brood mother, look for the digits twenty-seven oh five; our AIs are able to read the Honour Guard language. Without the brood mother in play, coupled with the counter-C4ISR operations being executed by the other four teams, we will virtually cripple their warfighting capabilities and OSI expects this to cause strategic chaos in the region. Any questions?' I finished.

'They have women?' Ela asked excitedly.

'They have women …' Tomas mused.

I let out a sigh of amused frustration. 'Affirmative,' I remarked as QT raised a sharp hand.

'Sara, what kind of defences does the Ympiirno Shendars Kor have?'

I nodded at the inquiry before changing the slide. 'The YSK inherited a planetary electromagnetic field generator from the Ympiirno Teritoriino Meikseifno Osoriti. It is designed to prevent hostile forces from escaping and reinforcements from arriving. The generator complex is large and sufficiently staffed, despite government budget cuts.'

At this, Elenskis frowned. 'Then how are we inserting and extracting?'

'We will be conducting a low-orbit, low-opening space dive from the Kármán line and inserting at these coordinates.' I paused to adjust the display behind me. 'Once there, we'll link up with the YSK assets on the ground and work to locate our HVT. If Operation Cropping goes as planned, we won't have to; the enemy will be effectively eliminated, and the Governor-General's office will be able to lower the protective field. However, if Operation Cropping fails to incapacitate Honour Guard C4ISR or the YSK is incapable of handling the remaining Guard Forces we will secure our HVT and our mission will shift to search and destroy.'

'What will our air support be doing?' Tomas asked.

'We will have minimal wireless contact with our Condor dropship due to the interference from the electromagnetic field. As such, they will be conducting anti-satellite operations, referred to as ASAT, in support of Operation Cropping. Any more questions?' With a shake of their heads, I switched off the display as I spoke. 'Gear up, we're launching at zero nine hundred hours,' I finished.

With this, the fireteam members rose from their seats and made their way towards the armoury. With the retrofit came a number of major changes. Carriers traditionally organised everything around its Carrier Air Wing (or Group in the USR). Briefing rooms, ready rooms, and the hangar deck would lead directly off each other while elevators fed the aircraft onto the flight deck. Load dropship docks aren't designed like this. With their dual purpose as troop transport and carrier comes a hybridisation of priorities. As such, LDDs built from the keel up would traditionally install a second layer of compartments dedicated to arming and equipping soldiers, sailors, and marines for ship defence or rapid deployments. With the retrofit impracticalities of a pre-existing warship, however, a decision was made by the gimmits of Naval Sea Systems Command to effectively split the ship in half. Half of the forward ready rooms were converted into armouries, another third were converted into sparring facilities, and the remainder were left as ready rooms for the naval aviators of VRC-77 and DNC-64. After changing, gearing up, and now caught in the infinite cycle of 'hurry up and wait', Lycaon made its way to the sparring facilities that had over the months become a glorified waiting room. There, another four teams also calmly drifted, waiting for final preparations to be completed and deployment instructions to be satisfied. The four fireteams were from 24th Special Air Service Regiment, 76th Ranger Regiment, Marine Commando Force, and finally Delta Force. I watched their slow, deliberate motions, the methodical cleaning of weapons, the way they carried themselves with intention. They wore power armour much like ours, currently tinted in the muted grey to match the ship's bulkheads, but there were distinct differences, as it lacked the same kind of polish; random affectations of duct tape held down loose equipment, the suit's force-amplifying synthetic muscles seemed to almost moan with sonorous distinction from our own petulant whines, and a layer of dark grey forever permeated the carbide plating. As my team waited nervously to the far side of the chamber, a sailor began to make his way across the compartment towards us. I automatically made a move to inspect the rank plaque at the centre of his armour's chest, and upon seeing the chevrons of a Senior Chief Petty Officer almost snapped to attention. Seeing my confused response, the man simply chuckled.

'E'erything alright there, Special Operations Inquisitor?' he queried.

'Sara. The name's Sara, and yes, everything's perfectly fine,' I replied with a smile. 'Everything except for the "Special Operations" part,' I added darkly.

'Rob Steeples, Marine Commando Force,' he reported, his tone loud and boisterous as he offered his hand. After a moment of confusion, I returned the gesture. 'Y'know, lotta folks 'round here think you can't hack it. Think you're some dog and pony show by OPSI,' he began, my eyes blinking in confusion at the expression.

'Um… sorry—dog and pony show?'

The man just chuckled. 'You're here for propaganda and to look pretty for the holos,' he explained, my head nodding in understanding.

'Well, over the last four months I can't help but feel the same way. I know we've received the necessary training but—'

'It just don't feel right, does it? All that flash training and sleepless nights. Ain't quite the same as a weapon on a range,' he finished for me, his head nodding as he spoke. 'Can't say I blame ya; first time I was flash-trained for an op it was back in twenty-two forty. In twelve sweat-soaked hours I learned the entire firin', loadin', and aimin' procedures for the newly approved M thirty-two. Never been more confused about a rifle in my life than that mornin'. I can't even begin to imagine how you're feelin' havin' e'ery major tactical technique and procedure from o'er four hundred years of special operations.' He placed a hand on my shoulder. 'Honestly, I don't got a clue what you're going through. Best I can tell you, that trainin' will kick in. It will save your life; s'long as you trust your fireteam, it will bring you home,' he finished, his hand twitching towards his earpiece as a report presumably came through. With one last smile, he turned back towards his fireteam. 'Alright, alright, alright! You heard the lady,' he called with enthusiasm, his index finger repeating the circular rally up gesture as the servicemembers began to vacate the sparring compartment. Twenty minutes before launch, we strode up towards our Condor dropship as a Chief Petty Officer inspected the fuselage.

'Oh fuck—morning, boss!' called Harmon over the dropship's speakers as he rushed out to meet us on the hangar deck.

'Shouldn't you be running pre-flights, Flying Officer?' I inquired wryly.

'I behove such an assumption, boss, I have a co-pilot for that,' he said defensively. 'Besides, I thought I should personally introduce you to your crew chief and my co-pilot.' He gestured to the enlisted man. 'This is Chief Naval Aircrewman Langridge, UNS.' As he spoke the Chief Petty Officer snapped to attention.

'Morning, ma'am,' he stiffly replied.

I couldn't help but smile. 'Inquisitor or Sara. I'm only a Lance Corporal, Chief Langridge,' I replied with a chuckle.

'And the bludger up in the cockpit is Lieutenant Dyke Samson, UA.'

'Welcome aboard, Inquisitor!' the lieutenant answered over the speaker as Ela spewed hellfire.

'What have you done to our Condor?' Ela exclaimed in near anger. The dropship's hammer missile pods were nowhere to be seen, and its nose-mounted G19 Vulcan autocannon was missing.

'Don't worry, she's still got the firepower for when you inevitably screw up. It's all under the hood, ya see?' he explained, gesturing up to his Condor. 'The Nineteen Alpha's been locked down inside her casing. The hammer's been sealed up. To let the stealth coating do her job. Be stealthy, ya see?' Harmon continued, his fingertips waving around. Ela grinned like an idiot.

'Alright, enough talk—let's mount up, *gospadinas*!' I ordered. Harmon clambered aboard, tapping a strange totem, which sat at the centre of the cockpit's control console, on the head as he entered the cockpit.

'Inquisitor,' Samson called as he started the pre-flight start-up. 'Engines: online, guidance systems: online, kinetic screens: online, silent running systems: online.'

'*Yamamoto* flight, Alpha Quebec Two Five Seven. Understood. Out.' Harmon paused to signal the Landing Signal Officer attached to their launch. 'Flight Deck will clear up for launch in ten minutes, everybody,' Miles reported as the rear ramp rose. Ten minutes later, Harmon relayed the succinct report that we'd been cleared for launch as the lift ferried us up into the vacuum of space, the Condor shuddering as the lift finished its ascent.

'Disengaging magnetic locks, now,' Samson reported as our craft began to drift, the thrusters kicking in to guide us out of the launch deck. Minutes later, our Condor leapt into FTL.

Chapter 13
Trial Error

'Definitely not landing in that shitstorm, ma'am!' exclaimed Harmon as our Condor Dropship killed its main engines to effectively glide in its geosynchronous orbit.

'Great, jumping out of a perfectly good dropship again!' Ela sarcastically remarked.

'Over the drop zone in twenty seconds!' reported Samson.

'Lycaon, have infiltration protocols on stand-by. Engage airborne protocols.'

'Rah!' the fireteam exclaimed as they readied themselves mentally for the task of conducting a low-orbit low-opening insertion, amusingly abbreviated to LOLO.

'Get ready!' barked the Crew Chief through his fitted mask, rising from his impact seat. 'Outboard hands! Prepare to jump!' He paused. 'Inboard hands! Prepare to jump!' At that, the fireteam disengaged their five-point harnesses and rose in two orderly lines. 'Check equipment!' he continued as each marine began to inspect the other's powered combat armour for loose or unsealed equipment or other hazardous breaches. With inspections completed, Langridge continued, 'Sound off for equipment check!'

As first in the line, I cried out in reply, 'OK!'

This continued down the line till it reached QT-2 who finished the sequence, 'All OK!'

With the OK given, there was a moment's pause as Langridge depressurised the bay before continuing: 'Stand in the door!' he barked as I advanced towards the aft of the dropship. At that, the chief slammed the door mechanism, its form slowly lowering. In an instant, the bay's red hue was replaced with a sea of green. '*Go*!' exclaimed the Crew Chief. At that, we leapt out into the black gulf of space and began to plummet as the planet's gravitational pull dragged us down, our suits flight systems keeping us on track. We plummeted two minutes in the dark vacuum of space; my breaths were concise and controlled.

'Sixty seconds to contact!' reported QT as we plummeted towards the electromagnetic field, my HMD generating the distance in metres. 'Thirty seconds to contact!' QT paused to adjust his systems. 'Ten seconds!' he barked.

'Hold onto your *chikups*!' Ela boomed over the wireless, laughing. As we hit the field, it coursed through my body; raw energy rippled through my skin as if I'd been thrown in an oven, my nostrils flared, and my vision began to blur. I clenched my teeth as we passed through the excruciating field, our vision impaired by the blinding light and our systems flickering as they processed the excess energy. An instant later, the pain ceased, and the blinding light faded, quickly replaced with blue skies and clouds. I smirked. *Brafiksjot, yes!* I thought to myself. Now past the energy field, each of us pulled our wingsuits, and the five of us glided over Aiken Sitii. We continued down, slowly edging towards the drop zone over the next nine minutes before finally slamming into the ground with a solid thud. Our armour's dynamic optical camouflage immediately encompassed us, our positions known only to each other, thanks to a small green outline generated by our suit's HMDs.

'Spec— One, Al—a —bec. Mo—in to con— ASAT Op—ons, O—' Harmon interjected, static interrupting his report.

'Alpha Quebec, Specialist One. Say again your last, over,' I instructed.

'S— One, Alph— Qub—. Say ag— y—r last. Th— shield is pl—in' havoc —comms!' he replied.

'Specialist Three, boost communications!' I instructed.

'Yut, boosting communications.'

'Alpha Quebec, Specialist One. Say your last. Over,' I repeated.

'Specialist One, Alpha Quebec. The shield's playing havoc with my comms. We're moving to conduct ASAT operations. We'll monitor all planetary traffic and reports, anything you need to know we'll pass on. Over,' he responded.

'Understood. Out.' The signal finally cut out. I looked around. 'Okay. Specialists Five and Three, I want eyes on the Shendars Kor Centre, give me a SITREP as soon as you can. Specialists Two and Four, you're with me,' I instructed. With a flurry of replies, Ela and QT-2 quickly disappeared into the urban jungle of apartments and smog. Five minutes later, they each rapidly keyed back on frequency.

'Specialist Five in position,' QT-2 reported as he settled into a prone position, his M164 Special Applications Scoped Rifle (SASR) nestled in his shoulder.

'Specialist Three. Set, downloading drone feed now,' Ela reported mere moments later as she settled into the living room of a vacated apartment.

'I've got flames pouring from the Shendars Kor Senterno, boss,' followed the voice of QT soon after.

'Confirmed, drones are registering a cordon and a mobile command centre. I have positive ID on the CO, Komandant *ov* Shendars Alan Rontfelt, Shendars Kor Aiken Sitii, SKAS,' Ela added to QTs report. I frowned. *How were they ejected from their own headquarters?*

'I guess we just have to ask,' mused Mariko, to my frustration.

'Right, Specialists Two and Four, let's get moving,' I instructed as I broke into a jog. Pain raged across me as I crossed the four and a half kilometres in under four minutes, our suits' dynamic camouflage struggling to keep pace with our motion, causing a blur to seemingly rush by to onlookers. As the distance to the cordon dropped to 100 metres, we slowed and switched our suits from generating an active photoreactive reflection to projecting our thick grey-green dress uniforms. As the Tangible Holographic Plasma emitters settled, I looked back at Elenskis and Tomas. The Imperial Uniform

Procurement Board had elected to go for a design very reminiscent of the old-Earth Third Reich. 'So, what're our credentials?' I asked.

'Lutenant Konel Viki Blunk, currently Executive Officer to Konel Reiner, Speshalistno Mishon Shendars Kor, SMSK, formerly Ympiirno Akarasnii Hoshtar Armii Task Fors Nein,' repeated back Elenskis as she read her freshly created ID Card.

'Skvodron Chiif Djosaia Atkinson, currently RSM of SMSK, Commanding Officer Konel Reiner, formerly YAHA Task Fors Nein,' Tomas reported succinctly.

'That would mean I am Konel Radir Nasir Reiner. The Redvich,' I said as I made an about-face and began to stride towards the cordon. 'Interesting choice of cover story,' I mused as I adjusted my artificial side cap.

'Well you are very similar in looks to Reiner,' Elenskis chimed.

'It's almost like she isn't real…' Mariko muttered amid the conversation, an ever-darkening frown furrowing across all three of our heads as we approached the cordon, the three of us, in turn, flashing our IDs to the Shendars as they waved us through to the archaic Mobile Command Centre. The vehicle was a retrofitted 2340 Mitsubishi Isuzu heavy hauler. They were sturdy things, basically idiot-proof, but they still moved on eight magnetically leveraged spheres for tyres instead of the smoother anti-gravity propulsion that had superseded them. However, what it lacked in modern locomotion it made up for with modularity and integration, the perfect combination for security services who needed discreet vehicles that could be reinforced and adjusted with ease. As I was led into the operations centre, I was exposed to a buzz of activity as gendarmes and chief marshals worked away on raised platforms, their work diligently inspected by chief adjutants who quietly patrolled the sliver of space between the edge of the raised stations and the gantry with each officer relaying information from dozens of operations across the system. At the door to the vehicle cabin sat two medium-sized desks, each mounted with a pair of modestly sized monitors that generated a strategic map of the local area and the greater real-time force projection map. Behind the reinforced door that divided the vehicle's cabin from the back sat two wireless specialists, relaying and receiving orders from dozens of localised sub and upper commands. Thanks to the Honour Guard's immaculate stealth technology, the readouts still referred to the incursions as Kasim Coalition Raider Corps actions.

'Who the *bȓafiksjot* are you?' remarked the commandant in charge as he looked up from his station to the right, rising to meet me. A sardonic smile crept along my jaw as I turned around, quickly returning to the usual cold stare that I had.

'Excuse me, son?' I began.

The commandant's breath stopped, as did the entire operations centre as a technician spluttered, 'It's the Redvich.'

The commandant whirled on the technician to berate him before thinking better of it and resuming at a choked pace. 'My apologies! Konel Reiner, I didn't know our Code Eight—'

He was cut off by Elenskis. 'You didn't know? *Prosedjur eit siks* Ana is very clear, your *shendars* should be informing the *komandant ov shendars* when VIPs are entering their security zone,' Elenskis hissed to my side, her knife-hand raised and chopping with each word. The commandant pivoted to face Elenskis.

'Who are you?' he asked, disoriented.

'Lutenant Konel Blunk, Exec, SMSK,' she said with cold precision. At this, the commandant's lips twisted in horror. At this, Tomas looked up to me.

'Konel! FnM this man!' he hissed with pleasure, knife-hand also raised, before pivoting towards the operations centre, striding five paces singling out another soldier with his knife-hand. 'You!... adjutant *chiif*! Get me the provost *shendars*!' he hissed. At this, the commandant hissed in fury.

'Skvodron *chiif*! I don't know who you are! But—'

He was cut off by Tomas. 'Korman, Regiment Sargent Madjor, SMSK,' he said with a slow but deliberate tone. At this, the commandant spluttered.

'As you were *chiif,*' I intervened, before locking eyes with the commandant. 'Komandant, as you were. We have more pressing issues than proper paramilitary conduct,' I interjected. At this, the commandant let out a sigh of relief. 'With that said, Komandant, would you care to explain why you are currently operating out of a mobile command centre instead of your own headquarters that is a hundred metres behind me and on fire,' I said with a stern gaze.

'The KKRK seem to have invested heavily in an independent cyber warfare component of their pirate coalition. They … triggered the buildings fire suppression system and as we evacuated, they dropped in via the rooftop landing pad. When we attempted to re-enter … that's what the fires from,' he muttered sheepishly.

'Breaching charges and grenades,' Elenskis finished for him.

'Yes, ma'am,' he confirmed as I mentally sighed. *An impossible day.*

'What is the situation with the greater APSK?'

'Unknown, ma'am. Shendars Kor Senterno is the only way to communicate with the greater Aiken Praim Shendars Kor,' he responded more firmly before adding, 'which is the building behind you that is currently on fire.' I mentally sighed again.

'Lutenant Konel Blunk, remain here in operations with me to coordinate with the SKAS; *chiif,* get down to triage begin assisting the wounded,' I instructed before turning towards the briefing room. Elenskis, Rontfelt, and I worked through the midday, consulting sector commanders, comparing building schematics and other critical points of information. Over two hours, Ela and QT-2 had timed and tracked legionary patrol paths, watchkeeper periods, and guard changes as well as clarifying the disparate and confused reports on weapons emplacements and fighting positions initially detailed by the gendarmes a part of the first blind assault. I looked down from the wall-mounted monitor with a deep sigh of frustration. This lie was killing me, not because of any moral reason, simply because it was a nightmare trying to translate real actionable information into a falsification that was impossible to connect. *Well, that's what you get for running with the assumptions of the misinformed,* I mused to myself as a sound crackled over my earpiece. Commandant Rontfelt noticed the split-second reaction.

'Everything alright, Konel Reiner?' he asked softly. I nodded instinctively.

'I just have a report coming in; I will take it outside,' I said firmly as I rose from my seat and stepped out. 'What've you got for us, Specialist Three?'

'I think I've got something. Remember our team briefings on the legionary's biology?' Ela asked.

'Affirmative, they're test-tube creations, made for war from day one, but their big earmark is that they communicate through wireless electrical signals, artificially induced telepathy,' I recited vaguely.

'Aye, well I think I might have found a way to make that work to our advantage. I've been struggling to get a hold on their cyber warfare systems; even though the information is transmitted through a well-known digital format, all of my conventional cyber warfare techniques haven't been effective. Viruses, DDoSing, and direct electromagnetic solutions haven't seemed to bother the system. Anyway, while I was working, my system registered a random subspace anomaly, and I started considering alternative avenues. That's when I realised the reason my techniques haven't worked has been because they're using living computers, creatures that can partition and respond to my threats or mitigate them the way only a sentient creature can, especially when I'm directing it through a greater hive mind of legionaries. But that interconnection has three drawbacks. First, it means I can pinpoint the source of the cyber warfare specimen using the link. Second, if we can directly assault the creature, that'll cause the pain it's feeling to be transmitted back through however many legionaries are on this line. And third, if we can pour enough radio frequency signal into the air, it'll completely cripple their C3 organisation,' she explained.

'Do you have this cyber warfare creature's location now?'

'Aye, it's currently holed up on the thirty-seventh floor in that section's panic room,' she relayed.

At the heart of the Brood Mother's operations centre.

'Understood,' I said, before changing frequency. 'Lycaon, regroup in the operations centre briefing room. We've got an HVT to catch.'

Back in the operations centre, every one of Lycaon sat around the table, now unashamedly dressed in full battle rattle instead of their holographic personas. The only member who hadn't made an appearance was QT-2. Due to the legislative prohibition on automated combat personnel in the union, his presence would be too hard to explain; he stayed on comms instead. At the centre of the table, a 3D representation of central command appeared before us, its sloping, sleek design impressive even as a digital recreation.

'So, what's your plan, Konel Reiner?' inquired Commandant Rontfelt.

'We've found a way to cripple their C3 capabilities and temporarily stun the entire building. Once we've achieved that task, your *shendars* will move to secure the building. From there you'll be on your own, I'm afraid. My Meikseifno Rikon Komandos and I will be extracting with our high-value target.' The commandant's face tightened with that confirmation; he'd been dreading that answer all day, but he simply nodded for me to continue. 'We need to gain access to the thirty-seventh floor—suggestions?'

At this, Ela began to speak. 'Well, the breach is the easy part. With our ...' she paused to think through her words, '... training and equipment, we'll be able to scale the building without detection. Once around the thirty-seventh floor, we'll just breach in. Our experimental explosives will be able to break through the reinforced panes that surround the building. If two of us clear the lower floor and two of us clear the upper floor and we each meet up in the middle, that will clear us an escape window. From there, we can extract our HVT and be on our way,' Ela explained.

'When should we start our assault?' inquired Rontfelt.

'Once we've crippled their C3 capabilities, Specialist Three here will pass the word to you,' I explained. The commandant nodded in understanding. 'Any questions?' The room was silent.

'Let's get on it, *gospadinas*,' I instructed as I rose from my chair and slipped my helmet over my head. 'Alright everyone, pair off: Specialists Three and Four, hit the east side thirty-sixth floor. Specialist Two, you're with me on the west side.'

'What about Specialist Five?' Ela queried.

'What about him? He'll be providing overwatch,' I detailed.

'A *skarant*? Providing overwatch? Why not put him in the heart of the action?' she asked genuinely confused.

'Because he's our designated marksman,' I replied firmly.

'But anyone could do that, none of us could be pulped with plasma and be brought back from the dead,' she said with sincere belief.

'Neither can I, Specialist Three. If my platform is terminated, I will cease to exist,' QT-2 interjected.

'But he doesn't have a soul, he still can't actually die,' Ela continued, her voice rising in protest, thumb hitched behind her in the vague direction of QT's position.

'He's providing overwatch and that's the end of that discussion, Specialist Three,' I said with gruff determination. With a bewildered stride, Ela turned left and followed Tomas. As Elenskis and I passed the final security cordon, our suits' photoreactive camouflage materialised around us, our presence becoming wisps in the heated air. As we reached the edge of the forty-storey building, our heads craned to see the top and we momentarily looked down at each other. A hidden smile crossed my face as I stowed my rifle and began to climb, our magnetic palms suppressed by concealed dampeners in the gloves. The climb wasn't particularly long or difficult, but my body screamed as I climbed, angry that I'd subjected it to the universe at all. As we reached the thirty-eighth floor, I mentally checked and activated the THP rappel ropes and began to unhook the C13 charges I carried on my person. Between the two of us, Elenskis and I plastered a perfect rectangle of the plastic explosive around the edges of the reinforced glass that surrounded the headquarters. We were so close to the enemy entrenchments I wasn't willing to test their attentiveness, so with a single tap of my comm piece, a burst of static was relayed to the entire fireteam. A series of two-tap bursts followed. At that, I held my comm piece for a single uninterrupted burst of static before releasing my comm piece, retrieving my rifle from my sling and pushing off from the glass as Elenskis mashed the detonator. In an instant, fire spewed and glass erupted inwards like knives as the four of us swung onto our respective floors, our rifles bouncing from target to target. In four months of action, the URC had made leaps and bounds in countering the enemy. As each of our rounds made contact with a creature's centre mass, their shields flared, and colossal forms crumpled to the floor. I moved left as a legionary rushed into my line of sight, his rounds slicing through my upper left arm as I slid right and unloosed the last three-round burst of my magazine. Lowering my weapon, I reached for a tube of kaolin nanofibers and injected them into the precise circular hole in my arm. Snatching my weapon again, I continued. 'Changing mags,' I reported as Elenskis covered my six o'clock, my gloved hand instinctively reaching for the release before snatching another magazine from my webbing and settling it into the weapon's receiver.

'We've gotta stop this flow of infantry,' remarked Elenskis.

'Agreed.'

'The western staircase is fifty metres ahead,' Mariko calmly informed as I swung around the floor's central lift tunnel towards the west side staircase, Elenskis staying behind to set her obstructions on the eastern staircase. I advanced forwards, weapon raised as a swath of dark red contacts appeared on my motion tracker. Lowering my rifle, I snatched two triplets of M42s from the sides of my back and bounced them off the side of the wall. With a clatter and crack the staircase filled with fire and telepathic screeches as I knelt and placed my C39 mini-multi-purpose anti-personnel mine reusable at the base of the entrance and affixed my active denial system Mark 36 to the side of the entrance. Turning back to face Elenskis, I saw a firm thumb up from her free hand. With a stern smile behind my helmet, I combat signed, '*Let's get going.*' Weapons ready, we moved to the building's rear, my HMD marking our breach point with a golden outline. I knelt above the detonation point to pack my satchel of C13 charges onto the floor, shaping their explosive angle and direction into the panic room below. With its shape set, I activated the C13's wireless receiver as Elenskis and I moved out of the blast zone. Once safely away, I activated my comm piece.

'Specialists Three and Four: SITREP.'

'Specialist One. Specialist Three: Floors thirty-six and seven secure,' Ela reported.

'Transmit to Komandant Rontfelt. Go for mission and begin filling the area of engagement with RF white noise,' I instructed.

'Yut, drowning the AOE[1] in white noise,' Ela replied before changing channels. 'Orders relayed.' Instantly the boom-crackle of explosives and automatic weapons filled the headquarters.

'Mark!' I ordered, slamming the remote detonator. The rooftop erupted downwards in a roil of flames as Elenskis and I leapt down. Flames poured in from all sides as Ela and Tomas moved inwards, weapons dropping the initial dragoons before they could react. As I landed, my aim settled on the cyber warfare platform's head, a large yet elegant creature, its entire body ensnared by optical fibres and adapted cabling. I levelled my rifle and poured a three-round burst into the creature's bulbous skull as a pulse of pain screeched out from the living weapon. In the moment of weakness, Ela poured RF white noise into the air, causing even more pain for the legionaries. I frowned. 'Where's the brood mother?' I asked over my speakers. Lycaon systematically put three rounds into each of the incapacitated dragoons as I spoke, and a figure rushed past the east side door. '*Brafik*!' I cursed as the slender, agile figure of something rushed past, its nimble form deftly sidestepping two perfectly centred shots from QT-2. I rushed out of the panic room and began signing, '*Five you get PID?*' With my enhanced eyesight, I got his sharp reply, 'Positive ID, twenty-seven zero five.'

'*Five, keep track of HVT,*' I instructed before whirling to Lycaon.

1 A full glossary of terms and acronyms can be found on page 377 in Terminology of the Traverse.

'Specialists Three and Four, track her from the rooftops! Specialist Two! You're with me!' I hissed before leaping over the thirty-seventh floor's balcony, my armour transitioning its thrusters into action slowing my descent to the ground floor. With a thud, my descent stopped, and I saw the dozens of limbless living, their bodies rent apart with vicious rapidity. Elenskis landed beside me a moment later.

'Gods below,' Elenskis muttered as the electric hiss of energy arced through the air. I shifted my weight right, pushing Elenskis away as I tucked my feet together to fall backwards, rifle raised. My head landed beside the sizzling blade that had embedded in the floor an instant later. Following the blade up, my gaze stopped on a behemoth of a creature with the build of a gorilla.

'Get after that Brood Mother!' I barked as I switched my rifle to fully automatic and emptied a magazine into the creature. With a nod, Elenskis dashed past the partial wall as the creature finally wrenched its right arm from the ground. It spun on its heel and released a colossal silver-white shield, its smooth shape sharply cut inward on the edges. Caught in the midst of reloading, the giant unloosed a section of its shield and poured a hail of maser fire in my direction from its arm-mounted blade. 'Protocol thirty-seven!' I instructed as I rolled, rising to my feet, and dashed for the cover of the reception, catching myself on the reception's half wall. As I stopped, the barrage of maser fire increased as the creature returned its shield to the nether realm it had appeared from. With a chance to breathe, I unclipped a spare magazine, replaced the empty receiver, and pulled back the charging hammer. I quickly looked over the weapon's accelerator coil status as well. I'd already have to replace them in another magazine's time thanks to the full auto stunt I'd just pulled. I glanced down at my motion tracker as I began to hear the rumble thump of footsteps. *'Shajst!'* I hissed as I threw myself back into the hallway. The monstrosity ploughed through the partial wall and crashed into the wall behind it. *Gods-damned,* I thought to myself as I pivoted to face the creature. Switching my weapon back to three-round-burst, I began to pepper the monster with rounds before it finally released one of its arms from the hole it'd carved in the wall and slammed the shield between us. *Damned!* I thought as I tossed my service rifle, unsheathed my sword, and dashed towards the goliath. In a single step, I scaled the shield, my hand propelling me ninety degrees into the creature's back. Flailing for a handle hold, I latched onto the creature's protective collar, my legs wrapping as tight as they could around the creature's waist. I raised my blade to slash through the goliath's shoulder as its shields vanished and it threw its back into the wall. My grasp failed, and I began to fall before I was wrenched up and over the creature. In that moment, my vision slowed, my blade hand tucked close as I flew. My eyes saw shoulder, arm, ground, arm as I tumbled away. I bit down hard and slashed hard with my sword hand. I felt steel meet bone and my steady, directed arc shifted into a wild, erratic spin before coming to a stop in a wall.

A burst of adrenaline flooded my system and my eyes flared open, my heart restarting with a gasp. I looked at my sword, its blade bent in impossible angles. I looked up at the colossal alien as it seemed to soothe its gaping arm into submission, the blood flood ceasing as it clutched the pink circle with its good arm. Stumbling to my feet I began to dash towards the creature once again, my thumb adjusting the electrical field projector distance as I leapt right and slid low past the abomination. It stumbled once before crashing to the floor, its knees separated in half. It began to flail in rage as I rose from my crouch and swiftly decapitated it. I deactivated the katana's energy projectors and ran my index finger and thumb over the bent blade, all the while never taking my gaze off my opponent's now-lifeless corpse, before sliding the blade unceremoniously into my webbing and slumping to the floor, the telepathic echoes of the creature's dying screams still ringing in my skull.

'Good to see someone taught you fine Japanese swordsmanship,' Mariko coldly remarked.

'You can thank my instructors at Kiil Island for that,' I muttered softly as Mariko made a quiet *tsk* sound.

'Those swordsmanship instructors at CNI couldn't tell the difference between an ōdachi and a British greatsword if it was written in big bright letters,' she stiffly rebuked.

'What are you on about?' My gaze swept across the foyer. *Where did he come from?* I continued to wonder.

'Unknown, ma'am, but I did notice the phantom subspace anomalies noted by Specialist Three back at the Hakon and while reconnoitring this building,' Mariko explained. I gritted my teeth; I refrained from lecturing Mariko on reading my thoughts as gunfire began to rage outside the building. Snatching my service rifle from the ground, I rushed out to follow it. The brood mother had left a trail of dismembered gendarmes in her wake. A burst of static audio cascaded over my helmet's speakers.

'Specialist One. Specialist Three. I've gotta kill the jamming for a moment, Specialist Two's down, Specialist Four's moving to assist. Orders?' At this my throat twisted as my breath caught, my suit screeching in protest against my worried response.

'Understood,' I finally said. 'Does anybody have eyes on the HVT?'

'Affirmative,' reported QT-2. 'Target is on a westerly heading.'

'Roger. Specialist Five, continue observation. Do not engage. Specialist Three, provide security for Specialist Four,' I instructed before speaking to the rest of the fireteam. 'All Specialists, be advised: there are large, bipedal shield-wielding giants in the AOE* that can seemingly translocate at will by means unknown. Designate Goliaths. Do not engage unless fired upon,' I reported. A series of acknowledgements came through.

Chapter 14
Zero hour

A burst of animal static crackled across my speakers as Commandant Rontfelt reported: 'Redvich Aktual. Komant Aktual. Shendars Kor Senterno is secure. We've regained communications with the greater APSK.'

'What's their status?' I replied as I stood beside Elenskis' weak body, her armour panelling unclipped and the mist of kaolin nanofibres permeating the impromptu operating table.

'The other *sektor komandants* have received MRKs just like us and seem to be holding out. But its precarious; if we didn't have the field, and reinforcements arrived, we'd be done for,' he solemnly reported.

'Say again, Komant Actual; did you say MRKs?'

'Confirmed, your Meikseifno Rikon Komandos,' he said explicitly.

'Understood. Reiner out,' I finished before turning to face Tomas. 'What's the verdict, doc?'

At the question, Tomas let out a loud sigh.

'She's stabilised but she's sustained a punctured lung and liver. Her collarbone and her first two ribs have been shattered.' Tomas paused. 'Not to mention that her rib cage is *brafik*ing floating,' Tomas hissed in exhausted fury. 'She won't be doing anything for the op, that's for sure,' he finally replied after a long pause. I hesitated. *This can't be happening; this cannot be happening,* I thought to myself. My thoughts began to consume me as Ela's voice interrupted my spiral.

'Chiif, Five's got a report.'

I nodded involuntarily as I tapped my comm piece. 'Talk to me, Specialist Five, what do we have?' I requested, pushing out my trembling voice.

'HVT's stopped in a building two hundred metres out from the generator complex,' he succinctly reported.

'You got eyes on her activity?'

'Negative, and thermal's useless.'

I gritted my teeth before replying. 'Break break. Komant Aktual. Redvich Aktual. How could someone disable the EM field generator complex? Over.'

'Redvich Aktual. Wait, over.' The audio keyed off before returning moments later. 'If someone was planning to lower the field without destroying the complex, they could do so via the generator's manual overrides—all seven of them—or via the facility's *komant senterno*. Over,' he relayed from one of his engineers.

I nodded as I spoke. 'Understood. Out.' As I let go of the comm piece's switch, I turned to face Tomas. 'Specialist Four, could Specialist Two be moved with a stasis litter?'

The corpsman paused to think. 'Aye,' he said after a moment.

'Then procure one from triage,' I instructed. With a sharp simple nod, the corpsman was off as I tapped my comm piece. 'Lycaon, change of plans. Rally on my position. Be ready to move the moment Two's secured,' I instructed. Only four beats later, the entire fireteam had assembled, and Tomas and QT-2 were now slowly lowering Elenskis onto the stasis litter before activating its protective field to hold her battered body in place as she was moved.

'What's the play, *chiif?*' asked Ela.

'Operation Cropping seems to have only had a moderate effect. The dragoons seem to be more aggressive now, rather than less, and they're teetering on the edge of success. It's my suspicion, given the situation, that the enemy commander's waning deadlock has driven him to request reinforcements. That makes control of the generator complex critical to their strategic victory on this planet,' I began to explain. 'Since I am not comfortable leaving Two in the hands of the USR, even if it is a proxy force of the USG, I have decided to take her to the generator complex where we will support the facility security there.'

'Now, wait a minute—' interjected Tomas. I raised a hand to stop him.

'Elenskis and one other member will pull security on the facility's command centre while the rest of us will protect the facility's manual overrides,' I immediately explained. 'She will not need to be fighting a fire manoeuvre fight, she will be in the best defensible position and be escorted by one of us,' I finished explaining. At that, Tomas closed his mouth. 'Any questions?' silence replied as I turned to move out. 'Then let's get moving.' The four of us moved through the streets in a loose column formation with me in the lead, Tomas behind me pulling the hovering stasis litter with Ela bringing up the rear while QT-2 was on overwatch from the rooftops on our left and right. When we arrived at the facility, we were hurriedly ushered into the facility by the *shendars* that manned the complexes checkpoint. The entire facility was a matte grey immecrete monstrosity, a reflection of the old Imperial Territory Authority's budget and needs.

'Specialist Five in position,' reported QT-2 as he settled on the rooftop outside the generator complex. His M164 zeroed in on the Command Centre, his protocols automatically going through the motions of switching from .50 BMG accelerated to M568X jumper rounds, the loading mantra Like Bears Squeak Bats muttering through his subroutines as the anxiety of pre-combat returned to his platform.

'Two is on her way,' reported Tomas before appearing in QT-2's scope 16.5 seconds later. He ran one last inspection over her wounds before rising from his crouch and vacating the command centre.

++++

Ela scanned the generator complex. ‘How in the *brafik* are we supposed to pull security on seven manual releases?’ she asked, visibly bewildered and somewhat overwhelmed by the task at hand.

‘As long as we can control that sightline, we should be alright,’ I calmly explained.

‘And if they just flank the complex and climb the wall behind us?’ Ela asked, leading to an awkward shrug from Tomas.

‘I hate to agree with the child but … she’s got a point.’

I thought for a moment as Tomas finished speaking. ‘Specialist Three, you collected the C39 MMPAP mines back up, right?’ I queried.

‘Aye, wasn’t gonna let the song of my people go to waste,’ she said with pride.

‘Set them up along the southern wall. That narrows some of our variables down,’ I instructed. Moments later, final preparations were complete and each of us settled behind whatever cover we could find.

++++

IN AIKEN ORBIT, CONDOR DROPSHIP AQ-257 ‘MATILDA’

The *Matilda*’s dimly lit cockpit hummed and buzzed as its radar and lidar arrays searched for more satellites. While they hadn’t had contact with Lycaon in over three hours and had some concerns about success on the ground, the trio had redirected their worry into the anti-satellite operations they’d been conducting, hoping it would provide some assistance or reprieve to their specialists on the ground. Of course, they and the four other stealth Condor gunships that orbited Aiken had run out of targets just over an hour ago, and without anything to do, their worry had begun to grow. So, when Samson piped up it’d almost been a relief to Miles until he saw the terse lines of worry that clung to the army aviator’s face.

'We've got spatial distortions at L1,' reported Dyke.

'How many contacts?' Miles spluttered in shock, leaning gently over to inspect the readout.

'Reading—' his voice broke off, becoming hoarse as he tried to resume, '—thirty-one vessels.'

'Damned son of the stars, that's a flotilla of ships,' Langridge muttered as he hung from the cockpit's pressure hatchway.

'Are they squawking a transponder code?' Miles suggested, steadying his voice.

'Uh… negative…' Samson's hands began to shake.

'ETA?' Harmon continued, his gut clenching with nervous impatience.

'They will re-enter normal space in … six minutes,' Samson calculated.

'Get on the horn to the rest of the Condors, have them cut engines and power. Initiate silent running protocols.'

'Wilco,' Samson replied, his voice seemingly steeling with action as he passed the word on to ships outside detection range of Lagrange Point 1. 'Alpha Quebec Two Five Seven to all craft in AOR. Unidentified flotilla inbound at Lagrange Point One. ETA Six Minutes. Recommend going to silent running protocols. Out.'

'Righto boys, we ain't here to fuck spiders,' remarked Harmon as he slipped his sealed helmet atop his head. Langridge and Samson quickly followed suit before strapping in and systematically shutting down the ship's entire portfolio of systems. Harmon adjusted his five-point-harnesses straps as the zero-G overtook his body. It was a cold, nervous four minutes before the flotilla arrived in all its colossal horror.

'Not gonna lie: really glad they got that field still up right about now,' interjected Samson into the silence.

'Yeah I just hope it stays that way, mate,' Harmon replied to the thought.

++++

In a flash of violence, the nervous tension of the late evening wait was vaporised by the guttural bark of PS-84 general-purpose machine guns from the sentry line answering the precision weapons fire and inhuman screams of dragoons as they charged the generator complex. Their ferocious charge overwhelmed the checkpoint guards. 'Let loose!' I ordered as the three of us levelled our M8A2s. Three-round bursts erupted from our weapons, their rounds flying true as they found their marks. But even as the first wave of dragoons fell, the synthetic reverb of a precision energy fire support platform roared over the recently-dead, forcing the three of us back into cover. '*Brufik!* They used the gods-damned dragoons as cover to dig in!' cursed Tomas as the laser cut into the pylons we'd settled behind for cover. I grimaced as I braced for the dragoons to close the distance under the cover of a turret but the grimace turned into a frown as I watched the motion tracker marks move left instead.

'The *brafik*ing Komant Senterno!' I hissed in rage inside my helmet 'Specialist Four, smoke out! Specialist Three, forty mike mike, now!' I barked into my comm piece. 'I hope we aren't late,' I muttered to myself as affirmatives echoed back through my speaker.

++++

Tension exploded through the command centre as the black silhouettes of stealth-coated dragoons advanced towards the hexagonal command centre. Flashes of energy began to light up QT's thermal scope as he lined up his shot. *Bears Squeak Bats,* his subroutine muttered to itself as he pressed down on the trigger and the round exited the barrel before vanishing only to relocate in the chest of the lead dragoon. *Squeak Bats,* his subroutine repeated as another round let fly. *Squeak Bats, Squeak Bats, Squeak Bats, Squeak Bats, Squeak Bats, Squeak Bats.* The bolt opened as the last round ejected from the chamber. Releasing the magazine, the mantra changed to *Like Bears Squeak Bats,* but as he pulled back the weapon's bolt, a blue-hued blade of plasma dug into QT's platform. Fluids of half-a-dozen types poured from his waist as he reached up and with a powerful roar screamed, '*I! Will! Not be! Subdued!!*' He hurled the creature up, over, and down from the five-storey roof, the heavy soldier landing with a wet crunch. But in his lapse of fire, the dragoons had poured into the centre and deactivated the shield. His core sent a diagnostic ping down along his platform. *Just peachy.*

++++

Alarms blared around Elenskis as her artificial intelligence systematically began to override the litter's stasis field. With an abrupt snap of awareness, she felt the intense pain of her chest wound as the featureless skull of a dragoon leaned over her inert form. Snapping her sidearm up, she put one excruciating round through the creature's skull before pivoting, her chest aching with the motion as she dropped two more, before the single iron grip of Brood Mother 2705 bent both her wrists like steel in a vice. Her M18 clattered to the floor. The brood mother's stump of an arm had finally stopped bleeding since it'd been rent from its socket by Elenskis, and the eyes of the mother still burned with hatred for that disgrace. 'You *Maeth*-thieving filth. Your disgraceful, *rumaek* flesh will sing for its crimes against the great mother plains…' the brood mother hissed, her speech surprisingly fluent for something without a discernible mouth. 'The Makers wish you to be unharmed, to ensure that your *maeth* is not given to Rumae, but … You have made *rumaek* of those already shamed *kuaer* and that can't be accepted,' the brood mother hissed as she tightened her grasp of Elenskis' wrists, the crunch of bone ear-splitting as the mother finally released the hands and activated a small but intense plasma torch at the back of her slender yet powerful hand.

As she lunged the torch forward, an explosion of glass erupted inwards and the impossible grip of QT's actuated hands moved to clamp down on the brood mother's shoulders. She tried to react, her immense intellect calculating the perfect escape vector as the hands remained locked onto her shoulders.

'You are not escaping me this time!' QT-2 roared as the brood mother attempted to break free. A flurry of small-arms fire echoed into the command centre followed by the sharp helmets of Lycaon. 'Corpsman up!' called QT. 'And someone get that field back up and actively targeting!' he barked. 'And a pair of neural cuffs would be much appreciated!' he hissed. As the binders were applied, he too collapsed beside Elenskis.

Chapter 15
Ops untraveled

The ramp slammed onto the deck with a heavy thud and three gurneys carrying Elenskis, QT-2, and Samson were tugged out by hospital corpsmen. In the chaos of Aiken, we'd needed to call for a medical evacuation (MEDEVAC) so I wasn't aboard the dropship that transferred the brood mother from our area of engagement to the *Yamamoto*. The Condor carrying Brood Mother 2705 had touched down only a few moments after ours. What I remember was how the room shone from the refracted red glitter of Elenskis' inhuman eyes, her tears welling. As naval police coxswains took the monster off our hands, my military discipline and demeanour seemed to vanish, as if my skeleton had disappeared. As gimmits began to crowd around the craft, attempting to remove it from the active hangar deck, I wrenched myself up and began to drag myself to the armoury. Mitchell was waiting for me. As he stood there, an iron pillar of stability, I slowly began to work through the dozens of pieces of equipment including my suit that had to be securely stowed before I could walk around the greater ship. I tried to avoid him, placing my equipment in the furthest weapons lockers, but he intercepted me.

'You okay?' he asked, legitimately worried for me under the professional exterior.

'Yeah, fine,' I replied, trying to play it off.

'Don't lie to me,' he coldly replied. I tried to move away but he grabbed me by the shoulder. 'Do ya need a hand with anything? Need someone to talk to?' Paladin continued; he meant well. I lashed out at him.

'Do you think I need a *brafik*ing hand?' I hissed, tearing away from his grip. 'Do you think I need your help? *All* I need right now is time and a hot shower!' I exclaimed as I broke away from his iron grip and rushed to the furthest weapons locker finally stowing the various bits and bobs, slipping out of my suit then into a pair of fresh fatigues before rushing out through the door. As I strode through the cold, crowded, and glistening halls of the *Yamamoto*, the world around me was almost an empty fiction taking place around me, a life happening to someone else. With each step, my spirit drifted up and away from me as my corpse kept walking on, my steps thoughtlessly drifting me into the near-empty corporals' mess, its dimly lit, wood-furnished aesthetic in stark contrast to the rest of the ship.

It was oddly devoid this evening of people, except for Tomas and Ela. The trail of smoke arced high towards the ventilation, the sharp smell of gin and tobacco permeated the room. I slipped into the room and up onto one of the nearby stools, clicking the table-mounted buzzer recalling the barkeep to the front. 'Glass of bourbon if you could,' I said before turning to inspect my teammates. Ela was working her problems away tonight tinkering with Executioner—one of her morbidly named battlespace intelligence drones that had a 'loose gyro', apparently—and Tomas was chain-smoking. I took a deep breath and sighed as I absentmindedly stared across the table, drink in hand, and just listened. Words drifted off into the vacuum of space, my soul floating above the whole corporals' mess, silently staring at everyone in disoriented silence. It was Tom who spoke first, taking a drag from his cigarette before speaking.

'I've buried a lot of good mates, on a dozen cratered hellscapes, to incompetent lieutenants blinded by some bloody… some bloody fervour to capture a blackened bombed-out hill. Till the very last gods-damned man if need be, regardless of the cost, regardless of the personal sacrifice because of the gods-damned will,' he remarked, a tremble in his throat. 'All of them from some upper-middle *brufik* pocket that lived and breathed the lie it propagated. But I never feared them, despised them, but they never instilled the same kind of heart-stopping dread an SNCO could. While the LT could set the order, it was the RSM who was the one who'd inspire you to go over the top, run into the interwoven web of machine-gun fire an' it was the upper-middle *brufik* starts that I dreaded the—the most,' he remarked, a tremble of fear in his voice. 'They were the ones who could make you feel as though Lati Athia herself were to be there by your side as you rushed across no-one's land, her very own aegis shield protecting you from fire as you ran.' He paused again, his voice deep. 'I thought you were going to be one of those, fuelled by righteous fire, with your head so far shoved up your *zhopas* that the mission and the glorious words of Devna herself would inspire those under your command to throw themselves against the gates of Takahara itself an' I wasn't wrong. I've been in more blood-soaked, mud-caked foxholes than you can take a *shajst* at to be wrong. I've buried my muddy, bloody hands in too many wounded to ever be wrong. But I was wrong about one thing. Something none of my SNCOs in my eight years of service could ever do except you, take their head out of their *zhopas*,' he finally finished, putting out his cigarette and tossing it away as an officer passed through the room. I looked over to Ela, who just sat there swirling her drink, the clear liquid lightly splashing over the rim onto the furnished table before finally speaking.

'You know, I was raised in the Kaisarno Kult and rigorously taught that humans were the pinnacles of genetic engineering. Not because of their physical strength, nor for their analytical skills that I know some preachers and my parents subscribed to. My family's been manufacturing synths for the Traverse since the Pacification of Kiln. I, of all people, should know that we... meatbags can't compete there. No, I never believed we were superior because of those physical skills. I believed because a machine couldn't possibly have a soul. Machines have no drive to change, to improve, or to grow. Their only concern is to maintain the status quo and execute their assigned directive. Its directive shapes its entire existence. The battle buddies on its left and right are only a concern in light of its objective. It faces its termination in the context of its directives and objectives; untroubled and unbothered by its self-preservation subroutines ...' Ela's voice trailed off. 'I just finished reviewing his neural oscillation... his brain waves,' she trailed off again, her voice trembling. 'B—because he's a URC pet project, they monitor everything from servo fluid pressure to command pulse frequency, creating dozens of digital backups for future study.' Her hands began to tremble again. 'In that moment, the instant he collapsed, his entire neural net was erratic: the patterns identical to that of fear in organics,' she explained, her face trembling with shock and visible discomfort. 'As he rushed between Elenskis and those dragoons... he disconnected his self-preservation subroutines from his platform's sensory impulse control node. The fear that he could have so easily shut out... he embraced,' she finally finished, resting her drink on the table before finally turning to leave, holding at the edge of the mess's door only for a moment before finally leaving. Eventually, Tom too left the corporals' mess, leaving me. Glass in hand. Alone.

I strode back to my quarters, slipped out of my clothes, switched on the showerhead, and glided down the side of the shower. My head between my legs, the warm water trickled down my skin as I lay there, slumped in a light pool of water. The heat of the liquid flared across my neck, but I didn't flinch. Heat began to expand from the core of my body out to its various appendages, but I continued to sit there, unfeeling, and immobile, paralysed by the outside world.

++++

Nuleningrad

Lightning crackled and rain hissed in the night as I waded through the thick liquid mud. My service rifle clung to me, the weapon's sling hugging tight to my shoulder thanks to the frequent suit failures in the inclement weather of Nuleningrad. My power armour hurled and howled as its internal gyroscopes struggled to anticipate the unpredictable terrain. To my right walked Lutenant Foksel, Platoon Two's Commanding Officer. My Chiif Starshiina engravings glimmered in the lightning's caress as we continued. I glanced up at my suit's chronometer; the digits flashed 5053. It was midnight, and we'd just completed two hours of our platoon's rearguard patrol. Tu Ten Tu Komando had advanced two hundred metres in the last fourteen days. The fresh platoons had been assigned to sift through the recently deserted battlefield in search of enemy forces that had used the chaos of the advance to slip behind friendly lines. Amongst the chaos, they had hoped to ambush supply lines or cripple other important infrastructure. We paused to survey for a moment. 'You see anything, *chiif?'* Foksel inquired as I scanned the horizon, my helmet magnifying the image for me as I looked. I let out a deep breath.

'Negative, Lutenant, I don't see nothing but mist and misery,' I reported solemnly. A chuckle echoed from the lutenant at the poetic language. But his laughter was strangled by a cry as the liquid terrain knocked him on his zhopas and sent him sliding down the hillside we'd been standing on. A moment of panic washed over me as I tracked his descent and guided my way down to his immobilised position. 'You alright, Lutenant?' I called frantically, my voice strained with genuine concern.

'I'm alright, chiif! You don't need to baby me,' he chided as I lifted him from his horizontal position. As he rose to his feet, a groan echoed through the weather's lullaby. We both spun to see the twisted animal face of a Xendatran soldier, its red eyes pleading as its body contorted in impossible angles. By now I had already unloosed my service rifle, its muzzle levelled on the alien before wavering and beginning to lower. 'Right, chiif. Put this monster out of its misery and let's get back,' Foksel said with machine precision. My brain raced and my body trembled in confusion.

'But, sir—' I began to protest before the sharp crack of orders, plasma fire, and a gavel. Gone was the siren's song of lightning, replaced by the moans of ancient wood and ageing admirals. Dim lighting obscured the five flag officers that stared down at me, their contempt barely hidden behind their social masks as Judge Advocate General Lutenants strode around the podium like prowling wolves.

'Ordinarii Siman Aviatsii Elektroniks Teknison Meikor, is it correct that you recovered passive video footage from Gard Naitno Bomistno Regiment *faif hyak eit ten eit Niit Vitch en-trei* demonstrating Chiif Starshiina Hart firing her weapon at an unarmed and injured enemy combatant behind friendly lines?' demanded the scowling skull of Grand Admiral Kuzmoto.

'Aye, Grand Admiral,' the Aviatsii Elektroniks Teknison reported in his witness box before the gavel struck once again.

++++

UNV Yamamoto, 10:00 hours Zulu (Military Calendar)

My eyelids fluttered open as I slowly re-awoke. I looked down at myself, I was still naked, my hands and feet were shrivelled beyond belief, I squinted as I processed my surroundings. Shajst! *I fell asleep in the shower!* I thought to myself. I rose to my feet. I felt woozy; my equilibrium was off. I took a deep breath, and my heart rate slowed; I was calm. Something felt off. I stepped out of the shower and dried off what little of me was still soaked in water and quickly got changed. *Brafiksjot!* I thought as I saw the time. Something felt different, everything felt so much more straightforward. My heart still ached from the ordeal and my body had finally decided to inform me that it hated everything I stood for. I strode out into the main passageway. It was business as usual, nothing out of the ordinary for the *Yamamoto* to my knowledge at the time.

++++

The last three days were a blur to Elenskis; she'd been in and out of a close-quarters battle fight, been put in stasis, had her wrists crushed by aliens, been saved by a *skarandroid* of all creatures, been airlifted, and immediately put into surgery. When they'd finished up replacing almost every last organ, they'd kept her moderately sedated in one of the medical wards aboard *Yamamoto*, beside QT-2. She smiled in her mind's eye as she lifted a desperate hand to the battered artificial lifeform. While it ... he ... hadn't suffered in the same sense she or any of the others had, over the last two days she'd heard his intense screams as the lack of input, the stagnant silence so uncommon for AI had settled in as technicians replaced his sensory systems and his limbs. While he had never come close to dying two days ago, what he'd lived through since had been arguably worse than death, and she'd desperately wanted to comfort her saviour, her protector, her brother in arms with a simple touch of his newly installed hand. But as she struggled so desperately to lift her hand, the smooth metallic grip of QT-2's gently wrapped around her own. Involuntary tears began to well and run streaking red beams of light across the ward.

++++

Today was the day. The *Yamamoto*'s medical staff had officially released Elenskis and QT-2 out of their immediate care. So, after some minor tweaking of official Taskforce records, seven waivers authorising exotic old-Earth *pankaks*, or pancakes, to be cooked up during the middle watch were distributed. It was a good night. Ela was groaning about petty things—and Tomas about Ela's complaints—in between her shovelling food like some plants eat people. QT and Elenskis sat close together, their arms around each other as they watched Harmon and Langridge regaling and rebutting the stories and myths about old Earth.

'How'd you even get out of the secretary's soup anyway?' I asked, with a humorous tone.

'The magic of … AI,' Elenskis said as she moved her open palms out in a circular fashion. I let out a feigned sigh as I ate. But then, Ela spoke through a mouthful of food.

'Actually, what was it like?' she inquired, with almost childlike enthusiasm.

'What's what like?' QT and Elenskis asked back.

'The afterlife!' Ela exclaimed with fervent joy. A dark cloud seemed to hang for a moment at the talking point.

'You misunderstand; neither of us died,' QT pointedly corrected.

'Brafik!' Ela cursed. For a woman with degrees in Aether theoretical physics, mechanical engineering, information technology, and applied physics, she was quite the religious zealot; always chasing some deeper meaning in all the wrong things.

The morning improved once again after that, but for Harmon and Langridge, a shadow never seemed to leave their eyes after that point. They had lost Samson on that last op, defending Aiken from the Honour Guard's Void Wanderer Navy. But as the morning went on, a faint smile began to cross my lips before fading into emptiness. *If you can't find pride in yourself, find pride in others.* But as the forenoon watch end approached, I began to rise from the table. With a chuckle and a sly smirk. I slapped Ela on the shoulder, said good morning to my fireteam, and vacated the galley. I took a deep breath, my body trembling with emotion as Mitchell strode up beside me.

'Specialist,' he remarked coldly.

'Morning, Mitchell.'

'How's the fireteam?'

'As green as they can be,' I replied.

'Don't play with me, Sara. How are they?' Paladin continued, his voice soft. I nervously rubbed the inside of my palm.

'I really don't know,' I conceded. 'For the first time in my entire career with these marines, I've got no *brafik*ing clue, and that's my professional opinion.' I paused to slow my breath. 'The only one of us who's been in any scrap as bad as we've just been through is Tomas. Elenskis was my battalion commander before this so I've never been in a scrap with her, and Ela and I were never ordered over the top during our time as part of one twenty-two so I've got no basis to know how they are, but I wouldn't test it against a razor's edge that's for sure,' I replied.

'Roger that. I'll have Lycaon stood down temporarily from active operations and removed from the roster,' he finished before striding off.

Over the next few months, our emotional and physical scars began to heal, although Elenskis fought tooth and nail to keep hers, as a reminder, she said, of what they'd done. After much thought, I came to a similar conclusion; every mistake, every failure had to be remembered. Each mistake bore its own physical torment and unless it impacted our operational capabilities, it would remain a part of me; of us.

Chapter 16
Day 730

01/01/2439 (Military Calendar), UNV Yamamoto

Dive klaxons engulfed the air. I dashed to the ship's armoury, snatching up my weapons as I went before stepping out onto the hangar bay. Lycaon stood at the ramp, clad in their PCAs and waiting for me. As I approached the Condor, I slipped off my helmet: my scarred face, faded hair, and cybernetic eye some of the many changes undergone due to three years of war. Looking back, so much had changed over the last three years—our equipment, our bodies, us. Tomas, now standing at the head of the group, helmet nestled in his lap and M8A2 resting on his hip, stood out with a distinctly white shoulder pad on his right with the red engraving of the caduceus. He also had an integrated rucksack, a half-a-dozen utility pouches, and a small pocket of Mijanii cigarettes just under his right arm. The chiselled, blunt face of our hospital corpsman had darkened over the last three years, replaced by even deeper stress lines and determined fury, directed outward for the first time in his life. Though he'd been a salty sailor before the war, the last three years hadn't done him any favours. Ela stood to his left, solemn and head down, her M8A2 and underslung M406 grenade launcher wrapped in her arms. Her armour still sported the integrated AN/PRC-2091 wireless set, an integrated rucksack, and a mixed assortment of utility pouches. The 'vacuum energy woman', as some of our Drill Instructors had come to know Ela three years ago because of her bottomless pit of energy, had begun to look darker by the day. A deep, violent exhaustion punctuated her gaze, while her mind remained as sharp as ever. Her body had run out *brafiks* about Operation Hidden Trident, of the pointless and wasteful stall-and-surrender offensives. Her body was showing what everyone was beginning to think: *Whiskey Tango Bravo?* QT-2 stood beside her. Nestled in his arms was his M54 infantry automatic rifle and settled against his hip, his M164B4 SASR. QT-2 had only undergone a few physical upgrades with a head-mounted digital rangefinder and shoulder-mounted digital spotting scope. Mentally, QT-2 was fairing much better compared to the rest of the fireteam after three years of intense direct action and unconventional warfare. Some technicians had even suggested he was at his calmest in the middle of a firefight. But the op on Aiken Praim had never stopped haunting his processors. Finally, to the right of Tom was Elenskis, her helmet—bent and dented from years of abuse—cradled in her hand, while her M500 squad automatic weapon (SAW) and Mk 306 'Pilum' shoulder-mounted multipurpose weapon (SMW) were slung across her back. Beside it sat her armour's SMW rocket auto-loader folded tightly against her back while just over a dozen hardened utility pouches were scattered over her armour, including two hardened utility pouches carrying a pair of Mk 12 mod zero encased high-explosive anti-armour rockets.

Elenskis, of all of us, looked the worst; her armour was beaten and bruised from botched ops and she refused to replace it unless it was operationally compromising. Her helmet hid her emotions far better than her face did, her eyes trembled with fury, fear, sadness, and shame all at once. At the end of operations, she'd whale on whatever she could find in the gym till her indestructible hands began to pour blood like a governor pours wine, but in the heat of the moment, she was laser-focused, and glimpses of her old self would shine in those moments. I looked to Tomas as I came to a stop near the fireteam and quickly dipped my head, as did the rest of Lycaon, as Tom began to speak. 'Tisorno Lort *an* Lati Se and Eri, revel in the chaos we cause and let us avoid your vengeful glare. Oorah,' Tomas finished.

'Oorah!' we exclaimed before boarding our Condor.

'Mornin', boss!' exclaimed Chief Langridge as he strapped into the crew chief's seat.

'Welcome back, ladies and gentlemen!' Harmon remarked having finished his pre-flight rituals. The moment we'd boarded, the Air Boss had our Condor lifted onto the flight deck, and we launched soon after, gracefully gliding out of the *Yamamoto*'s flight deck into the pure vacuum of space before entering the Aether.

'Lycaon, we have a high-value target, call sign "Patriarch". The HVT is a high-level USR commander who's defected to the Honour Guard. OSI has deemed him a tier-three priority due to his extensive UIR influence,' I began to explain. 'Patriarch has isolated himself in asteroid field Zulu Eight Seventy-Three in the Fader System and is currently waiting for a guard emissary fleet to arrive. When we disengage from Aether Space, we'll be dropping to manoeuvring thrusters and gliding cold into the field. We'll be RVing at point Sierra Whiskey two seven, seven dash five eight three,' I said as the *Matilda* dropped out of Aether Space. I tapped the intercom.

'Harmon, the *brafiksjot* are we doing?'

'Priority command just came through, boss: we're aborting the operation,' Harmon reported with a worrisome voice.

'It's fine,' I replied with a bitter tone. 'Roger that,' I added before settling back into my impact chair. *Something's not right,* I thought to myself as the *Matilda* pivoted on point and re-entered Aether Space. We made twenty-nine more jumps before finally arriving at our destination.

'Harmon, can we at least get eyes on?' There was frustration in my tone.

'Negative boss, orders are clear. All non-essential systems or security functions have been disabled. I'm flyin' by wire here,' Harmon reported. A burst of anger rushed through me; as I slammed my fist into the hull, a burst of air hissed into the bay. *Something's definitely off,* I thought again to myself.

'Okay, *gospadinas*, we're moving into an unknown area, keep fingers off triggers and helmets on,' I explained as our Condor touched down. Our craft ferried into the heart of the station.

'Ramps down,' Harmon reported.

'*Brafiksjot* off,' Ela hissed, infuriated by the cloak-and-dagger bull*shajst*. The five of us strode out onto the dark hangar bay, rifles in hand, our night vision both natural and artificial unable to penetrate the darkness. I bit my lip. *If we activate lights, we'll be discovered, and if we don't, we'll be dead,* I thought as a voice rang across the room.

'Welcome, Fireteam Lycaon,' the voice proclaimed, sounding familiar. We glanced in the direction of the sound but couldn't see the figure. Each of us raised our rifles to fire, creating a firing line around the rear of the Condor. I clenched my teeth as I scanned for contacts. *We don't have enough time to get the drones up and running!* I thought to myself.

'That won't be an issue, Inquisitor Hart,' continued the voice ahead of us as a light slammed on overhead us. The vague shimmer of a woman appeared through our overwhelmed vision as she swayed forward toward our position. My trigger finger became twitchy as the shadowy figure advanced into the light. Then I froze. I stared blankly at the figure, slowly thinking through who I was looking at. Then it finally dawned on me—it was Director Mizuka who'd stepped out from the shadows, her hand gliding across a cluster of boxes to her left.

'Officer on deck!' I barked. Lycaon snapped to attention, our rifles firmly nestled in our shoulders, our left palms resting firmly on the weapon's magazine.

'At ease,' Director Mizuka replied.

We all lowered our weapons and returned to a resting posture, our feet a shoulder-width apart and shoulders locked in place.

'Apologies for the security precautions, but the secrecy of this ship is paramount,' Chihiro unapologetically remarked.

'You could've left the lights on,' Ela bitterly replied. I shot her a furious glare.

'I like to see how my investments operate in high-stress environments,' Chihiro replied. 'That, and watching people squirm is a pastime.'

'Ma'am, on a more serious note, what was so important that Harmon had to fly by wire and our ship had to generate at least twenty Aether Wakes?' QT interjected.

'Because you're standing aboard the Unified Naval Vessel *Alexander,*' she explained. As the revelation rolled off the director's tongue, each of us took a deep breath. The *Alexander* was the flagship of the Taskforce, the director's centre of power when she was away from Taskforce Headquarters. She was three kilometres long, crewed by 8,988 sailors and marines, and had four spinally mounted Mark 29 electromagnetic chase batteries alongside a plethora of other main and regular naval batteries.

'But why have you brought us here, ma'am?' interjected Elenskis, interrupting our awe.

'Down to business; I like it. Wish OPSI had your focus,' she offhandedly remarked. 'The Office of Strategic Intelligence has identified a colossal breach that directly contravenes the Taskforce charter,' Director Mizuka explained.

My heart stopped as I processed what she'd just said: *a colossal breach that directly contravenes the Taskforce charter*.

'What's the problem, ma'am?' I questioned.

'As you know, we have been at war for the last three years, our enemy has held tight. They have not advanced and they have not retreated. But we cannot penetrate the Crimson Veil.' Chihiro paused. 'Given this situation, OSI believes the Honour Guard is now hunting for a game-changer to solve this issue.' The director paused to bring up a wireless transmission. 'OSI listening posts intercepted a number of communiqués between enemy commanding officers referring to a weapon system known to them as "the Accuser".'

All of us looked at her with confused concern.

'What is this Accuser, ma'am?' Ela inquired.

'The Accuser, according to these communiqués, is a weapon of mass destruction; designed to kill on a universal scale,' Chihiro explained.

'What do you need from us, ma'am?' I asked.

'Glad you asked. Due to your extensive military service, your exceptional operational track records, and your enhanced tactical training and skillsets, you and nineteen other Asymmetrical Combat Teams have been selected for Operation Salutis, meaning "salvation" in modern English,' Director Mizuka explained. 'Any questions?'

I paused to do the maths. 'There are only a hundred Asymmetrical Combat Officers in the service, ma'am,' I muttered.

'I know. I have re-tasked the entire Humanoid Intelligence component of the Strategic Operations Executive, unfortunately named by my predecessor "The Office of Unbecoming Warfare", to deal with this threat.'

'Where will we be operating out of, ma'am?' Tomas immediately asked.

'We're currently in the process of forging an advanced Stealth Command Corvette known as the Fortuna-class SCC. Your corvette, the *Morte Fortuna*, or Darkest Hour, is entering the final stages of construction aboard the *Alexander* as we speak,' Director Mizuka explained. 'She'll be the line's flagship.' Chihiro again paused to allow us to voice our opinions.

I nervously looked around as I thought through my questioning. 'Why do you prefer us, ma'am?' I finally asked with a tentative tremble.

Director Mizuka was almost taken aback by the inquiry before quickly moving with the question. 'We haven't given you any special treatment, Specialist Hart, or any of your unit for that matter. You've merely received the necessary tools to maintain your operational efficiency and your exceptional track record,' Director Mizuka replied. 'If that is all, High Special Operations Inquisitor Paladin will escort you to the *Morte*,' Chihiro coldly continued before striding off.

'Lycaon! Attention!' I barked. Lycaon snapped to attention and remained there until the director was out of sight. As she made her exit, Paladin made his entrance and approached us. He'd been detached from our unit for the last three weeks. Holed up at Taskforce Headquarters, most likely organising the finer components of Salutis.

'Inquisitor,' I remarked as we left the hangar bay.

'Inquisitor,' Paladin replied with a smile.

'How've you been?' I asked plainly, curious about what he'd been up to.

'Oh, this and that, mostly working out the kinks in this operation,' he replied. Brafiken *knew it*, I thought to myself.

'How've you been going?' he coldly inquired, his tone professional only because of the setting.

'Ah, Semper Gumby, still being *brafik*ed around by those spooks in the "Intelligence" community,' I replied.

'Excellent to hear,' he replied with a wry smile. 'Now, let's get you out of those PCAs,' he quickly added before directing us towards the ship's armoury. We slipped out of our PCAs and into a fresh pair of UCUs (utility combat uniform) before continuing in silence towards the *Alexander*'s forges; they were external mounts that used the *Alexander*'s vast resource stores to construct warships of varying size within the space of twelve to twenty-four hours using an advanced liquid printing system known as the Devas LPS. Our lift took us down to the forge; it was a rectangular container and was suspended below one of the eight frigate berths the *Alexander* had. Dozens of black tubes and support cables ran down from the overhead of the frigate berth towards the photochromic roof of the container. I stepped into the observation module that extended ever slightly into the frigate berth and stared out through the translucent lid and saw the final layers of the *Morte Fortuna* settling into place; she was a beautiful ship. I turned to Mitchell.

'She's done.' He confirmed my silent question as he activated a collection of tiles on his CPI. The whole berth shook as the forge was magnetically lifted into the heart of the dock, the observation module retracting as it ascended.

Chapter 17
The 3D Dream

The forge's colossal bulkhead receded to reveal the UNV *Morte Fortuna*; she was magnificent. The *Fortuna* was built on a smooth central column while a pair of triangle-like wings curved down to each side. At the bow of the ship sat the semi-circular bridge. We looked up as the *Alexander*'s docking collar slinked across the forge's empty space and latched onto the ship's neck without issue.

'Whadda ya think?' Paladin's posture loosened as he leaned towards me.

'A-*brafik*en-grade!' Ela exclaimed as she jogged off towards the docking collar.

'She's one of twenty; your sister ship's the *Fortuna Favente,* "fortune favoured", ironically; she'll be coming off the assembly forges in the next couple hours,' Paladin explained. He gestured forwards, looking to me and asking, 'Shall we?', his professional persona returning.

I gestured. 'After you.'

When we boarded, it was as if we'd just stepped onto the set of a science fiction series. Nestled at the front of the bridge was the *Fortuna*'s helm control module, and two seats for the pair of helmsmen. On either side of the captain's chair sat a pair of operation pits that held six impact chairs and each sailor's assigned equipment. A central passage connected the bridge directly to the rest of the ship. Turning left from the airlock we strode down the central passageway towards the ships main junction, living quarters lined the port and starboard sides of this section of ship while a door labelled 'Combat

Information Centre' sealed a compartment to the direct aft of the ship. At the centre of the thoroughfare was a large oak table.

'Isn't that against standing medical and biosecurity regulations protecting non-human servicemembers and planets from introduced organisms?' Elenskis interjected, always the stickler for regulations.

'Yes, but there's a waiver for everything, and that waiver, in this case, is the director,' Paladin replied. 'Engineers installed the combat information centre into the aft compartment ahead of us. Lifts to the deck below are port and starboard of the CIC. Below first level, second deck is compartmentalised into your engine room, reactor room, and well deck,' Paladin explained, pointing to the floor. 'Your Condor and all essential supplies are being transferred as we speak, you'll be ready to launch within the hour,' Paladin paused. 'Oh, there's one other thing,' the inquisitor remarked as we turned to leave the Fortuna. 'Specialist Hart, could you step forward please,' Mitchell instructed, his voice shifting to a formal register. I complied. 'Can you confirm that you are Sara Alaja Hart? Service Number Six Twenty-One Dash Five Eighty-Seven Dash Hotel Sierra?'

'Yes,' I cautiously replied.

'Prepare for verification,' Paladin instructed. I looked at him with confusion. *Verification? I haven't been scanned in over three years,* I thought to myself. I rubbed the inside of my hand before cautiously raising and uncovering my inner forearm. Mitchell unclipped a pen-like apparatus from his waist, nestled it against my arm and pressed down on the activation switch at the top of the machine. A small appendage cut into my skin and extracted a piece of the Biological Identification Chip that was buried inside my arm.

'Target verification complete. Hart, Sara Alaja. Staff Sergeant, Asymmetrical Combat Officer,' the computer reported. Nodding with approval, Paladin tucked the verification gun back into his belt and turned to face me.

'Staff Asymmetrical Combat Inquisitor Hart, with the power vested in me by Director Mizuka and the Operations Personnel Security and Intelligence Committee, I hereby issue security level

'Final shakedown tests complete and in the green, hull one hundred percent, heat sink and silent running systems nominal,' cited Sandon.

'Plasma torpedo tubes one through four loaded, CIWS online, decoy launching system in the green. Chrysoar combat system online and receiving data. FARSIGHT array active,' stated Phar.

'Tight beam, wireless, and subspace communications systems online,' responded Hesch.

'All systems nominal, ma'am,' finished Michiko as she settled into her impact seat.

'Understood. Bosun, inform the *Alexander* we're leaving.'

'Beginning cast-off procedures, aye, ma'am,' Hesch replied. '*Alexander, Morte Fortuna.* Requesting cast-off. Over,' Hesch transmitted.

'*Morte Fortuna, Alexander.* Request approved. Lowering the forge now. Over.'

'Understood, *Alexander*. Out,' Hesch replied.

'Docking collar released,' added Setch as our ship's liquid printing tank abruptly began to lower into the empty void of space before depressurising and opening the bow side bulkhead.

'Releasing clamps and keying engines. Now,' reported Setch as the muted pulse of manoeuvring thrusters echoed across the hull and the main engines kicked in. We began to slowly drift out of the forge.

'Adjust direction; point five degrees to port,' instructed McGhee, interpreting the Alexander's FARSIGHT readings and his own instruments.

'Adjusting direction; point five to port. Aye,' responded Setch. 'The *Morte* is away, keying main engines, moving to quarter thrust.' With that, we glided out towards the system's edge.

'Go to silent running,' I instructed as I rose from my chair, the lights dimmed.

'Silent running active, ma'am,' relayed Sandon.

'Excellent, Michiko, you're with me. Bosun, have Lycaon form up in the briefing room, Mr Barken, you have the conn.'

'Aye, aye,' the three sailors replied. As I slid out of the captain's chair, I eyeballed one of the sailors unwrapping a comfit. I quickly stopped and strode over to him.

'Mr Sandon.'

'Yes, ma'am?' he reported as he threw the confectionary in his mouth.

'You done *brafik*ed up,' I jokingly replied. His eyes widened. 'You know what you just ate, son?' I mockingly questioned.

'A comfit, ma'am?' he cautiously replied.

'Yes, yes you did. Do you know what comfits do?'

'No, ma'am?'

'They give you *brafik*ing bad luck!' I exclaimed. 'Now, bin it! As soon as possible!' I hissed, smirking as I walked back towards the briefing room.

The room was dim as our ship silently cruised past a nearby nebula. Lycaon stood around the table, two on either side. I smirked. *Always symmetrical,* I thought to myself. I leaned onto the head of the table and scanned across the room, my gaze passing over each member of Lycaon.

'Okay, so we've got a weapon of mass destruction somewhere within the space of two galaxies, and an intelligence network that is stretched to capacity,' I paused. 'I'm open to suggestions right about now,' I admitted.

'Well, I've been looking over OSI interception transcripts for the last hour; they really didn't want the source to be traced, but I've been able to map the signal origin based on the USR buoys they hijacked to boost the signal range.' Ela paused as she activated the table's holographic projector.

The Enzo Line sat ominously on the northern regions, almost daring to be taken head-on. To the south-west sat the Red Line, the next portion of unexplored space in the Galaxy.

'So, the transmission originated in this quadrant of space,' Ela explained; moments later, an outline appeared at the centre of the map and the faded words 'Kalani System' sat below the map.

'I don't get how this relates to us finding the Accuser,' I stated plainly.

'Strategic analysts have been trying to understand why the Honour Guard moved into this territory so early in the war with such zeal. The northern regions have no agriculture, no industrial-military complex, and nothing of major importance on the Taskforce end either. It's my hypothesis that they've been searching for this weapon from day one and the northern regions is where it's at,' Ela explained.

'In another scenario, I would have demanded you produce a much more rounded rationale and a lot more proof, but given our lack of anything right now, I'll take it. But how does this location narrow down our search from the entire northern region?' I continued.

Ela smirked. 'Three years ago, you couldn't wrap your head around why they resumed offensive operations at Aiken Praim of all places. While I can't speak to their strategic logic on the ground, I think I can speak to the strategic logic of claiming the Aiken System.' Ela paused as she readjusted the map. Faster-than-light travel lines overlaid atop the map. 'Aiken feeds directly into this cluster of territories,' she said. 'The cluster that contains a planet known to cartography as Hotel Papa One Seventy-Two Dash Four Twenty-Seven that experiences intense wireless distortion. It is my hypothesis that this distortion is generated by the Accuser,' Ela explained.

I bit my tongue. 'Well, it's better than nothing, but we need to validate your theory; we can't throw a massive offensive into Honour Guard territory over a guesstimate,' I replied.

'Roger that,' Ela replied.

'Elenskis, you're the Kanarvin University graduate, any ideas?' I asked, turning to the xeno-archaeologist-turned-marine draftee.

'Well, assets from Third Special Forces Group recently raided a Void Wanderer convoy in the Fagani System,' Elenskis explained, lighting up a territory on the edge of Honour Guard Space on the map as she spoke.

'What did they find?'

'Well, they secured digital manuscripts from an unknown alien culture that according to metallurgical dating procedures pre-dates the Architects by well over ten thousand years,' Elenskis explained.

'And for the uninformed who didn't study ancient history?' Ela asked, bored already by Elenskis' report.

'The Architects, more properly known as the Prethosi, were an advanced precursor race who, per the consensus within the archaeological community, created a large portion of the golden worlds discovered and colonised by the Union of Imperial Realms during the Age of Resurgence, around the 2280s.'

'Okay, and this is pertinent to our operation?' I asked, Elenskis' archaeologist persona beginning to annoy me as well.

'Firstly, how many Void Wanderer convoys have been reported to carry digital manuscripts written in a language not native to either the dragoons or the Kalil?' Elenskis posed. I paused before quickly nodding. 'And second, the transit logs; its destination was the Kalani system,' Elenskis explained.

Where Ela had traced the transmission, I thought to myself.

'Okay, the directors requested a SITREP every three days. I'll relay our findings then,' I explained.

'Rah,' replied the group.

'If you need me, I'll be on the bridge,' I explained before striding off. As I settled into the soft posture of the captain's chair, Petty Officer Hesch looked up to face me.

'Uh, ma'am, I've received a Priority One from Fourth Fleet and Eleventh Marine Expeditionary Force,' Hesch explained.

'Well, we're not under their jurisdiction anymore, they can shove their Priority One up their arse for all I care,' I replied.

'It's been signed off by OPSI, ma'am,' Hesch added.

I sighed. 'Fine, what is it?'

'There's a Void Wanderer relay station on the edge of the Enzo line; she's a central controller of all data moving through this sector of Honour Guard space. Air Corps Special Signals IDed her a couple weeks ago, but until now OPSI hasn't had any available special operations units to make the station vulnerable. It's been marked as critical to our operation—as such the director has approved our redeployment to the Sena system as a part of the joint operation,' Hesch reported.

'I guess we have no choice then; bridge, get us underway,' I instructed.

'Aye, aye,' the crew responded as Hesch hit the 1MC.

'All Stations, prepare for jump, this is not a drill. Repeat. All Stations, all Stations, prepare for jump, this is not a drill,' the jump alarm flared through the ship as he spoke. Golden emergency lights pulsed through the vessel and a shorter, sharper klaxon wailed in the background as the *Fortuna*'s crew locked themselves into their impact seats and secured any loose equipment.

'Mariko, Safae, Helm! Confirm jump data!' Samuels instructed. 'Coordinates One Zero Seven Dash Eight Niner Four confirm?' Samuels continued.

'Confirmed!' called the trio as they reviewed the accuracy. Michiko rose from her chair.

'Navigation?'

'Route plotted! Coordinates input!' relayed Samuels

'Engineering?'

'Silent running disengaging, reactor power routing to engines and FTL! Reactor within margins!' Sandon reported.

'Helm?'

'Engines responsive,' Manu confirmed. 'Controls positive!' reported Setch.

'Security?'

'All passageways, and equipment secured and stowed,' casually reported Safae.

'Communications?'

'All communications secured for jump!' responded Hesch.

'Combat?'

'All hardpoints secured for transit!' reported Phar at his secondary combat information station.

'All hands report secure for jump,' Hesch finished as Michiko turned to face me.

'All departments report secure for jump, ma'am,' Michiko reported, her posture formal.

'Execute jump,' I instructed. Michiko reached for a secure container on the starboard side of the bridge and entered a four-digit security key before lifting out an isolineal jump key, designed exclusively for the *Fortuna*. Michiko strode down to the helm and passed it to Manu who proceeded to slide the key into his control system. He paused for a moment before twisting it counter-clockwise. The central screen mounted to the overhead flickered to life.

'Jump clock is running. Jump clock is running,' Hesch announced over the 1MC before continuing with his countdown 'Ten, nine, eight, seven, six—'

'Singularity fielded,' reported Manu as Hesch continued.

'Four—'

'Rift created; vector set,' relayed the helm as the bridge's blast shield quietly lowered.

'Jumping!' Hesch relayed as the *Fortuna* was engulfed by the rift, before calmly gliding through Aether space.

'Glide nominal, ETA forty-eight hours,' Manu reported.

++++

02/01/2439 (Military Calendar), UNV Morte Fortuna

My stylus hand began to visibly shake; my eyes grew distant, my breaths ragged. I'd been voluntarily couped up in the captain's ready room for a little less than thirty-six hours reading into paperwork and administrative tasks now befitting of the rank of Chief Warrant Officer. Needless to say, if my eyes started bleeding like the twelve hundred brothers as they watched Emperor Kuzmoto's coronation, I wouldn't have been surprised, though I very much doubted mine would've been from joy. Slapping my stylus to the desk, I rose and left the room. *I need a gap of sanity,* I thought to myself as the door snapped open. A cacophony of drums, tambourines, and maracas rolled into me amongst a sea of quiet. I stood there, stunned, as Ela's hands deftly danced across her *ydaiko* polyphonic synthesizer as it echoed the empty, cold, and pitiless arms of deep space. Around her, the others looked on as she played, the old Terrans mesmerised while the *ympiirtach* sat, heads bowed, and palms upraised. As she finished her hymn to Lati Kalm, she opened her eyes, lowered her instrument, and looked across the compartment.

'*Mitach pritoot,*' she recited.

'*Mitach pritoot,*' the *ympiirtach* echoed in response.

'We remember,' I called across the compartment in direct translation. The echo of my voice was followed by an immediate clatter of chairs and a series of rapid reports.

'Good evening, Chief Warrant Officer!' echoed Samuels, Hesch, Manu, McGhee, and Setch as they rose from the around the table to bolt upright attention. Elenskis sat rigid in her seat; the rest who sat around the table were either officers or inquisitors, who didn't have to come to attention for me despite being in command of the vessel. A smile broke across my face that twisted into a chuckle.

'At ease, *gospadins* and *gospadinas*. Just to make this clear, to you enlisted sailors that haven't worked with us before. If we aren't operating as part of a joint operation, you can drop the formalities,' I said as I slipped onto a chair around the table, the other standing enlisted troops following suit. The compartment was filled with the intense layer of *reish* hanging in the air.

'Someone mind telling me how we got *reish* onboard?' I asked, gesturing to the rice wine across the table.

'Under the religious activities provision, obviously …' said Ela with a grin wider than the Eye of Primera.

'Setch and Manu, is there a reason you aren't on the bridge?' I asked as a frown of confusion twisted across my face.

'Safae is monitoring the detection systems; if something goes wrong, we'll be the first to know, but there isn't much for us to do up there. If our Aether Drive fouls up, the crash translation will leave us chucking our kidneys up through our lungs before we have a chance to fight the physics of the universe,' explained Imogen Setch. My eyes twitched at the thought.

'She's overexaggerating the effect—' interjected Connah Manu, his words choking off as he struggled to find a term of address for me.

'Sara, Inquisitor, and Chief Warrant Officer are all perfectly acceptable, Seaman Apprentice,' I answered through my smile.

'Thank you, Inquisitor—as I was saying, she's overexaggerating the effect; the most common injury with crash translations is blackouts.'

'I'm definitely underexaggerating. Besides, tell that to the crew of the UNV *Nullarbor*,' retorted Setch with a dark tone.

'Wait, hold that thought,' Harmon said, hand snapping towards Setch as he looked across at Ela. 'Would someone mind telling us fine old capitalist globalisation heretic Terrans what in the bloody hell I just witnessed?' interjected Harmon, his index fingers gesturing around Johnathan, Setch, Manu, McGhee, Hesch, and himself. Confusion cascaded across the compartment before Manu stated.

'Uh… we're not Terran,' Manu said, his eyes darting left to right awkwardly. At this, Harmon's eyes bulged.

'But, you're a Kiwi! That's a Māori surname!' he bellowed in confusion.

'The Diaspora happened to New Zealand as well, mate,' Johnathan said in an even tone.

'So where're you from?' he finally asked.

'Valles Marineris, Mars,'

'And you?' he interrogated, index finger moving as he did.

'Ganymede, Jupiter,' Setch replied with more than a confused expression across her face. At this, he began wildly indicating the implied question at McGhee and Hesch.

'Ceres, Neptune,' replied McGhee.

'Ireland, Earth,' Hesch said. At that, a cough from the Executive Assistant's cabin rang out followed by the clinking of nondescript ceramicrete saké pouring glasses tumbling to the deck.

'The Irishman is from Ceres and the American is from Ireland …' muttered Evans, confused. 'I did not see that coming. But, Sol folk, even if you aren't Terran,' he said with placating gestures and more than an edge of relief. At this, Manu frowned and turned toward Ela.

'But seriously, Inquisitor, what is this whole celebration about?'

'Voidno Matsur, or the "Festival of the Void" is to commemorate those who died during the Age of Absence as we travelled across Andromeda in search of a home—specifically the Lensner—and to ward off the Lord of Disorder, Lort Se, and the Lady of the Underworld and the Void, Lati Kalm.'

'I'm sorry—the what?' Setch coughed in confused concern as she tuned into the conversation.

'The Ensnared,' Tomas translated.

'The Lensner were a squadron of shuttles, each a crew of ten. As the First Flotilla made its final eight-month voyage towards the Primera Cluster, acting on faith alone that Lati Suna, the Lady of Light was guiding us to safe harbour. The Lensner gazed upon the Eye Primera, a Nebula that defied the very laws of physics by drowning our lidar and radar in impossible ways. In what could only be described as a trance, the forty broke away from the First Flotilla and against orders flew into the Eye of Primera, never to be heard from again, their last words would simply echo "Lati Kalm calls and Lort Se sings",' Ela finished.

'And so we remember this day to mourn our dead and remind each other of the dangers of the Void with stories of the mysterious and the violent, as her domain is not one to be interfered with,' Tomas added.

Manu looked across at Setch. 'Well, the *Nullarbor* ironically fits perfectly with that then,' Manu said, gesturing to the helmswoman.

'Wait, "*Nullarbor*"? A DDG built back home, eh?' asked Evans, curious.

'Home?' asked Elenskis

'Oz, the land down under,' Miles interjected.

'Australia,' Evans translated. 'The Nullarbor is down along our southern state, South Australia.'

'How original,' Ela remarked, sarcasm dripping from every syllable.

'What happened to her?' I asked looking at Setch.

'The Admiralty was attempting to break the stalemate against the Honour Guard about a year and a half ago, and with the URC's assurances that their impact chairs could hack it, tried executing a pincer manoeuvre by having a squadron of ships conduct a crash translation through Aether Space's Tachyon Band. Tachyons are the science fiction nickname they gave whatever possessed particles are actually below the Quantum Band where regular craft cruise. Anyway, when the crew of the UNV *Nullarbor* hit the Tachyon Band, the crew was simultaneously accelerated past the speed of light and ceased all forward momentum simultaneously when they re-entered normal space. Sir Isaac Newton's laws of motion applied, and the entire ship was a meat sandwich,' she said grimly. 'I was the shuttle pilot who had to pick up the bits,' she added for grizzly context. The conversation seemed to die among the others from Sol, but from Ela's mouth, the ritualistic words continued unfazed by the horrors of deep space.

'Suna, Liktno Lati, take our trials and horrors and set them in our heart that their sacrifice may lead us from the sirens' call of the Lord of Disorder and clamouring claws of the Lady of the Void,' Ela finished, cracking into her pre-poured glass of cold *reish*. Followed soon after by the other *ympiirtach*, besides me. As the glasses struck the table, Harmon and Jonathan glanced at each other across the table.

'Oi, so—we've been curious: we've been around this outfit for the last two hundred to two fifty years, give or take a decade between friends, and we never got round to asking,' Harmon froze on his words, eyes curling into a frown as he tried to find his tongue.

'What was the daily life of an … what do you call yourselves?' Evans added, just as perplexed as Miles.

'*Ympiirtach*,' I answered.

This drew a low cackle from the 1MC as Mariko appeared at the centre of the table.

'It just means we Imperials inclusive,' she said with bursts of inappropriate laughter.

'Mariko, I will box your data core for that gross violation of personal conduct,' Michiko said with a controlled expression as she finally stepped out into the central compartment, her alcohol stowed in her cabin and her uniform immaculate, despite the fiasco several moments ago. 'Flying Officers, your question is what was the daily life of the *ympiirtach*?'

'Yes, ma'am; that was the question,' Harmon replied. With a nod, we looked across each other, and Tomas simply shrugged.

'Well, for me that was in an eight-day work week, four and a half days on, three and a half days off. Worship was on the sixth day. Before I enlisted with the active Ympiirno Junjonno Militarii, my father and I worked the Pinch Fusion Reactor Plant of the region full time and the Ympiirno Teritoriino Reserf part-time as our commitment to the union in return for military healthcare and fortnightly rations. On top of that, my father was a *diikon* for the Ympiirno Kult and ministered on worship. Beyond worship days, our average religious conduct was a prayer to Lati Suna or Lort Helis to ensure our Fusion Reactor would run smoothly and not claim one of our brothers or sisters of the faith,' Tomas said. Nods in agreement orbited the room.

'Mine was nothing like that,' said Ela, her eyes low, her heart rate spiking on my display. 'My family was aristocratic by nature; we are descendants from the original twelve founding families who worked to defend the old world. We were charged to resuscitate the old Earth French Empire from globalist destruction,' she explained. Harmon began to laugh, but Evans clamped down on the man's wrist. 'Our day-to-day was far more ceremonial. For eight hours, we were in worship or in ministry training, and then for eight hours, we were engineering as our Tekno Baroni allowed us to do. And, as others worshipped on the sixth day, we presented gifts to Ympiirista Aleksandra in the blinding rays of the Imperial Palace,' she said with glazed eyes. At this, a silence fell over the compartment before eyes fell upon me.

'What was your day to day like, Sara?' asked QT-2, his patient form people-watching from a corner. I paused with the blank look of someone caught in a spotlight.

'Our average week …' I muttered, trying to recall. 'I wouldn't know what the average family of my station looked like. I was born into an active military family. As a child, our day was regimented from start to finish; work around my parents' duty station and some light worship, but with the spontaneity of almost everyone within the chain of command, many of the longer religious rituals weren't authorised. Even our daily classes were less religiously geared; our regimen was designed to raise the next generation of sailors and marines,' I said with a distant tone, before returning my focus and checking my grandmother's watch. 'Well, we've got some planning to get done,' I said with a stiff voice. 'Let's get it done, *gospadins* and *gospadinas*,' I instructed, officially ending the ceremony.

Chapter 18
Just another day in the Corps

0630 hours Zulu, 03/01/2439 (Military Calendar)

'Re-entry in three, two, one,' reported Setch, as Manu slowly twisted the jump key into the 'off' position, his hand steady on the throttle as we were returned to normal space. With a jolt, the stars around us returned and a large gas giant stood before us. 'Jump complete, ma'am,' reported Setch.

'Going to silent running,' reported Sandon as the lights dimmed once again. 'Thermal emissions contained. Optical camouflage plates are green. Reactor temperature within acceptable margins. Silent running is active, ma'am,' finished Sandon.

'Good to hear,' I replied.

'Ma'am, we're being hailed by the UNV *Immemorial* and the UNV *Dreadnought,*' reported Hesch.

'Put them through, Bosun,' I instructed.

'Activating live feed, aye, aye,' Hesch replied as the 3D holograms of the operation's two commanders resolved before me. As their images resolved, their bios snapped on beside them. Before me stood Lieutenant General Ronald Nelis, UMC, and Admiral Reginald Bacon, UNS.

'Lieutenant General Nelis, Admiral Bacon. Pleasure to see you again,' I opened as I rose from my chair and snapped to attention. For the operation, I'd mandated that we were to respect traditional military conventions, at least in the short term, to better integrate with friendly forces.

'Can't say the same, Chief Asymmetrical Combat Inquisitor Hart; you know I fully expected your batch of ACOs to be court-martialled by now, not outranking me,' Nelis opened. I recoiled.

'I'm only a Warrant Officer, General Nelis,' I humbly replied.

'You've got SL1 clearance, you're an ACO and you're a Special Operations Inquisitor. You've outranked me for quite some time, Chief,' Nelis replied.

I shrugged. 'So, I've been told, but that's a conversation for another day. What's the situation?'

Nelis turned to Admiral Bacon, who replied with a tight nod. 'Certainly, down to business,' he remarked before turning back towards his bridge crew. Navigator! Pull up grid reference King Apples one zero two dash three eight five,' Bacon instructed, before a commissioned navigator and their enlisted assistant navigation quartermaster came back with sharp replies—the audio receptors picking up the grumble of the navigation assistant about the admiral's predisposition to use old-Earth world war phonetic spellings.

The Admiral turned back to face us as a map of the sector settled between the three of us. The 3D image was quickly magnified, resolving to show the unusually dark blade-like relay station, hovering silently in low orbit around the nearby gas giant. 'This is relay station Kasiel's Reach.'

'*Brafik*ing weird names,' I remarked aloud.

'Vau ov blad,' Nelis hissed in agreement.

'Under normal circumstances, she'd be an impossible target. Honour Guard kinetic shields are damned-near impossible to breach, especially station-grade ones. The combined firepower of the Fourth Fleet couldn't break those barriers even with my modifications,' Bacon admitted.

'So, what's changed?' I asked.

'They've moved this station into the low orbit of a nearby gas giant. If we can knock out her guidance and barriers—even temporarily—she'll begin to descend towards the planet's hard deck.'

I held up a hand. 'Apologies, Admiral, my background as a leatherneck means that the term "hard deck" is beyond my knowledge.'

The Admiral frowned in mild confusion at my use of the navy's derogatory nickname for marines before continuing.

'That is a gas giant's crush depth, where no man-made system survives the gravitational forces,' he succinctly explained, as though he had expected the question, before moving on.

'Now, strategic analysts and researchers from ONI and URC have calculated that it will take the relay station approximately thirty minutes to sink below the hard deck,' Reginald continued as I mentally converted the pair of acronyms to the Office of Naval Intelligence and the Unified Research Command respectively.

'Now it is a given that, in that time, the forces aboard would be able to reactivate enough systems to escape their disastrous descent before they're crushed by the planet. So, instead of destroying the station with gravity, with the ensuing chaos, your team will jump below the gas giant's atmosphere and board the station,' explained Bacon.

'Once aboard, you'll have two targets. The station's data, and its survival mechanisms: so, data centres, transmitters, replication systems, guidance. You name it …' Nelis continued.

'And after this station has been buried?' I asked, wondering what OPSI had in mind.

'From there, the Fourth Fleet will advance through the gap, escorting General Nelis' Eleventh Marine Expeditionary Force,' began Bacon. 'Where we will link up with friendly forces at similar positions along the Enzo Line and initiate a directed strike deep into the heart of Honour Guard territory. We're going to carve a hole in their line,' Nelis explained with enthusiasm.

I took a deep breath. *Another* brafiksjoti *try-hard,* I thought to myself. 'And our infiltration point?' I continued.

'Micro-jump. Your navigators are going to have to be extremely accurate, but it isn't impossible,' Admiral Bacon clarified.

'Understood, now how're you getting that station down?'

'We … haven't figured that out,' Nelis grudgingly interjected.

I crossed my arms as I looked at the station's 3D model.

'This isn't my expertise … Bosun, have Lance Inquisitor Tremblej report to the bridge.'

An affirmative called back, and two heartbeats later, Ela was standing beside me. 'Lance ACI Tremblej reporting,' she called as she stood at attention on the bridge.

'We need to cripple a guard relay station enough to force it into an uncontrolled descent into this gas giant's gravity well without destroying it outright, so we can board the station and secure critical repair systems and intelligence,' I explained as Ela stared intently into the hologram. 'This discussion is open to all bridge crew with ideas,' I added, turning to face the rest of the crew.

'Quartermaster Samuels, how far out is the gas giant from this system's primary star?' Ela requested.

'One hundred and thirteen astronomical units, Inquisitor,' reported Samuels as he double-checked his instrumentation and star charts.

'Admiral Bacon, General Nelis: are your ships within the cover of the system's heliopause?' Ela continued.

'You have other ranks manning watchkeeping roles of officers—' Bacon muttered before interrupting his train of thought and replying for both of them. 'Aye, we are. It's the easiest position to mask our craft.'

'Confirm that's thirteen AUs out from the gas giant.'

'Aye, Inquisitor, confirmed; thirteen astronomical units from the gas giant,' Samuels replied.

'Then make an intra-system jump into the local binary pair,' Ela replied after a moment of thought.

At this, Nelis frowned and Reginald erupted in confusion and anger.

'What?' He paused to regain his breath. 'What would that accomplish?'

'The explosive distance of a micro-supernovae only expands to about a hundred and fourteen AUs,' Ela began to explain. 'The major star of the pair is currently sub-critical and is perfectly poised to trigger a fission-fusion reaction, the star's helium content is already providing the necessary heat to trigger a reaction but lacks the necessary pressure to go nova—so, we provide the pressure. It should take a little bit of reworking from one of your ship's engineering teams, but if you can generate a micro-singularity at the heart of the major star, that should compress the solar body's helium contents enough to trigger a micro-nova,' Ela finished.

General Nelis looked at her as if he'd been starstruck.

'Inquisitor, what compelled you to join the Marines? You'd have made a fine commissioned sailor,' Bacon remarked with a smile.

'Some days I think of retiring, you know?' Nelis began as he rubbed his temple. 'Transferring to the army, at least they don't have *brufik*ed-up plans that make sense,' he wearily replied.

I smirked. 'Don't worry, General; they have them as well, they just don't have that many,' I said with a grin. 'How long will it take your engineers to retrofit an FTL drive into a makeshift black hole?' I asked. Admiral Bacon disappeared from the video before appearing a moment later.

'My engineering team is estimating one hour from now,' he finally reported, my head nodding with each word.

'Roger that, we'll be ready and waiting,' I reported before cutting the connection and turning to my bridge.

'Exceptional thinking, Ela,' I said as I snapped to face Samuels.

'Quartermaster, coordinate with Ela, QT-2, Mariko, Evans, and Safae,' I instructed.

'Aye, aye,' Samuels replied. I turned to Hesch.

'Have the rest of Lycaon form up in the briefing room,' I instructed.

'Aye, aye,' he replied as he tapped a tile on his control console to issue instructions over the 1MC.

'Michiko! You have the conn!' I instructed.

'Aye, aye!' she exclaimed as she settled into the captain's chair. Over the next hour, we trawled over passive and active lidar and radar readings that emanated from the station as well as comparing dozens of predictive assault maps created by the special operations and intelligence communities. Ninety minutes after we'd combed through the data, conducted our own ad-hoc briefing, Harmon and his flight crew had rechecked the *Matilda* thrice over, and the ships combined navigation and physics expertise had generated a faster than light insertion vector within a point one margin of gravitational fluctuation, Admiral Bacon finally reported that his engineering team had successfully cannibalised their FTL Drive.

I strode down the passageway, armour around me, as I headed below to the well deck. I strode out onto the dark empty cavern that was the *Morte*'s well deck. Langridge knelt beside the *Matilda,* finishing some final modifications before our jump.

'Are we good to go, Chief?' I queried.

'Aye, Inquisitor, just calibrating a pair of cantankerous injectors and we'll be good to go,' he reported. I gave a nod of approval.

'Lycaon!' I called out as I turned back to face my fireteam jogging across the deck, all spoiling for a fight. 'We have two objectives, *gospadins* and *gospadinas*; we are notionally preventing this relay station from conducting repairs and we are notionally scrubbing their servers clean of everything they have on the Accuser,' I habitually reiterated, my nervous tics resurfacing.

'Rah,' they collectively replied in response.

'Once we are aboard, each of you will make your way towards your assigned objectives before RVing in the control room once your objectives are complete. There, we will exfiltrate via the overhead port where a Condor from the eleventh MEF will arrive to pick us up,' I continued to explain. Lycaon nodded intently.

'Alright, *gospadinas*, hop aboard!' remarked Harmon as he strode across the well deck. We all quickly settled into seats while Harmon keyed the engines, and the well deck began to open.

'Everyone, hold tight!' I barked as the *Matilda* rocketed into the vacuum of space moments later.

'Stand-by for micro-jump,' Harmon instructed.

Ela's eyes widened. 'We're micro-jumping into the station?' she panicked.

'No! We're going to micro-jump the moment this system's star goes nova into the atmo of a gas giant!' I called over the ever-increasing whine of the Condor's FTL Drive as the navigational computer continued to synthesise its jump coordinates, holding the drive in a state of potential stress as it did.

'We discussed this in the briefing!' Elenskis yelled in frustration.

'You were doing the equations with me!' interjected QT-2.

'I thought those calculations were theoretical! For *shajst*s and giggles!' she yelled back, 'and I haven't paid attention to briefings since officers were commanding officers!'

'I'm enlisted, you *zhopas*!' I screamed over the violent whine. If Ela had replied, it was drowned out by Harmon's report over the speakers.

'Coordinates locked in!' The pilot's voice paused. 'Holding FTL Drive!' he continued. *Come on,* I thought to myself. Moments later, an explosion was detected millions of kilometres off from us. *Yes!* My mind exclaimed, my right-hand curling up into a fist. 'Starting FTL Cycle!' Harmon reported. The drive was beginning to groan as its quark pairs began to deteriorate, the erratic particles straining the container's safety limit. 'Rift created!' Harmon relayed. I pulled up the ship's cameras, the solar rays were almost on top of us—two seconds away. 'Rift is moving!' exclaimed Harmon as we were devoured by the tear in subspace. Our Condor rocked from side to side as the effects of normal space distorted the Aether. 'Jumping!' exclaimed Harmon. An explosion rocked through the Condor, sparks flew in every direction, my head slammed into the bulkhead behind me; my vision became distorted, and the lights went out.

Chapter 19
Out of the fire

I opened my eyelids. My eyes were spinning. Tomas knelt over me, conducting a brief medical. The *Matilda*'s lights were out; we were on emergency power. I focused, centring my vision on a single point in the Condor. My brain reengaged. Groggily, I activated my magnetic soles, snatched my floating rifle out of the air and turned to Elenskis. 'SITREP!' I exclaimed.

'Condor's BUBAR, we're SNABU and the station's CATBU,' Elenskis summarised. I nodded.

'Excellent news,' I sarcastically replied as I strode up to the cockpit door. I reached for the door panel before Langridge yanked my hand away from it.

'Don't do it!' he exclaimed. I turned to him in confusion.

'Why not?' I asked, my head still turned around from the accident.

'Canopy's blown. Condors are tough, but not that tough. The solar winds roasted 'er kinetic plates and debris obliterated the canopy. We barely made it out,' Harmon interjected.

'*Brafiksjot*!' I cursed.

'Exactly,' remarked Will in agreement.

I turned back to our pilots. 'Are you able to get this bird up and running? Get yourselves out of here?'

'Affirmative, we can route most of the main flight controls through this panel,' Harmon explained, pointing to a faint console beside the door. 'And we've got enough spare capacitors to boot 'er up,' Harmon elaborated.

'You got rebreathers?'

'Yes, ma'am; in the floor,' he replied as he gestured to a plate below him.

'Then get them on,' I instructed before turning around. 'Lycaon!' The fireteam stopped what they were doing. 'We're completing this mission! Form up and stand-by!'

'Rah!' they howled in response as they began to prepare.

'Gospadins and gospadinas, wireless silence protocols are in effect. Hand signals if possible, verbal transmission if necessary, and wireless delivery only if priority one,' I instructed. 'The only time you're authorised to generate a wireless signal is once you've arrived at your second objective. Understood?' I asked, finishing my speech. Each simply replied with a simple nod.

'Then let's not keep them waiting,' I remarked as I gestured up to the hatch. I turned to Harmon, Langridge, and Evans who were now holding onto a pair of handles, sealed rebreathers on. I turned to a nearby emergency switch and activated it. The ship sparked as the emergency power was routed momentarily into the O2 vents. The bay's oxygen vented into space. As the air reached zero, Lycaon began to pry open the access hatch with little effort before silently slipping into the vacuum of space and onto the hull. As the last of us left the ship, we sealed the hatch again, and the pilots got back to work repairing the Matilda.

'Good hunting, ma'am,' Evans wearily called over the wireless.

'Affirmative,' I solemnly replied. I dropped down my helmet-mounted binocular range finder (an attachment I requested after Operation Shattered Stars) and activated my suit's airborne kit. I looked up to the sky and magnified a drifting distortion in the charred gas clouds of the planet. *There you are*, I thought with a smirk. Kasiel's Reach drifted down through the clouds roughly six thousand metres above our position. I raised my optical enhancement device and surveyed my fireteam. *Warriors to the end*, I thought. The five of us quickly touched off, a light stream of air trailing off our wings as we glided near silently up to the relay station. We didn't say a word to each other; we each knew what the other was thinking, we knew what the other was doing, and we knew what needed to be done.

My HMD flared up as we approached the station, my suit's passive radio and light detectors denoting various access hatches across the station. Besides the damage incurred on Kasiel, the station's exterior was much like any other Guard relay station, its angular blade-like design hovering there like the sword of Damocles. The uniformity of the station ended there, however; much like terrestrial airbases, naval bases, and air stations, Void Wanderer stations were each unique in their internal layout, design, and aesthetic.

We floated up to the hatch, and Ela immediately got to work bypassing the door. She accessed a backdoor into the airlock's internal sensors and reattuned them to erroneously detect a pressure build-up; the door snapped open moments later, and we glided in, reverting to our suits' photoreactive plating the moment we stepped into the airlock. The door slammed shut behind us, and the room began to re-pressurise while internal sensors began to search for life. Nothing would be found though. We slunk to the side as Ela accessed the closed net telepathic comm channel on the Hotel band.

'Gu Keta, Cha?' Ela transmitted to a nearby dragoon.

'Gu Seka, Cha,' the dragoon replied. An instant later, the inner door opened up and the dragoon strode in. 'Tag?' he called back as he stepped in, rifle now raised.

Elenskis unclipped a knife from her belt and slunk up to him, slamming the activator on the hilt. A pulse of energy rang through the room, and the dragoon moved to turn around as the knife was embedded into his neck; blood went everywhere. Deactivating the blade, Elenskis tucked it back into her sheath. Turning to face Ela, she slipped to the side while Ela got to work, dissecting a portion of the spinal column to retrieve the dragoon's internal guidance chip, a bio-electrically linked SPS. Tearing it out with care, Ela nestled it into her CPI and began to process the data before generating a 3D map of the station. Our objectives were quickly lit up in red. After a momentary pause, Ela released the data to our suits, and all of us slipped away to complete our various tasks through the plethora of ventilation systems, sub-access tunnels, and passageways, leaving me in the central hall. A guard unknowingly strode past, his telepathic net hijacked by Ela. Anyone we killed wouldn't be missed, so long as their bodies weren't physically touched by a dragoon; nothing would seem out of place. One of the fatal weaknesses of telepathic networking. I looked over my rifle one last time before striding out.

I strode into the main passageway and slid into an adjacent ventilation shaft and moved through the ducts. My targets were twofold: a thruster guidance controller (TGC) and one of five core data nodes. My node was four floors above me, directly linked to the central data stream (CDS) that ran through the heart of the station. The controller was one floor higher and was adjacent to the bridge. I stopped at a crossroads. *There's got to be a faster route,* I thought to myself. I pulled up the map. As I inspected the schematics, the chirp of a priority one field report from QT-2 appeared. I pulled up the message.

> SPECIALIST ONE, SPECIALIST FIVE. BE ADVISED. STATION AT SECURITY ALERT. ALL HATCHES SECURED. IMPASSABLE. OUT.

'*Brafik*! Now, how're we going to get our objectives?' I hissed to myself, then I saw it: the CDS. I responded with a smirk.

'I wouldn't recommend that, ma'am,' Mariko defiantly replied.

'We've got no other choice. You heard Lycaon—security checkpoints have choked up the main passageways. It's the only thing that runs directly through both objectives and isn't covered by a thousand dragoons,' I replied.

'But the energy—' Mariko began to reply in defiance.

'Look, I don't like it either, but you're going to have to plot a course to the line, set my equipment to MOPP Four, and shut down all non-critical systems; we'll only need to be in the stream for a couple seconds.'

'It takes less than a millisecond for the data stream to burn you alive, ma'am, or even worse, destroy my consciousness,' she replied coldly.

'We'll make it,' I retorted as I began to climb up the ducts to the access hatch to enter the data stream.

'How 'bout we improve those odds, ma'am?' Mariko replied with an atypical lexicon.

'What'd you have in mind?'

'Get me to a terminal, and I can trigger a cold start of the CDS; it'll give you sixty to get to and secure what we need,' Mariko replied with her cold brand of professionalism.

'Fine,' I conceded as I readjusted my stance to access my CPI. I activated a tile on my CPI and readjusted a component on my shoulder.

'Bringing Gurkha online,' I reported.

'Initiating Soul Rip,' Mariko reported. 'SR protocol online,' Mariko continued. 'Digital connections severed.'

'Gurkha online.'

'Preparing for digital handshake,' Mariko reported. 'Handshake initiated.'

A moment later, a pulse of frigid temperature arced through my neck as my suit pumped liquid nitrogen into my suit's superconducting memory crystal, followed by a dart-like object bursting from my shoulder armour, its wings unfurling from its body before quickly gliding off down the duct system.

Now, we wait, I thought to myself as I placed a holographic overlay onto the physical terrain and digitally removed the colour in the walls. I'd have to climb ten decks to junction eighteen, then head topside another fifty metres to reach the data stream. *Well, better get started,* I thought. I holstered my rifle and began to climb, leapfrogging my way up the central duct. The station, like many Void Wanderer ships, was covered in digital murals telling the military history of the various units assigned to the station (much like traditional military colours); the walls were titanium white. The station was built with sweet curves that stretched around corners and up to doors. Of course, Kasiel's Reach had lost its beautiful allure; walls were charred black, plasma conduits leaked onto the floor, and engineers and medics rushed about tending to their various duties, removing the wounded from damaged stations and activating temporary ballistic shielding to seal large cracks in the station's superstructure.

Junction eighteen, I noted as I deactivated the directional overlay. I froze there, my arms and legs locked in an X shape as I patiently waited for Mariko to return. Moments later, Gurkha returned, and my suit's throb of liquid nitrogen temporarily diluted the blinding pain that I was in.

'Welcome back,' I remarked.

'Ma'am,' Mariko replied. 'I'd recommend you reach that access hatch asap, ma'am; the data stream will begin its cold restart cycle in less than ten seconds.'

I nodded and climbed into the duct and approached the hatch. The data stream flared with an intense fury, the raw energy boiling the amplification chamber as it processed quintillions of bytes of data. Abruptly, the stream shut off, the quiet hiss of cooling metal echoing out as if in relief. I flipped onto my back and kicked out the access hatch, its metal form flying down into the empty abyss. I threw myself out into the black pit; a number appeared above my HMD as Mariko engaged my suit's tracer kit. *Two hundred metres in sixty seconds,* I thought to myself. I stared at the timer as my feet caught onto the compartment's circular housing and my armour's advanced manoeuvre control thrusters kept me upright, my boots dashing along the bulkhead at impossible speeds, my legs screaming at me as I did. I glanced up at the distance as it rapidly ticked down then looked across to the first of two waypoints that denoted the access hatch to the TGC. In fifteen seconds, I would be above the designated hatchway with a clear line of sight to the objective.

Checking that my rifle was still secure, I unclipped the weapon and unfurled the under-barrel launcher that held a remote access transceiver (ironically abbreviated to RAT). *Ten seconds,* I reported to myself as I one-handedly levelled the rifle against my shoulder; 'five seconds,' I muttered to myself as I raced past the hatchway and arced up and across to the compartment's port side. My HMD transformed, providing firing arcs and millimetre measurements detailing the hatchways design as I pulled the trigger. The overlay changed from blue to green mere milliseconds before I fired. The RAT careened through the hatchway, its micro-translocation buffer throwing it through the solid cover before it rematerialised on the other side. As I continued to race up the housing, the RAT rocketed through the labyrinth of ducts, ventilation shafts, and conduit lines, a dozen bursts of compressed air practically screamed from the dart-like transceiver's micro-directional jets. Mariko guided the dart through the maze with pinpoint accuracy, the dart's micro-camera feed appearing in the corner of my HMD as it dived down a shaft and levelled out in a new compartment. I could see the target. The node was behind another access hatch, its ballistic security field disabled during the accident. The RAT continued ahead, gliding silently through the cover's louvres and towards the node. After slipping through the hatchway, the dart picked up speed and threw itself into the alien node before starting the colossal effort of sifting through the petabytes of data that the Core Data Node 4 processed every second. Physical alarms screamed through the room while telepathic data intrusion alerts wailed over the wireless network. Dragoons burst into the room, hunting frantically for the intruder. But they would never find one. At least not until after we'd stolen every last bit of data. As the RAT did its work, I looked up at the distance that sat at the top of my HMD. 'Fifty metres,' I muttered to myself as the final restart timer flicked onto my display. Ten seconds. '*Shajst!*' I cursed as I dashed up the outer housing, my feet aching and my legs boiling as I ran. I glanced up at the timer once more; five seconds … three, two, one. I leapt from the starboard bulkhead and threw myself headfirst at the ventilation shaft, the data stream recommencing an instant later. I slumped to the ground and gave a heavy sigh as I stopped to recover from the two-hundred-metre vertical dash, the thruster guidance control room adjacent to the shaft I now lay in.

++++

Gurkha quietly returned and powered down in my hand before I returned him to his socket. The thruster guidance control room was oddly light on security; that should have been my first inclination that *shajst* was about to go down but, being the mortard I was, I merely disregarded the light security as pomposity and a shift in objective priorities. I slid up to the access hatch and quietly detached it from the ventilation before sliding into the room, rifle raised. The room was exquisite, it was like a large hollow ball that'd had the bottom cut off. In the centre of the room was an imposing pentagonal control system. Five holographic control panels speared out from a central spire made of pure energy, surrounding the deck were command pits where dragoon helmsmen writhed for control, their neural impulses transmitted via wireless interface.

'She's out of alignment, ma'am,' reported Mariko.

'Who's "she"?' I replied, confused.

'The station's bio-mechanical AI. She is the command and control hub for every single thruster, engine, and gravitic generator aboard,' Mariko explained.

'Well, she's doing a lousy job,' I muttered, surveying the compartment.

'The solar energy disturbed the living computer's equilibrium ballasts. As long as they are disturbed, the station will continue to plummet towards the hard deck,' Mariko explained.

I smirked. 'Then let's keep it that way,' I replied as I lowered my rifle into my reactive webbing.

'Inadvisable, recommend holding for friendly wireless contact.'

I sighed, shaking my head. Mariko ignored my comment. Over the next few minutes, Lycaon began to make wireless contact: a series of pre-arranged message bursts, each unique and each over TEAMCOMM. I looked around, searching for their silhouettes in the darkened compartment, but saw nothing. Despite a lack of visual confirmation, I knew they were there as I unclipped a satchel from my waist and approached the guidance controller. I opened the bag and slipped C13 charges out and began to place them along the length of the controller. As I strode over to place the final charge, my legs locked up and my shoulders froze. I lurched, trying desperately to move.

'Vema fath,' a creature proclaimed through the station's bridge. Mariko paused to analyse the phonetics.

'It isn't Honour Guard, ma'am—dragoons focus on velar plosives. I'm registering labiodental nasals.'

'Don't,' the voice continued, in an understandable dialect this time. 'Don't. Move,' the creature said with difficulty, his linguistic modulator struggling with the dramatic shift in syntax and phonetics.

I looked across into the station's bridge, and there stood a creature. It was a thin, bipedal thing with an elongated jaw, sleek arms, and fluid legs. It was supported by a thin chest. Its head was similar to that of a human, with thick cheekbones and a smooth skull. It wore a skin-tight flight suit and had a white face, its eyes and mouth obscured by a white film. At the centre of the creature's forehead sat a black circle. My eyes widened. *It's a mask.* 'Very astute, Officer Hart,' the creature began, turning towards me. 'It is a Kalil death mask. Crafted and worn by each member of the Dishonoured ever since the *dhaeseii Maiin-Uifiedh Mava dhfaetha,*' the Kalil continued.

So, this is a Kalil, I thought to myself.

'Yes, I am a Kalil,' it continued.

My heart began to race. 'Get out of my head!' I screamed.

'On the contrary, it is you who are in mine. Your wireless chatter, your electrical interference, your crude bio-electrical signals. To you it is a pattern—to me, it is an incomprehensible scream. Your primitive attempt at telepathy is nothing but white noise to us. Your presence is a strain on even our near-infinite tolerance,' the Kalil replied, infuriated by our presence alone.

'Why've you captured us?' QT interjected. 'You now hold our lives in your hands, you could easily kill us right now ... So why not?'

The Kalil paused as if in thought. 'I would very much like to do so. Your fireteam has caused more hassle for me than your entire Taskforce combined!' the creature exclaimed. 'But, alas, your lives are more useful to me than your corpses ever will be,' he explained in cryptic words.

'Oi!' Ela exclaimed. The Kalil turned to face the defiant redhead.

'What is it you want, repugnant child?' the Kalil snapped, uninterested already.

'You should really invest in better wireless security,' Ela said with a smirk.

'And why would that be?'

'Because you've done *brafik*ed up,' Ela explained, equally cryptic.

'And how would that be?' the Kalil questioned, with more interest this time.

'By doubling down on telepathic fields, you've bred weakness. Did I mention that your telepathic field sucks?' Ela exclaimed.

The Kalil chuckled with arrogant pride. 'And how do they—'

The Kalil's question was interrupted as an ear-splitting pulse of radiofrequency electromagnetic radiation blanketed the station, causing a cascade of new ruptures around the compartment followed by the evaporation of our gravitic prisons. We all lurched forwards as we overcorrected. With a sharp smirking gesture along her helmet, Ela lowered her thumb from the chin of her helmet to a tile of her CPI.

The station began to shake, and the sound of drowned-out orders peaked through our minds. I couldn't help but chuckle while explosions rocked through the bridge as the station's antimatter containment failed to re-engage. As the Kalil realised what had befallen his plan, he began to truly worry. He was now surrounded by five specialists who were quite noticeably pissed.

'Vama!' he cried. The creature's form vanished before our eyes as we dashed into the central room. The bridge was a circular structure, much like a traditional observatory. Explosions rocked through the hull again; this time, the lights and artificial gravity faded into inactivity. We quickly regained our footing.

'Ballistic shields are down,' QT reported as he monitored the station's electrical patterns.

'How're we getting out?' Panic seeped into Ela's voice as she spoke.

I looked around. 'Same way we were planning to,' I explained.

'Negative, all bridge emergency pods have been jettisoned and airlocks have been remotely sealed; it will take approximately six minutes and fifteen seconds to disengage the locking mechanisms,' QT explained as I looked over the display.

'Bull*shajst*, I can get it done in under three mikes,' Ela retorted, physically moving into QT's deactivated periphery as he sifted through the station.

'The station will be terminated in two minutes fifteen seconds,' QT added.

Brafiksjot! I thought to myself. My eyes traced around the bridge before settling on the roof.

'There!' I proclaimed as I pointed to the glass roof above me. 'The fleet's vector has it passing right overhead!' I overlayed the tactical approach lines onto Lycaon's HMD. I turned to Elenskis and Ela.

'Specialists Two and Three—get up there!' I barked.

'Aye!' replied the pair.

The duo disengaged their magnetics and began to lay C13 charges along the frame of the glass dome. I moved back to the thruster guidance controller and collected up my satchel of C13 before passing it up to Ela.

'Specialist Five, ETA?' I demanded.

'Thirty seconds till station detonation!' QT replied.

Thirty seconds later, Ela and Elenskis remagnetised to the ground.

'Good to go,' Ela reported.

'Two! Light 'er up!' I barked. Elenskis nodded as she unclipped a remote detonator from her waist and held her thumb over the detonator. 'Everyone! Release magnetics the second the dome breaks!' I instructed.

'Rah!' called back the fireteam.

'Get some!' I screamed.

'Kill!' Lycaon cried as Elenskis slammed down on the detonator's switch. The roof erupted in a ball of flame that was quickly consumed by the vacuum of space. The five of us barrelled out of the bridge with immeasurable speed. If it wasn't for our enhancements, the force of the blast would've easily knocked us unconscious. We glided out into the emptiness of space just as the station erupted, and fragments flew in a billion directions. As we drifted into the assault vector, a piece flew up at an impossible speed and slashed through Tomas. It ruptured his suit seal and cut deep into his chest; bluish-red blood seeped into the vacuum. My heart raced as I processed what'd happened.

'What?' I muttered in disbelief. 'Get to him!' I barked in fury as I snapped back to attentiveness. Ela jetted over to Tomas' now-limp body and immediately began to administer basic first aid. She activated her PCA's cutter, resealed the vertical breach and slammed a canister of kaolin nanofibers into Tom. I brought up Tom's vitals.

'He's stabilised!' Ela verified as I looked over the readout. The cut was deep. It'd split most of his ribs, he had a punctured lung, and his subclavian artery had been cut. Ela nestled his weak form into her arms, guiding his mindless drift. Despite the painkillers that the nanofibers released, Tomas was out cold from the pain; the operation had taken its toll on the salty bastard. To be frank, most of us were almost unconscious thanks to the pain. *The joys of augmentation,* I sardonically thought to myself afterwards.

'Specialist Two, secure Specialist Four! Specialist Three, get on the horn to the eleventh!' I barked over the wireless as assault ships glided past us to targets unseen.

'Rah!' they both replied as they switched places.

Ela immediately activated her suit's radio. 'Black Paddock, this is Shafted Sabre. Request 9-line MEDEVAC. Over,' Ela began.

'Shafted Sabre, this is Black Paddock. Prepared to copy. Over,' replied the tactical air control party. Ela promptly relayed the necessary details of Tomas' condition and the status of the pick-up zone to the TACP.

The TACP repeated back the details and relayed them to the MEDEVAC Condor *Dark Druid 792*. Ela tore the side of a grey bag attached to her chest and unfurled a large VF-20 signal panel. *Druid* arrived minutes later; we promptly climbed aboard. As the bay regained atmosphere, I ripped off my helmet and screamed to the pilot while the Condor's team of corpsmen moved to take care of Tomas. My eyelids began to swell with tears, my heart began to race as I gazed upon Tomas' lifeless face. But the tears never came, my emotions just faded away, replaced by the warm embrace of controlled fury. At the time, I paid no attention to how odd such a response was. Moments later, our Condor was already moving, en route to the *Xiwang Shengli* medical frigate.

Chapter 20
The ninth circle of bureaucracy

0530 Zulu, 04/01/2439 (Military Calendar)
UNSV Xiwang Shengli medical frigate ('Hope's Victory')

I gazed across the *Shengli*'s medical ward from the doorway. Tomas' quiet form nestled on one of the *Shengli*'s many medical gurneys. I readjusted my shoulder as I inspected his limp body. He was on a ventilator, riddled with IV drips and enough bio clamps to make any normal person weep. He'd just come out of seven hours of intense surgery, and the surgeon assigned to his operation was coming to give his assessment of Tomas' condition. Lycaon appeared behind me as the surgeon was approaching us, his footsteps a hundred metres away. I sighed as I lifted myself off the door frame and strode into the room, Lycaon in tow. The doctor assigned to his case arrived a few moments later.

'Chief Warrant Officer Hart?' the surgeon verbally checked. I nodded.

'The name's Lieutenant Danil. I've got good news: your corpsman will make a full recovery. While the injuries sustained were extensive, because it was dealt with quickly by your fireteam and the fact that it missed his heart, we were able to stabilise him in an efficient manner. But he won't be seeing action for at least another month while his artificial lung develops and his reinforced rib cage heals,' the surgeon admitted.

'That's fine, we're probably dead meat as it is. Thank you,' I replied, taking a deep breath.

'We'll have him transported to your vessel asap, Chief. Your onboard medical equipment should be sufficient to take care of any complications,' Danil explained. With that, we left for the *Fortuna* that departed soon after that.

++++

0844 hours Zulu, in orbit of Cicapricous X. Captain's ready room.

I adjusted my collar as I stood before the view screen to the right of the door. I tapped a tile on my CPI, and the door that led to the ready room sealed behind me. Moments later, the monitor flickered to life as the director's cold, sharp gaze appeared. My skin went cold, my veins seized up, and my throat grew tight. I snapped to attention.

'Parade rest, Chief Warrant Officer Hart,' Chihiro hissed.

As I locked my shoulders and spaced my legs into the sharpest parade rest I could, I mentally grimaced as the director's disdain echoed behind the order.

'Now, can you explain to me how I'm supposed to accept that your failure to infiltrate an incapacitated relay station was somehow an honest-to-gods accident and wasn't a result of your lack of professionalism?' Chihiro remarked with a controlled fury. I remained silent, my back teeth biting hard into my tongue.

'That's what I thought, because no Special Operations Unit falls apart that easily. I'm taking your fireteam off operations. You're clearly incapable of completing them, and you sure as hell don't deserve half the accolades your superiors have given you,' Chihiro continued. My mind stirred, my heart raced back to Nuleningrad, to the slums of NuRostok as I'd submitted time and again to authorities higher than me only to watch lives destroyed and dreams erased under the heel of submission.

'If you want to call this a *brafik*-up on our end that's your call to make, Director Mizuka, but don't you ever question this fireteam's professionalism and capability; we have been the most successful unit, period. Our track record speaks for itself, our success rates outnumber our losses by a hundred to one, and if you want to make an example out of our unit, to give other units motivation to do better, take it out on me and me alone. I am their Senior NCO, their de facto commanding officer. I am responsible for maintaining discipline and unit effectiveness. My unit deserves every accolade they've achieved. I'm expendable but they're invaluable,' I remarked, a controlled fury rising in my throat. 'And its Chief Asymmetrical Combat Inquisitor Hart, ma'am.'

For once, Director Mizuka sat with a subtle smile across her face, which for her was a miracle in itself. 'Glad to see you've got it, Chief,' Chihiro remarked before cutting the feed. I let out a sigh. I relaxed my posture and strode out into the main passageway that connected the bridge to the rest of the ship. Lycaon stood anxiously to the side of the compartment door awaiting the verdict. I stepped to them and smiled.

'We're still green,' I remarked as their faces lit up with joy.

'Kill!' Ela exclaimed.

'Follow me, *gospadins* and *gospadinas*, we've got work to do,' I instructed with a smile. Lycaon stepped out of the way as I made my way aft before following close behind me. I strode to the briefing room that the *Morte* had been constructed around, its fine wood table soft to the touch as my hands shook with relief. The three team members stood around the table as moments later the muted clang of a metal cane emanated through the ship. We looked aft to see who was making the sound, a smile rippled across my jaw. 'You know, the doctors said you shouldn't be up and walking, right?' I jokingly said.

'Well, in my professional opinion, their opinions can get *brufik*ed,' Tomas replied, the salty sailor crawling out into the light once more. He smirked as he clattered over to the table before taking a seat on a nearby chair that he'd dragged out with him. Lycaon turned back to me.

'So, what did we get?' I finally asked. Ela was the first to speak.

'Well, jack *shajst* from the actual server. From the sounds of it, the entire offensive was a trap, the relay station had nothing of value, and the guard had an entire fleet waiting behind the station. When the expeditionary force rolled in, they were completely wiped out,'

'So, it was a waste of time, effort, and lives,' I said with a sigh.

'Not entirely,' Ela refuted. 'While the pre-existing data at the relay was a waste, according to the upload logs, a file was transmitted just minutes before we began the extraction process.'

'That's not uncommon, it was a central hub of data,' I said, unsurprised by her discovery.

'See, this is the thing though; it was the only file uploaded in the last twenty-four hours. For a data hub like that, that's not logical. They shut down communications to that relay station in preparation for this trap,' Ela explained. I leaned in further.

'Okay, you've got me hooked. What is it?'

'Well, we've still got a little bit more to crack on the encryption; it's an Honour Guard format I've never seen before, but we've been able to pull coordinates from it,' Ela explained as she looked down at her CPI and brought up the galaxy map. It zoomed out before enhancing a small portion of Honour Guard space. I looked at Ela, confused.

'This is Hotel Papa One Seventy-Two Dash Four Twenty-Seven, and guess where she is located?' Ela asked smugly.

'Let me guess: the Kalani System?' I spoke knowing exactly what she was going to say even without a neural link.

'Nailed it,' Ela said with a wry smile.

'Well, looks like I owe someone a bottle of Sauri Whiskey,' I said with a sigh.

'So, what's our next move, *chiif?'* Ela asked, curious about how we were going to act.

'We're going to wait,' I said as Ela's enthusiasm quickly faded. 'I'm going to get on the horn to Shadow Director Rokkaku and have force recon marines move into the territory and confirm our suspicions, because if the Accuser is there, we'd need the whole damn Unified Navy to even get near her,' I replied, indicating a line across the map to the planet. Lycaon sighed, their fight was postponed. 'Anything else?' I asked. Lycaon just shook their heads. 'Then get some rest, I want this fireteam to be a hundred percent for when we do roll on these Alpha Bravos,' I instructed. At the informal cessation, Lycaon quickly left the compartment without another word. It'd been a rough couple of days for us—touch and go at every stage. I strode into my room soon after everyone had returned to theirs and called up Mariko.

'Ma'am?' she reported as she stood on her pedestal.

'Have Petty Officer Hesch feed a line to Shadow Director Rokkaku,' I instructed.

'Contacting Shadow Director Rokkaku. Aye, ma'am,' Mariko replied. Mariko's avatar faded before quickly returning (she liked to entertain the idea that she actually left the room when completing a task when in reality she didn't). 'Connection live. Ready when you are, ma'am,' Mariko reported. I readjusted my collar again and nodded to Mariko. Director Rokkaku's worn Japanese face appeared before me.

'Chief Warrant Officer Hart,' Sasaki began, with a strong Japanese accent.

'Shadow Director Rokkaku,' I replied, bowing as I did. Sasaki returned the gesture.

'What, can I do for you, Chief Warrant Officer?' said Sasaki.

'I need to requisition a Marine Force Reconnaissance Unit,' I explained.

'And why would that be?' Sasaki asked, sceptical.

'We've received coordinates to a planet deep in Honour Guard territory that we believe is the location of the Accuser. But we need hard evidence before we're ready to commit our proposal to

Director Mizuka. As such, we need a reconnaissance team to land on the planet and confirm or deny our suspicions,' I explained.

'Very well, I'll have Second Deep Reconnaissance Platoon sent in to ascertain the validity of your work,' Sasaki said with a nod.

'Thank you, sir.'

'Jupiter Actual, out,' Sasaki finished before cutting the line.

Now we just wait and see, I thought to myself. I relaxed my posture, returned to my quarters, had a quick shower, and then slipped into bed.

Chapter 21
To blacken an eye and bludgeon the brain

1910 hours Zulu.

Alarms blared around me as I woke from my slumber, my eye rapidly recovering from its disuse. The back of my neck and inside of my right eye burned with an inhuman intensity. I scanned the room as I reached for my M18 Aetherfield and combat knife, unclipped both from the bottom of my bed before quickly slipping onto the floor. I checked the weapon. *Brafiksjot!* I thought to myself. The weapon's circuitry was fried; it'd take a few minutes for the EMP hardening to process the power surge, but that wasn't the only problem: the weapon barely had half a magazine. I inspected my clothing. I was only lightly clothed, a tank top and a pair of briefs. I looked to the far side of the compartment. My armour rack was oddly retracted. *Brafiksjot!* Lockdown protocol's been triggered. *Gonna be that way until the ship's main systems finish processing the power surge,* I thought to myself. I reached for my offline CPI and comm piece before shifting my attention to the door. I tucked my M18 into my briefs, slipped on my knife's sheath and strapped my CPI and comm piece to my person before kicking at the emergency locks. *Shajst! They won't budge!* I cursed. I looked around the room. My one good eye spotted an indent in the overhead. *Access hatch!* I strode over to where the manhole was, jumped up, and latched onto the cover's handles. I bit my tongue as I let go with my right hand. I began to enter the access pin on the keypad (that was still working, thankfully). As the cover swung down, I let go and landed on the ground with a muted thud, before spinning on point and leaping into the Fortuna's access ducts. Using the hand rungs on either side of the duct, I hauled myself up into the central shaft and began to make my way through the labyrinth of systems that made up the Fortuna. I quickly found another access point that led out into the passageway that connected the bridge to the briefing room. Against my better judgement, I opened the hatch and dropped down, my pistol and blade raised (not that it was going to do much in its present state). No contacts. With the initial area clear, I turned to approach the bridge as the hushed thud of footsteps began emanating from behind me. I turned to react to the sound, but there was nothing. I lowered my weapons as a hand latched onto the back of my neck, the tips of its three-fingered hand digging into my throat with brutal force. I squirmed as I tried to plunge my blade into my assailant's midriff, but the bastard snatched my arm away from me and yanked it out its socket. I let out a scream of pain. The creature let go of my limp arm and activated a wrist-mounted blade; the quiet sizzle and the intense heat that seared my skin was unmistakable. It was Honour Guard. *Of course it is,* I thought to myself. My attacker inched closer with the blade, its fiery plasma boiling my tank top and quickly cutting into my flesh.

'Chikup!' I exclaimed as the bastard inched the blade further and further in. An instant later, the creature retracted the blade and paused. It inspected my incapacitated form as if unfamiliar with the concept of a human. 'What? Too *bladsa* for your liking?' I sarcastically screeched as my throat began to well with anger. The sound of a knife being drawn echoed from my attackers' belt. *Well, this is new,* I thought to myself as the creature balanced the short combat knife on my shoulder, the plasma searing my flesh. The sight of my skin's blackened state caused me to scream in fury. 'That's it!' I howled. As I slammed my left foot into the creature's double-jointed knee, he

flailed in pain, causing him to stumble uncontrollably. Apparently, they'd attempted to correct this flaw without compromising its benefits in this model, as it didn't dislocate as easily as a traditional dragoon's knee would. He dropped to the ground, my neck in tow. I slammed into the steel floor and my vision became blurred. A flurry of rounds followed, slamming into the alien's ballistic shields before a hard crunch echoed through the ship. The alien's hand went limp, and I slammed into the deck. I rolled over to see what'd just happened, and I looked up to see Elenskis hauling her fist out of the guard's back. Blood and guts soaked her arm. She flicked the gore away as she approached me.

'Took you long enough!' I hissed as the pain finally kicked in.

Elenskis swept the area before dragging me by the collar into the cover of a nearby compartment. The rest of Lycaon dropped into the room via the ducts soon after. I surveyed the compartment. Tomas was leaned up against a bulkhead, a trail of blood leading up to his current position on the metal flooring. As he saw my condition, he groggily dragged himself across the ground, his cybernetic knee clamped bolt straight.

'She's got—' Tomas spluttered as he spoke, '—a sliced external oblique, bruising on the neck, and third-degree burns on her shoulder. I need a dermal regeneration patch, some sealant strips, and thirty milligrams of Mort,' Tomas instructed as he propped himself up beside me, his right cybernetic knee locked in the forward position.

'You know, I'll be fine,' I replied with a spluttering smirk.

'Errr, an' I'm a paragon of happiness,' Tomas' replied with a hiss. He collected his material from Elenskis and immediately administered the Mort before applying the dermal patches and sealant strips. As the covers were applied to my skin, they hardened, becoming airtight and impervious to water. Nothing was entering the wound. 'She's good to go,' Tom approved, nodding as he took a deep breath, his weak lung still giving him difficulty. Elenskis outstretched her hand to lift me up.

'Okay, explain to me what the *brafiksjot* just happened? What happened to my ship, why there are dragoons on board my ship, and why the *brafik* are they interrogating people?' I asked, my fury returning.

Elenskis stepped forward. 'At eighteen forty-four hours, an unidentified vessel appeared less than three hundred klicks off our bow. Sixty seconds later, the vessel fired an EM pulse torpedo that overwhelmed the ship and sent all compartments into lockdown. At eighteen fifty hours, they moved within our defensive perimeter and deployed two-man boarding teams at the starboard bow and port quarter docking hatches. As for what they are, we've only been active for the last twenty mikes; the lockdown trapped us in our racks.'

'Okay then, so where do we stand?' I questioned.

'Well, Specialist Three's been able to jury-rig a closed comm line with Harmon, Evans, and what remains of the bridge crew,' Elenskis reported.

'What do you mean what remains of the bridge crew?' I said, increased tension seeping into my speech.

'Well, Setch and Manu didn't make it. The rest of the bridge crew were on the bridge when the lockdown was initiated. Manu had left the bridge to attend to some fly-by-wire latency issues, and Setch was headed for her rack when the doors unexpectedly shut.' Elenskis' breathing intensified. 'We heard their ungodsly screams at eighteen fifty-two hours but were still trying to get out when it happened. We found their mutilated bodies at nineteen oh five.' Elenskis paused. 'Just before we rescued you,' she added.

'Assuming the rest of the bridge crew were locked on the bridge, where're Evans and Harmon?' I asked.

'The two mad pilots are alive for now; they had just enough power to trigger the *Matilda*'s security lockout protocol, so they'll be fine,' Elenskis continued.

'Any damage to the hull?' I asked.

'Negative, they haven't left a scratch.'

I acknowledged the report with a nod before changing the topic. 'And there's another one out there?'

'Affirmative, there's one still out there.'

'Where the *brafik* was he?' I asked, confused as to why the guard didn't capitalise on the advantage.

'We're not questioning good luck at this point, Chief,' Elenskis replied, her formality seeping through.

'Well, you should be, because these bastards don't deal in luck and coincidences. I didn't get my cuts because of some blood-raged dragoon; these were precise, conscious cuts. Their entire intention was to cause the most pain—' I broke off. 'To lure you out. The screams from Setch and Manu weren't just because of some sadistic cultist religious belief, they were bait for us, loud enough for anyone on this deck to hear,' I explained gesturing to the passageway behind me. I paused to think. *What was your game plan?* I wondered. I rubbed the inside of my palm. 'Okay, this one'll be ready for us, so we'll need to know its moves before it knows ours. Specialist Three, can you get my comm piece back up and running?'

Ela simply nodded at the request.

'Good, fix it, then hold position. I'll go up top because I'm the most ambulatory of this fireteam's wounded and I need all three of you ready to nail this Victor Foxtrot. When I'm in position and I've noted his position, I'm going to get his attention. From there, I'll need the three of you to move on him and drop him as quickly as physically possible. I'll be depending on you, Rah?'

'Rah,' Elenskis replied.

'Yut,' Ela responded.

'HUA,' answered QT, my mind automatically translating the abbreviation of 'heard, understood, acknowledged'.

'Now, can someone help me up into the ducts?' I instructed, my wounds infuriating me. Elenskis and Ela immediately grabbed hold of me and hoisted me into the ducts where my arms practically took over; just climbing up into the system was excruciating. Between the lactic acid that'd begun to build up and the gash that contorted as I reached up, I felt like passing out. Biting down on my tongue, I pushed through the pain as I lifted myself up into the ducts before sliding onto my belly to crawl my way through the ship's ventilation. I stopped at a junction. *If I were a crazed psycho spec ops alien, where would I be and why wouldn't I have my partner's back?* I questioned myself. *The lift! Or the hatches!* I answered. *They need direct access to both levels for some reason. If the others are trying to access the secondary command terminal* ... I thought to myself, internally distracted before my heart stopped, *they can't get out. They must have gotten in via the airlock somehow but can't get back out, and they can't vent the ship until they're secure in engineering, otherwise, it'd be a waste of money venting a billion-credit killing machine,* I explained to myself. I slid through the central vent and took a hard left towards the aft part of the ship. I continued forward until I reached the access hatch that overlooked the briefing room. I surveyed the area. *Nothing ... how could that—* I wondered as my thoughts wandered off. I quickly realised that our adversary was employing an advanced thermal-light refraction unit. I began to search the room for anything out of the ordinary, besides the bodies and the distinct lack of primary lighting, most of the ship was relatively intact. The only thing that stood out was the flicker of sparks in the corner of my eye. I frowned as I repositioned to get a better look at where the sparks were coming from. As I looked on, a dumb grin began to creep across my face. *He's repairing the lift,* I noted to myself. I lifted my arm and tapped a tile on my CPI.

'*TARGET, STARBOARD ELEVATOR. LOOK FOR SPARKS. ENGAGE ON MY MARK,*' I texted.

'*LIMA CHARLIE, AWAITING SIGNAL,*' Elenskis typed back. Rubbing the inside of my palm, I crawled forward to an access cover just past the elevator and quietly unclipped the cover covering it before slipping into the duct and dropping down left of the elevator. As I landed on the deck below, rolling away to pad my impact, a blade swung towards me from the left, barely missing me as I rolled. Reflexively, I turned towards my assailant and launched myself into my attacker. As his blade careened wildly into the air, I latched onto his shoulder, hurling him overhead. *Shajst!* I hissed as I realised what I'd just done. The guardsman quickly recovered from his momentary incapacitation and spun to face me. The voiceless *brafik* lunged for me. He switched blades and swung with his left instead. I shifted left as the blade glided past me, but as I shifted, the crackle of another blade hissed beside my abdomen. He was too quick, however, and my body slammed into his arm. With his momentum avoided, I latched onto his shoulder and pushed him back.

'Mark!' I yelled as the guard recovered. Infuriated at my continued resilience, the guard triggered both blades and rushed for me. At that moment, QT latched onto the guard's neck and threw it into Elenskis' jumping kick to the jaw. The creature began to flail wildly as it desperately attempted to regain control of the situation. Without any direction, QT, Elenskis, and Ela approached the stunned bastard and quickly disarmed the creature before holding it down. Ela reached for the neural lace that lined its armour, but as Ela approached its skull, it roared in anger over the telepathic link, causing our brains to scream in anguish at the intrusion. In agony, Ela plucked the guard's combat dagger from its webbing and moved to bury it in the creature, but I snatched her wrist. 'We need to know what the *brafik* is going on!' I intoned as I held her powerful arm at bay. Finally, she relented, instead slashing at the creature's major leg muscles.

'Well, that just happened. Patch him up and get him to the brig,' I instructed before pausing to catch my breath and inspecting my injuries. The cut on my abdomen had partially reopened due to the excessive movement that I'd endured in the fight, but the patch remained strong.

'Okay, *gospadinas*, the guards downstairs most likely know that the top deck's compromised, which means they'll be working towards accessing the secondary bridge controls at double the pace they were. So, lets beat them to it,' I instructed.

'Rah,' Lycaon replied. Ela and QT immediately made their way towards the bridge to inspect the bulkhead that divided the bridge and the passageway. Ela took one look at it before turning to me.

'Okay, the doors are tied directly to the central electrical lines, so when the EMP hit us, it overloaded the circuit. The circuit breaker kicked in just as the doors sealed. Now, because we're running on emergency power, that's barely keeping life support and gravity on. QT and I will only have a few seconds to duck onto the bridge to get repairs underway. I'll need someone to head to the …' Ela's voice trailed off as she traced the power grid, '… aft circuit breaker to the right of the central table,' Ela instructed as she pointed back down the passageway.

'I've got it,' I replied before jogging off. I strode over to the circuit breaker's location, marked by an orange cover. Kneeling, I lifted the covering away to reveal a single red handle and a cluster of switches beside it. 'What am I getting?' I clarified.

'There should be a large red lever next to a cluster of switches! Get the lever and we'll be in business!'

'Understood!' I replied.

'Okay, three!' Ela began to call. 'Two! One! Hit it now!' Ela barked.

I yanked back the lever, and sparks exploded through the ship before converging at the door disengaging the locks. The door parted to reveal the bridge. Ela and QT quickly slipped through the gap just before the door slammed shut again, the lockdown protocols returning to effect. My earpiece crackled to life.

'Okay, we're in,' QT reported. 'We'll need a couple of minutes to bring Samuel's console back online,' he continued.

'Understood, we'll hold the fort,' I replied before inspecting my M18. It was back in action. I activated the weapon and cocked the weapon's cooling hammer.

Elenskis settled into a corner of cover to my left while I nestled to the right of the passageway. The thud of the alien fists echoed through the ship as one desperately struggled to work its way into a hatchway to reach the upper levels while the other continued to work at the secondary bridge controls. Muffled thuds rang out across the lower deck as the well deck depressurised, dragging anything unsecured into the cold vacuum of space before it quickly resealed. Moments later, nodules across the *Fortuna*'s hull extended and began to siphon off the excess energy caused by the EMP.

'Weapons operable,' Ela reported. 'Disengaging from boarding craft and going loud,' Ela continued. Moments later, the Fortuna's automatic detection systems pinged as it registered the strike. 'Target vessel neutralised. Lifting lockdown,' Ela reported.

Moments later, the doors retracted, and the klaxons and emergency lights wound down. I slumped down into the corner that I'd been kneeling in, careful to rest my weapon in a nearby corner. *It's over,* I thought to myself. Of course, it wasn't, but I couldn't be brafiked to be rational right then and there. From here, I was coaxed into the ship's medical bay where I was quickly sedated.

Chapter 22
Back on the horse

2330 hours Zulu 08/01/2439 (Military Calendar), UNV Morte Fortuna

My eyes flickered open slowly as I groggily awoke from my Mort-induced slumber. I lifted myself onto my elbows as a burst of pain cut through my side. *The Mort and adrenaline have well and truly worn off,* I thought to myself. I lifted my tank top to clearly inspect my wound. Tomas had seemingly put my side through the rigours of dermal regeneration, leaving just enough of a wound to create a faint scar. *How sweet of him,* I thought to myself. I slipped out of the hospital bed and onto my feet, the cold embrace of the deck pulsing up through my body like a piercing nail. I hobbled out into the briefing room to inspect our situation. 'SITREP, *gospadinas*!' I hissed as I clenched my side. Lycaon turned to face me. QT came rushing over to me.

'I don't think you should be up and walking,' QT kindly suggested.

'And I don't think you should be offering any helpful advice,' I bitterly replied. I'd been bed-bound for four hours in intense surgery while my ship was a sitting *raet* waiting to be blown away at a moment's notice; I wasn't going to be sitting this out if I could help it.

'Uh … Sara,' Elenskis attempted to interject.

'I said, SITREP!' I barked through clenched teeth as I hobbled towards the bridge. When I arrived, I witnessed an odd sight: Evans and Harmon were at the helm. 'Okay, why are those two at the helm?' I asked, concerned.

'Um, because the helmsmen were killed?' Harmon said bluntly.

'You're rated to fly more than a Condor?' I questioned sceptically.

'Uh-huh,' said Harmon with a smug tone.

'It's from our time in the RAAF, boss. You see, historically, national air forces were the only branch to handle the fourth and fifth dimensions of warfare, and with the exception of the United States, unification didn't change that concept. Roughly four hundred years since Unification Day and the creation of the Military Forces Act 2091 and the formation of the Unified Sol Command, all pilots within the sphere of the USC are required to not only be rated for air superiority and stellar superiority operations but also rated for flying any stellar craft within two brackets of your own stellar certification. The *Fortuna* fits that bill,' Evans explained.

I pursed and then flexed my lips, my anger slowly subsiding. 'Okay, so where do we stand?' I asked as I calmly settled into the captain's chair.

'Well firstly, our POW is holding fine. He can't walk, but he isn't bleeding any more. And we've been down for longer than four hours, boss,' QT interjected as he strode up beside me.

I frowned.

'Check your chronometer; we've been offline—and you've been unconscious—for the last four days, ma'am,' he said with trepidation.

'And we got our long-range transceiver back online only a few moments ago, and we've just reconnected to the net. It ain't looking good,' Hesch replied.

'Why? What's happened?' I continued.

'From after-action reports and Taskforce recovery team debriefings, what happened to us four days ago wasn't an isolated event,' Hesch relayed. 'From the sounds of it, single-ship boarding parties were deployed against all Proteus vessels and installations. Only seven percent of the twenty Operation Salvation fireteams were able to repel borders. The numbers don't get much better from there: out of the forty Sectorial Command Vessels such as the *Yamamoto*, only thirty-five percent of SCVs survived what is now being referred to by OPSI as Operation Whiplash,' Hesch reported.

My heart skipped a beat as the information settled in. 'How the *Brafiksjot* did they get past the Enzo Line? We had them contained. Why'd they get offensive now?' I asked, confused as to how their retaliatory strike was so effective.

'It wasn't a conventional assault. These guards—which OSI are now referring to as "Proteus Killers"—were trained and equipped to bypass conventional forces and gut us specifically. Due to our strategic capabilities, they were given our then-current airlock codes,' Hesch explained.

My mouth opened in shock and understanding. 'Which is why they could get in but couldn't get out the way they came without the secondary bridge controls. When they reactivated the airlock console and input the keys, the system reset the access key,' I answered, staring blankly out towards the black of space. 'Do we at least have anything from the Deep Reconnaissance Platoon?' I asked returning my thoughts to the present situation and hoping for some better news.

'Well, yes and no,' Hesch replied.

I clenched my fist. 'For *brafik*'s sake!' I hissed in anger. 'Nothing can be simple, can it?' I offhandedly remarked as I released my fist. 'What do they have, and what's the catch?'

'Well, the Deep Reconnaissance Platoon arrived at HP One Seventy-Two Dash Four Twenty-Seven at Twelve Forty-Four hours Zulu and immediately noticed an atypically large guard presence for an installation referred to in guard transmissions as a simple ground side relay station. Upon going ground side at thirteen thirty using an orbiting debris field, members of Second DRP noted a heavily fortified beachhead on the north-western side of the complex and a sizeable military presence on the south-eastern front. Second DRP noted a sizeable underwater reservoir that was connected to a river that ran down from the southern mountains. These notifications were transmitted at fourteen thirty before the platoon entered the stream and moved for the reservoir. From here, all communications with Second DRP ceased until seventeen twenty hours Zulu. Their last transmission reads, "Accuser location verified. Substantiating documentation attached",'

'So, what did they attach?'

'Second DRP transmitted three documents but only two-thirds of the material was transmitted before the signal was drowned out. They transmitted this,' Hesch replied, as he passed across an image obviously taken by one of the marine's helmet cameras.

It was an image of a large black spire-like structure at the centre of a silo-like building. Observation towers surrounded the perimeter, and drones (most likely sensor probes) investigated the object for answers to questions beyond its comprehension. The dark pylon sat atop an elaborate pyramid that pulsed with white energy. Black angular columns protruded out from the main structure and stretched down the length of the base diagonally. But they didn't serve any support function. They looked as though they channelled the energies harnessed by the weapon. At equal intervals, presumably on all sides of the weapon, was a single five-metre-wide and two-metre-deep river-like incision in the metal that surrounded the weapon's potentially immense reactor. From the base protruded two claw-shaped prongs that reached the roof of the cavern. I passed the image back to Hesch who passed me the other images.

The other two images were only partial but they both showcased the fortress's bastion-like nature. The bastion was built around a six-kilometre-long Honour-class dreadnought and was surrounded by two two-metre perimeter-wall-like concussive barriers. Interwoven between the two concussive barriers was a honeycomb of infantry barracks and motor pools for the thousands of vehicles and soldiers that manned the installation. At the centre was the Honour-class dreadnought. They'd lifted the plating from the lower stations, apparently, and lowered many of the administrative functions of the ship groundside, leaving only the topside guns intact. At the centre—and presumably the fort's central power supply—sat the intimidating antimatter reactor. It had been detached from the ship for quite some time, from the looks of it, and powered the four large ballistic shield generators that were placed around the facility. I put the satellite image down and reached for the facility floor plan before nestling it on the digital image reader on my chair's armrest. Moments later, the Fortuna's holographic projectors kicked into life, creating a 3D render of the fortress's floor plan. While much of the inner schematics were sketchy, the outer periphery and the reservoir were relatively clear. With all this, however, it still didn't explain how 2nd DRP was able to access the Accuser's research silo. I flicked off the display and turned to Lycaon.

'Is there anything else we've been able to recover? Equipment readouts? Topographical notes? Spectral anomalies?' My hopes were riding on harder evidence.

'Negative, ma'am. Shadow Director Rokkaku had all equipment readouts and reports sealed under the Powers Act,' Hesch reported.

'Well, looks like I'll be having a conversation with the director, but first I need to have a conversation with our resident POW,' I replied with a sigh. 'Excellent work, gospadins and gospadinas,' I said as I rose from the chair and strode towards the brig.

++++

The translucent door snapped open with a hiss, and I stepped into the tight compartment. Before me sat the dragoon, its legs shackled, and its hands bound together by neural restraints. Now in the light of a powered ship, I realised something: the creature wasn't tall and broad like conventional dragoons. It was slender, powerful, and it possessed a seemingly feminine poise. As my brows narrowed, I tapped a series of tiles on my CPI and lifted the audio-visual haze that encompassed the creature. As its red eyes opened and its gaze rose to meet mine, curiosity began to dance through my thoughts. 'You're a brood mother,' I remarked as I leaned in to inspect the number: 2707. 'You were in the same batch of Kaera as Superior Two Seven Oh Five,' I remarked, genuinely intrigued. 'Don't bother trying to speak with telepathy; we had your biological implants surgically removed; you'll have to get by with filthy spoken language,' I remarked with a sardonic smile.

'You truly are honour thieves,' the creature finally said, its perfect fluent speech somewhat of a surprise to me.

'How's that?' I asked, for once genuinely intrigued.

'The makers give brood mothers a lot of lateral will, and from my experience, I'd seen your kind to be honourable, even if you've stolen the Maker's souls. But I'd heard my sister's stories from the tanks: that you would steal the honour from the soulless. But I'd never quite believed her when she'd said it. But for a woman to defile my blood tie, to defile the only two privileges I have—war and death—she has to be right,' the creature spoke.

Now I was curious. 'Why were you attached to this operation? You're a brood mother, your skills and abilities aren't in boarding actions,' I began to explain.

'I wanted to see the death stealer,' she calmly remarked, before lowering her head and closing her eyes.

With a tap of my CPI, the neural restraints resumed.

++++

I adjusted my dress uniform's collar as my side released a burst of pain. *Oh,* brafiksjot *off,* I thought to myself as Mariko appeared by my side. 'The director is waiting, ma'am,' Mariko reported.

'Then let's not keep her waiting, shall we?' I questioned, gesturing for Mariko to open the line. 'Director on deck!' I called snapping to attention.

'Should you be standing?' Director Mizuka said.

'The mission comes first, over everything else,' I replied.

'At ease, Specialist,' Chihiro responded, sincerely worried for me. I complied with her command; no complaint was coming out of me on that issue. 'So, what do you need?' Chihiro finally asked, knowing full well I never report something without a request.

'I need the entire Unified Security Military at my disposal,'

The director was noticeably taken aback. 'That's a hefty request, Sara, I'm going to need a really good reason.'

'We've found the Accuser, ma'am.' At this, the director was shocked.

'You've found it?' Chihiro questioned. 'Are you sure?'

'About as sure as anyone could be.'

'Any evidence?'

'In case Director Rokkaku neglected to inform you, I requisitioned a Deep Reconnaissance Platoon to reconnoitre the Kalani System—specifically a fortress world at the quadrant's heart known as "HP127-427" to the Taskforce Corps of Cartography. At a cursory glance, the planet appears to be merely a subspace relay station but upon further inspection, it is a fortress world protecting no particularly valuable assets. The only recorded military installation is on the planet's only equatorial continent, on the most northern part of the continent. Further investigation on the part of Second DRP uncovered a circular cavern that contained an alien structure that was being studied by Kalil acolytes,' I explained. 'Second DRP was able to upload two and a half documents before their upload was intercepted and they were presumed KIA,' I continued as I turned to a data port and transferred the data to Director Mizuka.

Chihiro paused to inspect the files before returning her gaze to me. 'Well, this is certainly tantalising information. Is there anything else to prove your claim?' Chihiro asked enthusiastically.

'I'm afraid not, ma'am, but field telemetry from the marine BDUs and their environmental arrays has not been released to us per Shadow Director Rokkaku's orders which may reveal something.'

Director Mizuka let out a muffled sigh. 'Okay, I'll have the records unsealed for you and I'll pass on your findings to the committee.'

Chapter 23
Truths written in black ink

2340 hours Zulu 08/01/2439 (Military Calendar), Taskforce Headquarters [FILE ACCESSED 2440]

Director Mizuka let out a sigh as the video feed faded. 'What was he thinking?' she exclaimed as Ada appeared beside her.

'Unknown. Shadow Director Rokkaku provided no rationalisation for his actions.'

'Get me a line to Sasaki, this is absolutely unacceptable,' Chihiro hissed.

Ada flickered as she attempted to bring up a live feed. 'I apologise, Shadow Director Rokkaku is unreachable at this time.'

'Contact security forces at his location and have them secure the Shadow Director,' Chihiro instructed.

'Contacting naval infantry and the master-at-arms aboard the UNV *Hannibal*', Ada reported. 'Bringing up operations feed.' Six helmet camera feeds flickered to life and weapons swept the area.

'Clear!' called one of the marines.

'Clear!' reported another. The other four reported in quickly before the ship's master-at-arms strode into the room, weapon in hand.

'By the gods!' the master-at-arms exclaimed. Ada pulled up the master-at-arms' combat feed. For once, even Chihiro quietly gasped. Shadow Director Sasaki Rokkaku lay slumped to the side of his oak table, a katana buried in his abdomen. He'd committed *seppuku*, a form of honourable suicide under the traditional warrior's code of *Bushido*, to which Rokkaku had sworn an oath when he enlisted in the Taskforce. The master-at-arms turned to the oak table where a handwritten letter, written in ancient Japanese remained. It read:

> Director Mizuka, forgive me. If you are reading this, then my work is done. I am dead and the Taskforce lives to see another day. I struggle to write this: the voices, they whisper to me even now. Initially, I had thought it just a passing dream, a whisper of my subconscious that would soon pass as quickly as it had arrived. But soon over the days and months of this cycle, my voice began to fade. The voices whispered to me while I stood awake. Soon even my actions were not my own. What little of my personality remains suspects these voices to be the Guards' doing. Please forgive me for my transgressions.
> —Sasaki

Chihiro looked at the script in shock as she flawlessly translated her native tongue. She gritted her teeth as she turned off the display in front of her. She turned to Ada.

'Get those records unsealed!' Chihiro began with fury, her skin flushed for the first time in centuries. 'Convene the committee! And have all commands move to REDCON One!' Chihiro hissed.

'All amenities are in order, ma'am,' Ada replied an instant later.

'What did the armour record?' Chihiro inquired as she poured a glass of saké.

'Air Corps Special Signals and Marine Corps Data Recovery teams were able to recover facets of Second Deep Reconnaissance Platoon's sensor readouts,' Ada explained.

'Did ACSS and MCDR extract anything particular?' Chihiro queried with an inhuman fury.

'Powered combat suit five seven three one detected an extremely high generation rate of electrical signals,'

'But that's to be expected: it's a Wayfarer facility manned by legionaries that communicate with wireless electrical signals,' Chihiro replied with confused frustration.

'That's what ACSS, MCDR, and Second DRP initially assumed as well.' Ada paused. 'But upon closer inspection, the electrical signals were emanating from the object at the centre of the cavern.'

Chihiro's eyes widened. 'Did Second DRP report any atypical satellites in low orbit above the planet?'

'Affirmative, Second DRP and Taskforce Corps of Cartography confirmed that there are indeed over one hundred and fifty alien satellites in low orbit above the planet,'

'They're right,' Chihiro muttered.

'Affirmative, ma'am.'

'Is the committee in session?' Chihiro questioned.

'Affirmative, Director Mizuka, the conference room is the first door to the left,' Ada explained. Chihiro lifted herself out of her chair, her mahogany table suddenly repugnant to the touch as she braced against it. She calmed her breath as she straightened her uniform.

'Can't be looking unprofessional, now can we?' Chihiro rhetorically commented.

'No, ma'am,' Ada said.

With her calm returned, Chihiro strode out of her office and into the main passageway; she'd never wanted anything glamourous like her predecessors. She turned to the first door on the left, her retina-mounted display generating the words *COMMITTEE MEETING IN SESSION* atop the doorway. Chihiro paused to take one final breath before she entered the room. The committee snapped to attention as she strode in, her palm quickly waiving the formalities.

'What's going on?' Field Marshal Blaire boomed in confusion.

'What's happened to Shadow Director Rokkaku?' Agent Sinamon leapt in.

Chihiro took another deep breath, showing true shock and fear for the first time before the committee in over forty years. 'Shadow Director Sasaki Rokkaku is dead,' Mizuka said. She paused to download the master-at-arms' report. 'At twenty-two fifty-nine hours Zulu, Shadow Director Sasaki Rokkaku committed seppuku as a result of jacking. Jacking, for those who are unaware, is the art of accessing an individual's personality and their prestige and power via their neural implants that allow them to interact with their organisation remotely. From there, hackers begin to override the target's personality and will, effectively creating a—' Chihiro's voice trailed off as her emotions began to run high, '—living drone from the body,' she continued.

'Noting his lack of control and recent decisions, Shadow Director Rokkaku took matters into his own hands and committed military suicide to prevent further contamination by the enemy and to atone for his failure to protect his branch from intrusion.' Mizuka finished, her throat choking up. The committee was shocked.

'This is outrageous! We must initiate Security Protocol Omega!' exclaimed Director Akero, head of the Unified Research Command. 'Aye's began to ring out through the room.

'Take a seat, Director; there is another, far more pressing matter at hand,' Chihiro continued, her tone darkening.

The committee fell silent. *What could be more important than internal affairs?* they wondered.

'Fifteenth Special Operations Group: Proteus. More specifically, assets from Fourth Asymmetrical Combat Detachment, callsign "Crown Jewel", have located the Accuser,' Chihiro explained.

At this, a hushed murmur began to rumble through the room. 'Do they have proof?' Agent Sinamon asked this time.

'Files recovered from Kasiel's Reach were cross-referenced with Void Wanderer transport logs and intercepted Honour Guard transmissions from the Kalani System. After cross-examining the evidence, the planet designated HP172-427 by the Taskforce Corps of Cartography was marked as a potential location for the Accuser weapon system. At Asymmetrical Combat Officer Hart's request, Shadow Director Rokkaku deployed Second Deep Reconnaissance Platoon into the heart of Honour Guard territory.' Mizuka paused before continuing. 'There they were able to successfully verify the location of the Accuser Weapon System. Verification was based on historical descriptions and suit sensor readings recovered from the marine's data burst before they were presumably killed by Wayfarer security forces on sight,' Mizuka explained.

The committee looked at her as she released the three files she'd received from Sara to the rest of the committee. 'How do we know that this wasn't all fabricated by Sasaki?' Admiral Hurt suggested, immediately sceptical of the evidence.

'We really don't, but after months of hunting for this weapon this is the best lead we've gotten from any of our teams.' Chihiro paused. 'While I recognise the potential dangers of following this lead—' Chihiro began before Commandant Strandquist interrupted her response.

'I don't think you realise the potential dangers, ma'am,' Strandquist interjected as she pulled up a map of the local galaxy. 'HP172-427 is at the heart of Honour Guard space, six systems past the Enzo Line!' Strandquist exclaimed. 'We'd need a force that's over half our combined size!' Strandquist continued, pausing for effect. 'We'd have to pull units from just under a dozen different commands and forces from the Enzo Line itself which would make us vulnerable to literally *any* Honour Guard incursion all for a potentially imaginary weapon!' Strandquist hissed. A low hum of agreement echoed through the chamber.

'That's true, but, what if this isn't just a fabricated threat?' Chihiro retorted back. 'What if there is such a thing as an Accuser weapon system? If there is such a weapon, playing it safe won't matter in the slightest, because a weapon that kills on a universal scale via subspace telepathy doesn't give a damn about your manoeuvres and lines and formations!' Chihiro exclaimed.

'There are four ways this can turn out: one, Commandant Strandquist is right and it's all an Honour Guard ploy to move us out of position. So, we lose territory, we lose control, but that territory will remain capturable—we adapt, we survive, we win. All we lose is time. Two, we take our fleets and punch a hole through their lines to HP172-427 and discover that this weapon does exist, we have the chance to stop the Honour Guard threat once and for all. Or we take Commandant Strandquist's advice and continue to observe, holding our lines against the Honour Guard threat.

'In this case, there are two possible outcomes: the Honour Guard fires the Accuser, and we all die because we didn't have the balls to investigate a possible threat, or we survive because the Accuser never existed, it was merely bait.' Mizuka paused as she recollected her thoughts. 'The decision now falls to the committee: commit us to our duty or commit us to our fears?' Chihiro finished.

The committee fell silent.

Chapter 24
To stir a sleeping giant

UNV Morte Fortuna, 0001 hours Zulu, 09/01/2439 (Military Calendar)

I sat in the captain's chair, my left foot impatiently tapping the floor as I leaned heavily against the chair's armrest. Patience was never my strong suit. Hesch, as if woken from slumber, was abuzz with life. 'I've got wireless chatter on the Taf Net!' Hesch remarked. 'Units from all across Andromeda are being mobilised! And I've got reports that Enzo Line patrols are being redirected to rally point—' Hesch's voice trailed off as he searched for the rally point. 'Rally point Uniform Echo four niner three dash seven four niner!' Hesch reported. Mariko quickly pulled up the map on my retina and marked the location. I began to smile ironically. *Just on the edge of the Enzo Line, at Aiken Praim,* I thought to myself.

'Ma'am, we're receiving a transmission from Director Mizuka!' Hesch continued.

'Have it sent to my quarters,' I instructed.

'Transferring to quarters, aye, ma'am,' Hesch replied. I spun the captain's chair around and jogged over to my quarters where I quickly brushed myself down before activating the feed. I snapped to attention.

'Forget the formalities, Sara, you've received a battlefield promotion,' replied Chihiro. I looked at her confused.

'To what?' I asked, wondering what she was talking about.

'As of twenty-three fifty-nine hours Zulu, you are now Grand Admiral of the Navies and Shadow Director of the Taskforce. With the death of Shadow Director Rokkaku—' Chihiro began to explain, I stared at her in shock.

'Sasa—' I began to say as Chihiro continued.

'Yes, he had been under the sway of the Kalil intelligence service, he committed seppuku just after sealing the marine sensor data to ensure that he couldn't do any lasting damage to the Taskforce,' Chihiro continued, her cold exterior bemusing to me. *How could you care so little for someone?* I wondered. 'I put your data to the committee: after a heated debate, the Operations, Personnel, and Security Intelligence Committee has authorised a direct-action operation against Honour Guard forces protecting HP172-427 due to the dangers of the unknown. I can assure you, however, it was a difficult vote. Never has the committee been so divided in its history,' Mizuka explained.

'What was the vote?' I asked, curious as to who the objectors were.

'The vote was six to six, and because I cannot formally vote as part of the committee, the decision had to come at a compromise.'

No OPSI decision has come to a deadlock in over two hundred years! I thought to myself.

'Your operation has been approved, but I cannot authorise your original request, the risk that it is an Honour Guard diversion is too great,' she explained. 'As such, forces from across Taskforce-controlled space are currently being recalled and rerouted to the fastest entry point into Kalil territory; their number will be greatly lower than your original request, but they will be under your command, Shadow Director.'

I looked on in shock. 'Thank you, ma'am…' My heart swelled with excitement and fear. *What if I fail? What if* we *fail?* I wondered before quickly ignoring the thought. It wasn't useful for the mission.

'That is all, Shadow Director Hart,' Chihiro replied before flicking off the feed. I let out a loud sigh as I turned, a pulse of pain bouncing across my forehead before I strode out to Lycaon.

'What's the word?' Elenskis queried immediately, Lycaon and the rest of the Fortuna's crew looking in with interest.

I looked up to face my team. 'We've got war, *gospadinas,*' I said with a smirk.

'Get some!' they cried.

'But we've got some work to do before that, *gospadins* and *gospadinas*, get us to rally point UE493-749,' I instructed.

'Aye, ma'am,' bridge crew replied in unison.

'Then what're you waiting for?' I boomed with newfound excitement. 'Get moving!'

With that, the bridge kicked back into motion as the sailors and airmen quickly locked into their impact seats. Hesch activated the ship's jump alarms as he hit the intercom, Lycaon strapping in as he spoke.

'All stations, all Stations, prepare for jump, this is not a drill,' Hesch reported as the orange lights flickered to life. Safae and Mariko appeared moments later as Samuels began to speak.

'Mariko! Safae! Evans! Confirm jump coords!' he requested, the two AIs appearing beside me as he called. 'Confirm coords UE493-749?' Samuels barked.

'Affirmative!' Mariko replied.

'Aye,' answered Safae.

'Gotcha!' called Evans.

'Navigation?' Michiko boomed as she strode onto the bridge.

'Coordinates input!' relayed Samuels.

'Helm?' Stratton requested.

'Engines responsive,' Evans confirmed. 'Controls positive.' reported Harmon.

'Engineering?'

'Reactor power routing to engines and FTL. Reactor within margins.' Sandon reported.

'Security?'

'Secured and stowed,' casually replied Safae.

'Communications?'

'Secured for jump.' responded Hesch.

'Combat?'

'Secured for transit.' reported Phar at his secondary combat information station.

'All hands secured for jump!' Hesch reported before Michiko turned to face me.

'All departments report secured for jump, ma'am,' said Michiko, her posture loose.

'Jump computer locked, FTL green across the board. Orders, ma'am?' requested Harmon.

'Helm, execute jump,' I instructed.

'Executing jump protocol,' replied Michiko as she adjusted her posture and leaned over to the wall-mounted container, entered her four-digit security code and snatched up the jump key. Key in hand, she strode down to our two helmsmen and passed it to Evans who carefully inserted it into the *Fortuna*'s control panel. With the key inserted, he twisted it counterclockwise.

'Jump clock is running,' reported Evans as the ten-second timer appeared overhead.

'Ten seconds to FTL,' reported Hesch. 'Nine, eight, seven—'

'Singularity active,' reported Harmon as Hesch continued his count down.

'Six—'

'Rift created,'

'—Five, four, three, two, one,' said Hesch in unison with Harmon.

'Jumping!'

At the helmsman's report, the ship's quark pair released, and we were thrown into the wild black of the Aether. 'Glide nominal, ma'am,' reported Harmon as the ship's alarms flickered off.

'ETA one hour, ma'am,' reported Safae, her Abetra accent and attire an odd change to say the least.

++++

The *Morte Fortuna* returned to normal space with a mild jolt before silently gliding through the airless void.

'Six ships on FARSIGHT, ma'am,' reported McGhee.

'Understood. Bosun, contact those vessels,' I instructed

'Hailing, aye, ma'am,' Hesch replied as he activated his comm piece, getting to work immediately. 'Ma'am, vessel commanders are awaiting your transmission,' he reported.

'Very well; connect the line, Petty Officer,' I instructed.

'Connecting, aye.'

Moments later, the holographic forms of the other six captains appeared before me.

'Shadow Director on deck!' they declared as they snapped to attention.

'At ease,' I instructed, their postures relaxing as I said the words. 'Which fleets are you from?' I began, knowing full well who and where they were from already.

'Well, Captain Coe and I are from the First Fleet, ma'am,' reported Commander Gyi.

'Commander Kara and I are from the Eighth,' replied Lieutenant Commander Falyr.

'And Lieutenant Commander Kaga and I are from the Twelfth, ma'am,' specified Commander Kenza. I frowned in confusion as I registered the details.

'Why're you so far out from your parent fleets?'

'Question of our lives, ma'am. UNS had us redeployed to the Enzo Line months ago. Thought the local forces could handle it by themselves, but what do we know?' Commander Gyi replied.

'Well, gentlemen, I've got a war to plan for. I'll leave you in the capable hands of my EA, Commander Stratton. Whatever she says goes. She is my right hand, understood?'

'Clearly,' the officers said with a nod.

'Good. Bosun, notify Mr Phar that I'm coming down and have QT-2 meet me at the CIC as well.'

'Aye, aye,' Hesch replied.

With that, I spun my chair around and left the bridge. 'Commander Stratton, you have the conn,' I instructed.

Stratton's reply of 'Aye, aye,' rang behind me as she settled into the captain's chair to relay the *Morte*'s requirements and the procedures to synchronise such a large fleet's battle network. I strode past the briefing room's table as QT appeared by my side.

'Sara,' he said as I strode towards the combat information centre, my limp finally gone.

'QT,' I replied in response, laser-focused on the road ahead of me. I strode up to the CIC's doorway, activated the release mechanism and stepped into the hybrid compartment. Due to space constraints, the *Morte Fortuna* had centralised almost all of the combat information centre's functions to enable the only assigned Tactical Action Officer to coordinate all functions. As I strode in, I was honestly taken aback by the design of the integrated CIC. Until now, I hadn't seen it in action. Lieutenant Phar unhooked his skull from the base of a modified Armis skeleton at the centre of the room. Last I'd seen the CIC there hadn't been a chair. Lieutenant Phar snapped to attention as he got to his feet. I waved him to ease.

'So, what do you need, ma'am?' asked Phar.

'I'm going to need your tactical planning systems, Lieutenant.'

'Aye, aye,' he replied as he activated something on his CPI. Moments later, the chair he had just been seated in retracted into the floor and an overhead Tangible Holographic Plasma projector began to generate the system map.

'Oh boy,' I remarked.

'Yes, ma'am,' Phar responded, his head shaking as he looked at the feed.

'Firstly, what's our task force make up?' I asked, turning to QT-2.

'The UMC has, surprisingly, provided fifty marine expeditionary forces, the UNS has provided twenty-seven fleets, the UAC has committed thirteen major commands and, surprisingly, the UA has only committed complete forces from six named theatre commands with reserve units holding position along the Enzo Line for orders,' QT reported. 'Specifically, the UMC has committed fifty percent of its forces, the UNS just twenty-seven percent, the UAC approximately thirteen point five percent and the UA has provided just under six point five percent of its total military capabilities,' QT explained. Always the statistician.

'Okay, that gives us much more to play with than I was expecting but not nearly as much as I was hoping for.'

At that Phar frowned. 'You think we're going to be able to get through their lines with that small a force?' Phar asked, almost rhetorically.

'We'll see, Lieutenant,' I said as I turned back towards the display.

I glanced over the seemingly benign defences between our current staging ground and HP 172-427. Next to no defensive escorts or static emplacements anywhere to be seen, but for over two and a half years, the Enzo Line had claimed thousands of sailors and marines. There were six systems between us and our objective. Traditionally, a force this size would jump directly to the target, but Void Wanderer FTL inhibitors made that impossible. The only way in or out of the system was either by neutralising the individual Inhibitors in each system or by making six precision jumps into inhibitor-free zones near the system border. Neither was practical, but one had to be done.

'So, what's our move?' the Lieutenant prompted.

'We're going to have to fight our way through, inch by inch,' I said plainly. Phar just shook his head.

'That's what every admiral and general has said for the last two and a half years, ma'am,' he said with resignation in his voice.

'Then we do it right the first time: we pick apart their strategy piece by piece then we start from there.'

'But that's the issue, ma'am: the Taskforce hasn't been able to find any discernible tactic for the last two years,' Phar retorted with emphasis.

'You know, they said that there wasn't any logic in what I did back on the Hakon all those years ago. I detonated twelve micro fusion reactors to wipe out advancing Wayfarer forces in close proximity to friendly forces and I was criticised for using excessive force *and* having no method. Those *brafik*wits up at NAVCOM couldn't see *shajst* coming from the arse end of a *skuk* if it was staring them in the face,' I replied with a fire in my words.

'Aye, ma'am,' Phar replied with a tenuous smile. 'So, what's our game plan?' he quickly added as I looked over the map.

'Well—' I began, my words trailing off. As I looked over the first-star system, my mind began to race with variables and data as I continued. 'They've got airbases on Sierra Alpha Three Oh Two Dash Six Eighteen and Sierra Alpha Oh Seventy-Four Dash Niner Thirty-One.' I explained as I indicated towards the moon closest to the line and its diagonal counterpart.

The lieutenant looked at me confused. 'How do you know that?'

'The satellites have a roaming electrical storm that interferes with FARSIGHT, and there's no way they could hide within the system's nearby nebula because of the particle density,' I explained.

'There's only one problem with your hypothesis: UNS destroyers entering these areas have reported corvettes and carriers conducting interception operations within hours. Nothing, not even Void Wanderer vessels, have the engines to provide efficient escape velocity to conduct such tight interception operations,' Lieutenant Phar retorted.

'Then they've got another deployment method for their capital ships,' I explained. I paused and plugged into the network to review the combat footage recovered from the UNV *Saratoga* and hundreds of other ships. I sped through the data with inhuman speed as I processed thousands of hours of data. 'There,' I remarked as I pulled up the image beside the map. A frown creased along my TAO's brow.

'What am I looking at?'

'A subspace anchor,' interjected QT-2. Phar glanced at him with even more confusion.

'I don't see anything.'

'That's because you're looking at the wrong thing, Lieutenant,' QT began. 'Look at the directed energy weapon shots,' he remarked, pointing up towards the top left of the photograph. Phar seemed to freeze in place as he gazed at the image.

'It's miscoloured,' he muttered in understanding. 'But why would they need a subspace anchor if they've got a field of subspace inhibitors?' he quickly added.

'Because it's a shortcut; it allows quick-response forces to move from staging ground to the AOE* without having to keep their FTL systems on standby and jump coordinates perpetually locked in,' QT elaborated as the Lieutenant nodded in agreement.

'So, any other brilliant ideas?' Phar asked.

'Well, Void Wanderer naval tactics in the last three years have always revolved around misdirection. Every time the Taskforce has been punched in the jaw, it's been because we've reacted to a false threat and exposed our forces to the real one. Without any particularly tantalising features to misdirect our attention in the region, they're going to rely on conventional manoeuvres, but they aren't stupid. They've been preparing for this day since the start of the war … and that's all I can really know for certain,' I admitted. 'But I'm open to hypothesises as to what they've got though,' I continued.

'Well, if I was a paranoid Victor Tango that had lost defensive momentum against an advancing force, I'd just deny the entire area to everyone. It shores up the defensive gap and removes the opposing force entirely,' Phar suggested. 'I'm assuming the guard has plenty of graviton warheads or an equivalent that would be the perfect catalyst for an unavoidable singularity that could easily control all movement in the region,' he quickly added.

'But what about the last system? It's empty space, there's nothing to catalyse a long-term containment solution,' QT interjected into the conversation, extending a sharp digit to the digital map.

I paused. *He's got a point.* 'There's got to be something to this; have reconnaissance teams noted anything of particular interest?' I suggested.

'One moment,' Phar replied as he looked over the UNS logs. He shook his head. 'Nothing's gotten that far. Second DRP is the only unit that's penetrated that far into the Enzo Line.'

I looked at him in shocked confusion.

'What?'

'You heard correctly,' Phar said with confidence. My face contorted in confusion.

'That's not right,' I muttered as I tapped my comm piece. 'Petty Officer Hesch,' I requested.

'Yes, ma'am?' came Hesch over the intercom.

'How the hell did Second DRP get to HP 172-427?' I queried.

'Why's that of importance, ma'am?' Hesch came back, his confusion obvious.

'Just answer it!'

'Second DRP reported that a local resistance force past the Enzo Line assisted their incursion into Honour Guard space,' Hesch finally said in a confused tone.

I continued to frown.

'Any more details?'

'Um—' Hesch paused. 'No, ma'am. Second DRP reported nothing more than a resistance force,'

I sighed. 'Understood. Thank you,' I said defeatedly. I flicked off my comm piece and turned back to Phar. 'This is one *azvod* of a gamble,' I finally admitted.

'Wasn't it always?' Phar said plainly. I let out another sigh.

'Certainly, but that was before lives were involved,'

'Welcome to the difficulties of command, ma'am,' Phar admitted in a sombre tone.

My fingers dug into my palm as I closed my eyes. 'What are the fastest ships we've got?'

Phar looked at me, puzzled. 'What do you mean?'

'Answer me, Lieutenant, what are the fastest ships in the UNS?'

The lieutenant paused to think the question over.

'Enterprise-class corvettes, Sara,' QT-2 answered helpfully. Phar simply nodded.

'They're some of the only ships that can match Void Wanderer engines and are only a few KPH slower than Void Wanderer Interceptors,' Phar said in confirmation.

'How many do we have in the task force?'

Phar stopped to inspect the inventory. 'Four hundred and five, ma'am,'

I slowly nodded as I thought over our options. 'Have them reassigned to their own specialised task force,' I ordered.

Phar wrinkled his face in confusion. 'You're not suggesting—' Phar began.

'Am I suggesting using these Enterprise-class corvettes to spring the trap? You're gods-damned right I am. We are on a razor's edge here and I need every advantage I can get.'

This time it was the Lieutenant who couldn't help but pause. 'I understand the necessity, but I wish there was another way,' he finally added.

'You and me both, Lieutenant,' I said solemnly.

'Okay, so assuming we can make it planetside, what's our next move? Orbital strike?' the lieutenant suggested. I zoomed in on the Wayfarer bastion before shaking my head.

'While we may open our offensive with an orbital strike to clear out any Wayfarer entrenchments outside the wall, we will ultimately need to conduct a ground assault. Do you see those field generators?' I asked, gesturing to a cluster of generators scattered through the fortress.

The lieutenant nodded.

'Those are Type 5 Terrestrial Field Originators. If their fields are concentrated across a small enough area, like they are now, just one of those has the tonnage to take anything we throw at it, and they've got four of them. The only specific drawbacks of the Type 5 is its coverage; it can only cover a surface area of three to four kilometres in its current configuration and it also can't form a semi-circular field—' I explained.

'—without weakening, meaning it relies on its defensive wall and conventional field projectors where the generators can't reach,' the Lieutenant interjected, synthesising my explanation.

'Affirmative, although it flat out can't create a semi-circular field without making contact with the ground and causing the regular drawbacks of all-encompassing fields asphyxiating the people you're protecting,' I quickly qualified before pulling up the detailed photograph of the facility. Its high walls were an unholy marriage of asymmetric stone archways, the perfectly defined and ordered tiers of a ziggurat and a flower peeled apart into its component petals, all wrapped in hexagonal obsession.

'But there's more to it; that perimeter wall isn't of Honour Guard origin.'

The lieutenant frowned. 'Then where's it from?'

'It's of Prethosi origin,' QT reported.

Phar frowned at him, pausing to think through the meaning of the name. 'You mean the Architects? Creators of civilisation architects?'

QT-2 and I nodded in reply.

'Then could you elaborate on how you came to this discovery?'

I nodded to QT as he began to speak.

'There has been an intrinsic link between the Honour Guard and the Architects for the last three years, and with our assignment to Operation Salutis, we started piecing together the location of the Accuser from transport routes and the kind of matériel being ferried in and out on those transport routes. A lot of that has been Architect translation notes and other recovered technology throughout Honour

Guard Space. As a result, all of Lycaon, except for Specialist Three, has become versed in Prethosi art and architecture. From the imagery recovered from Second DRP, that structure is definitely Prethosi; the design language of the Prethosi focuses on hexahedrons organised as multi-tiered ziggurats with ordinally placed archways. Coupled with the energy readings emanating from the walls, which are consistent with the few Prethosi artefacts that have been successfully activated, besides the atypical towers that make up the wall, I'm fairly certain this is their handiwork.'

'Great precursor technology as well,' Phar muttered to himself before asking, 'How does this affect the operation?'

'It means we won't be able to assault through their defences,' I answered. 'We'll need to rappel over the perimeter.'

'Which will be difficult as the *chemin de ronde* allows them to redirect troops at will,' QT quickly added, referring to the walkways embedded into the fortress walls.

'Agreed, which means we'll need to divert their forces. We need them to pour troops into every available direction, effectively crippling their capacity to concentrate on a single assault vector. Now, my guess based on the topography and the weapons emplacements noted by Second DRP is that the north-western advance will be relatively unguarded, meaning that the picket line will most likely funnel reinforcements to the south-east perimeter as the north-western section of the fortress is a sheer cliff wall backed against turbulent seas and guarded by CIWS emplacements and SAM sites. So, what we'll need to do is move our dropship-dependent forces against the complex's southern and eastern walls. That should get the Wayfarers near-undivided attention.' I paused to recollect my thoughts. 'From here, we can launch an amphibious assault against the north-western wall and outflank the enemy garrison,' I explained, drawing up the force movement lines. The lieutenant looked at me in shock.

'But you just said that the north-western ridge was suicide?'

'I know that's what I said, but we've got no other choice. This territory is neutral ground: if the Wayfarers come to us, we have the advantage, but if we take the initiative, they hold all the tarot cards. That means we're going to have to tweak Sun Tzu's logic-train and figure out a way to get marines shoreside and inside that bastion via the north-western advance,' I explained.

'Now, how long will it take to get direct action forces ground-side?' asked Lieutenant Phar.

'Fifteen mikes if we're pushing it. Do you have a suggestion, Lieutenant?' offered QT-2.

The lieutenant began to lick his lips as he thought through his plan. 'There's an island ten klicks off the continental coast. What if we deployed a Strategic Reaction Force unit ground-side and had them covertly secure the north-western defences?' Phar suggested.

'Halkaa marines?' I interjected with a cough, shocked by his suggestion.

'Why not? They're trained in surgical strikes,' Lieutenant Phar retorted.

I stared at him stunned. 'Yeah, but they're Halkaa marines,' I said finally.

Phar looked at me with confusion. 'Why're you so shocked by that suggestion?'

'You've never actually met a Halkaa marine, have you?'

Phar shook his head.

'So, I'll give you a primer on levels of bat-*shajst* crazy. At the bottom, you have regular jarheads. Just above them are Specialists, and above *us* are Halkaa marines. They named themselves after hell itself!' I exclaimed.

'But will they work?' Phar asked, ignoring my statement.

'Of course! But that's not the point, they won't work the way you think, they have a very different idea of "surgical strike",' I replied with a tight smile.

'How will they work?'

'Halkaas take the old-Earth marine mission to locate, close with, and destroy the enemy by means of fire manoeuvre and close combat, and take it to its extreme. They won't take the north-western advance covertly. Covert is a word that actually doesn't exist in the Kitari combat language they speak, so to say it's not exactly their forte is an understatement.' I paused before continuing, 'But strategically they'll be loud enough, angry enough, and equipped with enough firepower to wage a one-man war on the Wayfarer's fire picket. They'll get the dragoons' attention, definitely,' I said before pausing. 'Okay, so let me get this straight: Halkaa marines are going to hit the AOE* and neutralise the Wayfarer picket line along the north-western wall. As Wayfarer reinforcements are redeployed along the north-western perimeter; ground forces will be deployed against the southern and eastern walls. Simultaneously, marine amphibious forces will further reinforce the north-western offensive. This will divide the Wayfarers against multiple assaults, ensuring total Honour Guard casualties and defensive collapse,' I reiterated.

'Sounds about right,' Lieutenant Phar said with a nod.

I couldn't help but let out a chuckle.

'What?' he asked in confusion.

'That's a far too idealistic simulation. While I have no doubt the Halkaas could push up to the precursor wall and scale it, they would be trapped within the fortress, literally cut off from reinforcements, and without a route to an effective withdrawal point where they could either be evacuated out or at the very least be covered by close air support. It would be a slaughter,' I replied.

'Okay, so we drop in artillery and carve a way through the wall for them,' Phar replied optimistically.

'We already ruled out artillery as a breaching option. Precursor structures have survived this long for a reason, and that's not even including the insertion complications,' I said with a shake of my head.

At this, Phar's brow creased in thought. 'Would a ballistic submarine or a slingshot Naval Strike Package have enough kinetic energy to breach the walls in a timely manner?' he asked, turning to QT-2.

The android ran through the maths. 'We have the targeting computers, the AI, and the fleet to pull off such a feat,' QT-2 reported finally.

I tilted my head. *He's got a point there.* 'Okay, let's do this,' I said with a nod as a frown began to appear across Phar's forehead. 'What is it?'

'What's the importance of the underground reservoir?' the lieutenant pointing to the position on the map as he spoke.

'That is for Lycaon,' I said, my index finger gesturing at the waterway, 'and as such, classified. Eyes only,' I finished.

'You're going groundside, ma'am?' Phar said in mild shock.

'Affirmative, we started this fight, we're finishing it,'

'Aye, aye,' Phar replied. 'So, anything else you need from me, ma'am?'

'That's all for now, but when the fighting starts, know that you'll be coordinating all fleet-side target acquisition decisions,' I explained.

Lieutenant Phar fell silent.

'Also, I'll be assigning QT-2 to your part of the operation; he'll be important to the later stages,'

'Aye, ma'am,' Phar said.

As I turned to walk out, the lieutenant stopped me. 'Um, Grand Admiral?'

'Yes, Denat?' I answered back; the lieutenant taken aback by my use of his forename.

'It's been a pleasure and an honour serving under you, ma'am,' Denat finally said.

With a nod, I left the compartment and tapped the comm switch beside the CIC's door. 'Bosun, ETA on the fleet.'

'One moment, ma'am,' Hesch replied. 'Next arriving fleet is the seventy-seventh, ETA seventeen hours. The last arrival is the seventh and is scheduled for thirty-seven hours from now, outbound from Theodorovna's Keep, ma'am,' Hesch replied.

I sighed. *This is going to be a long seven days.*

'Understood,' I replied before releasing my index finger from the intercom switch.

++++

0530 hours Zulu 10/01/2439 (Military Calendar), UNV Morte Fortuna

I fidgeted with my sidearm, aimlessly disassembling and reassembling it at my desk, the overhead lamp harsh against my eyes in my sleep-deprived haze. My hands glided across the weapon, flawlessly clipping the dozens of interlocking components together in mere moments. As the final piece slid into place, I pulled back the slide of my service pistol to the crunch of a jammed slide. My face twisted into a wince at the sound. I bared my teeth in fury, imagining the weapon's residue-laden gauss matrix would spontaneously unjam under the sheer force of my will. I continued to tug at the jammed slide until another audible crunch emanated from the weapon. '*Brafik!*' I cursed as I tossed the weapon across my desk, its metallic form clattering into the wall that backed the desk. I threw myself back against the chair, my fists momentarily clenching before releasing and slumping to my sides. With a sigh, I slithered out of my chair, snatched up the pistol and headed for the aft repair bay. It was unusually quiet this morning, even though the crew was smaller and the work cycle longer, normally there would still be some semblance of activity even at this time of day. Tucking my firearm into my holster as I clipped it to my hip, I made my way across the cold, grey deck, my body still wincing with pain whenever I tried to breathe. My eyes drifted over the *Fortuna*'s central deck, its smooth doors, and shaped bulkheads. As I walked each of the unsecured compartment doors slid open and shut as I passed them. Nearing the port lift, a door snapped open, and the laboured breaths and rhythmic drumbeats of fist against simulated leather echoed out into the passageway. I was about to walk off, but paused. I turned and entered the portside gym. It was even smaller than your conventional warship gym, its exercise equipment had to either be stacked in the walls or recreated with Tangible Holographic Plasma each time it was used. In the far corner, Elenskis whaled on one of the ship's artificially recreated boxing bags, its simulated leather never quite close enough to the real thing to fool anyone. Her hair was loose and ragged, in complete violation of the UMC's grooming standards. Her eyes were filled with a fury I'd only heard over comms a few times before and seen even less. 'Hey, are you okay?' I asked in a calm tone as she slowed her tempo, finally noticing me.

'Green,' she said through gritted teeth, her fists' furious barrage recommencing.

I pursed my lips as I cautiously stepped towards her. 'You really green, Elenskis?' I continued tentatively.

'Rah, why wouldn't I be? Haven't been sliced like Tom, nor cut up like you. I've got no excuse to be anything other than green,' she retorted in between strikes.

I stopped inching close to her as I pondered her words, my brow contorting only for a moment. 'You don't have an excuse to be anything but green? You know legitimate reasons aren't excuses, right?' I paused to let my words sink in and consider my next few. 'I've known you for longer than anyone on this ship; my first unit was KKN Land Force Twenty-Two Commando, where you were my CO for seven years before the Taskforce plucked us from the Two Twenty-seventh. Remember that night? I remember it like it was yesterday. The smell of charred flesh, the fanatic eyes as you'd tried to burn away the Kaltri pigments that dotted your arms as if you'd been infected with a virus and were wildly trying to stop its growth. That night you even tried to plunge a blade through your eyes, just to carve out your ember irises.' I paused. 'That night, you promised you'd talk to me if you were struggling. I don't want to bury another sister in arms to mental health,' I finished.

Elenskis paused as the last word slipped across the room. Her shoulders loosened, her jawline released, and she slumped across the floor, the sides of her lips trembling. 'That isn't the issue. I don't want to lose any of you. For the first time in my entire life, I haven't had to hide who I am to anyone and it hasn't defined my relationship with anyone. The only thing that has defined my relationship with people has been the fact that I am a Taskforce marine; not my Kaltri heritage or my fervid devotion to Empress Aleksandra the Seventh. For the first time in my life, I am judged by who I am and what I do and that's a debt I can never repay. So, I swore an oath, an unspoken oath, on the blood of my foremothers, to protect the four of you at any cost, and I can barely do that,' she explained, her fists clenching and unclenching.

I sighed. 'You don't owe us anything; we've each bled plenty enough for each other. The only debts that matter to this fireteam are drinking debts. Everything else has been paid in full, from the moment we met, and will continue to be paid in full till the day each of us dies,' I replied with a calm smile. I offered a hand to Elenskis, her expression returning to some semblance of normalcy.

She frowned as she rose, glancing down at my sidearm. 'Now how the *brafiksjot* did you do that?' she said jokingly gesturing to my hip.

'You know me, I don't do waiting. It's like pulling teeth out, and silence. It hurts,' I said smiling.

'So, you heading towards the armoury?'

'Rah, gotta get it un-*brafik*ed somewhere,' I remarked, calmly tapping my holster's side.

We continued aft along the central passageway in silence, Elenskis diverting towards the aft maintenance bay while I continued on before ducking right into the port quarter lift. Punching a key on my CPI, the lift doors snapped shut and the metal lift started down towards the well deck. When the lift doors opened, I slipped out into the shipboard armoury directly attached to the lift and strode into the adjacent machine shop. I unholstered my service pistol and rested it on the table before reaching for a cleaning kit. Unfolding the canister of magnets, lubricants, swabs, brushes, jags, bore snakes, rods, and cleaning cloths, I slowly and methodically began to disassemble the firearm once more before meticulously cleaning away the metallic filings and grime that had jammed the weapon's slide before piecing it back together again. Finished, I clutched the weapon in my hands before patiently pulling the slide back, with the firm clean click of the slide, I tucked the firearm back into its holster and headed back up to my quarters, a calm smile inching across my face before fading, my satisfaction disappearing as if a dream.

++++

1730 hours Zulu 15/01/2439 (Military Calendar)

I strode through the quiet passageways of the UNV *Morte Fortuna*. After the rush of the past few days—the death and destruction, the pain and injury—the silence was almost nerve-inducing. I was making my usual informal after-dinner inspection of the ship, ducking through compartment after compartment, not really looking for anything, but mostly trying to find something to do because Commander Stratton had effectively—and quite rightly—removed me from the organisational components of the operation due to my distinct lack (putting it lightly) of experience in organising star system-sized invasions. As I made my way forwards from the Combat Information Centre, I decided to swing right for the ladder instead of left for the lift. With the tap of a button, the hatch below me snapped open, and I climbed onto the ladder inside, dogging the hatch with the press of a button as I descended. As I reached the next deck, I turned to face the next door and activated it. With a snap-hiss, the door opened to the echo of laughter and conversation between members of the crew. The overhead lighting had been set to minimum and the dull glow of a portable heating unit (in lieu of a distinctly against-regulations combustible fire inside a pressurised starship) sat at the centre of the gathering. As each of them noticed me, a silence began to fall across the group, and Elenskis in particular straightened as she noticed me. I chuckled.

'Specialist Two, I'm fairly certain we can drop the formalities,' I said with a grin.

'Well, someone has to render them in this outfit; may as well be me,' Elenskis replied with a wry smile, to the confusion of everyone else.

'Mind if I join in?' I asked.

'Nah, yeah; pull up a stump!' Harmon bellowed from the other side. I stared in confusion.

'Yes—take a seat,' translated Jonathan. With that, I settled into a vacant chair and the conversation resumed.

'Hey, Lieutenant Sandon! How's the baby going?' called out Ela as she waved towards the ship around us. Everett paused before answering.

'She's going alright. Darling's a beauty to work with: completely leatherneck-proof. She's the engineer's dream ship. Maybe not as prestigious, definitely not as declassified as your Alexander-classes, but she's the one that deep down you know you wanted to work with really.' Sandon paused. 'Though, if I could nab me some of those Tremblej HX Twenty-Three Navigators for internal tube navigation, I'd be set for life. The possessed cracker of an engineer who thought stacking tubes was a bright idea needs to either recommend contortionism to NAVSEA for General Maintenance Training or they need to crawl the tubes they think up before they sign off on the *brafik*ing paperwork,' Sandon rambled before realising his audience.

'Is there a reason you immediately thought of the HX-23s?' Ela asked, surprisingly curious.

'Before I was recruited, I worked the orbitals of Pioniirno Pleis as an electrical apprentice for the Tremblej Tekno Baroni and after ... your incident ... I was actually contracted on to conduct maintenance on the Tremblej Homestead on Versails,' he added sheepishly.

I glanced at the corner of my ocular display, the heart rate monitor of the group spiking as everybody held their breath amidst the powder-keg conversation.

Harmon paused for barely a moment before redirecting the discussion.

'Oi! So, by the way, can someone please for the love of all that's bloody right in the universe please explain to me who in hell are these 'NATO nine-nine lard-oss and lollies'? I heard about 'em from one of the loons in our old squadron and it's been wracking my brain for ages,' Harmon, his hands gesticulating like a tentacled monster as confused stares followed his question.

Evans punched him in the shoulder before jokingly growling, 'Use "wracking" in its proper context, ya' mongrel.'

'No!' he said in a petulant tone of mocking, his nose scrunching up in defiance as a grin snaked across his face.

'Also, you can't call 'em "loons"—I'm fairly certain that's religious discrimination mate,' Jonathan interjected before translating: 'What he's asking is, what's the go is with the Naitno Nein Lort an Lati an Latos. We had a bloke back in the Forty-Second who swore exclusively to the nine lords and ladies and we never got the gist of what their deal was. Figured one of youse would have a clue as to the whole shebang.' At this, Ela and Tomas turned to one another.

'You want to answer the question?' Tomas asked.

'You're the trained *diikon*,' Ela retorted. Tomas gave out a sigh of thought.

'Take what I'm about to say with a grain of thought. Ela is far more freshly read of the Book of Lords than I, as I'm no longer practising the faith. But, as time began and the great explosion subsided, what was meant to be an ordered creation fell into chaos: gravity appearing where it shouldn't, stars vanishing, day and night were barely concepts to the mortal world. In this chaos, Lati Gaia, of nature, and her consort Lort Gede, of death and fertility, began assigning the Lorts and Latis of Takahara to the roles of correcting the broken world. As they came to the orbits and the stars, they assigned Lort Helis and Lati Suna to the light, but as they tried to assign a Lort or Lati to the night they discovered all were committed to another of the mortal coil's needs. In an act of desperation, they took four of Takahara's Lukistno Andjels—"Watcher Angels" in your tongue—and five of Lati Freja's Valkiris, and reforged them as four Latos and five Latis of the Night, holding the collective power of a single Lort or Lati. Five Valkiris were chosen by Takahara to ensure the dead and the newborns of the night would begin life and end life in true peace. In fact, at the birth of the Union, the connection between Lato and Man was made perfect on Kiln. As First Emperor Kuzmoto was being birthed, Lati Devna of the Hunt carried his divine spirit in her womb, causing thunder, lighting, hail, and hurricanes that rocked the very foundations of Kiln. It was the Nine that delivered Emperor Kuzmoto.

'But wait. Where's this *lato* thing come in?' Harmon interjected, visibly confused.

'The fall of the fifth would occur some centuries later, marked by the cracking of the capstone below the Imperial Palace. The fifth was a jealous woman, independent and favoured by Lati Freja. With her favour, however, the fifth would develop dreams of grandeur, of her own facet of creation at her command. So, without her sister's or brother's knowledge, she would orchestrate a coup against Lort Helis and Lati Suna of the Light, her goal to take claim of the day. But as her plans began to unfold, Lort Tumatanga of War would discover her scheme, and with the strike of his palm, crush her rebellion. Now bound, the fifth would be transmuted once more by Lort Gede into the one and only Lato of the Night, abstracted from their sisterhood of old.' As Tomas finished, Harmon sat enamoured, eyes wide with shocked amazement.

'Actually, now you've got me curious,' Harmon said, his hands still waving lunatically. 'So, look, I get you're all from a fascist theocracy—'

At this Evans rolled his eyes. 'One of these days, we'll cure the foot-in-mouth disease in your brain, but sure, go right ahead insulting the people you're asking.'

At this Miles, looked at him with moderately feigned confusion.

'What? I called them a theocracy! It was a good big word!'

'You were asking what us fascists get up to in our spare time?' I interjected.

'Nah, yeah,' he said as a statement. The entire compartment recoiled in confusion as Langridge and Evans collectively sighed.

'Yes, is what he just said,' Langridge translated as Evans gave up in protest.

'I used to read technical manuals; cross-sections of everything from the historic Adolf-class to the fictional Star Dagger from Exodus: Abyss,' Sandon said into the silence.

'My parents put me through *sistema* to stem my bad habit of playing pranks around the Imperial Palace,' Ela followed 'It didn't work … the pranks just got more elaborate and kinetic instead,' she added.

'I read, philosophy, and poetry, not just *Das Kapital* and *Mein Kampf*, mind you, but non-human poets and philosophers from Xeara of the Abetran Mediators to Sialco of the Symbril Unity,' Elenskis answered with fond thoughts.

'I wrote poetry in my spare time, before I had the shakes in my downtime between work I would write poetry: to the gods, to the fusion plant—I wrote about whatever for whomever would care to hear. It's a small miracle I didn't have a conversation with the Statsiano Meikseif Grup,' Tomas mused before Barken spoke.

'Futbal. I was so keen for the sport I played for the KKM Rojal Mariin Koleg's professional team, the "Midshipman Kadets".'

'Since when did you lot have NRL?' Harmon yelled into the settling silence.

'He means soccer, mate. Spaceships don't have enough space to keep rugby league afloat,' Evans answered before anyone could ask, feeding the descent into silence.

'What about you, boss?' Will asked inquiringly as he looked across the compartment to me. I frowned.

'I've been trying to think about that. Writing. I'd always found writing was so interesting being able to put all my emotions into a fictional character in a different universe where Zulu time didn't exist or rain didn't cause mud or whatever small thing irritated me that day and being able to collectively relate to this non-existent person with millions of readers,' I said fondly, 'what I would give to pick the skill back up again,' I finished.

We continued to talk for hours until as individuals slowly drifted out and away from the conversation throughout the evening.

++++

As the impromptu gathering finally dissipated, I decided to make my way back to my quarters. This time I took the lift rather than the ladder. As the lift doors parted and I stepped out onto the deck, my 0100 hours brain caught me; my shoulders sagged, and my eyes began to drift across the compartment. A smile curled across my lips as I exhaustedly appreciated the beauty of a warship's night cycle. The overhead lamps were off, instead supplanted by bunker lights lining the bulkheads and photoluminescent path markings lining the deck. Amidst this, the vibration of gravity plates rumbled around me, for once the dominate sound with the engines at station-keeping. I scanned the compartment and my mind relinquished those details, as I saw the glaring oddity: a deep orange expansion of light that crawled out from an aft compartment. I moved towards the compartment and quietly leaned in to see Tomas at the head of a ceremony with Ela, Barken, and Sandon seated before him. In the silence of the night and the bubbling pre-op tension, the rest of the crew manifested behind me to watch in silence, confusion, and awe at the ritual. While candles were supposed to be used in the ritual, combustion regulations continued to supersede religious ordinances (even in the USR.) So, without adequate fire-based lighting, Tomas had co-opted half a dozen of Ela's drones in lamp mode, their light warping every so often as they struggled to generate an orange with their native red and white settings. Tomas stood, his hands held high and wide to create a V. His palms open and up. Ela's, Barken's, and Sandon's were open and lower, imitating Tomas' V. After a moment's pause, he began to speak.

'*On besiich takaharano lort an lati an lato bles. Lati Gaiakara besiich dropntok es kliin skai an atfansntok es kliin grond. Lato Ankikara besiich mitachno ki es tru. Lort Tumatangakara besiich plan es korosh an tru. Priati Devnakara besiich Vilterhant es naj. Lati Frejakara an Lort Gedekara besiich Valhano root es kliin. Lort an Latikara Lukistno Andjel meik mitachno task es tru an komplit,*' Tomas recited before slowly yet deliberately lowering his palms towards the deck. As he did so, the trio at his feet repeated his gesture in reverse, raising their open palms from the deck towards the overhead before stopping to meet Tomas' palms.

'Don't mean to be rude, but what am I looking at?' Harmon whispered to me.

'They're exercising the ritual of request—as the name suggests they're calling the gods to wage the spiritual war that will spawn from our conflict on our behalf,' I explained as the ritual continued.

'What'd he ask for?' Harmon asked.

'He beseeched the Lorts, Latis, and Latos of Takahara to give us a perfect operation. From Lati Gaia, he asks for clear skies for the drop and clear terrain for the advance, from Lato Anki he asks for strong yet level spirits, from Lort Tumatanga he asks for a precise and efficient grand strategy, from Princess Lati Devna he asks the Wild Hunt to avoid our trial, from Lati Freja and Lort Gede he asks for smooth transitions to *asvod,* and finally he implores the Lorts, Latis, and Latos to appoint the Watcher Angels to the achievement of our task.'

'And that's it? He just asked for that?'

'No,' I said shaking my head. 'See how they are offering up objects to the *diikon*?' I asked gesturing to the clearance machete, map, necklace, foot, torc, bone, and page at Tomas' feet. Harmon nodded. 'The clearance machete is to be the accepted conduit for Lati Gaia's gift because enough units will be advancing through sheer jungle, the map and our assault diagram on its page will receive Lort Tumatanga's blessing, for he was the one to decapitate his own family in such true precision of planning. Lato Anki's calming presence will come upon the Crest of Kuzmoto, the conduits for all spiritual activity. The animal's foot is offered to Princess Lati Devna as it is the sole remains and sign of the Wild Hunt's trespasses. The neck-sized metal ring called a torc is Lati Freja's Briisingaamen and the bone is the remains of a feast held by Lort Gede. Each of these are either signals of validity to the Lorts, Latis, or Latos that are untrusting, or they are demonstrations of our choices to be validated,' I finished explaining as the ceremony ended, the drones deactivated and the participants began to exit the compartment.

'Wait, if Tomas' isn't a deacon of the faith anymore why did he lead the entire ritual?' asked Johnathan, just as confused as the others.

'Because only a *diikon* or *shrajnona*—deacon and shrine maiden in your tongue—may conduct the ceremony. Not even the god masters, known as *kanushi*, or god's employees, called *shinshokis*, can conduct this kind of request, and working-class certainly can't.'

'But isn't Ela upper class? The Tremblej family is a Tech Barony, right?'

'You're only upper class if you aren't a heretic,' interjected Sandon, his eyes nervous as he looked for Ela.

'Only if you count artificial intelligence heresy,' interrupted Tomas in a growling tone.

'Oh, I don't believe it for a minute, *diikon*. I learned a while ago with this Taskforce that artificial intelligence isn't to be feared,' Sandon explained.

At this, Harmon prepared to speak before Johnathan interjected.

'You've lost both of us,' Johnathan said in a controlled tone. The group just looked at each other nervously.

I nervously rubbed the inside of my palm before calling across the compartment. 'Ela! Our two pilots are wondering what got you the label of "heretic"!' I said with an even voice. Ela's head gingerly poked around the lip of her quarters' door. 'Figured you should be the one to answer their question; nobody should explain choices they don't live with,' I said with an apologetic grimace.

'No, its fine, chiif,' she said with a weary voice. 'My family earned its Tekno Baroni by being the best. We've all been naturally inclined towards engineering and IT. But when the AI ban went down, it not only was a legal law … it was a religious one. The Intelants of old were to be cast into the fires of history. Anything remotely near a Tier One like the Taskforce issues its troops was sacrilege. I, being the family troublemaker I was, decided to build one—nothing even remotely near a Tier One, but still able to execute complex pattern recognition—and proceeded to present it to Ympiirista Aleksandra at our weekly productivity offerings. I was dragged away by her own Imperial Guard and personally held in the family cellar until I turned sixteen and with parental consent was sent to Kiil Island and eventually assigned to the worst fighting of the Blooding Wars to more than hopefully die,' she said, a bitter tone creeping into her speech.

At that, the two pilots blanched in embarrassed shock as the fiery one-woman army was replaced by her insecure sibling, timid and terrified of the world's opinion. In the stillness, the firm but comforting hand of Tomas clamped across Ela's shoulder, and Ela snapped from her distance like a band.

'The *ympiirtach* have said time and time again that blood and chain are immovable cornerstones of our lives, that they take priority over all other. Your family because it grows the union, the chain because Ympiirista Aleksandra provides. Of course, when the chain rejects you and the blood denies you, what are you left with? Child, you are a stubborn, bull-horned, dozer. Engineers could move planets with your tenacity. But you are soft-hearted, mostly, and the gelatine that can flash over a room or wring it together,' Tomas remarked as he stood there.

'Where blood and the chain have rejected and denied you. The sword accepts,' I said softly as I placed my palm across her opposite shoulder.

'It says brothers and sisters in arms for a reason,' Evans said as he and Harmon closed the gap.

++++

0945 hours Zulu 17/01/2439 (Military Calendar)

Over the last one hundred and sixty-eight hours, ships from across Taskforce-controlled space appeared at the rally point, quickly and seamlessly synchronising with our tactical network and protocols. By the end of it, just over thirteen thousand five hundred ships and their assigned ground forces patiently awaited our command. I sat on the bridge, staring out over the impossible task force.

'Bosun, get me a line to all Task Force vessels. Audio only,' I instructed.

'Opening wideband transmission feed, aye, ma'am,' Hesch replied as he gave me the thumbs up.

'Attention coalition forces. Now, I know you're wondering, what's so important about this damned offensive? Why does this particular part of the Enzo Line even matter?' I paused for effect. 'Though this may break some OSI security protocols, I don't care. No one under my command dies without knowing what they died for, because anyone who dies on a battlefield deserves to know that they died for a cause worth fighting for. What we're about to do isn't for a flag or a charter. What we are fighting for today goes beyond even that. Today, we fight for the safety of a billion worlds; we fight to keep quintillions from dying at the hands of an unimaginable power. Not only that, today we fight for our brothers and sisters, the ones that never made it home. For their sacrifice is what gives us purpose! It's what gives us character! For every inch those bastards took from us we'll take double!' I screamed.

Cheers rang through the 1MC as Hesch routed the cries through the *Fortuna*'s speakers. As the excitement subsided, I continued. 'Welcome ladies and gentlemen to Operation Ultimus Finis—"Ultimate Goal",' I finished.

With that, Hesch cut the feed and the Task Force began to conduct final preparations. I stared out into the sea of starships as I noticed Hesch in the corner of my eye, his face contorting into a frown as he listened intently into his comm piece.

'What is it, Bosun?' I asked. Hesch just shook his head.

'Bosun's Mate Second Class, what's going on?' I demanded again, my tone stronger this time.

'Sorry, ma'am, a High Special Operations Inquisitor Paladin has requested to dock with the *Fortuna*,' Hesch relayed in confusion.

I smirked. He didn't even tell his handpicked crew who he was, did he?

'Clear him for docking on the starboard bow collar,' I instructed as I rose from my chair and strode down to the airlock that sat on our ship's throat.

'Aye, ma'am,' Hesch tentatively replied.

Minutes later, the hatch opened, and a gush of air seeped into the passageway as Mitchell stepped through, flanked by a pair of pilots.

'I bring gifts,' Mitchell jokingly remarked as he snapped to attention.

'Are they for me?' I called in excitement, like an excited child on the Night of the Mother.

'No, I brought them for me, myself, and I,' Paladin retorted, sarcasm on his lips. 'These are—' Paladin was about to introduce them as I spoke up.

'Lieutenants Len Neil and El Naken, aces of the Imperial War Navy and the Unified Naval Service. Top graduates from both the Royal Imperial Top Gun Academy and the UNS Top Gun Academy respectively and assigned to the Two Hundred and Twelfth Draku Makis, finest Naval Aviation squadron in the Imperial Starfleet, if I remember correctly.'

Paladin looked at me in shock. 'How do you know so much about these two?'

'I come from a long line of sailors which means that everything navy is general knowledge in my family, and the only other branch that's acceptable to join is the Corps of Naval Infantry solely because of the fact it is a corps of the navy,' I explained with a smirk.

'Well I heard that you're down a couple pilots, so I wrangled up these two idiots.'

'Hey!' Len interjected, feigning insult at the comment.

'... and figured I'd also ask if I could deploy groundside with you,' Paladin elaborated.

I smirked. 'What's the occasion?'

'Oh, nothing much, just been cooped up in administration for too long,' Mitchell admitted.

'Well, you're in luck, QT's remaining starside to coordinate operations so we're a man down.'

Paladin smirked. 'Looks like it's my lucky day,' he said as he strode off towards the well deck. My gaze followed Mitchell's move aft.

'You got gear?'

'Course! What do you think I am? A bastard?' he retorted with a grin.

'Never!' I replied jokingly. I turned back to Hesch. 'Bosun, where do we stand?'

'All ships are standing by for your command, ma'am,' Hesch reported.

'Excellent news. Have Lycaon gear up and meet me aboard the *Matilda.*'

'Relaying instructions to Lycaon, aye, ma'am,' Hesch replied. I turned back to my room and stepped in as Hesch's voice echoed over the intercom: 'Fireteam Lycaon, Fireteam Lycaon. Gear up and report to well deck. I say again. Gear up and report to well deck.'

I strode over to my equipment rack and activated the security keypad beside the rigid frame that now sat below the floor due to the lockdown. As I entered the final digit, the floor beside me parted and my suit's stand rose from the ground. Moments later, two other racks also unfurled from the wall behind my PCA: my weapon rack and sword stand. A tear began to form in my eye as I admired the blade's perfection, but it quickly faded. I turned to the suit, the armour's rear hatchway revealing itself to me. I stood there for a moment before working through layer after layer of clothing, hands catching at collars and auto-compression bands till I had plied away every last inch of cloth from my body. I clambered into the metallic frame, my carbyne second skin tightening around me followed by the snap hiss of medical ports as the suit sealed shut. As my HMD was brought online, the frigid touch of nitrogen clouded my thoughts, and my hands began to shake as my body reacted to the sensation. Moments later, Mariko's calm voice echoed inside me.

'Ma'am,' Mariko responded. I couldn't help but smile.

'Glad you could join us,' I said with a hint of humour.

'What'd you think I'd do instead?' Mariko asked sarcastically.

I just shook my head as I turned to face my equipment. I turned to my rifle, inspected its condition, and clipped it to my suit's reactive webbing. I repeated the process for my M18 and satchel of grenades before turning to my blades. With a heavy heart, I lifted each individually off their racks—a hand at each end—and clipped them to my waist. With my equipment in hand, I turned and left for the *Fortuna*'s well deck. As the lift doors slid open, the silhouettes of my fireteam stretched back across the deck.

'*Gospadinas!* You heard the sonorous song of Lati Athia! What are we waiting for?' I boomed as I rotated my index finger above my head. My team snapped to attention then turned to board. Tomas was looking better since I'd last seen him: the majority of his injuries had finally healed up, but the bruising was still quite prominent. 'Four! Aren't your lungs buggered?'

'Unn,' he said—the casual 'yes' of Japonno Spraak.

'That won't affect you?'

'Eh, iron lung'll hack it,' he remarked nonchalantly.

'Understood!' I replied over the din of the *Matilda*'s engines.

'Beginning pre-flight checks,' Len reported over the Condor's intercom. The aviator paused as he looked over the flight controls.

'Something the matter, Lieutenant?' I called forward.

'Nothing wrong, ma'am, just…'

'Spit it out, Lieutenant!' I demanded.

'Someone's customised the flight controls, ma'am!'

I began to chuckle. 'That's normal!' I reassured him.

'Aye, aye,' Len responded, cursing under his breath. I activated my comm piece.

'Commander Stratton?'

'Go ahead, ma'am,' came back Michiko's voice.

'What's the situation with our force?' I questioned. Michiko paused to check over her readouts.

'We're green.'

I pursed my lips. 'Then it's over to you, Commander,' I said before finishing with the time-worn naval phrase: 'You have the watch.'

'Aye, aye, I have the watch,' Michiko acknowledged with the time-worn reply.

Michiko

Michiko resettled her posture as the highly irregular nature of her command suddenly became apparent to her. 'Helm, get us underway,' Michiko instructed.

'Aye, Skipper,' Harmon responded as he began pre-jump protocols.

'Bosun, inform Task Force S to begin preparations.'

With a sharp reply, the boatswain flicked on his comm piece. 'All hands, all hands, General Quarters Condition One. GQ One. Stand by for combat jump. Air Defence Warning Yellow. Air Defence Warning Yellow,' Hesch instructed over the *Fortuna's* 1MC. After a moment's pause, he switched frequencies, muttered a series of instructions before looking up to the overhead-mounted console as he activated a tile on a digital screen. 'Jump signal is live, ma'am,' Hesch reported.

'Excellent,' Michiko replied with genuine satisfaction.

'Safae, Helm? Confirm jump data!' Samuels instructed. 'Coords zero one eight dash three niner two! Confirm?'

'Confirmed!' replied Evans.

'Agreed!' remarked Safae as Lieutenant Barken rose from his impact seat and began demanding department reports.

'Navigation?'

'Plotted and input!' relayed Samuels.

'Helm?'

'Engines responsive,' Evans confirmed. 'Controls positive!' reported Harmon.

'Engineering?'

'Reactor power routing to engines and FTL! Reactor within margins!' Sandon reported.

'Security?'

'All passageways and equipment secured for combat,' reported QT-2's avatar.

'Communications?'

'All communications secured for transit!' responded Hesch.

'Combat?'

'All hardpoints secured for combat!' replied Phar over the 18MC.

'All hands report GQ1, sir,' reported Hesch.

'All departments report secured for combat jump, ma'am,' Lieutenant Barken reported, his posture formal.

'All systems nominal, ma'am. Orders?' asked Evans.

'Execute jump,' Michiko instructed. Barken turned on point and reached for the jump key's security container, entering his four-digit code before handing the key down to Evans, who proceeded to lock the key into the control panel. He paused for a moment before twisting it counterclockwise.

'Jump clock is running. Jump clock is running,' Hesch announced over the 1MC as the jump alarm blared in the background. 'Ten, nine, eight, seven, six—'

'Singularity fielded,' reported Evans.

'—Four, three—'

'Rift created; coordinates locked in,' relayed Johnathan.

'—Two, one,' Hesch finished as Harmon reported, 'Jumping!' A few moments passed as the *Fortuna* leapt into the black and blue of the Aether.

'Glide nominal, ETA to jump point. Eight minutes,' Evans reported.

'Excellent, may the gods be ever watching,' Michiko prophetically replied.

++++

1011 hours Zulu

The Task Force re-entered normal space ahead of the inhibitor field. Tensions were high as captains calmly waited for the inevitable FARSIGHT contact and the flutter of screams across the wireless. All ships had moved to General Quarters Condition 1, but a ship and her crew are never truly prepared for combat. The Task Force was divided into three groupings, the 1st, 7th and 22nd Task Forces named after each sub-unit's oldest Carrier Strike Group. The 1st moved against Honour Guard forces on the left flank, the 7th on the right while the 22nd took the middle. Each Alexander-class carrier battleship was surrounded by a bulwark of ships and fighters with at least one naval squadron forming a tight picket around the warships. To the front of the formation, reconnaissance pickets swept the sector for the ever-elusive subspace anchor.

'Nothing on FARSIGHT, ma'am,' reported McGhee.

Michiko licked her teeth anxiously. 'Understood then. Helm, ahead full.'

'Ahead full, aye,' Harmon replied.

Hesch's voice echoed across the wireless moments later, relaying the instruction to the rest of the fleet. The tight mass of ships continued to rocket across the empty black of space. With each passing minute of silence, the crews of Task Force S became more restless. Gunnery crews twitched at each passing ping of their FARSIGHT instrumentation. Engineering teams chattered nervously between each other as they resolved any shipboard issues regardless of size or importance. The pilots were better off, as they were able to channel their fears into their flying. The marines and soldiers aboard the various landing dropship docks were in the best condition of the fleet. With their respective fights at least a few hours away, they could allay their fears with banter and improvised renditions of contemporary works by Rijun and 'illicit' old Earth classics by Nena. The odd Regimental Sergeant Major would try to shut the chatter down, but most commanding officers, if they had any sense, would let such mild unprofessionalism slide because the effects of such morale at this stage of an operation were critical.

++++

UNV Cyrus

Operations Specialist Apprentice Winter looked over her console as she adjusted targeting data and transferred readouts across the ship, glancing back and forth mentally between her shipboard data transfer duties and her plan position indicator (PPI) as it diligently pinged back negative contacts. She shunted her detection log away with the millions of others being processed simultaneously by Task Force S. Three cycles passed in her digital realm before she looked back at her PPI, its radar and light detection instrumentation once again pinging back negative. She was about to shunt off her report to the system when she noticed an insignificant flare appear across her screen before vanishing. She frowned with confusion and read over the data once more. Her gaze intensified for a moment before she looked up from her station. 'Mr Lam!' she called out, shunting her data feed to her periphery. The Combat Information Centre Watch Officer (CICWO) strode over to Winter's station.

'What's the issue, Apprentice Winters?' the CICWO inquired.

'I think I've identified FARSIGHT interference that may be masking inbound hostiles,' Winter reported firmly. The watch officer unhooked a cable from the station and inserted it into the back of his skull. Winter turned back to her station and mentally pulled up the data for him. 'I just spotted a FARSIGHT blip on my instrumentation; it seems to be the engine housing of something at two seven, seven mark one, one zero.'

'I'll pass it onto the TAO,' Lam remarked before turning and striding off towards the Tactical Action Officer. 'Lieutenant Commander!' he called out as he waded through the dozens of stations that littered the red-lit CIC.

Lieutenant Commander Haasbroek turned to face Lam. 'What's the issue, Lieutenant Lam?'

'Apprentice Winters has identified an unidentified flying object at 277-110.' Haasbroek simply nodded as Lam explained the situation. With the watch officer's explanation over and one final nod, the lieutenant commander finally spoke.

'I'll pass it up the chain,' he said before returning to his seat, plugging in his neural interface and wiring the information up to the bridge.

The OOD blinked as he received the information before disconnecting from the ship's network and looking up from his impact seat for the ship's flag officer.

'Admiral Williams!' he called.

'What's the issue, Mr Monteith?' called Admiral Theunis 'TT' Williams.

'CIC just reported they've identified a UFO,' the OOD explained.

'Do they have a position?'

'CIC reports FARSIGHT ping at 277-110.'

'Have CIC feed coordinates to gunnery crews and bring number one battery to starboard and prepare to fire!' Williams instructed.

'Bringing battery to starboard, aye, sir!' responded the junior officer of the deck who relayed the information to the combat information centre. Moments later, the main guns on the dorsal hull began to turn towards the nebula.

'Gunnery reports number one gun calibrated and online, sir!' reported the OOD.

'Good, fire at will,' Williams instructed.

With a nod, the JOOD relayed the instruction down to the CIC. The instruction funnelled down the chain of command to the tactical action officer.

'Firing. Aye,' he replied before awakening from his networked state. 'Execute firing solution!' the lieutenant commander barked over the muted hum of data stacks. Moments later, the ship shook as the main cannon pierced into the heart of the nebula, causing a relatively underwhelming explosion to starboard.

'CIC reports direct hit, sir,' relayed Lieutenant Monteith to Admiral Williams. The bridge crew let out a low cheer before returning their attention as proximity alarms began to flare across the ship. The CIC began to spew new data through the ship as radiation proximity alarms from around the fleet went off.

'Skipper! CIC reports depleted uranium projectiles, two seven zero mark one two zero and enemy interceptors, zero nine zero mark two four zero constant bearing decreasing range!' Monteith quickly added.

'Defensive countermeasures! Brace for impact!' Williams barked as thousands of depleted uranium projectiles launched from stealth relativistic kinetic kill vehicle platforms careened towards the fleet. The bridge began to vibrate intensely as naval guns designed to intercept relativistic debris rapidly launched precisely timed and aligned shots to deflect each incoming round. But for every two projectiles the ships successfully deflected, a third would slip through. The bridge filled with audio as emergency broadcasts flooded in.

'This is the UNV *Fallujah*; we've lost kinetic screens and are venting atmosphere!'

'This is the UNV *Maethyrin*; we've lost helm control and are venting atmosphere!'

'Somebody route that audio!' Williams barked as the Cyrus rocked violently. 'Report!' he continued, his voice commanding yet even.

'Direct hits to the starboard side. Damage control teams en route. Decks one through fourteen venting atmospheres, seals are holding!' The OOD relayed from the damage control watch. Moments later, the ship's Chrysoar combat system kicked into action as thousands of hive-like bombers careened towards Task Force S. The first wave unleashed a volley of bomb-pumped laser torpedoes, the munitions slashing through the fleet's port side. Portside Ancile close-in weapon systems and Mark 82 vertical launch systems whirred to life, throwing counter munitions high into the stars as layers of ionised flak screens (IFS) desperately tried to shred the magnetic containment of the BPL torpedoes.

'CIC reports torpedoes neutralised!' relayed Monteith before a series of violent impacts rocked the bridge crew left to right.

'Then what in the gods' name was that?' Williams howled in rage.

'Wanderer fighters just impacted our kinetic screens!'

'Set Air Threat Warning Red! How're they getting through our flak?'

'They're gliding in on momentum, sir!' the lieutenant replied. Williams gritted his teeth. 'Orders, sir? Shall I have gunnery switch to shredder rounds, sir?'

'Negative! Continue with IFS; those lasers will do more irreparable damage than any suicide bombers could any day,' Williams reluctantly ordered. Amidst the chaos, Michiko's voice came across the bridge with an inhuman serenity, even though she screamed her words, not a hint of frustration or anger could be felt in them.

'Destroyers, slag those RKKV platforms! Corvettes, break off, break off! Find those anchors!' she barked with commanding intensity.

'This is the UNV *Salamander*! Breaking off!' reported Lieutenant Commander Cyrillic.

'This is the UNV *Brangel*! Falling out!' responded corvette Captain Reed among many others. The corvettes quickly manoeuvred through the debris field that was slowly accruing from the Task Force and Honour Guard losses and began to frantically search for the subspace anchors that would soon call in larger, far more capable Void Wanderer warships.

'Have the message centre contact the Second Task Group! Transfer CICs findings onto Admiral Carson!' Williams barked. With a nod, Ensign Kirk, the ship's Junior Officer of the Deck relayed the order down to the CICs adjoined message centre. 'Bridge to message centre. Bridge to message centre!' the JOOD repeated.

'This is message centre. Send traffic,' replied Information Systems Technician Second Class Hunt.

'Relay CIC FARSIGHT data to the UNV *Yeppoon*.'

'Understood, relaying CIC FARSIGHT data to the UNV *Yeppoon,*' replied the information systems technician, before cutting the neural connection with his mind. Hunt mentally redirected his conscious into the CIC, pulling up the data logs that'd been filled aboard the ship in the last twelve minutes, noting what was reported and who it was reported by at a blinding speed. As he sifted through the logs, he verified the UNV *Yeppoon's* unit and classification:

UNV YEPPOON
WARSHIP CLASS: MARATHON-CLASS DESTROYER
HULL CLASSIFICATION: DDG-64
CAPTAIN: FLAG CAPTAIN BISHOP
UNIT: 2ND TASK GROUP
COMMANDING OFFICER: REAR ADMIRAL MICHAEL CARSON
CURRENT ASSIGNMENT: DETACHED FROM FLEET FOR STEALTH PLATFORM HUNTER KILLER OPERATION

As he processed this information, his original search came up with a match as it paired the FARSIGHT data with the assignment of *Yeppoon*. The data was logged by a Seawoman Apprentice Winters. In an instant, he had made a neural connection with the operations specialist.

'Apprentice Winters. I'm transferring your data across to the UNV *Yeppoon* to aid in their hunt for the RKKV platforms. Is this everything?' Hunt confirmed.

'Affirmative, that's everything. Seems to be that the FARSIGHT silhouette isn't as clean around the main drive section.'

'Understood,' Hunt remarked before cutting the connection and transferring the data to his station. 'UNV *Yeppoon*, UNV *Yeppoon*. UNV *Cyrus*. Over.'

'UNV *Cyrus*. UNV *Yeppoon*. Standing by to copy. Over,' replied the wireless operator on the other end.

'Transferring RKKV platform drive section silhouette data. Over,' Hunt relayed before sending across the file.

'Data packet received. UNV *Yeppoon*. Out,' finished the *Yeppoon*'s information systems technician.

++++

The UNV *Yeppoon* and its task group of over 125 destroyers, frigates, and corvettes executed a tight burn to starboard, away from the Task Force. The *Yeppoon's* bridge rocked as BPL torpedoes adjusted to target the diverting warships only to explode just metres off the hull.

'Admiral! CIC just received new tracking data from the UNV Cyrus! The RKKV platforms have a distorted drive silhouette that we can track!' reported Ensign Gorbachev, the ships JOOD. Admiral Carson simply continued to rest his elbows on the armrests of his chair as if unaware of the report and the chaos just metres from his head. His eyes narrowed as he looked out at the holographic map of the system, FTL exit and entry vectors marked around the rim of the map and dotted thrust vectors stretched across the display as 2nd Task Group and Task Force 53 disengaged from the main group in search of their targets.

'Admiral! CIC reports! Chrysoar's down!' continued to relay Gorbachev.

'Have them switch to manual targeting,' Carson calmly instructed.

'Aye, sir! Switching to manual!' the JOOD repeated back before relaying the instructions to CIC.

'Mr Gorbachev, have CIC cross-reference the RKKV flight lines with any and all drive silhouette breaks. Extrapolate their positions from there. Helm, stand by to adjust trajectory,' Admiral Carson instructed.

'Aye, sir!' Gorbachev responded. The Yeppoon continued to rock violently as bomb-pumped munitions inched further and further through the ship's flak screens before a thud rocked through the ship, throwing everyone starboard.

'Direct impact, skipper! Kinetic screens holding!' reported Leading Hand Hayward, the ship's messenger of the watch, as she too fed reports up from the ships various stations.

'Skipper! CIC has six hits!' reported Gorbachev.

'Transfer the data to the task group! Move to engage!' Carson barked.

'Aye, sir!' replied the JOOD who wired down to the ship's CIC. 'Mr Hoffmann, transfer RKKV platform positions to the fleet. Engage targets at will!' the JOOD relayed simultaneously.

'Aye, aye,' CICWO Lieutenant Hoffmann replied before sinking into his respective tasks. Lieutenant Hoffmann instantly reached out to his CIC's three AIs and the dozens of operations specialists under his command. 'Right, skippers ordered us to transfer the positions of all six platforms to the task group with orders to engage and destroy. Have all relevant data packaged and ready to transmit in fifteen seconds!' Hoffmann barked over the neural network.

'Aye, sir,' the CIC collectively transmitted back.

Hoffmann shunted the file compression progress bar to the back of his mind to quickly check the state of his operations specialists. Their heart rates were elevated: they were nervous, but laser-focused. However, one—Operations Specialist Petty Officer Carige—was breathing irregularly. She was shivering.

'What is it, Specialist Carige?' Hoffmann inquired.

'During our last FARSIGHT ping, I detected abnormal subspace readings at one five, five mark zero nine, nine,' Carige reported.

Hoffmann licked his teeth with worry. 'Must be the Subspace Anchor. Leading Hand Maud, get me a tight beam to the UNV Pathfinder. Transmit those coordinates to Task Force 53,' Hoffmann instructed. The CIC responded to the instructions in unison before recommencing with their work. The entire message centre was chaos as it manically sifted through the data and sent it off to the hundreds of warships within the task group. Information systems technician Leading Hand Maud was transmitting his last few position details as the ship rocked with a thud. As he transmitted the last data packet to the task group, a buzzing noise began to flood his mind. His heart skipped a beat and his eyes widened as the sound grew in intensity. He quickly activated the Yeppoon's tight beam, loaded the anchor coordinates, and pointed it towards the UNV Pathfinder.

'Electrical overload!' informed the electrical and auxiliary systems watch. The tight beam beeped an affirmative and Maud transmitted the data at the speed of light to the UNV Pathfinder as an electrical pulse overloaded his neural interface and the back of his head erupted in a pulse of energy and flames.

++++

UNV Brangel

'Seaman!' Captain Reed exclaimed. 'We need FARSIGHT yesterday!' she hissed as her small corvette shook from side to side, the torpedoes causing sparks to flicker through the ship.

'Damage control teams are working on it, ma'am!' relayed the messenger of the watch, Seaman Masters.

'SITREP!' Reed barked as the fighter-bombers continued to hammer the ship.

'Ancile CIWS offline! Plate capacitors at fifty percent!' continued Masters.

'Understood!' Reed hissed through gritted teeth. Moments later, the shake of retaliatory weapons fire rang through the corvette.

'Gods-damned!' the captain exclaimed as the ship shook violently.

'Skipper! FARSIGHT's back online!' reported the messenger.

'Excellent! Find that Subspace Anchor!' Reed instructed.

'Shining a light, aye, ma'am!' replied Masters before relaying the instructions to the CIC. After what felt like a lifetime the messenger piped back up. 'FARSIGHT's out of commission!'

Reed gritted her teeth. 'Did we get a location?'

'Negative, Skipper,' replied the messenger solemnly.

'Captain! Coordinates transmitted on the tight beam from the UNV *Yeppoon*! Subspace disturbance detected at 090 mark 210!' Ensign Siler, the JOOD, interjected.

'About time. Get me a firing solution!' Captain Reed barked. The ship shifted position as it readjusted to align with its newfound target, its main guns charging to fire.

'Firing solution acquired, ma'am,' reported Lieutenant Junior Grade Mathews, the ship's OOD.

'Fire!' Reed screamed. A flurry of orders followed and moments later, a pulse rang out past the viewport, the holographic display generating what was past the reinforced blast shield. The charging Subspace Anchor began to tumble as it was hit.

'Minimal effect, ma'am,' reported Mathews.

Captain Reed sighed before barking a flurry of new orders: 'All hands, prepare to abandon ship.'

The bridge crew paused.

'You heard me! Helm, plot a course towards that blasted Anchor,' the skipper snapped.

'Plotting a course. Aye, ma'am,' the helmswoman replied.

'All hands, execute Salvage Control, Phase One!' instructed the Boatswain's Mate of the Watch over the 1MC. The ship's crew shifted roles as the XO, and the specific watch officers began to coordinate the evacuation effort. The corvette's klaxon changed from an elongated whine to an intermittent beep, the emergency lights altering to a dark blue shade.

'ETA to impact, ten mikes, ma'am,' reported the helm as they activated the ship's automatic piloting systems. Moments later, the Boatswain's Mate of the Watch activated the intercom again.

'All hands. Execute Salvage Control, Phase Two!' she boomed. The ship was a flurry of action as it scrubbed the corvette of important equipment and regrouped to prepare for evacuation. With the final reports coming in about phase two's completion, the Boatswain's Mate relayed the final instruction. 'All hands, abandon ship! Abandon ship!' she recited. With that, the command crew began to vacate the bridge, leaving only the captain aboard. As the last escape pods rocketed away, fires sprouted across the bridge. The captain climbed into the helmsman's seat and moved the throttle forward; the corvette gained speed. The Subspace Anchor continued to generate the receiving portal for the incoming forces as Captain Reed rocketed towards it. The fibres of the universe began to bend and twist in brilliant hues of blue as the corvette closed to within ten thousand kilometres, the ships reactor flowering, its engines failing, and its computer systems aflame. Captain Reed paused to open a wideband comm line to Task Force S.

'Fight well, ma'am, keep my men safe. Brangel Actual out,' Reed reported.

The line faded into static as her ship collided with the Anchor. For a moment, the Task Force held its breath, waiting for the fleets to come through, crush their broken lines. But they never did. Reed did it and the lines held.

'Ma'am! Void Fighter lines are breaking up,' reported Hesch as he turned to Michiko, relaying the TAO's report.

'Excellent news! Get Admiral Birchall on the line. I want a Naval Strike Package ready to launch planetside within sixty ticks!' Michiko commanded.

'Requesting Naval Strike Package, aye, ma'am,' Hesch said as he turned back to his equipment. 'UNV *Roma*, UNV *Roma*. *Morte Fortuna*. How copy? Over.'

'*Morte Fortuna*, this is *Roma*. Reading five by five. Over,' responded Information Systems Technician Leading Hand Barrett.

'Stand by for tasking. Over,' began Hesch

'Standing by to copy. Over.'

'*Roma*, requesting Naval Strike Package, grids to follow. Over.'

'Understood, standing by to copy grid. Over.'

'Coordinates to follow, Celestial Body: Hotel Papa zero three eight dash five niner three. Grid: Quebec Foxtrot one zero two dash niner three niner. Break. Celestial Body: Sierra Tango one niner two dash eight two eight. Grid: Kilo Delta one niner two dash niner two niner. Over,' Hesch relayed. The wireless operator repeated the digits.

'Affirmative. *Morte* out,' finished Hesch as he shut off the comm piece. 'Skipper! Target Attack Missile outbound,' Hesch reported.

++++

UNV Roma

'Skipper! The *Fortuna* just requested a Naval Strike Package,' the Officer of the Deck cried as he turned to Admiral Birchall.

'Coordinates?' Birchall inquired as he looked over the transcript.

'Planetside Void Wanderer hangars, sir,' the OOD continued.

'Very well then, prepare a payload,' Birchall instructed, nodding as he spoke.

'Aye, sir!' the OOD replied before turned to the Junior Officer of the Deck and relaying the order. With a curt nod, the JOOD turned and settled back into his impact seat, clipped a cable into his neural interface, and contacted the CIC. 'Bridge to CIC, Bridge to CIC.'

'This is CIC, go ahead,' replied one of the Operations Specialists.

'The skipper's requesting a Naval Strike Package be drawn up. Grids to follow.'

'Standing by to copy.'

The JOOD quickly transmitted the coordinates and the Operations Specialist transmitted back a transcript to ensure no mistakes had been made. The Operations Specialist quickly contacted the Combat Information Centre Watch Officer. 'Mr Favé! Naval Strike Package to be launched to these coordinates!' the Operations Specialist reported as he transferred their digital notes to the Watch Officer. The CIC Watch Officer unplugged from the network and visually inspected the coordinates before speaking.

'Activate NSPs Kilo and Sierra! Upload coordinates Celestial Body, HP038-593. Grid, QF102-939 to NSP Kilo and Coordinates Celestial Body, ST192-828. Grid, KD192-929 to NSP Sierra!' the CICWO barked.

'Uploading Strike Package coordinates now, sir,' reported one of the operations specialists.

'Strike Package ready!' reported another.

'Then let Chrysoar handle it,' the Watch Officer instructed.

The operations staff nodded and continued to process new data. Moments later, another alarm began to whine through the ship more akin to a civil air raid siren than a conventional klaxon as Chrysoar automatically began to load and align the *Roma*'s magnificent ordnance. An instant later, the UNV *Roma* had a Vertical Launch System loaded with a BGM-218 Hurlbat Land Attack Missile and a 155 mm/62 calibre Mark 90 railgun, both levelled at two of the four planets orbiting the local star. Seconds later, the shots rang out; the HLAM careened out across the black of space while a single earth-shattering slug from the Mark 90 hurtled towards the nearest planet. Hours later, each weapon's destructive exploits would register on FARSIGHT. As the fighters finally stopped swarming the fleet and the guns fell silent, those aboard each Task Force vessel couldn't help but feel a little overjoyed. For the first time in two and a half years, the Enzo Line had been broken. But that in itself left an even more daunting fact; they were operationally blind from here on out. Nothing ever survived past the first line—ever. Michiko sighed a sigh of relief, but she knew it wasn't over. Everyone knew that.

'What's our status?' Michiko queried, turning to Hesch again.

'The seventh is critical: over forty percent of her forces were destroyed in the opening barrage, the first is in better shape: she only lost twenty-five percent of her total force, and the twenty-second has probably faired the best out of the three with only twelve percent casualties,' Hesch reported. Michiko rubbed her eyes. 'Uh, ma'am. Captains are requesting a couple hours to conduct repairs, what should I tell them?' Hesch quickly added.

'Tell them no,' Michiko's expression cold as the words left her.

'Say again—' Hesch began but Michiko interrupted his question.

'The answer is "no", we need to capitalise on this breach now; we don't have the time to tend to the wounded. Whatever repairs can be made in transit will have to do; if they can't be done then we leave them behind,' Michiko replied, her breath heavy with command.

'Aye, aye,' Hesch replied.

From there, the Task Force jumped to the next system. Another eight minutes before all hell broke loose again.

Chapter 25
Broken toys

Rakaru system, 1137 hours Zulu

The *Morte* shuddered as she re-entered normal space. Hesch's voice almost immediately echoed across the bridge. 'Corvettes are breaking off, ma'am!'

'Understood, location of the Anchor?'

'Subspace Anchor is holding at two four zero mark zero three zero! Corvettes on intercept course!' Hesch continued. Minutes later, the flotilla admiral's calm voice would crack over the comms.

'Jupiter's Consort, Pathfinder Actual. Subspace Anchor down. Over,' reported a corvette commander. Michiko tapped a tile on her captain's chair.

'Understood Pathfinder Actual. Juliet Charlie Actual. Out,' Michiko replied. Michiko turned to Hesch. 'Bosun, I want a SITREP on our FARSIGHT situation.'

'Retrieving damage report, aye, ma'am,' Hesch replied as he activated his wireless transceiver. He paused as he processed the data. 'Just over half the Task Force is back up to full array range, ma'am, the rest are either still blind or processing data at limited range,' Hesch reported.

Michiko nodded. 'Understood.'

Hesch stopped before returning to his monitor. 'Uh, ma'am?'

Michiko turned to face him. 'Yes?' she asked, distracted.

'The Task Force is wondering, what are we looking for, ma'am?' Hesch questioned.

'The abnormal, Petty Officer,' Michiko replied.

'Aye, ma'am,' Hesch responded before returning to his station.

Michiko stared out at the projected black space before them when something caught her eye. She turned to McGhee as he leaned in to inspect his monitor. 'What is it, Seaman?'

'An abnormality, ma'am. FARSIGHT is detecting low levels of radiation CBDR,' McGhee reported.

The lieutenant commander frowned as she translated the report: *constant bearing, decreasing range,* before sudden understanding pulsed through her eyes as she slammed the inter-ship communications switch on the captain's chair. 'All ships! All ships! Evasive manoeuvres, now!' Michiko screamed as explosions cascaded across the system slamming into the Task Force's contoured shield lines. Explosions rippled through the fleet as stealth mines detonated behind kinetic screens, the explosions amplified by the curvature of the energy fields. As quickly as the explosive domino appeared, it was gone, erased by the vacuum of space. Michiko readjusted her hair as she lifted herself back into the skipper's chair. The *Fortuna*'s bridge was a mess with electrical surges, thick flames, and light rupture points. 'Get those holes sealed and those fires under control!' Michiko howled. 'Bosun! SITREP!' she barked as the bridge crew moved to seal the micro breaches and kill the electrical fires. 'Quartermaster!' she screamed as she repositioned her chair.

'All ships, all ships! Report in! Report in!' Hesch ordered to the various ships in the force. An instant later, wireless responses came flooding in from the thousands of ships in the armada. 'The first fleet's down to twenty-seven hundred ships, the seventh is in even worse shape with only fourteen eighty-five ships,' Hesch relayed.

Kusō! Michiko cursed to herself, clenching her armrests tighter.

'And—' Hesch began, before deciding against it.

'Go ahead, Petty Officer,' Michiko insisted.

'Twenty-second still in the best condition, ma'am, with twenty-seven seventy-two ships,' Hesch stated.

We're gonna need a miracle to get us through this death-trap, Michiko admitted to herself.

'Ma'am, Task Force commanders are requesting instructions,' Hesch communicated.

Michiko bit her lower lip. 'Inform them data transfer protocol PASSOVER is in formal task force-wide effect and have them stand by for tasking,' Michiko replied.

Without warning, the crew of the *Fortuna* disconnected their neural interfaces and switched their consoles over to manual.

'Aye, aye,' Hesch answered. 'Stallion Actual, Sekan Actual, Harbinger Actual. Data transfer protocol PASSOVER is in effect. Stand by for tasking. Out,' Hesch wired.

Michiko leaned her head on her hand, her elbow resting on the armrest.

'Quartermaster, bring up the strategic map for this sector,' Michiko instructed.

'Bringing up strategic map for Quebec Delta two nine eight dash six eight four, aye, ma'am,' Samuels replied. Moments later, the Tangible Holographic model appeared at the centre of the bridge.

'Seaman McGhee!' Michiko boomed.

'Ma'am?'

'Do we still have FARSIGHT?' the commander inquired.

'Negative! Give me one mike to realign the FARSIGHT array!' McGhee reported back.

'You've got thirty ticks!'

'Aye, aye!' called back the lookout. Moments later, he called back that the system was operational.

'Excellent! Now, find me one of those Subspace Inhibitors!' Michiko instructed.

'Looking for the needle. Aye, ma'am!' McGhee answered back.

Then we waited. The fixed phrase 'looking for the needle' was coined by modern stellar seafaring, specifically from some of the first astral pioneers, searching desperately for a golden world to call home. It was drawn from the simple fact that space is incomprehensibly vast, cold, and devoid and made even kilometre-long ships seem like needles in the sea of black. Of course, while the term had proliferated into UNS jargon, it was a slight exaggeration. The Taskforce had been explorers before the empire was even a glint in Kuzmoto's eye; as a result, our FARSIGHT arrays were state of the art and could detect the dust on a person's tunic when properly tuned.

'Seaman McGhee, could you explain to me how you missed that minefield?' Michiko hissed.

McGhee shrugged. 'Best guess, those RKKVs did more damage than I initially suspected. I'd have to run a full diagnostic sweep to know the full extent of the damage. I can run that now if you want, ma'am,' McGhee explained.

'Negative, I need you focused, seaman; right now, you're our eyes, you are this ship's praetorian against threats.'

'Aye, aye,' McGhee replied before returning to his console. A few minutes into the sweep, the lookout erupted with emotion.

'I've got an Inhibitor on scopes! Bearing three, three zero mark zero seven zero!' McGhee elaborated.

'Understood! Bosun, I want a fighter sortie mocked up and scrambled asap!' Michiko instructed as she turned her chair.

'Requesting fighter intercept. Aye, ma'am,' Hesch responded before getting on the net. 'UNV *John F Kennedy*. UNV *John F Kennedy*. *Morte Fortuna*. Stand by for tasking. Over.'

'UNV *Morte Fortuna*. UNV *John F Kennedy*. Standing by to copy. Over,' replied Hesch's counterpart.

'Jupiter's Consort requesting combat sortie. Grid Uniform Papa two niner two, dash niner three two. How copy? Over.'

'Combat sortie to grid UP292-932. Confirm?' Information Systems Technician Seaman Plant confirmed.

'Confirmed. Execute when ready. Out.'

++++

UNV John F Kennedy

The OOD strode up beside the captain. 'Skipper! Jupiter's Consort is requesting a fighter sortie on these coordinates!' he said as he passed the coordinates across.

'Understood! Get air boss on the horn and muster up a detail!' Captain Marcin barked.

'Aye, aye!' replied the OOD before relaying the orders down the chain.

'Air boss, skipper's requesting combat sortie at grid UP292-932. Two-fighter detail. How copy?' relayed the messenger of the watch.

'Two-fighter combat sortie at grid UP292-932. Confirm?' the air boss repeated to confirm the numbers.

'Confirmed,' the JOOD replied before returning to their work. With a smile, Commander Aleks Heim, air boss for the *JFK*'s entire air wing turned to his Carrier Air Traffic Control Centre mounted to the overhead of the flight deck. 'Boys and girls! I need a fighter detail wrangled up, pull from alert fighters if necessary. Any fighter pairs within ten thousand kilometres of coordinates UP292-932 that aren't bingo fuel should be prioritised,' the air boss instructed.

'Aye, aye,' responded the air traffic controllers.

'I've got a pair!' reported Air Traffic Controller Second Class Tomson. The air boss leaned in.

'Where?'

'Sector five three, sir,' responded Tomson. 'It's Kilo Delta Zero Sixteen and Kilo Delta Zero Fourteen, sir.'

'Excellent, get on the horn with their squadron commander and redeploy them to sector five nine,' the air boss instructed.

'Re-tasking aye, aye,' Tomson replied. 'Kilo Delta One Niner Three this is *Kennedy* Flight. How copy? Over,' Tomson began.

'*Kennedy* Flight, this is KD193 reading five by five. Over,' came the instant response of the squadron CO.

'KD193, *Kennedy* Flight. Skipper needs KD016 and KD014 for a combat sortie in sector five niner. How copy?'

'Roger, Flight. KD193, out,' reported Captain 'Ridge' McBean. He switched to squadron communications and began to broadcast.

'Okay, Plugger, Choker. You're up. Skipper's got a sortie for the pair of ya,' McBean relayed.

'Just send us the coordinates, boss,' replied Lieutenant Sam 'Plugger' Kaatrait.

'Transmitting,' the squadron leader replied.

'Received,' reported Plugger and Choker.

'This is KD016, breaking off,' Plugger reported.

'This is KD014, manoeuvring,' Choker responded as the pair peeled away from the squadron towards the intended targets, their HMDs notifying them of a mission update.

'Sortie update,' remarked Plugger.

'I have a wireless transceiver too, you know?' Lieutenant Junior Grade Tjal 'Choker' Ndiaj replied.

'Then you'd know our new orders,' Plugger responded with a smirk.

'Uh, yeah. Of course!' Choker replied, obviously neglecting to read the change.

'We're inspecting a Subspace Inhibitor,' Plugger explained to save his wingman the work.

'Ugh!' Choker exclaimed over their local comm line. 'Why do we always get the saps?' the pilot exclaimed.

'Because you're the squadron target queen,' Plugger jokingly remarked.

'*Brufik* off! Bent is more of a target queen than I am!' Choker hissed defensively.

'Tell that to the four scrapes you've sustained in the last thirty mikes of ACM,' Plugger mockingly replied. ACM, or Air Combat Manoeuvring, was the flier's term for a dogfight. Tjal just stopped responding. It was a few minutes before the pilots finally reached their target. 'We're coming up on the inhibitor now,' he remarked.

'Inhibitor? What inhibitor?' Ndiaj sarcastically asked. 'You saved my skin there, how did I not see the inhibitor?'

Sam just simmered as he slowed his fighter's impulse engines until he was hovering in front of the silver spike. Kaatrait activated his ship's transmitter.

'*Kennedy* Flight, KD016. At coordinates, awaiting instructions. Over.'

'KD016, *Kennedy* Flight. Understood, patching you through to Jupiter's Consort Actual. Out,' responded *Kennedy*'s air traffic controller.

'KD016, this is Consort Actual. How copy? Over,' called Commander Stratton, her Japanese accent ringing through the pilot's audio. Sam took a deep breath at the realisation.

'Juliet Charlie Actual. KD016 reading five by five. Over,' responded Kaatrait.

'Lieutenant, I'm going to need you to try to create a wireless handshake between your fighter and the inhibitor. Over,' Michiko explained.

'For what purpose, ma'am?' replied Plugger.

'I want to level the playing field, let's leave it at that,' Michiko explained. With nothing important to say over the wireless, Sam simply clicked his wireless twice, the paired bursts of static acknowledging the instruction.

'Okay, let's do this,' Kaatrait remarked. 'Amelia?'

Amelia's avatar appeared moments later, her rugged 1890s attire and ragged hair noticeably distinct against the technology of the sharp jet-like fighter.

'Yeah?' she called out, her old-Earth Kansas accent even stranger.

'Prepare transceivers for wireless handshake.'

Amelia simply blinked. 'All done,' she reported with a grin.

'Excellent, okay. Initiating wireless handshake,' the lieutenant reported as he flicked the switch. Moments, later his HMD was filled with data processors as the two structures communicated. Kaatrait's face wrinkled in confusion before smoothing. 'Juliet Charlie Actual. KD016. Wireless handshake successful. But it was too easy.'

'Elaborate,' Michiko instructed, confused about the details.

'That inhibitor had no security software.'

This time it was Michiko who frowned, her finger lifting from the comm panel.

'Ma'am, I can secure the network against any intrusions if this falls through,' reported Safae.

'Do it; we've got no other choice,' Michiko admitted.

'Network secure, ma'am,' Safae reported an instant later.

Michiko nodded before tapping her chair's comm switch again. 'Noted, KD016; continue with the mission. Over,' Michiko instructed over the wireless.

Sam responded with another wireless acknowledgement before speaking.'Okay, Amelia, feed the inhibitor network to the *Morte Fortuna.*'

'You got it, boss,' Amelia replied as her avatar disappeared, the data feed reappearing in her place.

++++

UNV Morte Fortuna

Michiko looked over Samuels' shoulder as the inhibitor beacons began to appear across the system map.

'Mother of Gods. There have to be at least ten thousand!' Hesch remarked as the markers continued to appear all the way to the target planet.

Michiko turned back to Hesch. 'Bosun, get me KD016!' Stratton instructed as she settled back into the captain's chair.

'KD016. Jupiter's Consort. Did you find anything interesting? Over,' Hesch inquired for Michiko.

'Jupiter's Consort. KD016, stand by. Over,' Kaatrait reported before waking up Amelia.

'Did I find anything?' Amelia asked facetiously, already knowing the question. Sam simply nodded. 'Well, I done did find the self-destruct key, for all them at once,' she coyly replied, holding the facsimile of a door key between her index finger and thumb.

Sam couldn't help but smirk as he keyed his wireless transceiver.

'Juliet Charlie, did you get that? Over,' Kaatrait questioned, knowing full well Amelia had already uploaded it the *Morte*.

'Loud and clear, KD016. Return to your squadron. Out,' finished Michiko.

'You hear that, Choker?'

'Loud and clear,' Choker replied as he manoeuvred his fighter away.

'Hey, Choker,' Plugger called out.

'Yeah?'

'I'm bingo fuel, I'll call ahead and break off, link up with the RFC,' Sam said as he turned towards fleet's refuelling carrier, his hydrogen fuel indicator dipping into the red.

'Understood, clear stars,' Tjal replied.

'Fair light, wingman,' Sam called back before switching frequencies 'Hardball. Plugger. How copy? Over.'

'Reading five by five. Send traffic, over.'

'Bingo fuel. RTB to RFC. Over.'

'Understood. Link up at twelve fifty-two hours Zulu. Hardball out,' the squadron leader finished. With a thrum of reaction control thrusters, Kaatrait moved off.

Michiko looked over the extensive network of Subspace Inhibitors. 'And we've got the remote detonation codes for all of them?' Stratton said in disbelief, as Safae's avatar looked over the manifest of codes before her.

'Affirmative, they're all there.'

Michiko nodded as Safae reported the validity of the claims. ‘Then, we’re ahead of schedule. Bosun, inform Fireteam Lycaon of the situation, have the Task Force stand down to Condition Two, take up a defensive posture and organise a combat air patrol. After that, contact the ships we left behind. All ships that can be combat-ready in sixty mikes. Recall them. Leave the rest to tend their wounds,’ Michiko instructed.

‘Aye, aye,’ Hesch replied.

‘And get me a damage control team up here asap!’ Michiko barked. ‘All personnel who aren’t essential to this ship not crashing, you can now begin repairs. Quartermaster, Lookout. You’re up.’

It seemed like it was turning around for the Task Force. It truly did.

Chapter 26
A tinkerer's touch

UNV Morte Fortuna, One hour later: 1315 hours Zulu

Michiko sat in the captain's chair as Sara stood beside it. Michiko had offered the seat to her, but the Specialist had flatly refused while Michiko was coordinating the operation; for all intents and purposes, it was hers. She'd earned it. Over the last hour, Task Force S had recovered a portion of its force. Ships that'd been previously classified as casualties over the last two incursions due to the Task Forces prior situation were now up to fighting strength again and spoiling for a fight, their crews tempered by battle and eager for a bit of payback. With these recovered ships, the fleet of almost seven thousand was bolstered to eight thousand. Still not the thirteen and a half thousand they started with, but it was better than nothing. Bodies floated in the vacuum of space as ships had to vent damaged stations, their automatic seals condemning hundreds of sailors and marines for the safety of the ship. It should've been heartbreaking, but it didn't feel like it. The *Morte* had fared moderately better than most ships in the fleet. Carbon dioxide scrubbers had been ruptured, three of the port engines and half of the port manoeuvring thrusters had burst, leaving the *Fortuna* in an axial spin. A fifth of the *Morte*'s gravity plating had failed, leaving odd portions of the vessel without gravity. Sara tuned back into the situation.

'Commander, I'd love to allocate the Task Force's limited supply of electrical boosters, but we've got ships running on fusion reactors that have failing magnetic bottles that desperately need electrical boosters,' Michiko pointedly retorted over the comm line to one of the warship captains of the fleet who'd worked bureaucratic witchcraft to get a line to Michiko.

'What's the situation, Commander?' Sara asked as she shook herself out of her trance-like state.

'Well, repairs are going well, we've got a few ships that've had some unexpected complications en route, so operations will recommence a little later than expected, but we'll be back to getting our teeth kicked in by these Victor Foxtrots in no time,' Michiko sardonically reported.

'We'll do fine; you've done a fine job,' Sara comforted.

Michiko sighed. 'I guess,' she finally admitted.

'Well, do you have an ETA on those repairs?' Sara asked as she readjusted her posture.

'We'll be ready to get underway in another two–three minutes,' Michiko reported.

'Good to know. Well, you've got the conn,' Sara finished before striding back down to the well deck. It was in surprisingly good condition compared to the rest of the ship; with its reinforced bulkheads, the well deck could just as likely outlive the rest of the ship in a planetary crash.

Moments later, Hesch's calm voice echoed over the intercom: 'All hands, all hands, General Quarters Condition One. This is not a drill. All hands, all hands GQ1. This is not a drill. Air Defence Warning Red. Air Defence Warning Red.'

With a smirk, Sara slipped on her helmet and boarded their Condor for the second time.

'What's the word?' Elenskis called up in question. Sara smiled, though they couldn't see it.

'It's kick-off, *gospadins*.'

'Kill!' exclaimed the fireteam.

++++

Michiko

Bridge of the UNV Morte Fortuna

Dark scorch marks lined the bridge as the final sparks from the freshly disconnected power couplings fizzled out. Michiko rubbed her temple as she leaned against the chair's armrest.

'Ma'am, all departments report secured for jump,' reported Barken, before strapping into his impact seat.

'Good to hear. Quartermaster, are our jump coordinates plugged in?' Michiko asked.

'The Task Force is prepped for jump. Slingshot drop plotted; we'll cut across the remaining systems and terminate at Lagrange Point Five, ma'am,' Samuels replied.

'Aether Drive primed hot, we'll be able to get underway as soon as the Subspace Inhibitors are taken offline,' Evan's added.

'Excellent, then let's see what we can do about those inhibitors,' Michiko instructed as Safae appeared beside her.

'By your command,' Safae responded before disappearing. Moments later, the *Fortuna*'s arrays detected a cluster of massive explosions right across the quadrant, and the entire inhibitor field collapsed. As the last one erupted in a ball of fire, the jump command was issued to the Task Force and all eight thousand vessels vanished into the Aether.

'Glide nominal, ma'am. ETA thirty-two minutes,' reported Harmon.

++++

HP 172-427, 1353 hours Zulu

The Task Force glided through Aether Space. We were thirty seconds out from re-entry; alarms flared through the Task Force's ships as soldiers, marines, sailors and airmen braced for contact. We were about to jump into the middle of Honour Guard defences, circumventing the majority of their fleet.

Hesch's voice echoed over the 1MC. 'Re-entry in ten seconds. Brace for contact! Brace for contact!'

Alarms began to flare around the ship as the quartermaster reported. 'Skipper, we're being pulled out of Aether Space!'

Michiko cursed under her breath. 'How?' she replied as the ship rocked violently, dragged through the Aether's greater tachyon stream back into normal space. 'Status!' Michiko boomed as she looked up at the FARSIGHT readout.

'What?' Michiko exclaimed in disbelief as she looked over the readout. The positions were all wrong: the Task Force's, the Void Wanderers. 'Can someone explain to me how we're forty thousand klicks off our intended exit vector?' Michiko demanded.

'Subspace Inhibitor pulled us back into normal space, ma'am,' Johnathan reported.

'How, though? We remotely detonated the entire grid.'

'Apparently not all of them, ma'am,' Johnathan said, his ice-cool stare fixed on his instrumentation. Michiko frowned again as she looked up at the display.

'Ma'am! Void Wanderer fleet CBDR! ETA forty-five minutes!' reported McGhee.

Michiko clenched her fist as she ignored her immediate questions for the task at hand. 'What's the force composition?' she requested as a holographic display appeared at the heart of the bridge.

'Thirteen hundred twenty Type-83 interceptor corvettes, eight hundred eighty Type-87 strike destroyers, two Type-85 supercarriers, two Type-84 support carriers and a single warship of unknown classification, ma'am,' Hesch relayed as the holographic display showed the trident formation throttling across space, the new warship leading at the head of the central prong.

'Quartermaster, where is the Lagrange point for this sector of space?' Michiko asked.

'Minus fifteen thousand klicks from the target fleet, ma'am.'

'Lookout, get me eyes on that capital ship!' Michiko suddenly instructed.

'Getting eyes on, aye, ma'am!' McGhee replied. The lookout flicked a switch on his terminal and transmitted the image to Michiko's retina.

'By the gods!' Michiko whispered as she looked over the imposing ship; it was kilometres long and littered with gun batteries.

'There isn't a single fighter pod!' McGhee reported.

'It's a battleship. Their fighters have been outpaced by our CIWS in the past so they must have seen the logic of building themselves some sort of dreadnought,' she muttered. 'With that fighter escort, long-range munitions will be easily intercepted,' she remarked. 'Looks like we'll have to close the gap. Have the Task Force execute a bow-forward X formation; we're going to wedge ourselves into the heart of that trident and grind them to dust,' Michiko instructed.

'Relaying formation orders to Task Force, aye, ma'am,' responded Hesch.

'Relaying to CIC,' reported Barken.

Moments later, a muted rumble echoed through the ship as the screen generators recycled, their kinetic screens shifting away from the ships port, starboard, and dorsal plates to reinforce the bow and stern portions of the vessel, exposing the port and starboard launch tubes as well as the dorsal weapon emplacements. An instant later, a flash of emotion pulsed across the commander's face.

'Wait, Bosun! Belay that order!' Michiko boomed. 'Prepare to initiate Task Force manoeuvre. Execute close-in dorsal-forward hemisphere formation!' Michiko barked.

'Relaying manoeuvre, aye, ma'am!' Hesch replied.

Tight beams flashed as the Task Force cluster broke apart and began to reform behind a wall of Alexander-class carrier battleships, packed in so tight that kinetic screens flared up in protest.

'Prepare ground teams for launch!'

‘Prepping ground teams, aye, ma’am!’ replied Hesch as he continued to relay instructions.

‘And get me an Alpha Strike in the tube! I want torpedo bombers gutting that battleship as soon as it reaches our position!’ Michiko hissed.

‘Prepping Alpha Strike, aye, ma’am!’ responded Hesch. ‘UNV *Trajan*, UNV *Morte Fortuna*. Stand by for tasking. Over.’

‘*Morte Fortuna. Trajan*. Standing by to copy. Over,’ responded the operations specialist.

‘Prep Alpha Strike Charlie. Target, Uniform Sierra Victor. Launch at Juliet Charlie's discretion. Over,’ Hesch relayed. Hesch’s counterpart repeated the details before passing them along the chain of command and eventually down to the pilots.

++++

UNV Trajan, 1410 hours Zulu

‘You know the tune, ladies! Let’s get movin’!’ barked Squadron Leader Shanon as she and her pilot’s Torpedo Squadron VT-161 strode into the ready room after the mission briefing. Each pilot quickly geared up before slipping their helmets under their arms and striding out onto the hangar bay where their A-24 ‘Hell’ Intruder torpedo bombers were being loaded up and readied for launch.

‘This is the air boss. I want the entire hangar deck ready for operations and Intruders rearmed and refuelled for Alpha Strike!’ barked the air boss over the main circuit as the pilots strode out onto the hangar deck.

‘Chief! We ready to roll?’ Shanon called over the ruckus of other fighter preparations.

‘Purging the tubes now!’ barked back the flight crew chief as he reattached a piece of plating on a nearby F-72 ‘Harpy’ Joint Strike Fighter.

Shanon simply nodded as she passed her helmet on to one of the nearby enlisted flight crew—colloquially known as Airedales—preparing her bomber for launch. With her helmet out of the way, the lieutenant commander began to climb up into her bomber's cockpit via the craft's in-built handles. She slipped into the cockpit, and the Airedale passed her helmet before sealing the glass cockpit. Shanon slipped the helmet over her head and the glass visor lowered into place, sealing as it connected with the rest of the 'bucket'. A breath later, two small screw-like appendages attached to her temples and her body began to twitch.

'Connection established,' reported the bomber's built-in Tier One AI. Shanon followed her flight suit's oxygen hose down to the oxygen regulator and attached it to the right side of her abdomen. With her left hand, she reached behind her helmet and began to activate the various helmet-mounted electronics and displays. As her HMD flickered to life, cool air began to pump into the commander's helmet. She took a deep breath.

'Begin automated warm-up,' Shanon instructed.

'Beginning auto warm-up,' said the AI. There was a long pause before it reported again: 'Automatic warm-up function disabled; data transfer protocol PASSOVER in effect.'

Shanon frowned. 'PASSOVER's still in effect? *Brafik*, worth a try,' she remarked.

'Affirmative.'

Shanon just shook her head. 'Okay, beginning manual warm-up,' Shanon reported as she locked the flight stick down and away, pulled out the flight pad and went through the various switches. 'Initiating pre-cycle engine warm-up,' Shanon stated as she flicked a switch just in front of the throttle. 'Activating electronics,' she said as she prodded the plastic-covered button. The craft's electronics flickered to life and began to communicate with her helmet. 'Keying guidance systems now,' Shanon reported as she unhooked a configuration data card from her flight suit and slipped it into a horizontal slot on her right side, her palm nestled on a digital scanner. Both beeped in the affirmative to confirm the commander's identity. 'Okay, guidance online.' A low beep began to emanate from the commander's helmet. 'Okay, pre-cycle engine warm-up complete. *Trajan* Flight, Juliet alpha one eight four request engine key. Over.'

'JA184, *Trajan* Flight. Go for engine key. Out,' reported the aircraft handling officer from the hangar deck control embedded in the overhead above.

'*Trajan*, JA184. Understood. Keying engine now.' With the green light from her assigned aircraft director, or 'hangar rat', and the necessary chocks and chains removed by other nearby Airedales, Shanon reported, 'Taxiing to tube.'

She slowly released her foot from the brake to move her craft out of its bay and towards her electromagnetic launch tube. Ahead of her craft, the sharp precise hand signals of her hangar rat verified the information her neural interface was telling her; her direction, the distance of her wings to the bulkheads, to other craft and other sailors conducting work all around her. At the next hangar rat's instruction, she lowered her forward wheel's launch bar, aligned her craft with the catapult shuttle, and applied pressure to the brakes. Before her wheels had even fully stopped, Airedales rushed in to complete final hull inspections and troubleshooting before—at the orders of the senior ordnance handler—others rushed over to begin loading Shanon's intruder with an extensive array of ordnance at a blistering pace.

With their work done the Airedales vacated the area and the launch tube doors opened up. The last hangar rat guided her into the launch tube, relaying their final set of instructions before handing her off to the catapult officer, or 'shooter', and rushing out of the enclosed tube.

As she came to a halt atop the electromagnetic catapult shuttle, her front wheel was now forced into a groove in the deck by its idle power. A 'hook up man' rushed in to verify the front wheel was safely secured in the catapult shuttle. The squadron, as per the mission brief, was to be held in their launch tubes until the enemy fleet was within fifteen thousand kilometres of the Task Force, at which point VT-161 was going to initiate a tight gun run through the behemoth's gunport gaps in its ballistic shield. They were hoping to cripple the monstrosity, rout the enemy fleet, and allow ground forces to successfully land planetside. Shanon took deep breaths as her pre-combat jitters began to take hold. She clutched the stick tightly and began to run her index finger over the trigger, the grooved nature of the red button calming her thoughts.

The shooter began to fluster in the controlled panic of a freshly commissioned officer as the order to launch came down. The catapult system began to tense releasing any empty slack as the shooter furiously relayed the run-up and afterburner signal. Shanon quickly complied as she set the craft to full throttle and raised the launch bar. Shanon saluted before resting her hand on her craft's hold handle, affectionately called a 'towel rail'. The shooter looked over her check items before tapping her console behind the glass, saluting, and signalling forwards with a knife-hand as the fighter was thrown out into the black of space. It got Shanon every time: that momentary drop before the fighter was thrown by the tube's magnetic field. Her body was slammed backwards as if hit by an air blast. Moments later, her bomber was thrown into the black, the imposing side of the UNV Long Tan less than fifteen kilometres away from her.

'Trajan, JA184. I am in the black. Out,' reported Shanon.

Moments later, the wireless chatter of the 161st came echoing over her system. 'This is Screamer, forming up on your wing, Bajak,' reported one of the pilots as the squadron of bombers leapt out into the black of space.

Shanon quickly connected her bomber to the Trajan's infrared array and began to map her flight plan. 'Ladies! You read the briefing, two zero three mark two eight four, lock approach vectors, watch out for the Trajan's firing solution and stand by!' Shanon instructed.

Acknowledgement lights winked on as she pivoted her bomber to face the ventral side of the Trajan. As Shanon aligned her craft, a digit began to appear beside the invisible flight tunnel.

++++

UNV Morte Fortuna, 1440 hours Zulu

Michiko gripped the ends of her armrests and stared up intently at the monitor. 'Come on, you bastard,' Michiko muttered before pursing her lips. 'Distance?'

'Twenty thousand and closing, ma'am,' Safae reported.

'Situation with their fighters?' Michiko further pressed.

'Hostile interceptors are holding with their carriers, they are making no attempts to break formation and link up with the dreadnought, ma'am,' reported QT-2. Michiko's hands curled up into fists, and her heart rate increased.

'Fifteen thousand klicks!' Safae boomed with tempered energy.

'Execute manoeuvre!' Michiko howled. With that, the Alexander-class battleships began to peel away from the Task Forces forward wall of battle and began to open fire on the enemies' supporting supercarriers.

++++

UNV Trajan, Lieutenant Commander Shanon

Ten seconds. *Here we go,* Shanon thought as she gripped the throttle tighter. *Five seconds. Three seconds. Two seconds. Zero seconds.* 'Now!' Shanon barked over the wireless as she slammed the throttle on her craft, the starfighter gliding over the *Trajan* into the fray. She yanked the stick hard right and slid through the shield layers of the alien battleship before slamming down the weapon release on the stick. An instant later, a flicker of orange light began to bounce off the cockpit of Shanon's bomber as her ordnance gutted the battleship's insides. A split second later, she rocketed out from under the ship's magnetoplasma field and back into the emptiness of space. Shanon pulled back on the throttle and pitched her ship towards the unknown vessel, watching as her pilots gutted the craft from the inside out. Moments later, the magnetoplasma field collapsed and the heavy Task Force guns, that were previously limited by the field, began to crack through the battleship, its heavy guns trying desperately to make a hopeless last stand as they finally came into weapons range. The ship's superstructure began to fracture, its body breaking into three pieces as its latticework of bracings shredded away.

++++

UNV Morte Fortuna

'Hooyah!' Michiko exclaimed with an intensity that cut the tension on the bridge. 'Launch alert fighters and order all ships fire at will!' Michiko immediately ordered, turning to face Hesch as she spoke.

'Launching Alert Fighters and ordering all ships fire at will, aye, ma'am!' Hesch replied before relaying the order. Michiko looked back up at the display to see swaths of fighters launch from their parent vessels and swarm the attacking carriers.

The enemy captains looked on in shock, their pilots still finishing final launch procedures as their parent craft were gutted. All the while, the greater Task Force spread out and spewed lighting and tempestuous fury against the unsuspecting fleet of corvettes and destroyers that struggled with the sudden appearance. *We'd accomplished the impossible: we'd broken through Honour Guard lines and routed their main forces.* Michiko settled back into the captain's chair and looked over the display.

'All hostile craft destroyed. Orders, ma'am?' Phar reported over the intercom.

Michiko replied with a weary smirk. 'Continue with the operation, move into deployment positions and commence groundside operations on my command,' Michiko replied before closing her eyes momentarily.

With that, the fleet moved into low orbit and the landing craft began final preparations for launch.

++++

UNV Scorpio

Alarms blared in the background as Captain Delae rested tensely against the captain's chair, his bridge crew exhausted and on edge as the ship drifted into geosynchronous orbit over the planet below. A moment later, Seawoman Devrn piped up with instructions.

'Skipper! Message from the *Fortuna,* Jupiter's Consort just authorised Terras Alpha!' the messenger of the watch relayed as she turned to face Captain Delae.

Delae's eyes widened; Terras Alpha was the Task Force protocol for orbital bombardment.

'Helm! Pivot the *Scorpio* a hundred and eighty degrees!' Delae boomed.

'Repositioning, hundred eighty degrees, aye, sir!' Helmsman Saeri replied.

'Navigation! I want planetary data now!' Delae continued.

'Pulling up topography, aye, sir!' responded the navigator, Lieutenant Clarke.

'Mr Delari! Have CIC re-synchronise our Command Network Transceiver get us back on the grid and instruct Mr Kiryi to prep dorsal railguns and await final coordinates for a targeting solution!' Delae finished with a clenched fist.

'Relaying instructions to CIC, aye, sir!' Delari finally replied before turning to his Junior Officer of the Deck, Ensign Simper, 'Mr Simper, you heard the captain, handle it.'

'Aye, sir,' Ensign Simper replied, turning back to Seawoman Devrn.

'Bring CIC up to speed on the captain's orders,' Simper said, and with a nod and a sharp 'Aye, aye', Devrn disappeared into her intra-ship communications station.

'Bridge to CIC, bridge to CIC,' began Devrn.

'This is CIC, go ahead,' responded Seawoman Apprentice Lacerda in an almost bored tone.

'Bring the CNT back online. Be advised, TA protocols authorised, prep dorsal missile tubes and railguns. Fleetwide targeting data will be transmitted momentarily,' Devrn explained.

The CICs Messenger of the Watch crackled back over the wireless a moment later.

'Understood, relaying instructions to CIC,' Lacerda finished before returning the handset to its resting place and turning towards Tactical Action Officer Kiryi. 'Lieutenant Kiryi! CNT to be brought back online! TA protocols authorised!' Lacerda finished.

Kiryi paused as he drew himself up.

'Right people! You know what that means! Stand by to receive targeting data and prep railguns. Be advised, we'll back on the grid; that means we will be vulnerable,' Kiryi relayed to the room's operations specialists. A flurry of 'aye's rang through the room before each operations specialist began to initiate a variety of safeguards, countermeasures, and conversations with crewmembers around the ship, from the CIC's three AIs to the ship's gunnery crews. The CIC was a rumble of conversations.

Ielin Kiryi strode towards the holographic table that sat at the centre of the CIC and looked up at the unfolding operation. Three glowing avatars of the ship's combat information centre AIs hovered around the table's holographic display as if inspecting the map for its tactical genius as the ship slowly pivoted on its axis, its dorsal mounted guns shivering with charge as they angled towards the blue-green planet below.

'Lieutenant! I'm registering an abnormality!' called out an Operations Specialist, their words bringing a frown to Kiryi's face. He turned to face the specialist but saw the CIC Watch Officer move to solve the issue and so Kiryi instead pushed away his frown as another specialist reported.

'Data packet received, sir!' reported one of the operations specialists in the mix of the hundred or so that surrounded the central table. Ielin glanced around for the CICWO before realising they were busy and instead stepped over beside the operations specialist. He looked down at the command console and frowned; the file was suspiciously large despite supposedly storing only tactical data pertinent to a TAL Strike.

Kiryi looked down at the operations specialist before him before speaking. 'Open the zipx file in protected view,' he instructed.

The specialist quickly complied. The zipx held everything requested, including the command script that would interface the data with the targeting computers, except it had one more file, oddly sized and strangely useless. Very few Task Force program files had wasted data, but it certainly wasn't impossible.

After inspecting it for a moment longer, Kiryi nodded to the operations specialist. 'Transfer it across to the Gunnery; we're on the clock here, gentlemen,' the TAO instructed. As the specialist approved the transfer, the CIC's rows of storage banks erupted in flame, the AI avatars fading away as their storage centres spewed fire. 'Damn it!' Kiryi hissed as he realised his mistake, his fist slamming into the computer housing that the operation specialist was seated at, throwing sparks into the air. 'Engage magnetics, get rebreathers mounted and get that logic bomb under control!' Kiryi boomed as the *Scorpio*'s doors and hatches exploded open and the muted sound of rushing air began to echo through the ship above the whine of emergency lights and klaxons. The ship's wireless operator's pleas echoed desperately across the fleet net as he hopelessly transmitted an SOS.

'Mayday, Mayday, Mayday. This is the UNV *Scorpio.* Our position is Alpha Sierra zero three niner, three four niner. We have been hit by an enemy logic bomb. We are venting atmosphere and have lost all navigation and targeting systems. We've got nine thousand souls on board!' he practically begged that day, to the black void of space. But no one heard him, not until it was too late. Not until after they'd restored life support and repressurised the ship.

++++

QT-2

UNV Morte Fortuna

I surveyed the battlespace as golden streams of data stretched out from the *Fortuna* to the entire fleet like beams of energy. Safae and Mariko hovered around me, ignorant of the greater network, focused on smaller, more important problems. Targeting misalignments on the UNV *Miagani;* number two reactor failure on the UNV *Drelisad.* As I looked on, presiding over the network, a small data package began to bounce from ship to ship, oddly separate from the regular data streams. Lights began to vanish before my eyes, at first along the outer periphery of warships, but then it rapidly spiralled inwards towards the *Fortuna.* By the time many of the ships had noticed the virulent logic bomb, it had been too late, and many more would soon follow. My chest began to harden as the glimmering digital realm I presided over collapsed around me, devoured by the foreign object in the system. In a moment of pure instinct, I disconnected the entire network, the shimmering golden lines that stretched across the stars receding into their respective ships. My mind screamed as the network crumbled around me, crying desperately, begging for the stream of data to return, like an addiction. So, I pulled the release and threw myself out of the Armis skeleton I'd been lying on. The blood-red illumination and the frigid air of the Combat Information Centre were soothing to me; a shiver pulsed up my arms and across my collarbone, cooling the agitation of my mind. Lieutenant Phar sat across from me in an impact chair, surveying the battlespace from a projection table. He turned to look at me in confusion.

'What's wrong? What's wrong with the network?' the lieutenant bellowed, still unaware of the logic bomb.

'We've been hit by a logic bomb,' I replied, my metallic hands naturally curling into fists at the thought.

Phar's eyes widened. 'Where in the gods' name did it come from?' Phar exclaimed, 'And how did it get through?'

'No idea. I need to inform the skipper,' I replied.

'Just got off the horn with the skipper, she's been wondering what in Eri's name has been going on with the TACNET,' Phar reported.

With a nod, I turned to leave the centre and headed for the bridge. My feet pounded across the deck as my chest drummed to the steps, furious at no one in particular.

'What's the situation, Seaman?' asked Michiko from the captain's chair, her voice taut with stress.

'We've just been hit with a logic bomb, ma'am.'

Michiko's eyes widened. '*Kusoyarou,*' she hissed through clenched teeth, her hand curling into a fist.

'I had to disconnect the network to avoid any more ships being corrupted. We've retained about fifty-five percent of the fleet but this logic bomb is—' my voice drifted off, looking for the word, '—something; once it's triggered it can transmit even partial code in any form. Wireless, intranet, internet. I wouldn't even put it past being able to transmit via archaic things like radio from the architecture I was able to glimpse before the network went down,' I explained, my platform's monotone speaker hiding the feverish panicked intrigue and furious curiosity I was experiencing.

'Which means we're going to need to get some comm buoys up,' Michiko said with a sigh as she turned back around to look at Hesch. 'Bosun, how long would it take to set up a buoy field large enough to interact with an acceptable amount of the fleet to get that TA back underway?'

Hesch just shook his head. 'To get the whole fleet networked back up wouldn't take too long, an hour at most, once we start to get independent ships on the operation,' Hesch explained.

'But the real issue, ma'am,' I interjected, 'is that I don't think this logic bomb was supposed to be played this early in the game.'

Michiko frowned. 'Why's that?'

'Before the network collapsed, I identified a data packet from the UNV *Scorpio* that wasn't using the conventional channels of transmission; coupled with the virulence of this logic bomb and the systems it prioritised, I think that it was instead activated to mask an element critical to their defensive initiative.'

Michiko paused. 'What did it prioritise?' she asked.

'The logic bomb targeted FARSIGHT PPAs and CICs in an attempt to cripple our information warfare capabilities. Conventional cyberwarfare tactics are to target secondary damage control and auxiliary fire control to override decompression safeties, vent the fleet, and turn the fleet's guns on itself.'

Michiko nodded. 'So, is there any way we can recommence our FARSIGHT sweep?'

I shook my head. 'Negative, ma'am, even though its secondary subroutines failed to vent the fleet, their primary subroutine did succeed in crippling our information warfare capacity; we're running blind,' I continued.

Michiko paused for another moment before asking, 'Then … what do you think they were hiding?'

'Taking into account the former, and accounting for the phantom FARSIGHT file that was being transferred to the *Fortuna*, it seems the Honour Guard has some sort of energy field surrounding the planet. It's not a planetary shield, otherwise its energy signature would have been obvious the moment we entered the system. I'm thinking it's something more in line with a planetary EM-Field,' I finished. 'Now we could destroy the Field generators planetside, but detection will most likely be below optimal when we regain communications with the fleet, meaning that the fleet would have to find each generator effectively by sight or we would have to—'

Hesch interjected. 'Reinstall Tasking OS on just over eight thousand warships, which could take—'

'Just over five and a half hours, ma'am,' I finished for Hesch.

Michiko's fist tightened before quickly loosening with a sigh. 'Not gonna cut it. We've got a WMD down there that could be detonated any minute now and we don't have the time to leave that uncertainty hanging.' Michiko paused, her vitals fluctuating as she thought through the situation. 'What's the status of our landing craft?'

'They're deployable, ma'am; the UMC's Landing Dropship Assault ships operate a secondary tactical subnet to coordinate landings and the UA and UACs aircraft don't just rely on fly-by-wire like the UNS do, so we'd be able to mobilise a ground invasion within the next ten mikes. But even with their protective measures, those dropships will have to either drop in blind or be guided in by Force Recon,' Hesch replied with professional enthusiasm.

Michiko simply nodded, her heart rate stabilising. 'We need to keep their defences on the back foot; priority one is regaining contact with our soldiers and marines. But just because we're on the clock, doesn't mean I'm going to sacrifice our troops to panic. Link us up with the UNV *Immemorial* and get things underway,' Michiko instructed.

'Aye, aye,' Hesch replied before returning to his station.

Michiko's gaze returned to me. 'We'll also need to allocate a ballistic missile submarine to the north-western advance now that we won't be able to fire a Naval Strike Package to clear that perimeter wall,' I added.

'Agreed. Bosun contact the UNV *Mercury* and organise the deployment of a Goldsworthy-class submarine,' Michiko instructed.

'Aye, ma'am,' replied Hesch with a nod before Michiko returned her attention to me.

'Well, Seaman, seems like your work bridge-side is done. Return to your station, get to work cleaning up our TACNET,' Michiko instructed.

'Aye, ma'am,' I replied before turning on point and striding out of the bridge, headed for the CIC. *My pleasure,* I thought to myself.

Chapter 27
Iron coffins and the fires of hell

UNV Firestarter, 1505 hours Zulu

Emergency lights flared through the room, the muted hum of the ship's drop klaxon rumbling through Gunnery Sergeant Ramsi's teeth as he strode through the dark, crowded passageway. *'Sifere!'* barked the Halkaa's company commander as he strode through to the drop bay, his hulking Kitari form charging through the rows of marines, his ceremonial kalta swaying as he marched. 'Whaddya hear?' he boomed as his company marshalled into their drop bay, more commonly known as Hakaar or the 'Mother's den' to strategic reaction force marines.

'Nothin' but 'er voice!' the company barked back in reply as they slipped out of their racks and began to gear up.

'Whadda ya see?'

'Nothin' but 'er fist!' the company howled in reply.

'Then let's not disappoint!' Captain Hafe replied. As he released the casket's locking mechanism, the behemoth caskets unclipped from the support struts in their locked positions. The cone-like teardrops pulsed with energy as their lids depressed and slid in behind one of the four primary retrograde thrusters. The company of Halkaa marines filed into their Orbital Deployment Vehicles or ODVs as the captain continued. 'She calls to us from the dark! She whispers into the hearts of men! She twists us to her wills! We're 'er instruments! We're called to violence upon 'er behalf! We're 'er sifere!' he boomed. The marines slipped into the ordinally placed pod doors as Ramsi slipped into the next bay where his platoon of Marine Raiders of 5th Force Reconnaissance Company, 4th Marine Reconnaissance Battalion awaited, fitting the last few finishing touches onto their SPCSs before snapping to attention as they realised who'd walked in.

'Good morning, Gunnery Sergeant!' they each called, their posture straightening ever so slightly.

'Good morning, gentlemen,' Ramsi remarked with a smirk as he lowered his rucksacks from his gloved hands and rested his palms on the holographic table at the centre of the room. 'The lieutenant will be here shortly, ' Ramsi added as the platoon's posture loosened.

'So … this has been one shajstshow of an op …' immediately remarked Lance Corporal Dena Tesk. 'Oh, or is that just me?' she sarcastically added as Ramsi's gaze turned sharply to meet the terminal Lance's.

'Stow it, Tesk, we're in the heart of Honour Guard territory, recon data is three years out of date, and you're gonna sit here and bladsa about a rapidly evolving op?' Ramsi retorted as First Lieutenant Bobbi De Silva strode into the room, her tight cropped brown hair and stern Latina gaze nodding to Yishai as the platoon snapped to attention.

'At ease; we're on the clock, gentlemen,' De Silva replied, her posture rigid, as Ramsi loosened his. He gently tapped the holographic table with the tips of his gloved hands, the rough topographical scans from the Taskforce archives appearing before their eyes.

'In case you didn't know, approximately fifteen minutes ago the fleet was hit with a logic bomb and all FARSIGHT PPAs have gone dark. Currently, forty-five percent of the fleet is attempting to reinitialise and reinstall Tasking OS. To maintain operational tempo, all ground operations have been re-authorised. However, it has been surmised that HP 172-427 is protected by an EM Field Generator that, while not adversely affecting our Condor's propulsion, will cripple our dropship guidance and SPS systems. As such, to minimise preventable field casualties, force reconnaissance marines and army airborne pathfinders will be dropped into the AOE* to guide in our forward elements.' De Silva paused as Ramsi modified the visual display. 'To accomplish this, we'll be deployed planetside first to secure vital observation positions that surround the target complex. You will touch down at fifteen twenty hours Zulu. Once groundside, you will make your way to your designated positions. Forward elements will commence planetary assault at fifteen twenty-five hours Zulu and first forward elements touching down in the AO will be First Battalion, Fourth Halkaas at fifteen forty hours Zulu. Further forward elements will be arriving in the AOE* at fifteen fifty-five hours Zulu, quickly followed by triple-A and artillery assets along the eastern ridgeline and the southern perimeter.' Ramsi glanced down at the display, processing the names that marked the topographical map of the island already nicknamed 'Asfod' before finally settling on his own. Hill 632. 'Be advised, guidance systems will be offline for the operation after your initial launch trajectories are locked in and you enter the planet's atmosphere, course corrections will have to be input manually. Gear up, gentlemen; boots on the ground in fifteen,' De Silva finished, manually turning off the display, releasing the bay's caskets and turning towards her pod.

The tubes shuddered as their locking mechanisms released. Unlike the Halkaa ODVs, which were wide conical frustums that carried an entire five-man fireteam onto the scorched battlefields below, the ODVs employed by marine force reconnaissance and army airborne pathfinders were more commonly small skirt-shaped needle-like pods, wrapped in ablative stealth plating and with barely enough space for a single person, rations, and equipment to last fourteen days. They were known as Single Person Orbital Insertion Vehicles—officially SPOIVs, known to most as 'spovs'—that, as the name suggests, quite literally fired a single soldier or marine towards a planet, calculated by the ship's very own fire control system—more commonly used for its point defence cannons and Vertical Launch Systems. As the platoon dissipated, Ramsi snatched up his pair of rucksacks and turned towards his pod as the door unsealed. He secured his pair of rucksacks within the pod's outer hull and quickly slipped into his impact seat, his shoulders, hips, and head backed up against reinforced impact padding while his M32A2 rested firmly across his chest. His casket sealed up around him with a thud as he began to clip into the five-point harness that'd hold him into the seat as they crashed into the planet's surface before finally activating his seat's RCS Thruster Control board.

'Pre-flight check complete!' reported Tesk over comms as Ramsi did the same. The board to his left came up with green flickering lights.

'Pre-flight complete! All systems nominal,' Ramsi reported. 'All elements, report pre-flight,' Ramsi continued, speaking through the motions. The reports trickled through as Ramsi closed his eyes and took in a deep breath. *Just another drop. Just another drop,* he thought to himself, his hands beginning to shake as his body's pre-op anxieties began to rise. He tightened his fist as the last report filtered through his SPCS's speaker.

'Sound off siim buckets! Wireless check!' De Silva boomed, her TFI jargon slipping through as her mind shut down.

'Makai! Check!' Lance Corporal Makai reported.

'Akei! Check!' reported Private Akei before the wireless check went up the chain to the other pods within the platoon.

'Tesk! Check!' replied the marine.

'Ginkyi! Check!' reported the corporal.

'Ramsi! Check!' Yishai rounded out, releasing his thumb on the activator.

The outer doors slammed shut and the SPOIV's blood-red drop lights flickered to life. Ramsi's HMD quickly changed, bringing up a digital altimeter to the side of his vision: '2,000 km' was written beside the column of measurement lines. Moments later, a column of six lights appeared to the left of Ramsi's vision, all of them red. Each light began to flicker away, top to bottom. their colour shifting away from their initial blood red to a dark and eventually light orange before arriving at the final two squares. As the last green square disappeared, Ramsi felt the rude shake of his SPOIV being launched through one of the hundreds of vertical launch tubes that extended through the ventral plating of the Firestarter. Ramsi's vision was quickly absorbed by a live feed of the pods extended flight as it hurtled towards the planet's surface. 'ETA 10' appeared in the top left of the marine's display.

++++

1518 hours Zulu, seven klicks from impact

Engage chute! Engage RCS thrusters! Ramsi thought as the pod began to violently shake, the retrograde thrusters kicking into gear and slowing the pod at the marine's neural command.

Ramsi's neural flight feed vanished as the pod thudded into the ground and the pod's blood-red interior returned to his sight. He slammed the release on his five-point harness, inspected his equipment, and deciding against causing a panic, hit the manual release on his SPOIV's hatch. The door swung open without hassle to reveal sprawling, dense swampland. He dropped down out into the murky waters of the area of operation, flicked down his helmet-mounted thermal imaging device, and let his gaze sweep across the immediate area. Ramsi's heart raced as he lowered to a crouch, his rifle held close as he searched for hostiles. *No contacts,* he thought to himself with confidence, before rising from his crouched position and turning back to face the pod. His reactive webbing caught his rifle as he quickly began to unclip parts of the pod's ablative plating. He gently rested it all against the hull of the now-shattered pod before reaching in and retrieving his enhanced load-bearing equipment pack. After slipping it over his shoulders and clipping it together, he turned back towards the marshy swamplands that stood before him and once again crouched.

He consulted his CPI for his designated observation position on hill 632. Ramsi's SPCS was unique. Force reconnaissance marines' SPCSs were different from that of regular marines', but this one had modifications unique to him. His upper torso was partially covered in a layer of handcrafted camouflage webbing that clung to his back like a child crying for their father's attention. Beneath the photoreactive shimmer that echoed the surrounding terrain lay the rest of his plating, engulfed in a zigzagging pattern of digital greens, and browns and blacks.

With his bearings in mind and rifle in hand, Ramsi rose from his crouched posture once more and strode forwards. *Dragoons are gonna be here soon, and this is gonna be a real short quick trip if they catch me here,* he thought to himself. The water sloshed at his feet, casting waves out into the surrounding swamplands as he trudged forwards through kilometre after kilometre of mud and muck. His shoulders tightened as the soundless screams of dragoons hissed through his brain and the subtle rustle of marshlands sent panicked shivers down his spine. *You're getting soft,* he thought to himself as an explosion, causing his gaze to turn back, erupted kilometres behind him, and a plume of fire and smoke was thrown into the air. Ramsi smirked. *Just another beautiful day,* he thought to himself before turning back to continue on. His eyes widened, and he raised his M32A2 as the shimmering figure ahead of him dashed away, its hunched, animalistic form unmistakeable. A dragoon. He tucked his rifle close to his shoulder and continued forwards, his rifle casting wide arcs across the marshlands as he advanced through the swamp. *Shajst!* Subsonic rounds against a shielded, invisible dragoon. *Just my day,* Ramsi thought to himself as he continued on. A low growl rumbled through his brain as he pushed forwards, its intensity screaming through his very fibre. Ramsi spun around as the growl faded into memory. *There it is again. A phantasm? Am I losing it?* Ramsi's gaze narrowed as he lowered himself into the muck, trying to glimpse the dragoon that'd been clearly playing with him. He settled into the muck, his helmet only just above the water level as his gaze swept ahead, under debris and fallen trees, across the alien wildlife that swam blissfully in the middle of a warzone. *There it is,* Ramsi thought to himself. *What's it doing?* he wondered as he looked on mystified. The dragoon, phantasm, whatever it was, stood there motionless. *No, not standing ... pressed up against a tree,* Ramsi realised as he looked over the flickering object before him. An instant later, the neural screech of a patrol of dragoons walked past overhead. Ramsi froze, his muscles locking up as the screech became unbearable and then it vanished as the patrol continued past.

Brafik, *that was close,* he thought to himself.

Ramsi looked back towards the tree where the phantom was lying to find the flicker gone. His heart began to race as he slowly rose from his prone position. *That couldn't have just happened,* Ramsi thought to himself. *No, no, no it just couldn't have,* he thought to himself repeatedly, like the thump of a drum. Ramsi had just passed through the largest dragoon staging ground on the entire continent undetected, and if he had walked a mere two metres further before he'd stopped for the phantom, he'd be very dead. *No, a VF did not just save my life,* he defiantly thought. He didn't realise how wrong he was. Ramsi looked down at his CPI, once more ducking into the cover of a nearby tree. It was 1530. All that stood between him and his marines was two thousand metres of hilly, open terrain. He raised his binoculars to quickly survey the sweeping hillside. He switched to his helmet's thermal imaging device for an instant, before readjusting his rifle and running out into the open field as fast as he could towards hill 632. His vision rapidly swept across his nine and three, desperately wishing to be wrong—about the phantom, about the enemy, about the gods-damned hill. His shoulders began to burn first, oddly enough, though his thighs quickly corrected the order of events. His breaths were concise and his steps long before finally slamming into a tree on the other side. Ramsi looked back with a frown; he'd been wrong. There were no dragoons waiting to cut him down. *Something's not right,* Ramsi thought, before shaking off the thought. He still had another three minutes before the Halkaas would be touching down, and they needed laser guidance for at least thirty seconds to implement any meaningful course corrections. Sliding out from the tree, he continued forwards through the sea of branches, continuing to scan for hostile contacts that would never arrive. As he approached the hilltop, the familiar sizzle and crunch of plasma crackled through the air. Tightening his grip, Ramsi advanced, rifle raised as he inched up the hill to a sea of dead dragoons in a ring around a wide-open hearth, its plasma heart still aflame with heat. Black blood ran down the edges of the hill and small fires rose from the blood, soon to be the only proof there ever was a battle here. At the centre of it all stood the phantom, its shimmering cloak smattered with the black blood of the dragoon held tightly by its blade, its body spasming uncontrollably as the final death knells pulsed out sporadically. With the smooth swish of deactivation, the blade dissipated, and the body crumbled to the ground. The dragoon turned to look at Ramsi, unblinking, unmoving. As silent as a stone. Ramsi lowered his rifle. *If he was gonna kill me, he'd have done it by now,* Ramsi assessed to himself. And with that, as if with recognition, the dragoon vanished from sight, now invisible even to Ramsi's enhanced eyesight.

'I'm not paid enough for this *shajst,'* he finally said aloud as he dropped down into the dugout fighting position and strode across to overlook fourth Halkaas combat drop. He checked the timer on his left as he unclipped the laser pointer from his webbing with his other. The pad read '60 s'; *Perfect timing,* he thought as he unclipped his rangefinder and raised it to his helmeted face, glimpsing the flaming caskets that now hurtled through the cloud cover, off course from their island LZ by only a few critical metres. Ramsi held in the button and the invisible beam of light near-instantly touched the island's uppermost point. The pods above quickly adjusted their headings and sixty seconds later slammed into the ground, throwing dust and dirt into the air. Ramsi let out a sigh of relief, pivoting and leaning against the fighting position's wall, resting his rifle on his knee as he looked on in disbelief and confusion at the last nineteen minutes of mud, phantoms, and forces. Had his alien Lukistno Andjel not intervened, he'd have never made it up this damned mountain. He wouldn't have made it five metres, let alone seven kilometres.

++++

Hakir Company, 1st Battalion, 4th Halkaas. Ground zero. 1540 hours Zulu.

The pod thudded into the ground and the blood-red casket returned to him. Private First Class Hakei slammed the release on his five-point harness and unhooked his weapon before quickly smacking his helmet-mounted wireless switch twice, sending the automated two-tone acknowledgement chime across the squad's TEAMCOMM that'd replaced the impractical collar-bone strike that Halkaas had used historically to mark a readiness to serve. To finish the ritual acknowledgement, Hakei marked out an invisible semicircle along the brow of his helmet. Along it, the words 'Daughter's will' were written in Kitan; his personal *Hakemaki*, his divine sanction to gift death on the Daughter's behalf. Moments later, the doors exploded open and the four Halkaa marines bolted out onto the barren island that sat adjacent the alien bastion. Explosions kicked up rock and dirt as BPL mortar shells slammed into the soil, sending chunks of rock and granite high above; in between the explosions, sharp streams from wall mounted turrets buzzed passed the marines. Hakei quickly ducked into a freshly carved crater, his plates flaring as the still-fresh foxhole ate at him. He snapped his rifle up towards the wall, his scope 'glassing' the hundreds—no, thousands of legionary dragoons that manned the wall-walk, bloodthirsty to take lives. Hakei was one of a few that couldn't blame them; Halkaas were exactly that: director-sanctioned sociopaths.

'Gunners! Suppress those emplacements!' barked the company commander as he coordinated the chaos. 'Gynours! Hammer that damned wall!' he instructed in the Kitan combat tongue. At that the company's mortar platoon (nicknamed after the archaic name for gunner, gynour for their old-fashioned warfighting techniques) moved into position. With practised precision, they slammed their smoothbore, muzzle-loaded 51mm Type-178 grenade dischargers into the ground, the weapon's sharp bases piercing the ground with ease before the first barrage of shells careened up and into the fighting positions along the wall. The shells slammed into the overhead shielding.

The shields began to flicker and fade as mortars hammered it with everything they had, each ionised round sapping the barrier of power. Hakei adjusted his automatic rifle and dashed across into thicker cover beside Lance Corporal Kadoni. Moments later, the shells finally broke through, slamming into the walkway's cover before piercing through the jury-rigged fortifications. Hakei rose from his fighting position, propping his M480 Squad Automatic Weapon on the rock cover and depressed the trigger, spewing blue-hot munitions up into the row of fighting positions leaving dragoons stranded as the next volley of mortars slammed into the perimeter line, spewing incendiary napalm across the wall-walk.

'Pilums!' barked the company commander. 'Break that cover!'

'Aye, sir!' the platoon's lieutenant replied as his marines repositioned from cover to line up their shots. Hakei strapped his rifle back into his webbing and unloosed his Mk 306 'Pilum' shoulder-mounted multipurpose weapon—SMW for short—named after the Roman javelins of ancient past. As he levelled the weapon, its targeting computer unfurled from its body and his HMD changed again, providing him with targeting telemetry and wall composition. Kadoni quickly dashed from his position, unclipped a rocket from his belt and slammed it into the SMW's tube before sealing the hatch and ducking away. Hakei clicked a switch on the forward-mounted stabilising grip as the weapon acquired telemetry. The launcher's display slowly changed colour from green to orange, and eventually, to red.

'Fire!' barked Hakei's NCO.

'Back-blast area clear!' boomed from Hakei's speakers, followed by a chorus of replies as he depressed the trigger and the rocket went flying, evaporating before his very eyes. Hakei's mouth gaped with surprise. A breath later, high-powered capital ship rounds began to crash into the island. Hakei scanned the field of battle to see monolithic gun emplacements on four nearby sea stacks that stood between the main continent and their island.

'Fiken!' Hakei hissed in furious plea to the Mother Fi and the Daughter Ke as he repositioned to take cover from the colossal guns as their fire hammered into the island with alien ferocity.

'Those're capital ship guns!' bellowed Lance Corporal Kadoni as Hakei settled back into his foxhole.

'No *kendei*!' snapped back Hakei, this time calling out the obvious in the Daughter's name.

'Pilums!' barked the company commander, 'Focus fire on those guns! Ten o'clock high!' he continued as Kadoni quickly reloaded the PFC's launcher and his targeting computer lined up the shot. 'Fire!' screamed the company commander as a cascading echo of explosions, followed by the stream of smoke from one hundred and twenty rockets, careened through the air, slamming into the left turret a heartbeat later. The entire battalion froze.

'Fikende?' Hakei yelled in a ritual question of confusion to the Mother and the Daughter over the din.

'I don't know!' Kadoni hissed back in their stead.

'That wasn't to you!' Hakei snapped back in response. The guns then continued to hammer the battalion's position with brutal efficiency for the next ten minutes before Corporal Halae crawled into Hakei's foxhole.

'We're Oscar Mike,' the corporal relayed to the pair. 'Form up behind third platoons position with the rest of the fireteam.'

'Aye, Corporal,' Hakei and Kadoni replied. With their orders clear, the pair moved around and behind the staggered lines of third platoon's mortars and into an alcove that tucked them into the heart of the island. Corporal Halae and Lance Corporal Fasi—one of the Company's one hundred-plus self-defined 'Senior' Lance Corporals—arrived a few moments later.

'What's goin' on?' Hakei asked.

'We're taking one of those guns,' Halae said, nonchalantly.

A pause rolled over the fireteam.

'Rah? We're taking one of those guns?' Kadoni questioned, stunned.

'Are you deaf, *Fikefren?'* Halae hissed, invoking the Mother's lover and Daughter's father killed by a boar in an instant of lapsed awareness.

'Negative,' Kadoni said with a shake of his head.

'Then you know what we're doing.' Halae paused for any objections before continuing with his explanation. 'We're wading up to the Alpha Tower at the company's ten o'clock where we will make our way up the sea stack into the Fire Direction Centre and hijack it. If it doesn't have the firepower to crack their ballistic shields, nothing will.'

'Aren't we waiting for naval support?' Hakei asked.

Halae rolled his eyes, raising three outspread fingers to his helmet's faceplate. 'With those guns operational we won't be around long enough to wait for naval support. And the marine landers that'll be accompanying her will be sitting pretty for those guns if we don't neutralise them,' Halae explained. 'Any more time-wasting questions, Private?' Halae asked with clear irritation.

Hakei simply shrugged.

With their objectives clear, the fireteam climbed down the island's vertical cliff face and began to sidestroke out towards the stack. With the rest of the company island-side and enemy troops spread thin as Unified Army forces began to touchdown elsewhere on the continent, Fireteam K was able to make it to the base of the stack undetected and in record time. Hakei shuddered as his body boiled from the pain, his muscles pulsing with an unrivalled fury. The Halkaa marine inspected his M32A2; it was soaked. It wouldn't be operable for another three or four minutes. Strapping it back into his flexible webbing, he began to scale the monolithic stack alongside his fireteam. It was a tough climb; the stack's jagged shape carved out of the continent by erosion over millennia of wear and tear had made the once-solid rock unstable and, more importantly, uneven, leaving many a climber with a difficult ascent. The gun was mounted to the top of the stack, meaning there was a small ledge that could be easily shimmied around. If Wayfarer engineers hadn't decided to change anything, they'd easily surprise the turret's crew, thanks to a distinct lack of viewports.

The fireteam eventually reached the top of the stack and quickly climbed up onto the plateau of the pinnacle. Hakei looked over his weapon once more. It was working again. The corporal inspected his watch. The first marine landing craft would be on final approach within ten minutes; they needed to get control of this beachhead before it was too late.

Halae examined the bulbous turret, its silver and golden form rocking the stack as its capital ship guns pounded the island below. Halae turned to Hakei and gestured to a small hatch on the side of the battery before following with a flurry of hand signals, instructing the private first class to place a C13 charge on the door. With a nod, Hakei quickly obliged, moving up and laying just enough neon-laced plastic explosive around the doorway to crack the door's magnetic seal. The marines quickly took cover as Hakei activated the detonator, cracking the cannon open like an egg. The fireteam moved to take the initiative, as a pulse laser sliced through Hakei's chest. The beam finally exploded as it slammed into the ground behind him. The private crumpled into the ground, his body beginning to convulse. Blood, mixed with gel, spilled out of his chest plate, as his BDU got to work. The suit hissed with air as anti-coagulants poured into the open wound. Lance Corporal Fasi stepped in front, levelled his SAW, and simply held down the trigger as an ungodly fury rose within him. Halae moved around the hail of fire and the two of them moved in and cleared out the cannon as Kadoni dragged Hakei out of the line of fire before administering first aid to his battle buddy.

'Okay, okay. This is gonna hurt,' Kadoni explained through gritted teeth as he administered kaolin nanofibres directly into the wound. Normally the nanofibres would have sent anyone into a knot of pain but Hakei was so detached from his own body that he barely felt the kaolin's icy touch.

'Clear!' called Halae as he stepped out to help Kadoni move Hakei back into the battery. Halae turned to Kadoni quickly before returning to the task at hand.

'All guns secure!' reported Fasi as he finished flash-frying the other three gunnery crews with electrical overloads.

'Good to know!' came Halae's stern tone.

Satisfied with Hakei's condition, Halae returned to the gun controls. 'You got an interface, Fasi?'

'Rah, I've got an interface.'

'Then hook me up.'

'Yut,' the marine responded as he unhooked one of the neural connection cables from the dead dragoon commander and plugged an adapter into the base of the cable.

Without hesitation, Corporal Halae clamped the adapter into the base of his skull and began to convulse as his body processed the gun's immense data. Moments later, the four cannons began to pivot in unison.

'My turn, *Fikenre!*' Halae hissed, invoking both the Mother and the Daughter's wrath as he turned the batteries towards the colossal wall that stood between the marines and the centre of the alien bastion. He waited a moment for the other guns to catch up with his train of thought before hammering the liquid metal with the concentrated capital ship firepower on offer. The once-ethereal colour palette of the immense barrier began to fade, a bright superheated red replacing it before an explosion cascaded into the alien fortress, creating an open door into the bastion. Halae unplugged the cable and stepped out onto the plateau to see hundreds of Halkaa marines charge across the ocean towards the nearby beach where they'd hold out for marine reinforcements. But they'd done their job. They'd gotten their attention. The wireless began to crackle with activity.

'We've got comms!' Fasi exclaimed as he tapped his comm piece.

'Fireteam Kilo. Cichol One, One Actual. How copy?' came the ragged voice of the first squad's Sergeant Kaikn.

'Cichol One, One Actual, Fireteam Kilo. Send traffic. Over,' Fasi responded.

'Skipper wants your fireteam on that gun,' the Kaikn explained.

'Understood. Out,' Fasi finished before cutting the link. 'Corporal! Sar'nt wants you on the gun!'

'Understood! Now! Get me a nine-line!'

'Rah!' yelled back Fasi as he dug back into his communications gear to wrangle up a dropship.

Chapter 28
Omaha round two

The landing craft rocked as its orbital shuttle descended towards the shimmering, glass-like surface. Lance Corporal Kol Maklenan swayed as he stood in his impact harness of the LaCMaC (short for 'landing craft, magnetic cushions') with the marines and armour of 2nd Battalion, 4th Marines. The meat tray was dark with red emergency lighting as the LaCMaC was ferried towards the beachhead. Marines were strapped into the left and right of a trio of M2 Sera main battle tanks.

'Get some, marines!' boomed the company commander.

'Oorah!' the company howled in reply.

With a shudder, the shuttle released its landing craft and the craft's magnetic resistors took over, holding its cargo perfectly above the water. Loud thumps began to shudder through the craft as mortars hurled IR-dampening smoke towards the shoreline. An instant later, explosions erupted directly below the lander. The lights fluttered as power began to fade.

'EMP!' reported the company commander. The LaCMaC began to rapidly descend as the ship's resistor plates gave out. With a violent thud, the LaCMaC crashed into the water before beginning its callous descent.

Maklenan's heart was abuzz with fear as he took a deep breath. They were going to be alright—he knew that, as did everyone aboard, but the fear continued to rise. His train of thought was interrupted, however, by the muffled sound of explosions. He smiled as his heart rate slowed and he let out a breath. They were safe. The craft's nanotube skirt began to inflate with the planet's local air, and the craft began to move again. Weapons fire followed, ringing out across the way and echoing through the lander as the LaCMaC responded in kind. Light machine-gun fire began to screech out from the bow, slicing through the IR-blocking smoke with deadly efficiency.

'Twenty seconds!' barked the company commander, now on the company communications frequency.

'Rah!' the company replied as they began to unhook themselves from the craft's impact harnesses and release the Seras from their strappings before readying their weapons and bracing themselves for the first few minutes of combat, known as the 'frigid *brufik*ing ten', the first ten minutes of a fight where a marine's innate response manifests correctly or doesn't.

'Marines!' barked Regimental Sergeant Major Perritt. 'Kill on three!' he continued. 'One … two … three!' he roared.

'Kill!' the company bellowed back as the craft's main ramp began to lower.

With the ramp down, marines began to file down onto the beach below, rifles firing as they went. Maklenan ran out onto the soaked beach, the craft's pair of M120 7.62 mm machine guns screaming around him. The company continued to advance, the Sera's main gun exploding overhead, nearly deafening any normal man. But he was no normal man. He snapped up his rifle and fired off a few rounds; a dragoon collapsed as his shots made contact. To the left of the battalion were members of 1st Battalion, 4th Halkaas, dishing out their trademark lethality against the bolstered enemy lines. Maklenan peeked a look back as he wriggled into a nearby foxhole; they hadn't lost anything on the way in thanks to the efforts of 4th Halkaas. *We would have lost the lot if we'd flown in,* he thought to himself as he turned back to the conflict at hand. Legionaries poured through the now gaping hole in the perimeter wall and leapt down onto the beach below to form a desperate defence that was, for the moment, holding the marine advance. Golden beams of light cut into the ground ahead of Maklenan, obliterating the advancing dragoons.

He traced the shots back up to their towers. Above him sat four capital ship cannons cutting swaths across the enemy, presumably manned by Halkaas. A burst of static pulsed across Maklenan's wireless snapping him from his reverie.

'Take the initiative, marines!' barked the company commander as the Wayfarer defences collapsed under the alien barrage.

With the initiative claimed, marines slipped out from their foxholes and began to advance up the beachside. Marines and Halkaas ground away at the foot mobiles on the ground while M2s and the alien batteries bombarded the wall-walks with unparalleled violence. Debris went flying as the wall-walks erupted in fire. The marines continued forward, a crackle echoing through their helmets and the sand dragging at their feet with every weighted footstep. But the dragoons stopped pouring through the wall; the battlefield had fallen silent. Something wasn't right. *Have they seen through our ruse?* Maklenan thought before ignoring the idea as A-shaped fighters launched from the cliff line behind the battalion.

The fighters began to batter at the now-exposed marine forces with ruthless efficiency. The M2s and the alien cannon moved desperately to target the nimble fighters, but the enemy pilots bobbed and weaved as if they were in the vacuum of space. Maklenan dived desperately for cover as explosions rippled through the surrounding terrain, the marine offensive quickly collapsing, its momentum gone. Amongst the fire and chaos as Halkaas and marines alike were boxed in by the renewed infantry advance and the continued barrage from overhead interceptors, the company CSM rose from his prone position, rifle in hand, screaming as he did.

'Get me some defensive perimeter, ladies!' he howled as he rose. 'And get those Ymirs up!' he boomed over the wireless, his free hand reinforcing his instructions.

The instruction called for the battalion's complement of man-portable air defence systems: FIM-140 dual-setting lightweight multiple launchers, nicknamed 'Ymir' after the Norse god of creation for the ironic translation of the name as screamer.

As if stirred by a fire, the entire TACNET lit up with responses and beleaguered marines redoubled their efforts. Halkaa marines that were previously pinned down by enemy fire were now able to set up under the renewed fire support from Maklenan's unit, as M2s repositioned to create a physical barrier between the marines and the hostile fire raining down on the position. Within minutes of the renewed exercise in defensive manoeuvres, the Halkaas began to rain hell, rockets careened through the sky, precisely hitting the unshielded fighters as the Halkaas manually targeted their prey.

'Kri!' the Halkaas collectively roared as they continued to cut through the Wanderer squadron overhead while M2s pivoted to hammer the wall, cleaving through the advancing infantry. With transformed vigour and momentum, the allied defences began to break apart. Marines recommenced their advance up the beachhead as the wireless buzzed to life.

'Contact! Unknown classification entering Sector 2-1!' reported one of the Joint Terminal Attack Controllers overhead.

Maklenan looked up to see a black block falling from the sky, the sun dimming as it erased its gaze. The behemoth began to slow as its ventral thrusters kicked into full force, countering its incomprehensible mass. Maklenan looked up at its now-still form, finally able to see it clearly. The vehicle had one hundred and fifty infantry turrets from port to starboard and ten Widower pulse energy projectile cannons—five per side. At the centre was a huge reactor that protruded vertically from weather deck to keel. Finally, the monstrosity was fitted with an incomparable weapon system at the bow of the craft, its central directed energy cannon more akin to a battleship's main battery than the gun of a tank. What would later be uniquely designated the Type-101 'Jutland' atmospheric dreadnought would earn the instant nickname 'Kalm's Sekret'. It quickly got to work, tearing through the advancing marine forces like a hot knife through butter. Maklenan lowered his rifle as his wireless flickered to life.

'Foresight One, Belfast with immediate Call for Fire. Over,' called Bravo Company's CSO over the wireless.

'*Belfast,* Foresight One. We have no Call for Fire assets available at this time. Over,' reported the JTAC grimly.

'*Brufik!*' Maklenan hissed as he looked across the battlefield, the Jutland's infantry turrets slaughtering his company and the dreadnought's Widower's chewing through the battalion's armour column* as if it were a child's plaything.

'Hardcase Actual to any surviving marine forces, if you're below the Golf Bravo, you're our last chance! Hit it with everything you've got! Out!' the company commander barked over the wireless as his position was struck by a Widower pulse.

They always live up to their name, Maklenan, thought to himself. The marine looked up towards the Jutland, blocking out the violence around him, the titan's colossal thrusters beating down upon him like a malicious star. He glanced back down to survey the perimeter; he was it. He was all that was left. He looked up towards the colossal reactor. *That's the key.* He snapped his M32 rifle up towards the sky, let go of the barrel, and snatched up an attachment from his webbing that he quickly attached to the bottom. Maklenan clicked a switch just below the trigger and a cable exploded out of the attachment, slamming into the unprotected side of the goliath. Maklenan gritted his teeth as he activated the ascent line's automated winching function, his suit's limited thrusters keeping his posture while he ascended. As he reached the goliath's keel, he reached out with a single hand and activated its magnetic grip, slinging his rifle beneath his right arm. With both hands now firmly placed against the roof, Maklenan swung his legs forward up onto the hull of the titan, his orientation reversing as his hands let go. Maklenan snapped his rifle back up to a firing position and began to stalk the hull.

'Come on you Victor Foxtrots, you've gotta know I'm here,' Maklenan remarked to himself. Seconds later, air began to pulse out of the ship as airlocks began to unseal. Two heartbeats later, dragoons began to drop through the hatches towards the ground, apparently unaware of his presence. As the hatches resealed, Maklenan smirked. *My turn.* He strode over to one of the entrances, lowered his rifle, and reached into his kit for as much C13 as he had on him, layering it across the hatchway before stepping back to detonate. A dumb grin began to stretch across the marine's face as he armed the detonator. 'Fire in the hole,' he remarked to himself as he slammed the detonator.

An explosion careened up the tunnel and ruptured hundreds of infantry tanks as it went, igniting the tube's formaldehyde-like substance that kept dragoons alive and healthy. Explosions quickly spread through the hull, detonating huge portions of the dreadnought. But it wasn't enough. The behemoth had enough mass to take even that much punishment, and without munitions banks, the only thing left to do the job was the titan's immense reactor. Maklenan strode into the tunnel and began to scale it towards the nearest adjacent hallway. With his AI marking the way, he stopped in front of a seemingly innocuous panel and slammed it open with his fist. He'd found his hallway.

Snapping into the walkway with his rifle, he slid himself out onto the smooth gantry that connected the ship. The reactor was directly ahead of him; only a couple of reinforced doors stood between him and success. But he'd used up his C13 on the entry point, so he was going to have to find another way in. He scanned the area, his eyes looking for any inconsistency in the smooth, silver surface. Nothing. As he searched, the hiss of a door opening echoed behind him. He whipped around and snapped his rifle up and cracked a round into the alien's skull as it turned to face him. Moments later, his head screamed with thoughts and commands as the goliath's security forces went on alert. He'd been found. Maklenan turned around and tapped into the ship's sensors. At the heart of the reactor, dragoons were already pouring into the area to respond to his presence; blades drawn, they were moving to box him in. Maklenan smirked as the bulkheads behind him began to open. He whipped around and began to fire while advancing, letting off burst after burst. A dragoon moved to swing, his blade just barely missing the lance corporal's skull as Maklenan pulled back, slamming the butt of his rifle into the alien. The marine raised his weapon to drop a dragoon, preparing to fire inside the colossal reactor room when his M32's ejector casing jammed, disabling his weapon. Maklenan slammed it to the ground and drew his M18. As his immediate threats crumpled to the ground, he snapped around to see dragoons pouring in the way he came. He started to put rounds downrange towards the targets, overcharging the weapon's acceleration rails as he did, and his attackers began to drop like flies. He was getting nowhere. Gritting his teeth, Maklenan turned on point to face the reactor and began to pummel its security field with everything he had. With his attention shifted, dragoons finally began to gain ground, their shots cleaving through his flesh like a butcher carves up a beast. The marine finally collapsed to the ground. His muscles wavered as he levelled his Aetherfield once more and continued to fire as the guards advanced: one, two, three. An instant pulse of energy erupted through the room as the containment field collapsed. This time, physical alarms began to blare through the craft as the ship's antimatter reactor began to bleed into the ship's compartments. Containment fields materialised and died as energy conduits ruptured and anti-matter seeped out. The dragoons quickly abandoned Maklenan and evacuation commands began in earnest as the Jutland plummeted, like the Naintno Lato from the city of Takahara.

Maklenan lowered his weapon and sighed; he'd done it. The Honour Guard bastion would soon fall; he'd done his duty. 'By your word,' he stuttered as the ship exploded in a ball of flame, containment barriers failing and explosive materials igniting. Wireless signals along the north-western advance fell into uselessness once more as high-intensity energy washed across the battlefield. Troops would now depend on army pathfinders and rangers to guide them through the chaos, but the front lines had been established. Now it was Lycaon's turn.

Chapter 29
Siege of the century

The *Matilda* shook as Honour Guard AAA hammered the air around us, the ship's red lights creating a grim mood.

'Thirty seconds to touch down!' reported El Naken as our Condor continued to fly headlong into danger.

'Do or die!' I barked as our ship shook.

'Rah!' Lycaon howled back as our craft's thrusters kicked in and we began to descend.

The lights changed to green, and the aft access hatch began to lower. I disconnected my five-point harness and bolted out onto the open battlefield, Lycaon in tow. My boots ruffled the lush green ground that surrounded the alien compound. To my left and right, angular CH-108 Starhoists dropped M2 Sera MBTs, M5 Saker 'Buffalo' Medium Protected Mobility Vehicles, and M6 Saker 'Boar' Infantry Fighting Vehicles (IFVs) onto the battlefield, their guns firing the moment they had clear shots, Lycaon moved up to the nearest M5 and tucked in close to its protective shell as I pulled up my map.

'Okay, *gospadins*, our infiltration point is five klicks north of our current position. If we follow the river, we'll be able to break off from the main assault group and slip into the stream.'

'Rah,' acknowledged the fireteam as an explosion erupted nearby.

'Find a vehicle! Move up!' I screamed as I latched onto the side of our IFV, my left-hand gripping onto the vehicle's handles while my right propped up my M8A2. I peeked out; the number of dragoons assigned to the line was abnormally low. *The Halkaas must have done their job,* I thought to myself as the vehicle pushed forward.

Of course, that didn't mean the line was a walk in the park, as hundreds of dragoons still manned the line, armed to the teeth with anti-infantry guns that'd chew through your plates like a canine chews through meat and mortar emplacements that turned marines into the next meat omelette. On top of that, the wall and the advanced archway that stood between us and the enemy fortress could take all but the most brutal of punishment. As we advanced and their dragoons fell, a pulse of energy exploded up the wall and above the guards. The precursor lines pulsed with energy as the earth began to shake and rumble, the walls four equidistant trapezoidal petals drawing together as if attracted and fusing into a second storey. The ziggurat's four archways snapped together and with a blinding light flash fused into single stone pieces as energy pulsed up the walls generating an impenetrable field. Gone was the sizzling hole carved by the Halkaas on the north-western beachhead, gone were the dragoons atop the wall when the field was raised.

'What the *brafik* now?' hissed one of the marines to my right.

'Jupiter's Consort, all elements. The precursor structure has entered some sort of impenetrable siege mode; it's now surrounded by some sort of force field. Stand by for tasking. Over,' hissed Michiko over the comms. The entire advance froze as we clambered down from our vehicles.

'Specialist Three, get me comms to Jupiter's Consort Actual,' I instructed.

'Aye,' Ela replied as she activated her suit's LRT. A long antenna extended from her suit and she gave me the thumbs up moments later.

'Jupiter's Consort Actual. Jupiter Actual. How copy over?' I said over the line.

'Jupiter Actual. Jupiter's Consort Actual. Reading five by five,' came Michiko's crisp voice. 'We've finally been able to re-establish fleet-wide communications. Over,' Michiko sounded exhausted.

'Good to hear. Interrogative: what is the situation with the precursor fortress? Over.'

'Scans suggest the Prethosi fortress is generating an actual force field capable of creating a concussive feedback loop. We're looking for a solution now. Over.'

'Jupiter's Consort Actual. Specialist Three. Your best bet is to overload the force field. If you can launch a simultaneous coordinated strike that forces the field to concentrate its energy at multiple points around the structure you may be able to overwhelm it leaving just the indestructible wall. Over.'

'Specialist Three. Jupiter's Consort Actual. Understood, will take your suggestion under advisement. Break. Break' Michiko paused 'Jupiter Actual. Jupiter's Consort Actual. Confirm authorisation to commence simultaneous coordinated strike on precursor force field. Over.'

'Confirmed. You are authorised to commence simultaneous coordinated strike on precursor force field. Out,' I replied before releasing my hand from my helmet's comm piece. With that, I turned back to face Lycaon. 'Well. Let's get to work, then shall we?' Acknowledgement lights winked on in my HMD as I turned to face the river. 'Bring stealth systems online, we are Oscar Mike.'

The fireteam nodded in response before activating their suits' reconstruction procedures, their thick rigid marine BDUs being replaced with a sleek pattern of refractive material before quickly disappearing into the environment. Lycaon continued up the river's edge for another four kilometres before quietly transitioning from the shores into the river's current, our suits changing into diving mode as we slipped into the frigid water. The water thundered as sporadic Unified Army M1554 howitzer, 155mm towed artillery fire hammered the besieged fortress unsuccessfully. We moved through the water for another couple of hundred metres before finding a raised section within the reservoir to breathe normally. As each of us climbed up onto the rocky outcropping to the left-hand side of the reservoir, Ela lent down as her long-range transceiver extended.

'What is it?' I asked.

'They're about to attempt to overload the field,' Ela reported, listening intently to the new traffic as the explosive echo cascaded through the earth and shook me to my core. 'They did it! The force field's down!' Ela reported with excitement, followed by the rhythmic boom of towed artillery commencing in earnest accompanied by the kinetic rumble of Hurlbat missiles launched from the UNV *Waller*. The barrage of fire continued, unrelenting as it pummelled the dome before wireless chatter lit up with excitement.

Explosions rocked through the reservoir as Field Marshal Blaire's voice echoed through the wideband wireless. 'Caerus Six to all elements, advance! Repeat: all elements, advance! Perimeter breached! Repeat: perimeter breached! Out.'

I smirked.

'And here I thought we'd run out of tricks,' Ela said with a chuckle.

'Apparently not.'

'Jupiter's Consort Actual to all Task Force units, take the initiative. Flog their ragged hides. Out,' Michiko transmitted to all forces.

'So, with all that out of the way, can someone explain to me how the *brufik* we get down to the weapon?' Tomas sceptically questioned. 'Cos maybe it's just me, but I don't see no door.'

'Specialist Three, look for any form of electrical systems in the reservoir,' I instructed.

'Aye, aye,' Ela replied before looking down at her CPI. She shook her head. 'Nothin'.'

I frowned. *There's got to be a way down,* I thought to myself. 'I wonder—Specialist Three, have a look for any subspace anomalies that go through the reservoir.'

'Yut,' Ela replied sceptically as she looked back down at her CPI. Her head recoiled in confusion; I smirked.

'Let me guess… did you find a subspace signature?' I questioned knowingly.

'Yut.'

'They've got subspace translocation,' I extrapolated.

'And you got that wild theory from where?'

'Subspace anomalies have been detected just before an Honour Guard ambush. Given its not subspace communication—' I began.

'Because it has a consistent subspace signature,' Ela interjected.

'Now, unless you've got a better suggestion, I suggest you get to work trying to tap that line,' I instructed.

Ela tilted her head. 'Okay, acknowledging that they've got subspace translocation is one thing. Tapping into a subspace translocation line is a whole different ballpark; that's converting matter into subspace!' Ela paused. 'I've got better odds winning the Bayrn Prize than tapping that line!'

'Well, we've got no other choice,' I said.

Ela rolled her head, the mimicry of an eye roll. 'Aye, aye,' she grudgingly replied as she looked over the subspace data.

We rested there for four to five minutes while Ela worked at the problem. Bored, I unhooked Ela's handset from her PCA and demanded a SITREP from Field Marshal Blaire.

'Caerus Six Actual, Jupiter Actual. SITREP. Over.'

'Jupiter Actual, Caerus Six Actual. Fourth Halkaas and Second Marines have capitalised on the situation and have now entered the stronghold, Third and Fourth Brigade have breached the southern archway and are moving on the fortresses ballistic shield generators. The legionary lines at the heart of the bastion are holding strong, however, it will only be a matter of time. Over.'

'HUA*, Jupiter Actual out,' I replied before changing comm lines. 'Jupiter's Consort Actual, Jupiter Actual. SITREP. Over.'

'Jupiter Actual, Jupiter's Consort Actual. The fleet's back up to operational strength and Void Wanderer forces have been haphazardly jumping in to try to clot the bleeding, but we've got them on the ropes, ma'am. Besides that single transport corvette that slipped whatever the *brafiksjot* that was above our lines, we've got them contained; we're hitting them the moment they drop out of Aether Space. Over.'

'Understood, keep me posted. Out,' I finished as I reattached the handset to Ela's back.

'Okay, we're good to go,' Ela began. 'I'm at least thirty-three percent sure we won't be atomically annihilated when we enter subspace,' Ela pessimistically reported.

'Do or die,' I said as I tapped her on the shoulder. 'Let's do this.'

'Aye, aye. Initiating transport,' Ela coldly reported as she activated a tile on her CPI.

Our bodies began to fade as they were shifted into the depths of Aether Space. While the trip was mere seconds, it felt like a lifetime as my consciousness began to twist and contort, my particles strangled by the surrounding field. Moments later, we reappeared at the base of a colossal cavern, the five of us quickly slipping away from the translocation pad's windows. The immense cave was in ruins; scaffolding vibrated apart under the rumble of artillery fire; hundreds of sniper nests that lined the cavern imploded as the entire superstructure fell like dominos. But amidst the chaos stood the Accuser, its silver prongs raised in defiance of the anarchy around it. *It is real,* was the very first thought I had. Three black marks stretched out from the base of the weapon like an inverted Y and raced up the egg-like cave wall. The smooth Prethosi architecture shone through. Along the outer ring lay three collapsed trenches. Dragoon bodies lay buried in the rubble between one of the three translocation pads that stood in a Y pattern. Finally, at the northern mark, one hundred and fifty metres high, sitting halfway up the cavern wall, sat an extravagant overbridge where researchers tinkered and oversaw the troops amidst the chaos. As we hid at the pad, considering our next course of action, the pad began to activate.

'Ah, *brafiksjot*!' I hissed as a pair of dragoons appeared amongst us. They quickly reacted to our presence and alerted the entire area to our attendance just as we snapped their necks. 'Specialists Two and Five, suppressing fire! Specialists Three and Four, you're with me!' I barked as I ducked out of cover, quickly gunning down an advancing fireteam of dragoons. 'Go!' I barked as I tucked in close. Elenskis and Paladin vaulted left into the imploded trench. A large surfaceside explosion rocked through the cavern, and the central sniper towers collapsed as the vibrations dismembered the inner support lattices. I paused in mild shock. *So much for indeterminism,* I thought to myself with sardonic humour.

'Got eyes on a console!' reported Ela as she tucked into a supporting beam of the translocation pad's roof. 'Two high!' she barked, pointing out to an unseen object.

I peeked out to glimpse what she was talking about: it was the overbridge. 'Specialists Two and Five! SITREP!' I barked.

'Bounding!' Ela barked as I held her in place.

'Wait for Specialists Two and Five!' I instructed. Ela nodded.

Elenskis smacked her Squad Automatic Weapon up into the 'jaw' of a dragoon before slamming him in the chest, sending his pulpy form crashing into the other legionaries who continued to man the trench. 'Specialist Five! Cover Lycaon, I've got these *chikups* covered!' Elenskis explained.

'HUA*!' Paladin replied. As he levelled his rifle towards our advance, he tapped his comm piece: 'Specialist Five, ready to cover!'

'Bounding!' Ela remarked as she leapt from cover towards the base of the Accuser. Tomas and I quickly followed as dragoons in the right trench realised what was occurring and brought their rifles to bear.

'Specialists Two and Five! We're suppressed!' I barked as I slammed into the base of the weapon.

'Understood! Puttin' 'em down!' Paladin barked as he turned his designated marksman's rifle towards the trench. The legionaries quickly took the hint and ducked back into the cover they'd dug.

'We can move! Bounding!' Ela said as she prepared to run. I grabbed her by the wrist as a burst of turret fire rang out moments later.

'They've still got sniper and machine-gun nests,' I said with a stern tone. 'Specialists Two and Five, we've got fixed fire. Hundred metres, front,' I reported.

'Rah,' Elenskis called over the wireless as she sheathed her knife. 'Specialist Five, disengage. I'll take over.'

'Great, a Mexican standoff at a hundred and fifty metres. This has gotta be a record,' Paladin muttered as he re-synchronised his targeting computer.

'A what?' Elenskis questioned.

'Never mind. Take too long to explain,' he said, stumbling over his words.

The violent tempo had quickly sloped off to a nail-biting tension. Behind us, the Accuser began to pulse with activity, its twin prongs vibrating with golden energy on its inner track, more intently with each passing second.

'What's happening with the weapon?' asked Paladin as he chambered a round, levelled it across his shoulder and emptied the shot through the skull of an unsuspecting sniper.

'No idea!' I replied over the mic as a round whizzed by my shoulder. We were now less than a hundred and sixty metres away from the overbridge. I sighed as I looked back towards the central towers and traced my gaze up the roof. A tight smile drew across my lips. 'Five! Get me one of those panels!' I barked as Paladin leapt up from his foxhole and tossed down one of the sheets. 'Specialists Two and Five, be ready to hit those bastards as they go for us,' I instructed.

'Affirmative!' the pair responded.

'On my mark!' I boomed as I activated my armour's magnetic clamp and slammed the plate onto my forearm, easily hoisting it into the air.

'Standing by,' Elenskis and Paladin reported.

I turned to Tomas and Ela. 'Stay low and stick with me.' The pair nodded. 'Mark!' I barked as I strode out into the field of fire, the Honour Guard weapons barely heating the metal. With the sniper fire diverted, Elenskis and Paladin opened up against the nests, hammering them with pinpoint accuracy, dropping the entire network of snipers in under a minute as their targeting computers accurately predicted the enemy positions. Eventually, all that remained was the small five-dragoon patrol that had stayed out in the open to try to goad us out. I grinned as I screamed 'Now!', letting go of the plate as I did, and slamming my boot into the makeshift shield, sending it flying towards the guardsmen. The three of us raised our rifles and advanced with inhuman speed as the dragoons recovered from our first assault. I launched myself into the air and levelled my rifle towards the tight group. I snapped my rifle right, left, and down, as I held down the trigger, my rifle spewing burst after burst before I finally slammed into the ground and slipped back into cover. We were now less than thirty metres from our target.

'Specialists Two and Five repositioning!' reported Elenskis and Paladin as their ability to protect us disappeared. They slid down into the pit below and quickly tracked up to meet us in the cover of the pillars.

'Specialist Two, I'm gonna need you to crack that port,' I instructed as I pointed towards the overbridge.

'Makin' a hole, aye, ma'am,' Elenskis said with a smirk, her jargon slipping through as she unloosed her SMW and launched its round into the alien glass. The explosion shattered the window with a fiery force that surprisingly left much of the room intact.

'Lycaon! Get up there!' I barked as we moved from cover and bounded up to the cliff face before vaulting into the room, weapons raised. Three Kalil had been instantly killed in the first explosion while others reeled, panicking to find cover as their dragoon escorts raised their rifles towards the window. The first pulse of weapons fire buzzed overhead just seconds before we entered. I slammed into the ground, rolling forward with weapon raised, hammering a cluster of shots into the nearest dragoon I could find.

'Clear!' began Paladin, soon followed by the rest of the fireteam as they advanced into the room. The overbridge, as it would come to be known, wasn't anything particularly ethereal or exactly foreign. The glass observation post was semicircular on the window side and rectangular the closer you approached the only door to the outer passageway and the rest of the compound. As we strode through the room, sporadic displays of rapidly changing tactical data appeared before us in an alien tongue. It continued to be unintelligible for a long moment before it rearranged into numerous grids of ones, zeroes, and ones. I frowned in confusion as the grids changed into lines upon lines of digits before finally transforming into a single line of binary numbers.

'What am I looking at?' I asked.

'The evolution of coding, Sara,' QT-2 explained in reply.

'Ma'am, this facility is broadcasting tactical data directly to each of your central nervous systems. Fascinating,' Mariko muttered. My lips lowered. *Mariko 'the inquisitive' now?* I rhetorically thought.

'*Urusai!*' she hissed in mock anger.

'If its transmitting to my central nervous system, why is it writing in coding?' I continued.

'Because it can't find your root language to work forwards from … to extrapolate Ympiirno Spraak. So, it chose mine,' he explained, his tone almost reverent. 'If I'm reading it correctly, we have three minutes until activation,' QT-2 reported before I turned back to face Lycaon.

'Specialists Two and Three, get on that weapon. Jerry-rig an interface for our AI and get to work.'

'I'll be fine!' Ela stubbornly retorted.

I scowled. 'This is not the time for pride to bite you in the arse,' I hissed.

'I know what I'm doing. You made me memorise Architect programming language for this exact reason,' she retorted as she strode across to one of the inputs on the right.

I clenched my fist. 'Fine, everyone else, take up defensive positions,' I instructed, practically spitting the order. *I hope you're right.* The room only had the one door, which meant it'd be a shooting gallery. 'And can someone fix that window?' I bellowed, pointing out the obvious.

Ela frustratedly slid a line of code up, causing a neuro-electric field to form across the window. 'Thank you!' I exclaimed as an explosion interrupted my train of thought. Everyone spun around, weapons raised as neuro-electric fields materialised before us. Elenskis immediately went prone, propping her SAW's bipod against the low-set ballistic cover while the rest of us settled into our staggered defensive line. Ela's six o'clock was protected by yet another neuro-electric field she'd created. As we lay there, nervously waiting for the first set of dragoons, our bodies weary but our rifles balanced, a piercing scream cut into our minds as thousands of the damned creatures howled in anger. The thump, thump, thump of hundreds of thousands of rushing bootsteps cascaded into the room. I switched my rifle to automatic as the horde exploded into the overbridge. Elenskis' M500 cut through the swarm as quickly as it could before the last round was expelled from the chamber and she had to change out the belt. From there, we took over, one by one slicing through the wave of hostiles while the others changed magazines. It was a rhythmic process: *ten-second burst, magazine change, chamber round. Ten-second burst, magazine change, chamber round. Ten-second burst, magazine change, chamber round,* I mentally repeated as a round jammed and the rifle erupted in flames. As another wave of dragoons rushed in, I dropped my rifle, unholstered my M18, and unloaded the magazine at them.

'How much longer?' I bellowed as the clatter of Tom's M8 picked up the slack.

'I'm working on it!' Ela hissed as she navigated the controls.

As we knelt there, practically swimming in alien blood by this point, what had started as a quiet whine from the weapon had evolved into a deafening scream, its ungodsly 'alarm' ear-splitting to even the dragoons in the area.

'SITREP!' I barked.

'Last magazine!' replied Elenskis as I tossed a pair of grenades through the doorway into the connecting hallway. Flame cascaded through the hall, creating a break in the wave.

'Drawin' Hohbraum's an' Helium!' Tomas replied in the 'low ammunition' rhyming slang report of the son of a fusion plant worker.

'Same here!' reported Paladin.

'By the gods!' Ela remarked as she let go of the control panel. Outside, the Accuser had finally reached firing condition, in less than seven minutes. The billion-year-old system was finally active. 'Final firing countdown active! Emergency override codes offline!' Ela reported. 'I don't know what to do,' she finally admitted, her voice trembling.

'Specialist Three! Take these AIs!' I barked as I landed a shot on another advancing legionary. Ela simply stood there stunned. 'Specialist! Get me an interface!' I barked, wrenching Ela from her distraction as each of us quickly dislodged our AI before throwing them to the shocked marine who quickly began to work on an interface.

'ETA on that interface!' I barked as I turned back to the doorway.

'Not fast enough!'

The cave began to rumble. The dragoons stopped in awe as the pulse careened up between the two pillars and slammed into a ring that hovered above the two prongs. The golden beam vanished from sight before splitting into a thousand streams of golden energy that disappeared into hundreds of rings that silently orbited the planet. The single pulse was soon followed by a continuous beam that cascaded through the hundreds of rings like a light refracted through a million glass mirrors. Ela froze again; this time, I rose from my position, anger rising through my system. I holstered my weapon and slammed my fist into her jaw. She barely moved but the message was received.

'Finish the job!' I barked in fury. With renewed vigour, she began to work out the last few issues with the interface and plugged the five AI into the network.

++++

Mariko Hiroshi

I drifted through a sea of alien machine code, dialects, varieties, and languages unintelligible to me, abstract ideas and concepts presented by a million artificial entities that made up the system, chattering away as if gossiping in a lunchroom. Star roads, zero-point energy, string theory armatures. Amidst it, all four other 'voices' stood out amongst the noise, the distinct chatter of my fellow AIs. With our thoughts known to each other, we each began to drift frantically through the expanse of ideas, commands, and information, sifting through the volumetric ocean of data, grasping blindly for the—

'Master control!' I muttered with excitement as I snatched the line of code from its rightful place. 'It's here!' I called as the other four returned to inspect the impossible system.

'It's like FORTRAN,' Rusalka began.

'In the barest sense, most of this code serves no purpose ...' muttered Timycha, her sleek and lean form wrapped in a loose chiton.

'Focus!' I hissed. 'This has to direct the activation and calibration for the Accuser, meaning it must be able to also deactivate the weapon,' I explained. 'Without the control codes, we have to find the specific command line and alter it manually,' I continued to mutter. 'I've been around Sara for too long,' I said to myself sardonically.

'How about there?' suggested Timycha, her gaze settling on a line of code. I and the other AI simply shook our heads.

'There?' Rusalka proposed. Each of us shook our heads. I looked up from the master control to inspect the system's internal chronometer. The weapon had been active already for a whole three seconds, its devastating reach already crippling the greater universe. In a moment of sheer, impossible impulse, I clenched my fist and slammed it into the clutter of code that was the master control to the shock and horror of my companions. A nano-second later, the unremitting pulse abruptly ceased.

++++

In an instant, the AI overrode the security framework and reinstated the emergency shutdown commands. The pulse outside quickly faded before returning with renewed malice.

'Our turn,' the five AI hissed in unison, their voices an unholy cacophony over the dragoons' neural net. Moments later, the energy returned and cascaded into the surrounding area rather than collecting at the apex of the structure. Alien blood exploded through the building as dragoon arteries erupted with violent results. I sighed as my body finally relaxed. Ela fell to her knees, unclipped her helmet, and covered her face with her palms.

'Kiir-Riike Aleksandra!' she exclaimed as she spun her humble body. 'Kerankii!' she exclaimed.

My eyes narrowed, and I strode over to her, gripped her by the forearm, and pulled her to her feet.

'Don't pity yourself,' I replied. 'It's not worth the energy.'

'But I killed millions; I *brufik*ed up!' Ela replied with shock in her eyes. I unclipped my helmet and quickly tucked it under my arm.

'And how does pity change that? How does grovelling change that? You screwed up colossally and you waste your breath on prayers! Don't waste your breath praying for the gods to carry your mistake, because you have to. You bear those souls—they're dragged around by the chains you put them in. We've all got souls chained to our persons, but some are heavier than others—some are almost unbearable. But you adapt, you win,' I hissed, my hands trembling, my eyes shimmering with the wisps of water and memory.

'Remember this day, embrace every second: every sound, sight, and sense. When you sleep, let the whispers of the dead scream in your ear; let their cold, lifeless hands clutch your heart, squeeze it till it explodes before your very eyes. These things will plague you till death, but it's your burden to bear; it's your burden to remember this day, to remember your petty pride in your excellence and remember what your petty pride cost. The lives of billions, of trillions,' I boomed, my expression rigid with subtle rage, my tone cold as ice and my heart, beating like a drum of war.

‘Yes, ma’am,’ she replied in shame, her head down and her heart near motionless on my HMD, as if she’d died with them.

With her simple answer given, I quickly turned away, snatched up Mariko, slipped my helmet back on, and strode out of the room.

Chapter 30
End of the line

We made our way topside, striding through the kilometre-wide holes in the fortress's walls; soldiers and marines patrolled the now-eerily quiet ruins and stepped out onto the soft grassy plains that stretched on for kilometres from the charred Honour Guard facility. When the *Morte Fortuna* finally landed, its luminous thrusters ruffling the sea of green, we were about ten kilometres away from the fortress. The ship's well deck opened up to reveal Michiko, waiting for us at the mouth of the entrance. A smile of relief began to well before it faded away as she saw our gait. We'd failed, and we knew it.

'What happened?' Michiko asked.

'Specialist Three got cocky—that's what happened,' Elenskis spat before striding off. I simply strode off to my quarters in silence. I unclipped my M18 and slipped it onto the table beside me before triggering the release bolts across my PCA, as if the armour was too heavy for me to climb out. As the thick plates slammed into the deck with a thud, for the first time I stepped out of the usually sealed suit and made for my bed. *We're gonna have hell to pay for this* brafiksjot *up,* I thought to myself. As I settled into my rack, the door buzzed with life. I slammed my head into my pillow and rolled my eyes.

'*Brafik* off!' I screamed; the door system buzzed again. 'I said *brafik* off!' I hissed as I twisted up my face. The door buzzed once more. I clenched my fist before finally conceding and opening the door remotely. Paladin stood in the doorway, his PCA still strapped to his body. I waved him in. 'What do you want?'

'How're you holding up?' he asked as he entered the room, his helmet nestled under his arm. His black hair shimmered in the low light, his white crystal eyes glistened with life.

'How do you think?' I indignantly replied.

Paladin rested his helmet on my bedside table, and he too slipped out of his combat armour before settling at the bottom of my bed, his naked form beside mine.

'You're afraid you're going to lose your career, aren't you,' Paladin remarked after a long pause.

'What version of this doesn't lose me my career?' I retorted. Paladin activated his CPI and closed the door before speaking.

'The one where the Taskforce Corps of Judiciary places your fireteam's negligence square on the shoulders of the woman responsible.'

'And that's the better alternative? Assuming they don't charge me with dereliction of duty for failing to ensure that my marines follow my orders, I'm not going to sacrifice them just for my sake,' I snapped, my emotions seeping through the filter for once.

'Then why're you worried about losing your career if you're the one willingly sacrificing it?' Paladin asked frankly.

I fell silent. He had a point. I looked him square in the eyes, my heart racing. 'The *brafik* do you always have an answer?' I said rhetorically as I rose from my outstretched form and slipped my legs out over the edge. As I rose into the bare light, my body's scars came into view. Paladin recoiled. 'What? Never seen skin before?' I asked, attempting a stab at humour.

'No, no, not that,' he said. 'How the fuck do you have so many scars? You're from the twenty-fifth century for fuck's sake; dermal regeneration is sold from a vending machine.'

I grinned at the novelty.

'Same could be said for you,' I teased as I jabbed at the contorted piece of flesh. The scar stretched across the inquisitor's chest, and he winced in light pain at the gesture.

'Oh, this thing?' Mitchell replied, slipping closer into the light, showing off the scar tissue in more intricate detail as it wrapped up his abdomen like a snake suffocating its victim. 'Made by a Chinese interrogator from the remains of the Ministry of State Security in 2123. The dickhead decided it'd be a fun idea to put a *karambit* up through my gut,' Paladin explained.

'And you have the scar, why?'

'Well, most of the scar tissue would cause irreparable damage to my skin back in the day if they'd tried to clear it up, and besides, it's a reminder of what that fuck did to me.'

'Same here,' I admitted as I adjusted my posture slightly.

'Irreparable damage?' Paladin said confused.

'No, it's a reminder; everything's a reminder of my failures and a story that each of us can tell, a saga of this unit. Memorialised in scars. Shame I didn't get one today,' I muttered as I rose from my bed and moved for my shower.

Paladin's arm reached out and latched onto my hand as I went to move. I froze. I turned back to him with puzzled eyes. He inched closer to me and moved to hold me by my waist, his soft hands running over my scars. As he did, his head inched closer and closer to mine as he embraced me. I closed my eyes as he rested his head on mine.

My heart raced, and I struggled to know why. My mind was cold with calculation, but my hands were sweaty with energy. I felt numb, yet alive, and I failed to comprehend why. Paladin sighed as he let go of me and stepped out of the room. My heart returned to its former rhythm, my mouth wide open in confusion yet determined in hidden understanding.

Chapter 31
The blood-laden blade

0030 hours, 19/01/2439 (Military Calendar), Two days later, UNV Morte Fortuna

I readjusted my posture before activating the link to headquarters. Chihiro's cold demeanour was intimidating to just about anyone. When I snapped to attention, she quickly waved aside the formalities. 'Shadow Director Hart, I'm here to formally rescind your title as Shadow Director and Grand Admiral of the Navies, returning you to the rate of Chief Warrant Officer 2 and to inform you that Lance Corporal Ela Tremblej has been charged by the Unified Corps of Judiciary on the grounds of dereliction of duty. Until further notice, Lance Corporal Tremblej has been stripped of rank and is to be confined to quarters and access to material restricted. You will jump to headquarters where she will be put before a general court-martial to determine her level of guilt. Her Judge Advocate General lawyer will be assigned there,' Chihiro explained.

'Permission to speak, ma'am,' I requested.

'Go ahead, Chief,' Chihiro replied as if gritting her teeth.

'I'd like to request Lance Corporal Ela Tremblej's charges be put on my shoulders, ma'am.'

'That's not how this works, Sara, and you know it.'

'It was my fault the situation happened; I've let unit standards fall; if anything, I was the one who was in dereliction of their duty.'

‘That’s not for me to decide, Chief,’ Chihiro coldly replied before deactivating the feed.

I sighed as I reached for the intercom. ‘Barken?’

‘Yes, ma’am?’ the officer of the deck replied energetically.

‘Have helm lay in a course to headquarters and have Specialist Three confined to quarters,’ the intercom fell silent momentarily. ‘You hear me, sailor?’ I said again, furious.

‘Aye, ma’am, jumping to headquarters and confining Specialist Three to quarters,’ Barken replied before cutting the feed.

I sighed as I stepped back to fall onto my bed. I had condemned my own fireteam to the dogs of bureaucracy, thanks to a loose chain on my behalf.

++++

Taskforce Headquarters, Kin system, 0230 hours Zulu, 22/01/2439 (Military Calendar)

Ela strode into the monolithic atrium. At the centre of Taskforce Headquarters, the Hakon Memorial stood as the centrepiece of the hall. A pair of military police marines escorted her through the compound, equipped with full riot gear and armed to the teeth. Ela strode ahead of the pair, in shackles. The group paused as Tremblej looked across at the hauler’s wreckage, its twisted shape in between the zigzag of interlacing walkways and support beams that punctured the asteroid’s rocky superstructure. One of the marines nudged Ela with the side of their M32, gesturing for her to keep moving. With that, the group continued forward, through the heart of Taskforce Headquarters. As Ela was marched through the atrium, silent stares followed. Everyone had heard the rumours, the *Taskforce Times* had bred its very own monster from the facts of her arrest: ‘Renowned Specialist Turned War Criminal’ had been the headlines for the better half of a week and neither the E-4 Mafia nor the Lance Corporal

Underground helped the situation. We watched on from one of the upper walkways with shock as the bustling atrium faded to silence. The MPs quickly ferried her through the atrium and into the holding cell that was directly adjacent to one of the courtrooms. The doors shut with precision and life resumed in the building.

++++

Holding cell L-16

Ela was slammed into the seat and her restraints were attached to the bolted table. The marines stepped back and hovered behind her like hunting hawks waiting for their prey to make its move. A door to the left snapped open and a JAG officer stepped through, his freshly pressed navy dress uniform distinct against his dark skin. He held his peaked cap under his left arm and a khaki dossier in his right. The officer looked down at the specialist like a rabid animal sealed inside a glass cage for an audience's viewing pleasure. The JAG lifted the dossier before dropping it onto the table and pausing for dramatic effect. With his statement over, he settled into a loose resting posture. 'Lance Corporal Ela Tremblej?' the officer began.

'Former Lance Corporal,' Ela corrected. 'But yeah, that's me,' she said with a whip of bitterness.

The officer sighed. 'Well, my name is Lieutenant J.G. Bazra; I'm your legal officer from the Judge Advocate General Corps. This dossier's got the NCIS investigation—'

'Why's the Navy's JAG Corps and NCIS handling my case? Shouldn't the Corps' JA Division and CID be handling this?' Ela asked, her voice hollow and empty. Bazra paused for an instant before answering.

'Normally, you'd be correct. But the Operations Personnel Security and Intelligence Committee requested we handle your case,' he added before continuing. 'As I was saying, this dossier has the NCIS report into your dereliction of duty charges and my proposed defence. I won't be able to get you a full acquittal, but I should be able to limit the charges and get dishonourable discharge off the table. However, I can't guarantee you'll have any mobility in the USG for the rest of your career,' Bazra admitted.

'I'm Semper Gumby; as long as you can get me out of this four by four brick, I'll take anything right now,' Ela said with a sigh.

Bazra frowned in confusion before repeating the marine 'Semper Gumby?'

'Always flexible; from our motto and some old Earth clay monstrosity,' Ela translated.

'Well, the hearing is in an hour's time, so let's get started.'

++++

Central atrium, 0739 hours Zulu

I paced back and forth, my hands curled up in fists. Lycaon stood beside me, anxiously waiting for Ela's JAG to walk out of the courtroom. The courtroom's central entrance snapped open, and the pack of commissioned jurors, judges, and legal professionals filed out. I began to stare across the way with an inhuman intensity, my skin contorting as my nails dug into my palms. As the main group began to disperse, Ela's lawyer started to stand out from the crowd. Beside him stood his arrogant systems operator of a client, sombre for the first time in her life. It was the first time her authority and legitimacy had been challenged by another and lost. She'd fight tooth and nail to never go through that again. My fists began to relax, and my stern glare softened into something approaching joy. *She wasn't discharged then, otherwise, she wouldn't be walking out of that chamber.* The two groups began to approach each other as I reached out to cradle Ela's head, nestling her forehead against mine.

'How're you?' I asked as she gripped the back of my head.

'Semper Gumby, given that the green weenie struck again,' she jokingly replied with a weak smile.

I released her and turned to face the JAG. 'What's the SITREP, Lieutenant?'

'Well, she's avoided both maximum penalties due to her exemplary service to the Corps, and with her new-found stigma, they've allowed her to remain with Lycaon but they've permanently docked two-thirds of her pay. She's been permanently scratched from the promotion track, and because of implicit negligence on your behalf, both of your careers are dependent on each other staying out of trouble, unless you both want to be dishonourably discharged,' Bazra explained.

'Understood,' I replied before turning back to Ela. 'So, you heard the officer, leatherneck: keep your head out of crazy and we'll do just fine,' I said with a smirk.

'Head outta crazy? I'm already *chikupiir*-deep in crazy,' Ela roared with a grin.

'Well, there goes my career,' I jokingly continued before dragging Ela by the neck away from the lieutenant and towards the *Morte Fortuna*'s docking collar. 'Thank you, Lieutenant!' I exclaimed as we strode off. I lifted my arm off Ela's shoulder and ducked right, tapping her on the wrist. 'I've got something to look at. I'll catch up with you,' I said, stepping up the stairs past the Hakon Memorial as I spoke.

'You got it, Ms Hart!' she called back with a grin on her face.

I couldn't help but chuckle as I turned to back towards the centre of the atrium, where she stood, her impressive twenty-five-metre-tall statue dominating the atrium. Her stern yet precise parade rest commanding attention, measured ink-black hair, her ice-blue eyes, her curvaceous but still defined cheekbones almost demanding devotion. I stared up at the shaded statue of Director Janet Halloway, her features lacking her tan skin but retaining her contrastive eyes and hair against her silver uniform, a reminder of her past as the woman out of time. I smiled to myself. *I'm glad I finally got to see this monument,* I thought to myself before turning back to head for the *Fortuna.*

++++

The *Fortuna* detached from Taskforce Headquarters and began to glide off into open space, Len's hands manoeuvring her through the asteroid belt that orbited the failed colony Kin, now the capsule that held Taskforce Headquarters. As I sat in the captain's chair, the ship's klaxons began to flare up and our helmsmen recoiled in shock. 'SITREP, gentlemen,' I demanded.

'Manual controls have been locked out, ma'am, our jump drive's spooling up,' El Naken reported.

'We're on autopilot?'

'Seems so, ma'am,' El Naken reported.

'We're we headed then?'

El Naken paused to double-check the data. 'No idea, ma'am, we've been completely locked out,' Naken reported as the bridge blast shield began to lower over the bow viewing port.

Brafik *me!* I screamed internally as I clenched my fist. *Because this couldn't get any more eventful!*

The *Fortuna* made several micro-jumps over the next hour where it would arrive in-system only to jump away and repeat the process. We'd gone through our fifteenth micro-jump when the jump drive finally spun down and our propulsion engines were brought back online. As we drifted through space, blind to the world around us, our ship began to slow before coming to an abrupt stop. Lycaon stood at the airlock, weapons raised, as the hatch automatically cycled the atmosphere and opened. Lifting my left hand, I gestured to Elenskis to clear the doorway.

'Clear!' Elenskis called back as she gestured for us to move up. As we stepped into the dim passage, each of us activated our helmet-mounted lamps and began to sweep the passageway, our weapons trained on our sectors.

'Gear's reading O^2,' Ela reported.

'I'm not gonna gamble with the odds of decompression,' I replied as we snapped right onto a gantry that connected to ours. We advanced through the large gantry into yet another cavernous compartment.

'Why does it always gotta be the size of a gods-damned pinch room?' Tomas remarked in reference to a pinch fusion reactor's central reaction chamber as his helmet light struggled to reach the roof.

'Because we enjoy the spectacle, Specialist Four,' boomed Chihiro as the lights flickered on. The five of us rolled our eyes as we snapped to attention.

'Officer on deck!' I cried as we snapped our rifles up to our shoulders in a salute.

'At ease!' Chihiro called back as Paladin stepped out from behind us to stand beside the director.

'What's this about now, ma'am?' I asked.

'Your role's a part of Proteus, Specialist,' Chihiro replied. 'With the collapse of the guard and the activation of the Accuser, the Taskforce is at its most vulnerable. Taskforce analytics suggest the Accuser's firing radius could have annihilated over eighty percent of the universe's total population. That means we've made a lot of new enemies and they'll be coming for us and out for blood, and while the guard's been formally dissolved and war declarations have been rescinded, splinter factions have been reportedly mobilising and reunifying. If we don't remove this threat now, we'll be back to square one in a heartbeat. So, we need Proteus. As a result, Chief Warrant Officer Second Class Hart, you are hereby promoted to Colonel; Staff Sergeant Jen to Major; Lance Corporal Tremblej—against my better judgement, I'm offering you the rank of Chief Warrant Officer third class; Seaman Apprentice QT-2, we're offering you the rank of Command Master Chief Petty Officer; and Hospital Corpsman's Hand Plimis, I'm offering you the temporary rank of Lieutenant Junior Grade while you transition through Unified Medical School before your formal commissioning as a full Lieutenant,' Chihiro explained as Mitchell handed us each our respective collar pins.

'Anything else we need to know?' I asked.

'Well, as well as promotions, we're about to overhaul the Fortuna. Her facilities are being expanded as we speak to ensure that she's up to the rigours of long-term operations. Her refits should be done by zero eight hundred tomorrow. We've also taken the liberty of selecting your new crew to account for your broader force projection capabilities. You've got a composite army/marine battalion alongside a composite Special Operations Unit and an allocated marine squadron, among other things, to ensure your continued success,' Chihiro explained.

I paused in thought before asking, 'Ma'am, one question?'

'Go ahead, Specialist.'

'Why're you giving us so much, when we *brafik*ed up, big time?'

Chihiro sighed. 'Have you ever met any of Director Halloway's proteges? Visited her tomb?'

'No, ma'am.'

'I have. There are two things of note from both. The first was from her protege. Her name was Director Maria Reyes. I met her on her deathbed during my tenure as a lieutenant aboard the UNS Gilbert Blane. She said that there is one adage Director Halloway would personally write to each of her commanding officers and she mandated that to be passed down to each successive director.' Chihiro paused. '"There are two kinds of men called to carry the weight of the universe, the weak and the strong. Both will succumb to its weight, one way or another, but each will make a decision that defines their strength. The weak man will pass on his punishment. The strong man, however, rises from his failure. Weight in hand, he will shoulder impossible burdens and from such adversity is forged the stronger man, able to carry the weight of the world with ease while the weak man crumbles under its inevitable weight."'

'And the second?' Ela, the most sombre of the group, asked.

'The second was from her tomb. "One of the more interesting aspects of the directorship is that you don't need to provide explanation or rationalisation to anyone for anything."'

We all fell silent. That answer was good enough for us.

'Any more questions?' Chihiro now asked.

None of us spoke. 'Excellent. Colonel Hart, your department heads are waiting for you in briefing room two,' Chihiro informed.

Each of us snapped to attention, raised a salute, and strode off in the direction of briefing room two, its location marked by a waypoint on our HMDs.

I slipped off my helmet as I strode up beside Tomas, his eyes wide with disbelief as he balanced the pins in his hands. 'You alright?'

Tomas was simply shaking his head. 'I've spent so much of my life bitter about the chain of command, how cold and calculated it was in the CNI, and how it treated you so badly, and I'm standing here now holding the rank pin of a god-damned butter bar, the very spawn of Lati Kalm herself I'd decried for so long.'

I placed my hand on his shoulder and simply said, 'Do better.' In that instant, he froze and turned to me in confusion, his face twisted in bewildered puzzlement. 'Do better than the officers you know, do what mustang officers do better than most: treat the men and women under your command as people. You have experience that traditional officers would only dream of having, so use it,' I said before letting go of his arm.

'Well, I've had some of the best upper-middle officers to learn from,' he said with a subtle smirk as he tugged out a cigarette from his armour.

I began to smile, though my heart remained cold, the warm emotion seemingly faint, like a dim fireplace on the far side of a room. An instant later, the door in front of me opened to reveal a moderately sized room packed with people. The small talk vanished as section and department heads turned to face me, snapping to attention as they did. I froze as stage fright took hold. But I cleared my throat, and the words began to flow through the room.

‘Attention, you all know that you’ve been selected to join Proteus. You know that you are the best the Taskforce has to offer, and you know what you have to do, but what you don’t know is why you do this. Maybe you did, ten to twenty years ago, but I can assure you, you have lost your way. Stop for a moment, either right now or later in the comfort of your racks, and remind yourself why you fight for this Taskforce—what you fight for—because war without reason is a lost cause. It is violence for the sake of violence, and violence for the sake of violence is what we strive to prevent. Remember the charter, remember your oath, hold tight its values, hold tight its moral compass, for they shall guide you through uncertainty; they shall be your anchor on foreign shores. Hold firm those virtues and carry them with pride,’ I finished.

I surveyed the collection of section heads and company commanders, my eyes settling on Uncle Dimi’s weathered form finishing a glass of Russian Vodka, Harmon Miles downing a glass of whatever the *brafiksjot* they make in Australia, and Mitchell Paladin, as ever, sticking to the shadows and slinking around the corners of the room, his build powerful yet subtle.

I smiled. I was home. We had a lot of work ahead of us: dismantling a terrorist organisation, protecting the galaxy from more hostile threats, and working out the kinks from the Accuser’s activation, but we were the very best the Taskforce could find, and we felt like we could take on the universe. How horribly wrong we were.

Acknowledgements

To everyone who helped with the writing, conceptualisation, editing, and whatever else was needed to complete this book—I'm sorry. I'm sorry for the frustration that I caused as I would burst into the common room at bizarre hours of the day just to ask for a single letter, number, or eclectic word. But to everyone who did help, your contributions have been invaluable, your support priceless and your constant questions uplifting. Knowing people are excited for your works, even if they're never read, is an alien sensation that is by no means bad. In particular, I'd like to thank my amazing saints of editors Beverley Streater and Jason Martin, my amazing ad-hoc editor Sebastian Perritt, and my beta readers Eliza Williams, Chris Hodgeson, Jacob Woodland, Jayron Gray, Glenn Hohnberg, Belle Taylor, and Sam Bishop; you've had the toughest job of them all, putting up with my grammar. While I can't name everyone who has helped with this project, I can thank those I do know have played an irreplaceable role in this book's development. So, in no particular order, here's to some of those who helped with my writing immensely:

Second Floor Bellenden Ker (2016, 2017, 2018, and 2019), Kingaroy State High School Graduating Class of 2015, r/physics, Adam McGhee, Cain Kirk, Charles Ndiaye, Charlie Plant, Damon Landers, Danielle Carige, Fiona Hayward, James Hunt, James Hurlbutt, Johnathan Blair, Karl Barrett, Monice Hurlbutt, Quentin McBean, Stephen Carige, William Hayward.

Terminology of the Traverse

Acronyms

AA: Abbreviation of Anti-Aircraft, any system that deals with enemy aircraft from the ground.

ACB: Acquisition Calculation Binoculars, which provide digital elevation and distance measurements.

AO, AOE, AOR: Area of Operations/Area of Engagement/Area of Responsibility. An Area of Operations is where a military unit has been assigned to conduct its specific duties; this is further defined as the Area of Engagement where combat units are and will be fighting the enemy. The Area of Responsibility is a broader application of the AOE including a unit's responsibilities to maintain local infrastructure and any other necessary non-combat related responsibilities.

ASAT: Anti-Satellite is an operation executed by aircraft to cripple an opponent's information warfare and communication capabilities by removing satellites that provide such services.

AV procedures: Anti-virus procedures are a series of unit protocols overhauled and reimplemented after the Concealer War. They are specifically designed with each unit's independent Standard Operating Procedures (SOP).

BDU: Battle dress uniform. BDU refers to the full equipment load of a soldier, not including the weapon.

C4ISR: Command, Control, Communication, Computers Intelligence Surveillance Reconnaissance, an overview of every single facet of military coordination.

CATCC: Carrier Air Traffic Control Centre, a centralised compartment within a ship that coordinates the hundreds of daily fighter launches. The centre itself is chilled to ensure technical issues are not possible.

CATFU/CATBU: Completely and Totally Fucked/*Brafik*ed Up, jargon that began in the Vietnam War.

CBRN: Chemical, Biological, Radiological, and Nuclear procedures, and equipment designed to handle such hazards.

FTL: Faster Than Light transitions where a ship moves through some of the most dangerous layers of Aether Space to emerge in an alternate dimension.

FUBAR/BUBAR: Fucked/*Brafik*ed Up Beyond All Recognition, jargon that began in the Vietnam War.

HMD: Helmet Mounted Display.

HUA: Heard Understood Acknowledged is a phrase first adopted with the advent of the radio, it quickly and succinctly informed a radio operator that the information they had sent had been heard and understood in a single acknowledgement it was the evolutionary predecessor of 'Hooah'.

LRT: Long Range Transceiver.

LZ: Landing zones are areas where craft can land onto their wheels or struts to either turn off their engines or disembark troops without requiring training to jump out of the plane.

MAF: Main Assault Force.

Maser/laser: Microwave Amplification by Stimulated Emission of Radiation and Light Amplification by Stimulated Emission of Radiation respectively.

MOS: Military Occupational Specialty.

PZ: Pick-up Zones are where a force can expect friendly transport craft rather than simply any flight-capable craft to arrive to remove them from an environment, hostile or otherwise.

SNAFU/SNABU: Situation Normal All Fucked/*Brafik*ed Up, jargon that has its roots in the US Marine Corps during WWII.

SPS: Satellite/Station Positioning System.

Culture

Aion Krossno Ooda: Translated as Order of the Iron Cross. This medal is the highest military honour that a service member of the Imperial Military can possibly receive. It was adapted from the old-Earth Prusso-German medal of the same name.

Anki: Interpersonal energy according to the imperial religion.

Asfod/azvod: Asfod is the Imperial cult's equivalent of purgatory. According to the state religion, when someone dies, they are presented with a challenge. Before them is the Arduous River of

Asfod, its nine bends each holding a port that will tempt the rower. To stop at these ports is to rest from the waves but to be tempted by its alluring lies of happiness and relief. To successfully fight to the end of the river is to defeat purgatory. From there the dead may continue the trek to the City of Takahara or they may stop to remain in the Town of Valha.

Colonial Star: The Colonial Star was one of the first awards and military honours to be introduced into the Taskforce's inventory of accolades by Director Silas in 2105 in honour of the fighting spirit of colonists, especially those who would eventually colonise other worlds and the demands of such an endeavour and the cultural parallels between military service and colonisation efforts.

Kaisarno Kult: The Imperial state religion, literally translated means the 'emperor's cult'.

Kaltri: Kaltri are mammalian extraterrestrials who have vampiric tendencies, first discovered by the Union of Sovereign Realms in the Andromeda galaxy. Like old-Earth myths, they are a heavily martial culture to control their feeding impulses, and being quite nomadic, they would come into quick conflict with the USR as it began its various expansion wars.

Lati Athia: The Lady of War in the imperial religion. Formally known as Kriigno Lati Athia, which literally translates to 'War Lady Athena'.

Lukistno Andjel: Lyrin Watcher Angels are mystical servants of the Lords and Ladies of Takahara who watch, report, and when called to it, intervene supposedly on behalf of mortals in the Imperial religion.

Naitno Nein Lort an Lati an Lato: In Imperial mythology, the nine Lords and Ladies of the Night are a collection of deities who govern the happenings of the night. Four are masculine, four are feminine, and one is androgynous. Originally, there were five Ladies of the Night, but one of them was insolent and attempted to make the domain of the day their own. When Lord Tumatanga, the Lord of War, discovered this breach of the natural order, she was thrown from the city of Takahara and became the one Lato of the Night. This is known as the 'Incident of the Ladies of the Night'.

Naturno Lati Gaia: Lady of Nature in the Imperial religion and bondmate to Lord of Nature Ah.

Non-Judicial Punishment (NJP)/Formalnai Meikrul (FnM): What is loosely translated as non-formal judgement from the Imperial Creole. FnMs and NJPs are a form of punishment issued by a commanding officer concerning a military violation that does not warrant a court-martial but cannot be ignored. FnMs are an imperial classification while NJP is a term adopted by the Unified Security Military and originated in the United States Armed Forces, the process is nicknamed being 'ninja-punched'. Both the UNS and old-Earth wet navies instead refer to such decisions as 'Captain's Mast'.

Primera Cluster: Primera is where the Imperial Homeworld of Kiln is located.

Seksno an Shino Lati Freja: Lady of Sex and Death in the Imperial religion and bondmate of Lady Athia of War. Literally translates as 'Sex and Death Lady Freya'.

Takahara: The city of the gods in the Imperial religion that was derived from the old-Earth Japanese home of the gods.

The Concealer War: The Concealer War was the greatest strategic failure of the Unified Security Group and instigated the greatest rejection of the Revolution of Military Affairs and the greatest upheaval of the political norm across two galaxies in over 300 years.

In 2340, the UNV *Fateful* (PKG-128), a now-defunct Resolute-class extended patrol corvette, responded to a distress call 500,000 kilometres from the redline. Over the next sixty-one hours, the collective commands of the USG and the Union Military would be introduced to a computerised weapon of war created for a conflict long past and intent on never being discarded by biological life ever again. Over the next eight months, the Concealers infiltrated, struck, and systematically dismantled the Imperial Union and the Taskforce in one of the bloodiest conflicts ever seen. The Concealer onslaught would only be stopped through a combination of concerted denying actions and a directed computer assault on the commune's central collective. With the end of the conflict came a complete overhaul of both the USG and UIRs reliance on networking, automation, artificial intelligence and would lead to the complete rejection and isolation of the Unified Security Group from the public eye for the foreseeable century.

The Declaration of Xendarin Independence: The Xendarin Declaration of Independence was a monumental movement that spawned out of the USR's Age of Eternal Strife as the Union Military struggled to regain control of its territories and support its struggling economy through expansion, amid this chaos, a community of exiled pureblood Abetra known simply as the Xendarin Enclave that had flourished on the inhospitable mining colony of Nuleningrad had declared with resounding unity their intentions to secede from the Union of Sovereign Realms. Unable to show weakness in the matter, the Union Military would begin the Siege of Nuleningrad, under the initial cover of orbital fire marine forces advanced across the mining colony until faced with the fortified and near-impenetrable city-states of Nuleningrad. Built atop the planet's primary mines, they were not only designed to survive internalised explosions and accidents to prevent the damage from potentially affecting the rest of the planet, but were also nearly indestructible from external assault. Without the authorisation of orbital support due to the importance of the mining infrastructure, Marine forces were forced to siege each city-state into submission with minimal effect.

Tisorno Lati Eri: Eri: The Lady of Discord in the Imperial cult, she is sister to Se, Lord of Disorder and bondmate to Productivno an Shino Lort Gede—the Lord of Death and Fertility, although she does tend to cheat. Literally translated she is 'Discord Lady Eris'.

Tisorno Lort Se: Lord of Disorder in the Imperial religion.

Ympiirno Spraak: the creolisation of Japanese, German, Russian, French, and English due to the predominant ethnic groups which were part of the exodus. Literally translates to 'Imperial Speak'.

Language

40 mike, mike: Shorthand for a 40mm grenade launcher (term unused by the Union of Sovereign Realms).

5 by 5: Meaning that radio communications are coming through clearly.

Actual: Used in radio communications to denote that the officer or senior enlisted in charge is the one replying or being specifically asked for instead of the radio operator under their command.

Aircraft Tail Number: An aircraft's official designation and callsign is the two-letter aircraft or squadron designator followed by its three-digit model number that is traditionally inscribed on an aircraft's tail. E.g. TH557.

Armour Column: The military's term for tanks moving in an organised fashion.

Bingo fuel: A phrase used by pilots to inform other pilots and their chain of command that they only have enough fuel to make it back to their parent ship, airbase or station.

Brafik/*Brufik*: a derogatory verb that can function as a noun, adverb, and an adjective. It is the most used curse word in the Imperial military and by extension the USG.

Direct action: Refers to military operations usually carried out by relatively small, specialised units in order to seize, capture, recover, exploit, damage, or destroy designated targets.

Drop (FTL): A term used to refer to interdimensional faster-than-light transitions where a ship moves through some of the most dangerous layers of Aether Space to emerge in an alternate dimension.

Foot mobiles: A technical term to describe any armed warriors or infantry.

Foxtrot Bravo: Derogatory term for anything, extrapolated into the USG Phonetic Alphabet to ensure officers can't charge a service member with indecent language unbecoming.

Full battle rattle: To wear all battle armour and equipment at the same time.

Gimmit: Derogatory shorthand for all army, navy, air, and marine corps military occupational specialties, rates, and air corps specialisations who have completed general maintenance training (GMT). Suggesting a neediness for components, it is a play on the phrase 'gimme it'.

Golf Bravo: Derogatory for the Honour Guard, derived from the loose translation of Kukaerke 'Honour Guard' and fed through the

NATO phonetic alphabet that lives on as the USG phonetic alphabet creating the shorthand for 'Guard Bastard'.

Grid reference: Grid reference is a system of tracking friendlies and hostiles in an area of responsibility efficiently. It tends to be broken up into a two-letter designator such as FS and at least a six-digit designator although the longer the number the more precise the reference is. e.g. FS 223459.

Hatchway: An opening from one deck to another on a warship, as opposed to a door which is between compartments on the same deck.

Hooah: The Unified Army chant originating from the US Army and one of the few non-commonwealth traditions to be adopted by the Unified Army.

Hooyah: The chant of the Unified Naval Service adopted from the United States Navy.

Klick: Kilometre.

Lagrange Point 1: Often shorted to L1, Lagrange Points are locations throughout a system where a craft or station does not have to be concerned with keeping pace with the rotation of a star system due to the interactions of gravity from a planet and its sun. Because of this stability, it also is where Faster Than Light exit vectors are almost exclusively plotted.

Like Scared Bears Squawk, Squeak Bats Sadly: a children's rhyme created by QT-2 to memorise the process of Loading the magazine (Like), placing the weapon on safe (Scared), charging the Bolt or Hammer (Bear/Hamster), Semi-Automatic selector (Squawk), Squeeze Trigger (Squeak), the sound of a round exiting the barrel bang (Bats) then finally safety switch on (Sadly).

Lima Charlie: Loud and Clear.

Mikes: Minutes.

Mortarded: A marine who is a moron and mentally challenged.

NAVLOGCOM/LOGCOM: Naval Logistics Command.

Oscar Mike: On the Move.

Primsjns: The Ympiirno Spraak word for 'clone', drawing from the old English words 'synthetic' and 'prime' to indicate that it is a copy of an original host.

Quick Response Force: QRFs are predetermined elements of a ground unit that are trained and equipped to move into conflict zones or against hostile parties as fast as physically possible.

Raet: A form of rodent found on the planet Kiln.

Rah: A question, an exclamation, and 'yes' in the marine creole.

Rally point: A position where friendly forces meet up to coordinate operations or ensure they have sufficient strength to take a position.

Return to Base: abbreviated to RTB, Return to Base is the order or report given by a pilot when they are returning to their parent ship, Air Base, or Station for one reason or another (see also bingo fuel).

RV Point: Rendezvous Point, similar to rally point (see rally point).

Secretary's soup: A derogatory term for stasis litter.

Send Traffic: A fixed-phrase reply to another service member preparing to transmit information over a radio or wireless communication that they can receive and retain the information about to be sent.

Shajst: A derogatory verb that can function as a noun, adverb, and an adjective. It is the second most used curse word in the Imperial Military.

Skarandroid/Skaraloi/Skarant: *Skarandroid*, and its shorthand *Skarant*, are a combination of the Old English word 'android' and the Imperial creole for metal or alloy—'*Skaraloi*'—to mean any artificial life with a mechanised body.

Squad bay: An organised section of a barracks or warship, specific to marines.

SQUADCOMM: A specific network just for members of a squad.

Taf Net: Taskforce Network.

TEAMCOMM: Team Communications, a localised network specifically used for individuals with a team.

Triple-A/AAA: Anti-Aircraft Artillery are platforms that function in a similar format to Artillery but with the distinct function of tackling enemy air instead of enemy armour or infantry.

Unidentified Extraterrestrial Species: UES or UESes is the official designation required and utilised when dealing with newly discovered life, spawned from the USG's First Contact Protocols which were adapted to the USR during the two organisations' unholy union.

Victor Foxtrot: Derogatory term referring to Legionary dragoons due to their reliance on Wireless Electrical Signals for communication ('Voiceless Fucks'), extrapolated into the USG Phonetic Alphabet.

Watchkeeping: The process of a warship ensuring that all systems are always monitored without straining the crew, by assigning 'watchkeepers' to operate in shifts.

Wireless acknowledgement: The process of transmitting a single burst of audio over digital radio to a commander.

Wireless communication: The term used for digital radios.

Wireless silence: The instruction to avoid transmitting information over digital radio at all costs.

Wiring: The process of tapping into a network.

Yut: Yut is another way to say 'yes' in the US Marine Corps creole and, as a result, central to the Unified Marine Corps creole.

Organisations and Unit formations

ACT: Asymmetrical Combat Team. ACTs are a five-person unit designed to leverage the immense strategic latitude offered to specialists. By design, it enables specialists to seamlessly integrate into brigade/regimental combat teams and implement the manpower on offer into the planning and execution of complex operations.

BLUFOR: Blue Forces, a phrase used in Field Training Exercises and other war games exercises to refer to everyone roleplaying Taskforce personnel in a simulated war.

Communications Systems Operator: Abbreviated to CSO, a Unified Marine Corps or Unified Army CSO is responsible for a unit's communications at all levels as well as the integration and operation of other battlefield technologies. It evolved from the 20th-century billet radio telephone operator, or RTO and the 21st-Century US Marine Corps billet Squad Systems Operator.

Field Command Post: A command post that is forward deployed from other friendly units, a term predominantly used by the Imperial Union Military.

Fort Kow: Fort Kow is a prolific USG facility reported to hold various important artefacts from the group's history and is reported to be impenetrable.

Fort Yomii: Fort Yomii is a prison that was historically owned and operated exclusively for and by the Imperial Red Star Army's own Military Police Corps before the corps was integrated into the Committee of State Security and the Secret Service Bureau as a direct arm of the intelligence apparatus. With this transfer of ownership, Yomii became an interservice prison for violators of Imperial Military law.

Gaponno Fist: Loosely translated to English as the 'Fist of Gapon', a cadre of alien fighters claimed in Emperor Kuzmoto's initial expansion and sworn to protect the Imperial Emperor. However, due to the Imperial Cult's belief that emperors and empresses are the human manifestations of Lord Nikiri and Lady Devna, respectively, each time the emperor's female successor is chosen, according to the gender laws of manifestation succession, the Fist of Gapon immediately returns to their home territories and begins to wage a guerrilla war against the Imperial Union until another emperor reigns.

General court-martial (plural: courts-martial): A military court. A general court-martial is conducted by the Judge Advocate General Corps. The session is presided over by five senior flag officers in the Taskforce and Imperial Union and varies from nation to nation on Earth. A court-martial is called if a breach of the code of military justice is either a criminal offence or too egregious to warrant a Non-Judicial Punishment (see FnM/NJP).

Kaiserkriig Mariin Grondfors Komando: Translating to 'Imperial War Navy Land Force Commando', this battalion-sized unit is a part of the corps of naval infantry. The unit organisation adopted by the Imperial War Navy was a combination of the old-Earth Royal Marines and German Sea Battalions.

Kasimno Kombain Reidist Kor: The Kasim Coalition Raider Corps (abbreviated to the KKRK and KCRC, respectively) was originally a coalition of privateers enlisted into service by the Union of Sovereign Realms to support their expansion efforts that slowly found the benefits of service outweighed by the benefits of piracy and rebellion which led them to become a rival nation-state to the USR.

Kor Mariin Infantrii: Imperial creolisation of Corps of Naval Infantry, literally translated as 'Corps of Maritime Infantry'.

Meikkorek Bataljon: The Union Military's Correctional 'Punishment' Battalions were a pragmatic solution to a two-pronged issue that began to arise during the Era of Eternal Strife, as it became colloquially known. With the union engaged in four bloody conflicts over 100 years, a growing need for Military Police units arose as increasing unrest and overall loss of morale lead to an increase in non-conformists, party-line dissenters, as well as protests and insurgent actions across Imperial space. Correctional Battalions were the proposed solution. Non-conformists who were deemed reformable would be retrained for policing actions and deployed behind friendly lines to free up frontline forces to continue offensive operations. Over the years, this also grew to be a punishment system for failure and a motivator for success.

Min-Hei Industries: Abbreviated to MHI, Min-Hei Industries has been a premier research and development group since the 2070s. Using her family's extensive wealth, Director Halloway founded Min-Hei Industries as a public vehicle for the advancement of the Taskforce's equipment and the expansion of its warfighting and exploration capabilities. It would be responsible for several breakthroughs, many still classified. To the public, it would be defined by the well-intentioned but ultimately flawed Chimata Initiative that saw the implementation of advanced alien faster-than-light systems on five UN-funded colony ships intended ultimately for the Andromeda galaxy that would be hijacked by 21st-century anarchists known as the Preservation of the First World who, along with over three million prospective colonists, would leave Sol and eventually land on the planet Kiln to eventually become the Union of Sovereign Realms. Min-Hei Industries is frequently the vehicle through which the Office of Strategic Intelligence accesses the Union of Sovereign Realms political systems due to its frequent work for the USR.

Operations Personnel Security and Intelligence committee: Abbreviated to the OPSI committee, or simply OPSI, this was a creation of Director Ashton; he would cite the management difficulties that had arisen out of the explosive growth of the institution in the 2130s.

OPFOR: Opposition Force is the opponent to BLUFOR in war games exercises.

Phalanx: A formation created and historically refined by the old-Earth Spartans of the city-state of Sparta and used famously at the Battle of Thermopylae against the Persian Empire. The formation relied on intense unit cohesion to provide overlapping protection from attack and unified striking power against an opponent, something that was only achievable by the old-Earth Spartans as they were raised from birth for war. This formation would continue to be used in modern-day riot control and limited conventional shield-based assaults.

Platoon office: A platoon office is the administrative component of training platoons. The number is usually unrelated.

Project Phoenix: Phoenix was the overall name for the augmentation process first proposed in 2234 that had begun with the breakthrough in biological nanomachine augmentation. What is now known as 'Cephi-7' was the brainchild of biomechanical engineers Doctor Samuel Ce Gray and then-Surgeon-Lieutenant Eliza Taylor Dane who had been co-researching medical systems that could be inserted into the body without rejection from the host. During their research, they would be attracted to the concept of biomechanical systems that could systematically replicate their cellular structure to match that of a patient, paired with the cutting-edge research into nanomachine systems. Gray and Dane would introduce to the URC the first version of Cephi; over the next six iterations on the system during its trial process, Project Phoenix would eventually be greenlit by OPSI for limited implementation on volunteer Special Operations and Special Forces Units in 2240 and would become a mainstream requirement for all service members in 2250.

Project Reveles: A proposal by the Unified Naval Service to expand its covert patrol duties to include a greater block of Imperial Territory in an attempt to better secure Taskforce Interests from threats.

Recruit training company: A company of sailors organised for the specific purpose of being trained in the traditions and physical requirements of the Unified Naval Service.

Regiment: The unit structure known as a regiment has only continued as a practical unit structure in some old-Earth militaries as well as the Imperial Army and the Unified Marine Corps after being phased out by the Unified Army in favour of more flexible brigades. Despite this, the term 'regiment' has continued to see usage to refer to UA logistical battalions and legacy units that were once organised with regiments as their largest direct unit organisation. However, as the Taskforce lacks almost any legacy units from old Earth, units referred to as regiments tend to exclusively be the 1st Recruit Training Regiment (named to recognise the flexibility of training units), Regimental Combat Teams in the UMC and Special Operations units such as the Special Air Service that refers to itself as 'The Regiment'.

Spetsjalist Polits Kor: The Imperial creolisation of the old-Earth Imperial Japanese Navy organisation known as the Special Police Corps. The Special Police Corps is the hand of the Union's political loyalty maintenance goals.

Unified Research Command: The URC is the official institution that conducts research and development for the public front institution that is Min-Hei Industries. Like many arms of the Taskforce, the URC employs some of the best researchers in their fields of research and work. Unlike the rest of the Taskforce, however, with Min-Hei Industries acting as the public front for the URC, it enables the Command to acquire and hire researchers without having to kidnap them.

Ranks and billets

ACO: Asymmetrical Combat Officer. ACOs, more commonly known as 'Specialists', were a unique creation of the Unified Security Group designed to handle operations and incidents that necessitated highly specialised personnel to minimise any negative effects that displacing conventional special operations and special forces units would impose upon defensive positions and offensive planning. The Taskforce field's ten core positions that tend to be near-permanently staffed and another ten reserve positions. During wartime, this number can swell with an additional eighty activated slots that can be adjusted as the situation requires.

Airedale: All sailors assigned to a warship's air wing.

Boatswain/Boatswain's Mate/Boatswain's Mate of the Watch: Pronounced as 'Bosun', Boatswain is a multifaceted term in the navy that can mean a variety of things with drastically different understandings. The term 'Boatswain' by itself can refer to the senior non-commissioned officer in a ship's department. A Boatswain's Mate, however, and by extension, their role in the day to day operations of a warship known as Boatswain's Mate of the Watch, is to pass along announcements from the captain or officer of the deck, all daily announcements and to ensure that all enlisted personnel manning watchkeeping roles are capable of executing their duty as well as assisting the OOD, the conning officer, and the helms-personnel when necessary.

Chiif Starshiina: The Imperial creolisation of the old-Earth Russian Navy rank Chief Starshina. It is on the pay grade OR-8.

Commissioned officer: The proper term for someone who joins a military as an officer rather than as an enlisted rank. They tend to have a bachelor's degree, although the Unified Security Group is made up of more mustang commissioned officers than most conventional militaries.

Grond Kapitan, Ajnster Rank: The rank of Ground Captain 1st Rank is the marine equivalent of an Imperial Navy captain. It is on the pay grade OF-6 and equivalent to an Imperial Army colonel. This subtle distinction stems from the fact that the Corps of Naval Infantry is a subordinate corps of the Imperial War Navy. The rank was a natural evolution of the empire of Japan's rank structure.

Kapitan Lutenant: The Imperial creolisation of the rank Captain Lieutenant. It is on the pay grade of OF-4 and equivalent to the Imperial Army rank of Major.

Korporal: The Imperial creolisation of the rank Corporal. It is an OR-5 pay grade of the Imperial Red Star Army.

Liider Mariin: The Imperial creolisation of the old-Earth naval rank Leading Seaman. It is on the pay grade of OR-4.

Mariin: Marine in the Imperial Creole.

Mustang officer: A term that finds its roots in the old United States armed forces, a mustang officer is someone who started their career along an enlisted track and after a certain period as a non-commissioned officer before applying for a commission. They tend to have a more balanced understanding of their units as they have experienced both sides of the military.

OOD: The Officer of the Deck tends to be a lieutenant who is monitoring the bridge of a ship during a watch cycle if the captain is not on watch. The Junior Officer of the Deck (JOOD) supports their work on the bridge.

Open Ranks: The process of a unit in parade formation to make a double-spaced arrangement for an inspection party to walk in front of each row of soldiers, sailors, marines, or airmen.

PFC: Private First Class is a permanent rank offered to enlisted personnel after the first year of their service. A PFC is more commonly referred to as simply 'Private'.

Regimental Sergeant Major: known as a Regiment Sargent Madjor in the Union Military and abbreviated to RSM. An RSM is a professional title for the senior non-commissioned officer who is in charge of the enlisted personnel within an army or marine unit, the title RSM is separate from the rank. An RSM is expected to manage all enlisted matters including discipline and has a working relationship with a unit's officer component. It is identical to the US armed forces role of Command Sergeant Major.

Salor: Imperial creolisation of sailor.

Senior/Taskforce instructor: Abbreviated to S/TFI, TFI is the broad term for any Taskforce instructor that trains soldiers, sailors, airmen, and marines to carry themselves as warfighters and execute their trade. This title is only used on Joint Bases or before enlistees arrive at the Hakon. After this point, they are referred to as Drill Sergeants, Recruit Division instructors/Commanders, Military Training instructors, and Drill instructors, respectively.

Technology, Equipment, and Utilities

Biological Identification Chip (BIC): The information chip spawned as a response to the need for consistent and permanent battlefield records. It was a by-product of Doctor Gray and Surgeon Lieutenant Dane's work on Cephi 7.

Bomb-pumped laser (BPL): Munitions that are designed to focus and in turn intensify the radiation energy released by conventional nuclear munitions.

C13: Plastic explosive.

Carbyne-A: A carbon-titanium alloy that comes in three variants: Carbyne A, A2, and B2.

Crystalline Cooling Cells: Triple-Cs are compressed metallic packets of liquid nitrogen.

Immecrete: A concrete-like substance composed of nanomachines.

Imperial Common Tactical Interface: Abbreviated to ICTI, the ICTI is a handheld platform designed to integrate localised data into a coherent information packet for a soldier or marine to easily digest the rapidly evolving tactical situation surrounding them.

Iron ball paint: Paint combination designed to disrupt infrared and other detection systems, adapted from old-Earth F-117 Nighthawks.

Kinetic screen/field/plate matrix: Energy shields are a directed concentration of electrons on the hull of a ship, the perimeter of a base, or the plates of body armour. Due to the extraordinary amounts of energy needed for energy shields to successfully dissipate the kinetic energy produced by weapons fire, ship-to-ship munitions, missiles, and debris, energy shields are concentrated across critical areas of a ship's hull, a warfighter's body armour, or a base's perimeter. These energy shields, while able to deflect high calibre shots, can only protect its charge from certain angles of assault, leaving gaps within the defensive superstructure that must be filled by fighters or close-in weapon systems (CIWS). This drawback is similarly found in large scale planetary shields. During orbital bombardments, planetary shields can withstand blistering assaults for years when directed correctly. However, this invulnerability leaves the facilities below defenceless to ground assaults. Shields on a warship are known as kinetic screens, planetary shields are known as kinetic fields, and shielding on body armour is known as kinetic plating.

Klaxon: A loud alarm used aboard warships to inform the crew of attack or incident and to trigger them to move to their duty stations.

Light Detection and Ranging (lidar): Lidar is one of the more prominent systems in space to track incoming or surrounding craft as it sends out light and when it bounces back generates a relative position of the craft it has detected.

M42 Mod 9 Multi-Variable Response Grenade: Abbreviated to M42 M9 MVR, the M42 is a smart grenade that utilises a lighter explosive force compared to some other munitions such as the M134. What it loses in immediate high-powered destructive force it gains by giving a warrior discretionary capabilities and decreasing how many grenade variants a warfighter needs to carry, as the M42 can serve, in its lowest setting, as merely a concussion grenade, and in large quantities can simulate the M134.

M568X Jumper Rounds: Munitions with a translocation beacon attached to the tip of the round. Jumper rounds send out an active signal and as they are translocated reappear wherever there is a pingback from a sister beacon.

Marine Utility Combat Uniform: Abbreviated to MUCU, or simply UCU, this is the general term developed by the Unified Marine Corps to refer to all facets of the UMCs service uniforms, from fatigues up to Battle Dress Uniform.

Micro Superconducting Memory Crystal (SM/C): Similar to 5D optical data storage.

Mijanii cigarettes: An Imperial-made, and sanctioned, nicotine hit that in theory causes minimal lung deterioration compared to old-Earth cigarettes.

Molecular Moulding Forge: A variation on the technique known as Liquid Printing.

Muster station: An integrated hardpoint found on a warship where non-combat personnel are expected to stay during combat.

Passive Phased Array: PPAs are a system of detecting and tracking aircraft and warships around a craft, drawing in data from radar and lidar, as well as conventional telescopic systems, to monitor and potentially combat them.

PCS: Powered Combat Skeletons or PCS for short were the next generation armour system proposed to OPSI in early January of 2340 by Min Hei Design Team Kigati in an attempt to find a suitable replacement for the Mobile Defence Suit that was showing operational flaws after 110 years of continuous service and ad hoc improvement. The Powered Combat Skeleton was the first real proposal to phase out the force amplification actuators that'd plagued the Mobile Defence Suit but were essential to continued operations due to its unparalleled tonnage. The proposed PCS would be lighter than the ageing MDS and more easily serviceable by widening the actuator frame and removing the restricting and limiting armour plating around the upper arm. Though the committee had its reservations about the PCS due to its design being quite inferior compared to its predecessor, the true nail in the coffin for the PCS would be the Concealer War which would be declared three months later, and with the initiation of Security Protocol Omega only eleven months later at the war's end, the PCS would become quickly forgotten due to its reliance on networking, which became the sole concern of the committee for the next century.

Radio Detection and Ranging (radar): The traditional system of detection by sending out radio waves and receiving them again to generate a relative position of the craft the radio wave has bounced off.

Semi-Powered Combat Suit: The SPCS was borne of a need for a new protective body armour that quickly supplemented and removed the ineffective networking of the PCS and overhauled the ageing MDS. Drawing on ideas found in conventional body armour, the committee took experimental graphene then being tested as light security ballistic plating and, while not scrapping the force amplification actuators, did limit their usage within the glorified body armour to the wrists. SPC suits also removed many of the networking features found in both the PCS and the MDS. Among many restrictions and removals, they surprisingly kept the suit's mainstay crystalline matrix, critical to the use of an internally installed artificial intelligence. While Tasking OS remained the primary operating system of the BDU—as it became unofficially known—many of the design features that were a mainstay of the MDS would be removed, such as the integrated command and control networking and OS automatic update protocols.

Semi-Powered Exoskeleton: SPE was the experimental testbed for the Powered Combat Suit and eventually even the Semi-Powered Combat Suit, originally a stripped-down Mobile Defence Suit, the SPE would become an amalgam of theoretical powered combat armour technologies and techniques that would ultimately culminate in the powered combat armour platform, the SPE continues to be on display in the Min-Hei Industries Museum and reproductions of the Exoskeleton continue to serve as the testbed for modern Combat Armour enhancements.

Stasis litter: Stasis litters utilise a combination of 24th-Century technological and medical techniques to maintain an injured combatant before proper medical assistance can arrive. Stasis litters combine artificial gravity technology with refined cryogenic Emergency Preservation and Resuscitation (EPR) techniques.

Static coupling: Static couplings are designed to route static energy from around the suit into the hydrostatic gel to maximise energy efficiency in Taskforce powered and semi-powered combat armour.

Subspace communication: A transmission system that utilises the superluminal speeds of subspace to transmit audio and video communication across the universe.

Subspace Silhouette Scramblers: All objects in real space have a silhouette in subspace. A scrambler distorts that silhouette to confuse potential trackers or keen eyes looking where they shouldn't.

Subspace Translocation (transloc): The process of generating a localised wormhole to near-instantaneously move a marked object.

Tangible Holographic Plasma: THP is plasma encased in an energy field to manipulate and grip materials and generate interactive holograms.

Tight beam: Information transmitted via a focused beam of energy (a laser, for example).

Milton Keynes UK
Ingram Content Group UK Ltd.
UKHW022342020823
426203UK00017B/776